"I came for a drink of water."

"Come on in." Dori pulled a glass out of the cupboard, filled it at the sink and handed it to Eli.

"Danki."

She gifted him with a smile. *"Bitte.* How's it going out there?"

He smiled back. "Fine." He gulped half the glass, then slowed down to sips. No sense rushing.

After a minute, she folded her arms. "Go ahead. Ask your question."

"What?"

"You obviously want to ask me something. What is it? Why do I color my hair all different colors? Why do I dress like this? Why did I leave? What is it?"

She posed all *gut* questions, but not the one he needed an answer to. A question that was no business of his to ask.

"Go ahead. Ask. I don't mind." Very un-Amish, but she'd offered. Insisted.

He cleared his throat. "Are you going to stay?"

She stared for a moment and then looked away. Obviously, not the question she'd expected, nor one she wanted to answer.

Mary Davis is an award-winning author of more than a dozen novels. She is a member of American Christian Fiction Writers and is active in two critique groups. Mary lives in the Colorado Rocky Mountains with her husband of thirty years and three cats. She has three adult children and one grandchild. Her hobbies are quilting, porcelain-doll making, sewing, crafts, crocheting and knitting. Please visit her website, marydavisbooks.com.

Marie E. Bast grew up on a farm in northern Illinois. In the solitude of country life, she often read or made up stories. She earned a BA, an MBA and an MA in general theology and enjoyed a career with the federal government, but characters kept whispering her name. She retired and now pursues her passion of full-time writing. Marie loves walking, golfing with her husband of twenty-seven years and baking. Visit Marie at mariebastauthor.com and mariebast.Blogspot.com.

MARY DAVIS
Courting Her Prodigal Heart

&

MARIE E. BAST
The Amish Baker

LOVE INSPIRED
INSPIRATIONAL ROMANCE

LOVE INSPIRED®

INSPIRATIONAL ROMANCE

Recycling programs
for this product may
not exist in your area.

ISBN-13: 978-1-335-22981-6

Courting Her Prodigal Heart and The Amish Baker

Copyright © 2020 by Harlequin Books S.A.

Courting Her Prodigal Heart
First published in 2018. This edition published in 2020.
Copyright © 2018 by Mary Davis

The Amish Baker
First published in 2019. This edition published in 2020.
Copyright © 2019 by Marie Elizabeth Bast

This edition published by arrangement with Harlequin Books S.A.

For questions and comments about the quality of this book,
please contact us at CustomerService@Harlequin.com.

Harlequin Enterprises ULC
22 Adelaide St. West, 40th Floor
Toronto, Ontario M5H 4E3, Canada
www.Harlequin.com

Printed in U.S.A.

CONTENTS

COURTING HER PRODIGAL HEART

Mary Davis

To my son Josh

It was meet that we should make merry, and be glad: for this thy brother...was lost, and is found.
—*Luke* 15:32

German Proverb
Mer sott em sei Eegne net verlosse;
Gott verlosst die Seine nicht.
One should not abandon one's own;
God does not abandon His own.

Chapter One

Goshen, Indiana

With the reins in hand, Eli Hochstetler drove his *vater*'s supply-hauling wagon through Goshen in the early-June sun. Dutch's hooves clip-clopped on the pavement.

Daniel Burkholder sat on the seat next to him. "Have the church leaders given you permission to purchase a computer and make a website?"

Eli shook his head. "I haven't asked yet."

"Why not? The summer is going to be over before you know it."

"I need to have more items made first." Eli had branched out his blacksmithing from the practical horseshoes, weather vanes and herb choppers to decorative items like napkin holders, door knockers and small animal figures. This second group of items would be marketed toward *Englishers*, hence the need for a computer and website. Not everyone who requested such privileges were granted them.

"Shouldn't you make sure they'll let you before you go to the trouble?"

"I want to show them I have a need and *meine* work can support a business. I also need to learn about websites and such."

"You can't create your own website. They wouldn't allow that. You'll need an *Englisher* to do that."

"I know. I'm not sure how to go about finding one."

"Doesn't every *Englisher* know about computers?"

Eli shrugged. "I think so. If I know a little, I'll know how to talk to an *Englisher* about *meine* website."

His attention gravitated toward Rainbow Girl. That was what he called the young woman with rainbow-colored hair. His gaze automatically followed her.

For the past six months, he'd seen this same girl every time he came to town, without fail. Her multicolored hair made her hard to miss, but she held herself differently today. Not the usual bounce in her step. Not the usual head held high. Not the usual carefree swing of her arms. Her head hung low, and her shoulders hunched over. Her fancy black knee boots scuffed the sidewalk, and her body shook as though she was crying.

What drew him to this stranger? An *Englisher*, no less. It made no sense.

Inasmuch as ye have done it unto one of the least of these my brethren, ye have done it unto me.

Ne, this verse didn't apply.

Not for an *Englisher*. Therefore, not his responsibility. And none of his business.

"You aren't going to ask *her* for help, are you?"

Daniel's question brought Eli back to his right

mind. "Of course not." He snapped the reins to hurry up Dutch. He had errands to complete and work to do.

"What is it about that *Englisher* that makes you stare?"

Eli shook his head. "I don't know what you mean."

"The last three times I've ridden into town with you, you've watched her. You don't do that with other *Englishers*."

Eli hadn't realized he'd been so obvious. "Who wouldn't notice someone with hair like that? You've obviously noticed her also."

"That's different. You stare like you're trying to figure her out." Daniel's assessment was too accurate.

Eli struggled to figure out what drew him to this one *Englisher*. He didn't want to talk about her anymore. "We should get the lumber first, then the feed."

A while later, with his errands done and the wagon loaded down, Eli drove back through town. Would he see Rainbow Girl once more? He hoped not. He didn't want Daniel bringing her up again.

But there she sat. Alone. Huddled on the curb in front of a sandwich shop with her arms wrapped around her bent legs.

He guided Dutch into the small strip mall parking lot, pulled the draft horse and wagon through two adjoining spaces and hauled back on the reins.

Daniel elbowed him. "What are you doing?"

"I'll be right back." After setting the brake, he jumped down and headed toward Rainbow Girl.

He hesitated a few feet away. What did an Amish man say to such a person?

One side of her hair had been cropped very short while the other side hung down to her shoulder. The

short side shone bright red, and her ear had *five* earrings. Purple bangs swooped across her forehead and
partially covered one eye. Then came sections of blue,
green, yellow, orange and around to the red again. All
of it had about an inch of brown close to her head. Why
would anyone do that to her hair?

Her jeans had several large holes up and down the entire fronts in various sizes. With her legs bent, her black-
net-covered knees poked out the biggest openings. A
green army-style jacket hung loose over a baggy T-shirt.

Englishers were strange.

His heart raced being this close to her after all these
months and now contemplating speaking to her. He
should leave, but instead, he said, "Are you all right?"

Slowly, her head rose, and she stared at him as
though she'd seen something out of the ordinary. Perhaps she had. Amish didn't normally talk to *Englishers* like her.

Her lips were purple, similar in color to the hair that
covered part of her face. Above her upper lip sat a dot
of silver metal. She had a small silver hoop hanging
from the one eyebrow he could now see. Heavy black
makeup encircled her eyes as though she'd used soot.
Below them, the black had run and smeared. Why did
Englisher women choose to cover up their beauty with
so much paint?

"I'm fine. Leave me alone."

All her makeup couldn't disguise the pain in her
eyes. Pain that came from deep inside. From her heart
and soul. "You don't look fine." There must be something he could do. Why he felt a need to help her, he
didn't know. He pointed to his own face. "Your eye…
The black stuff… Never mind."

She wiped her fingers below each eye, further smearing the inky mess. "I'm fine."

This woman obviously didn't want anything to do with him. He shouldn't bother her any longer. He should leave. Instead, he sat on the curb near her, keeping a respectable distance, at least four feet. He glanced toward Daniel, who shook his head.

Eli needed to make sure she was all right. "My name is Eli." He'd never imagined ever being so close to her. The nerves in his fingers and toes tingled. He clasped his hands together to dull the sensation.

She turned toward him and raked the purple hair from her face with her hand. "What are you doing?"

He wasn't sure himself. "You're clearly upset about something. Maybe you need some company."

"I am, and I don't."

Even though she dismissed him, he couldn't bring himself to sever the tenuous connection with her and stand. "What's your name?" Something about her struck him as familiar, but he couldn't imagine what. Probably by seeing her frequently, he'd become accustomed to her.

"If you weren't Amish, I'd think you were some sort of creepy stalker." Did she have a lilt of an accent?

He placed his palm on his chest. "I mean you no harm. Won't you tell me your name?"

She changed her focus to her purple painted nails and picked at them. "Dori. Why did you sit down with me? That's not very Amish."

He gave a chuckle. "You probably won't understand this, but I felt *Gott* leading me to come over to you."

She chuffed out a breath. "God? God doesn't care about me."

"He does. Very much."

Her words rushed out. "Then why has my boyfriend kicked me out? I lost my stupid low-paying job. And I have no place to live. Trust me, God does *not* care about me."

"What about your family? You could ask them for help."

She pulled a tight smile. "Trust me, my family doesn't want anything to do with me."

"Have you asked them?"

"There's no point."

"You don't know until you try. Your family may be waiting to hear from you. Waiting for you to come home."

She shook her head. "It was nice of you to stop and try to help. You've done your good deed. You can go now."

Gut deed? Was that what she thought? If he simply needed to complete a *gut* deed, he had many neighbors he could help.

This had not been his idea. But had he done all that *Gott* had in mind for him to do?

She inclined her head toward his wagon. "Your friend is waiting for you."

"He will wait." Eli considered her. She had no job and no place to live. That likely meant she had nothing in her stomach. He stood and took a retreating step. "Come."

She glanced over her shoulder and up at him. "Why?"

He poked his thumb behind him at the sub shop. "I will buy you a sandwich."

The one visible eyebrow shifted down. "What? Really?"

"*Ja.* Come in and pick out what you want. If you don't, I'll pick for you." He reached for the door handle.

"You're serious." She scrambled to her feet.

He held the door. "Pick whatever kind of sandwich you want." With his other hand, he held up his index finger to Daniel to let him know he'd be a minute.

The male server behind the counter pulled on clear plastic gloves. "Welcome. What can I make for you?"

Rainbow Girl's voice came out small and uncertain. "I'd like the sweet onion chicken teriyaki."

"Six-inch or twelve?"

Rainbow Girl said, "Six—"

Eli spoke over her. "Twelve-inch, please."

She looked at him sideways.

He knew she had to be hungry. She could eat the other half later if she didn't want it now. She chose her bread and veggies.

He ordered two more twelve-inch sandwiches, one for himself, the other for Daniel, and got them all chips and chocolate milk. He set her food and drink on a table but didn't sit.

"I need to go now."

"Thank you. I really appreciate this." Her mouth curved up a little bit, and his insides responded happily. "I won't tell anyone you helped the strange *Englisher*—" she lifted her hands and flipped them around in tight circles "—with the colorful hair."

He should do more but didn't know what. "You should talk to your family. I'm sure they miss you." *Englisher* parents had to love their children too, didn't they?

"I'm sure they don't. I've done things they'll never be able to forgive."

This poor woman had next to nothing.

"Give them a chance." He dug in his pocket and put a ten-dollar bill on the table. "Spend this on food." But there was no guarantee she would.

She stared at him.

Though he wanted to stay longer with her, he turned and hurried out before she could refuse it. He cast a glance over his shoulder. What was it he felt for this stranger? Pity? *Ja.* But there was something more to it. Compassion? *Ja.* But still more. He continued to mull it over as he approached the wagon, and the impossible truth hit him. *Attraction.*

How could that be? It certainly wasn't her appearance. It had been when she'd thanked him and smiled. It had caused his insides to wriggle like a fish trying to get away.

He couldn't deny it. She was someone he wanted to get to know better, but that would be ill-advised. The best thing to happen would be to never see her again.

Dori. Knowing her real name dispelled some of the mystery about her. He would always think of her as Rainbow Girl though.

He suspected it would be a while before he could shake her from his thoughts.

Something inside Dori ached for the handsome Amish man to stay with her a little longer. He headed out the door and toward his horse and wagon. Eli Hochstetler hadn't recognized her. Nor had the other Amish man with him. Just as well. She'd worked hard to erase any trace of her former Amish self. Eli made her long for...for... What? Something more. But what was that something? Craig? No. Then what? She stared after his retreating wagon and wanted to call him back.

How weird to see and talk to an Amish person. She hadn't done so in four years, avoiding them whenever possible.

Eli had surprised her when he bought her—an *Englisher*—a sandwich. He had always been kind even though a bit rigid and unbending with people's actions, like his father and her grandfather. The three of them would have plenty to say about all her poor choices. Choices that had been right for her at the time.

He likely had many thoughts about her hair, makeup and clothing. And what had he thought of her piercings? She chuckled to herself. If he had recognized her, no doubt he would have been horrified and wouldn't have spoken to her at all. She'd thought she'd blown it by calling herself an *Englisher*, but it seemed to have sailed right by him. She was glad he hadn't recognized her. This way she could keep this little moment she'd had with him special.

He'd looked so uncomfortable talking to her. It had been kind of cute. Eli had always been appealing. His intense brown eyes still captivated her. She'd almost told him who she was and that she knew him, but she feared it would have put him off, and she'd appreciated his kindness. He would have judged her actions as vulgar and unacceptable, but as an *Englisher*, anything she did would be viewed as merely an example of their strange ways.

Tears welled in her eyes at the thought of him being repulsed by her if he knew. She desperately didn't want him to think poorly of her. She wanted him to like her again. What was she thinking? It must be her out of whack hormones.

With her stomach satisfied and the other half of the sandwich tucked inside her backpack, she headed down the street.

After two weeks of morning sickness and fighting with Craig, Dori had packed suitcases with her clothes, books, and various items from around the apartment, and checked herself in at a women's shelter. How pitiful her life had become.

How could Craig not want his own child?

The following morning at the shelter, she shoved her damp toothbrush into her backpack in preparation to leave for the day. Her hand hit something hard. She gripped the cold, curved metal and pulled it out. At the sight of the iron door knocker, she froze. Even though she had put it there, it surprised her. Why? Because she'd seen and talked to Eli yesterday? He'd created this in his forge. She gripped it hard. The prodigal son story came to mind.

And when he came to himself, he said, How many hired servants of my father's have bread enough and to spare, and I perish with hunger! I will arise and go to my father—

She sucked in a breath. No, she could never go back there. Would her father even let her return? He might, but her grandfather never would. Amish had a propensity for forgiveness, but her grandfather had quit speaking to her even before she'd left because of her wild ways. If he saw her now, would he even recognize her? Would any of them? Eli hadn't. She smiled at his sweetness yesterday. Thoughts of returning to the Amish people were Eli's fault. He'd put the idea in her head.

Dori shoved the iron door knocker back into her backpack.

—and will say unto him, Father, I have sinned against heaven, and before thee.

Boy, had she ever sinned.

Even shunned, as she would be if she returned, the Amish would treat her better than this. They would feed her, give her a clean bed and take care of her, even if she had to eat at a separate table from the rest of her family. Though no one would be allowed to talk to her, she would be provided for. Her child would be treated well and taken care of. Her child wouldn't go hungry if Dori was forced to remain there for an extended period, nor would it go without clothes or a bed, and it would have a roof over its head. What more did either of them need right now?

She would go back to the community until she could get a job and support herself and her child. Only a temporary solution.

And she would get to see Eli again. That thought made her insides smile.

Chapter Two

Later that morning, Dori stood in the buggy-filled yard of her parents' Amish home.

The shelter manager had told Dori that being homeless was no life for her child. She even specifically said that the Amish community would be a good place for both her and her baby.

Dori doubted that. It was strict and overshadowed by so many rules. Too many to keep track of.

She wanted to run after the car that had dropped her off but instead stood in the midst of the buggies for several minutes, contemplating what to do. The vehicles mocked her, reminding her that she didn't belong. But somewhere beyond them, inside the house, sat Eli Hochstetler. Had she not run into him and seen the potential for the Amish to treat her with even a small amount of compassion, she doubted she would have come.

She stepped between the buggies, and her breathing came in catches. She didn't want to go inside and have everyone stare at her. She'd hoped to arrive unnoticed. Just her family would know she had come. Not only would they be surprised but shocked. She couldn't turn back now. No way did she want to return to the unpredictable women's homeless shelter. The one thing she could say about the *Ordnung* rules, they made life here predictable.

She ventured toward the house she'd grown up in and climbed the porch. Sweat broke out on her upper lip. *Just look for Eli. He will welcome me.* She was sure of it.

Voices rose in a cappella with the words from hymn 131, *"Das Loblied,"* "Hymn of Praise." Always the second song.

The words floated back to her like a gentle breeze, and she mouthed the all-too-familiar hymn as she stowed her suitcases at the end of the porch. As though being drawn forward by something outside herself, she moved toward the open doorway. With a deep breath, she slipped inside at the back of the room. Fortunately, everyone was on their feet for singing. Wouldn't Eli be surprised to see her?

And there he stood in the last row on the far side in the corner. His usual place. He looked in her direction and stared for a moment with wide eyes, probably wondering why she—an *Englisher*—had invaded an Amish service. He motioned her over and pointed to his place.

Her stomach twisted even more. She shook her head, undeserving to take his seat and preferring to stand by the door for a quick exit if she needed it.

He crossed to her, causing several of the single men who always inhabited the back of the room to turn. He guided her to the bench.

She wanted to refuse, but more than that she didn't want to draw attention to herself. No going unnoticed now. She stood where he'd been, and he positioned himself between the end of the bench and the wall.

"Thanks," she whispered and turned from him. She had been right about him welcoming her. At least until he found out who she was.

The man she stood next to jerked his attention forward. He'd obviously been staring. Was he the same one with Eli yesterday? She knew him but couldn't pull his name out of her tumultuous brain. It would come to her later. Rather than singing, she hummed along with the other voices, not wanting to give away her heritage. People would know all too soon who had invaded their midst.

After the next hymn ended, everyone sat. She did so as well, now grateful for a seat. She would blend in better sitting as opposed to standing by the door. As much as she could blend in with brightly colored hair and *Englisher* clothes.

How unorthodox for a woman to be among the young, unmarried men. This would cause a stir. Without enough room on the bench, Eli stood against the wall, as did a few other young men. Having him near gave her courage. Several of the men along the bench glanced in her direction. She tried to feign invisibility.

The bishop stood in the front of the room, Bishop Bontrager, her grandfather. Strict. Inflexible. Judgmental.

She held her breath. Would he see her? Of course he would with her hair. How could he miss her? She might as well be wearing a flashing neon sign on her head. But would he recognize her? Would he accept her back? He and the other leaders were hard on young people who indulged too much during *Rumspringa* or left the faith altogether. Both of which she had done. She'd never planned to return, but here she sat. She wished she'd worn a dark beanie hat to hide her hair.

He was giving one of the three sermons that would be preached by three different men this morning. Though his voice didn't have the edge to it she remembered, it still grated on her nerves, hearing his years of admonishments echoing in her head.

Please, don't have him see me. Now she wished she *had* waited on the porch. She could've listened from there just as well.

She glanced up at Eli, who was staring at her, and her heart skipped a beat. He jerked his gaze away and to the front where it should have been. Had he been trying to figure out why an *Englisher* was here? Or had he recognized her?

She turned her attention to the bishop, who spoke about the woman caught in sin.

Strange. Dori tilted her head. Was that compassion for the woman in his voice? In times past, he would pound the point home that the *woman* had been caught in sin and would focus on *her* sin and how wrong *she'd* been.

His gaze flitted over his flock but kept returning to Dori, and finally, it rested on her. His words halted momentarily. Could he have recognized her? Even with her strange hair and makeup? What would he do now? Single her out as the sinful woman she was?

His eyes softened even more, and his lips pulled up ever so slightly at the corners. He didn't take his eyes off her as he went on. He thumped his fingertips on his chest when he emphasized that the eldest among the accusers dropped his stone first and walked away.

"'Neither do *I* condemn *thee*.'" He spoke the words as though they were just for Dori.

She swore she could see a tear roll down his cheek. Had he changed in the years she'd been gone? She couldn't imagine that he had. Too much to hope for.

When he was through, he sat in one of the chairs up front off to the side reserved for the church leaders but kept his gaze on her.

She couldn't tell if he was chastising her for being the biggest sinner of them all or if he was… Dare she hope he forgave her?

It didn't matter. Even shunned here with the Amish was better than being in the shelter out there, wondering where her next meal would come from. Scared. Alone. She would actually prefer to have people not speak to her rather than face their condemnation.

When the service concluded, Dori remained seated while others filed outside to eat lunch in the late-spring sunshine. People glanced at her on their way past or pretended not to see her at all. Just as well. Dori kept her head down when her parents passed by. Everyone left except Dori, Eli Hochstetler and the bishop.

Eli motioned toward the door and spoke in English. "We eat a meal together. You're welcome to join us."

She delighted in his kindness and wanted to savor it. The fact that he was handsome didn't hurt. His nearness fortified her nerves.

Bishop Bontrager approached and spoke in *Deutsch*. "I'll see to this young lady."

Though Eli appeared reluctant, he gave a nod and left without protest.

She wanted to call back her benefactor. Her champion.

The bishop held out his hands, palms up, continuing in *Deutsch*. "You've come home. At long last." He *had* recognized her. What was this welcoming attitude?

"Ja. Ne." But she *was* here, and this *had* once been her home. *"Ja."* Dori stared at his hands a moment, then put hers in his. She didn't know what else to say. Should she come right out and tell him she was going to have a baby? She should tell him, but he seemed genuinely pleased to see her. She didn't want to destroy that. Didn't want to see the disappointment on his face when he learned how far she'd fallen. She wanted to bask in the joy and love she felt at this moment. What must he think of her wild appearance?

"You've grown up in the years you've been away." He squeezed her hands. "Let's go tell your *vater* and *mutter* you've returned."

Dori pulled free. *"Ne.* Not out there. Not in front of everyone. I didn't realize it was service Sunday. I hadn't even realized it was Sunday at all."

He pulled his eyebrows down. "You didn't know it was Sunday?"

She shouldn't have admitted that. She braced herself for a lecture about going to church.

But instead, he held up a hand. "Wait here, and I'll bring them to you." He walked out, but stopped at the door and stared at her. "Welcome home, *meine enkelin.*" He left.

Was she welcome? Would she be welcomed by her *vater* and *mutter*? If the bishop could welcome her, then certainly her parents would. She put one hand on her stomach. But would she still be welcomed when she told them? Even the New Order Amish here in Elkhart County, Indiana, had their limitations of what they would tolerate. She had gone far outside those boundaries.

She should leave. Before the bishop and her parents returned. But how could she escape without being seen? If she left now, where would she go? Return to the shelter? To Craig? He'd made it clear that the only way he'd have her back was if she "got rid of it" as he put it. She caressed her growing stomach. Her baby was a person to be loved and who would love her. Not something to be gotten rid of.

When the door opened, Dori jumped and spun around. She faced her parents.

Bishop Bontrager motioned toward her. "Our Dorcas has come home."

She cringed at her given name.

Mutter's face lit up, and she rushed to Dori and hugged her. "You're home. You're finally home."

Dori hugged her in return. She'd missed her. "I'm back." Sort of. No sense clouding the moment by telling them she didn't plan to stay.

Vater hung back. "Until the next time she doesn't like the *Ordnung* rules."

Two out of three people happy to see her wasn't so bad. Or was that three out of four if she counted Eli?

Would she be forced to abide by the *Ordnung* if her stay was only temporary? Would she follow the rules for the sake of her child? The *Ordnung* offered a degree of safety and security. Two things she needed most right now. "I will try." She couldn't promise anything more than that.

He gave a nod. "Then welcome home." But his words weren't filled with cheer or even pleasure, only resignation. "Come eat."

She couldn't have pretense and secrets if she was going to live under her *vater*'s roof. When he found out, it would be worse. "Wait. I have to tell you something first."

Three sets of questioning eyes stared at her.

Best to get it over with quickly. "I'm going to have a baby."

Mutter clapped her hands together and put them to her lips. "Our first grandchild."

Vater glanced around and then narrowed his eyes at her. "Where is your husband?"

The temptation to tell him that her "husband" had died tickled her tongue. He would accept that, and everything would be fine. No one would have any reason to shun her or hate her.

But she couldn't.

"I have no husband."

Mutter gasped.

Vater glared. "So this is why you have returned. Where is the *vater*?"

"He doesn't want us anymore." Craig's rejection had hurt more than anything.

"See where your sin has gotten you?"

"Andrew," Bishop Bontrager said.

Her *vater* narrowed his gaze at his own *vater*, the *bishop* of the whole community. "She has brought this on herself. I want no part of her."

Mutter gasped again. "Andrew, you can't mean that."

"I do. And you are to have nothing to do with her either."

The bishop put his hand on his son's shoulder. "We must all forgive trespasses as the *Vater* in heaven forgives us."

Her *vater* shot his hand out to the side, pointing at the floor. "Not this. If we forgive her, what does it say to all the other young people going on *Rumspringa*?"

The bishop straightened. "That we show grace and mercy as our Heavenly *Vater* shows grace and mercy to us."

"*Ne*. It shows we condone their actions. Then every girl will return pregnant and every boy a *vater*-to-be."

"Release the rock in your hand, Andrew."

Her *vater* glared. "You might be able to forgive her, but I can't." He wheeled around and walked to the door. He stopped and turned. "Come, Leah."

Dori's *mutter* glanced between her daughter and her husband.

Dori gave *Mutter* a nod that she understood her *mutter* wasn't abandoning her like *Vater*.

Her *mutter* gave her a weak smile and followed her husband out.

Dori blinked, freeing the tears pooled in her eyes. Then she turned to the bishop. "What do I do now? I thought my parents would allow me to come back. I have no place to live, no money and no job. I assumed I'd be shunned, but I'd at least have a roof over my head."

"You have a roof."

"I don't want to be in my *vater*'s *haus* if he can't tolerate my presence."

"You'll come and live under *meine* roof. I'm across the yard in the *dawdy haus*."

This was a turnaround. She'd thought her *grossvater*, the bishop, would be the one to reject her and her *vater* to welcome her. "The *dawdy haus* isn't big enough. It has only one bedroom."

"We'll manage. I'll hear no arguing over the matter."

"Danki." She needed to know where she stood in the community. "Am I to be shunned?"

The bishop smiled. Or was that her *grossvater* smiling at her? "Did you join church before you left?"

"Ne." But he knew that already.

"Then there are no grounds on which to shun you. You don't fall under the *Ordnung* or church rules." He smiled broadly. "So we can eat together."

"Don't you eat at the big *haus* with *Vater, Mutter* and the rest of the family?"

"I did. But now that you're here, you can cook for the two of us."

"Are you sure?" It was as though he was choosing to be cut off like one who was shunned.

"Let's call it your rent for staying in *meine* home."

"Danki. I appreciate this so much, but I have to ask. Why this change of heart? You never would have accepted me home before."

"You aren't the only one who did some growing up while you were gone. I'm an old man. I don't want to spend what few years I have left at odds with *meine* family."

"But you are at odds with your son because of me."

"Andrew will come around. Given enough time."

Would she be here long enough to see his change? And when she left again, it would confirm that he'd been right about her.

Eli Hochstetler had stared in wonder when Bishop Bontrager left the *haus* and then returned with his son Andrew Bontrager and his son's wife, Leah. Why had the Bontragers gone back inside? Why would the bishop want them to meet Rainbow Girl? Unless…they knew her? But how could they? Who was she?

He thought hard and could come up with only one name. Dorcas?

Couldn't be. But the twisting in the pit of his stomach and the leap of his heart said otherwise.

Rainbow Girl *had* seemed familiar, and now he knew why. She *was* Dorcas Bontrager, the sweet girl who had turned her back on her Amish life.

And him.

Anger boiled inside him. Why hadn't she told him? Why had she returned? Was she here to stay?

Someone nudged him. "Did you invite that *Englisher* here to make a website for you?"

Eli turned to Daniel. "*Ne.* I had no idea she would show up."

"Did you tell her you needed a website? Maybe she decided to see if she could persuade you. *Englishers* can be pushy that way. Thinking they know better than we do."

"Don't talk about her like that. I told her to go to her family." Apparently, she'd taken his advice.

"I wonder why she came."

Eli held his tongue.

"Are you coming to eat?"

"Not yet. You go on."

Daniel walked away.

Soon, the door to the *haus* opened, and Andrew Bontrager stood in the threshold. Quickly, his wife joined him, and they left. Neither happy. One angry, the other on the verge of tears.

Where were the bishop and Rainbow Girl?

He longed to see her, to make sure it was indeed

her—or that it wasn't. Which did he want? Both. Neither. So he stood at the bottom of the steps, anticipating. Debating. Should he go inside?

Eli startled at the appearance of the bishop and Rainbow Girl in the doorway, and he stuttered out words. "B-Bishop Bontrager."

The bishop's eyes widened. "Ah, Eli. This is *meine enkelin*, Dorcas. And this is Eli Hochstetler. But you two already know each other."

His gut twisted, and his heart leaped. He stared hard to find some glint of the Amish girl who'd once lived among them. "Dorcas?"

She spoke in *Deutsch*. "*Ja*. It's me. I'm Dori now."

Even after all this time, he'd still imagined her very Amish. Not…*this*. "Nice to see you. Again."

Dorcas smiled a smile to rattle a man's nerves. "Good to see you again too, Eli."

Eli understood. The lilt of an accent he'd heard came from her Amish roots.

The bishop stepped forward and pointed to the other end of the porch. "Eli, would you get *meine enkelin*'s suitcases and take them to the *dawdy haus*?"

He glanced down at the stoop. "She's staying?"

"*Ja. Meine enkelin* has come home."

Dorcas's expression said she wasn't pleased about it.

Bishop Bontrager gave him a pointed look. "Will you bring them?"

Eli wanted to take them for the Amish girl who had left him behind but not for the outrageous *Englisher* who had returned in her place.

"I can get my own things." Dorcas stepped in that direction.

"Of course, I'll get them." Eli bounded up the four

steps in two strides. He gripped the two side handles and hoisted the suitcases.

Rainbow Girl pointed. "They have wheels."

He extended one index finger. "They'll bounce around too much going over the grass." For some strange reason, having her back in the community both excited and repelled him. How could Dorcas—the rebel—interest him? He followed Bishop Bontrager and Rainbow Girl.

As they passed the crowd dishing up food and eating, many stared at Dorcas.

Eli wanted to tell everyone to stop gawking, that they were being rude. He wanted to protect her.

Inside the *dawdy haus*, Bishop Bontrager indicated next to the door. "You can set them there."

He didn't want to be dismissed so soon. He wanted to stay with Rainbow Girl a little longer. "I can take them—"

The bishop lifted his hand. "Here will be fine."

He set down the suitcases. "Is there anything else I can do to help?" He glanced at Rainbow Girl, who was watching him.

She gave him a small smile in return that delighted him.

The bishop said, "*Ne*. That will be all. *Danki*."

Though Eli wanted to stay, he backed out the door and continued until he stumbled down the two steps. He didn't need this, any of this. He needed to stop thinking about Rainbow Girl and focus on getting his ironworks business going this summer. And he wouldn't be asking her for any help whatsoever.

He'd also planned to start courting this summer. He

hadn't decided who to court yet. But it was high time he took a wife.

Dorcas returning changed everything.

Not necessarily for the *gut*.

Chapter Three

A hole widened inside Dori after Eli left. She glanced around the tiny *dawdy haus*. Her and Craig's apartment had been bigger. And she might have been able to mistake this dwelling for any apartment except for the lack of a big flat-screen TV and a laptop.

The bishop grasped the roller handle of one of the suitcases and aimed for the short hallway with three doors. "The bedroom's back here."

She gripped the side of the extended handle. "I won't take your bedroom. I'll be fine out here." Fortunately, the full-size couch looked comfortable enough. Couldn't be any worse than the shelter beds.

He stared at the couch. "But… I… I want you to feel welcome."

She patted his hand, still on her roller bag. "I do. *Danki.*" She wouldn't be staying for long and didn't want to put him out. The less comfortable she was, the better.

He released his hold on the bag.

How surreal to be here. It was as though she were walking through some bizarre dream. "I appreciate you letting me stay with you for a few days." Strange that she'd so easily slipped back into speaking *Deutsch*. Almost natural. The rest of her short stay wouldn't be so effortless.

"I can't begin to express how pleased I am you've returned."

"I haven't *returned*. I just need a place to stay until I can get things sorted out." Or until Craig came for her.

"But you're here, and I'm grateful for that."

"I'm grateful too. If you hadn't taken me in, I would've had to return to the homeless shelter."

"Homeless?" His eyes widened. "You are never homeless. You always have a place with me. Let's go get some food."

Dori's insides turned cold. "You go. I'll stay here." Though hungry, she didn't want to face the others and be stared at again. Walking from the big *haus* to the *dawdy haus* had been bad enough, like running a gauntlet or being an oddity in a freak show.

"You have to eat."

She was about to lie and say she wasn't hungry when her stomach growled loudly. Why couldn't it have waited a minute or two? "I can't. You go."

He hesitated. "Everyone will be glad for your return."

Dori shook her head. "You saw the way *Vater* reacted."

"But your *mutter* was pleased, as others will be."

"She's not allowed to be pleased." That was clear enough.

"It will be fine. You'll see."

She wasn't convinced. Chances were that more people than not would have a mind-set like her *vater*'s. If

Eli were here to go with her, she might be brave enough to risk it. "I'll pass."

After a moment, he nodded. "I'll bring you a plate of food. Make yourself at home." He scuttled out the door.

Eli ignored the smells of food and the buzz of people talking around the lunch tables in the yard. Instead, he stood, leaning against a large, blooming fruit tree that had been grafted to bear three different varieties of apples in season. Waiting. For what, he wasn't sure. To catch a glimpse of Rainbow Girl? *Ne.* Her unruly image was seared into his brain. The bishop to come out? *Ne.* He would wonder why Eli was standing around and not filling a plate. Eli had no idea why he stood here, just that he couldn't tear his gaze from the *dawdy haus* she'd disappeared into.

Daniel once again came up to him, holding a plate heaped with food this time. "Who is she? And why has she gone into the bishop's *haus*? Is she planning to convert?"

Eli doubted that. Should he tell Daniel who she was? He would find out soon enough. "She's Dorcas Bontrager, the bishop's *enkelin*."

"Are you serious?"

Eli wished he wasn't.

"Weren't you sweet on her?"

Dorcas? *Ja.* This *Englisher*? *Ne.* "That was a long time ago. I've gotten over her." But had he? His flip-floppy emotions told him there was still something there. But what?

"You better get some food before all the *gut* stuff is gone." Daniel took a big bite of the chicken that was on his plate.

"I'll be there in a few minutes. You go on."

Though Daniel seemed reluctant, he walked off.

When the bishop exited, Eli pushed away from the trunk.

Bishop Bontrager made eye contact and headed in his direction. "Why aren't you eating?"

"Um... I didn't know if you would need any more help."

The old man's eyes brightened. "I do have something. Let's fill plates and take them back to *meine haus* and discuss what I have in mind."

Back to where *she* was. This was a change from being dismissed a few minutes ago. The bishop wanted Eli to help him? An honor.

At the table laden with food, Eli loaded a plate for himself, then carried the second plate the bishop had filled. For Rainbow Girl, no doubt. He would get to eat lunch with her. His heart skipped a beat. Maybe figure out how the Amish girl he'd known could turn into the *Englisher* one who'd returned.

Before they reached the *dawdy haus*, Andrew Bontrager, the bishop's son and Rainbow Girl's *vater*, approached. "You're feeding her in there? Is she too embarrassed to eat with everyone else?"

She did need to eat, and she couldn't exactly blend in. No Amish liked to stand out from the others. But then, she wasn't Amish. She had designed her appearance to draw attention to herself.

The bishop held up his hand. "Give her time. Our ways are a lot to get used to."

Andrew scowled. "She was raised with our ways and threw them away. She knew exactly what it would be like returning in her state." He strode away, shaking his head.

The old man sighed. "Dorcas isn't the only one who needs a little time to adjust." He opened the *dawdy haus* door and walked in.

If Rainbow Girl planned to stay for any length of time, everyone would need time to adjust. Eli followed and froze just inside. His breath caught.

Rainbow Girl lay curled up on one end of the sofa. Eyes closed. Even, slow breathing. Out of place in an Amish home. Though she gave an unreal feel to the room, his insides felt happy to see her here. He could almost see the sweet, pretty girl from his youth.

Bishop Bontrager put a finger to his lips, then pointed at the table and whispered, "Let's sit."

Eli set the two plates he held on to the table. A sound from across the room drew him around.

Rainbow Girl swung her legs off the couch and sat up.

His mouth reacted by pulling into a smile. He straightened it.

Bishop Bontrager waved her over. "I'm sorry we disturbed you, but since you're up, come eat."

"I learned to sleep light at the shelter." She padded over in stocking feet, socks that were like gloves with a different color for each individual toe. She sat in one of the chairs.

The shelter?

The bishop looked at the one remaining chair, then at Eli. "Would you go to the big *haus* and bring another chair?"

Eli shook his head. "I'll stand."

"Are you sure?"

Nodding, Eli picked up his plate and leaned against the counter. If he left, she might disappear like a mirage. Something inside him needed her to stay.

Bishop Bontrager gave a nod and sat. "I'll say a blessing for our food."

Rainbow Girl's fork, with a chunk of potato on it, hovered an inch from her open mouth. She set the utensil on her plate. After the bishop prayed, she picked up her fork once more. "I've missed really good potato salad." She put the bite into her mouth.

Eli stared at Rainbow Girl's lip. How could she eat with that piece of metal in her upper lip? His own lip twitched. The loop in the side of her nose made his itch, but he resisted the urge to scratch it.

He studied her to find some vestige of the girl she once was. What had happened to that girl he grew up with who bested him in math every time? Where had the girl gone who'd brought him a handicapped puppy? How had she turned into...this?

She didn't stop eating until her plate had nothing left. Hungry, indeed. It had been *gut* that he bought her the larger sandwich yesterday.

Eli hurriedly took bites and swallowed the barely chewed food. "Bishop, what is it you need me to do?"

"Let's finish our food first. It'll be better to show you." In other words, eat, no talking.

Eli ate without looking at *her* again so she wouldn't realize he'd been paying more attention to her than his food.

When finished, the bishop pushed his plate away from him. "Now, Eli, about that project I have in mind."

Project? That sounded big. Would it take away from Eli getting his business started?

The bishop stood and retrieved a measuring tape from a kitchen drawer. "Follow me." He walked down the short hallway to the back door opposite the front one. Hooks hung on the walls leading to the exit. A bedroom door to the right and bathroom to the left.

Eli had actually helped build this little *haus* many years ago when the bishop had turned over his farm to Andrew. Eli glanced at Rainbow Girl, who shrugged. He supposed he should follow and headed down the hall. She trailed behind.

The bishop stopped at the end of the hall and indicated the door. "I want to extend this another eight to ten feet." He opened the door and walked down the steps outside onto the grass and turned around. "Come."

The rear of the *dawdy haus* faced away from the crowd of people eating and playing.

Eli stepped aside to let Rainbow Girl exit ahead of him. She did. In stocking feet.

He followed this time. "Why do you want a longer hallway out into the yard?"

The old man smiled like a little boy. "For the extra bedroom, of course." He strode about ten feet straight out from the *haus*. "Move the door to here. I still want to get cross ventilation. No sense being impractical."

Eli's mind whirled. Building onto his *dawdy haus* seemed impractical. What could he possibly need another bedroom for? Maybe he'd heard wrong. "You... want to make...*your* bedroom bigger?" That didn't make sense either.

"*Ne*. A bedroom for Dorcas." He turned to the right and held out his hands to indicate the space.

So she planned to stay for quite some time. Or at

least, the bishop thought she would stay long enough to need a room.

Rainbow Girl stepped forward. "You can't do this. I'll be fine on the couch."

He waggled his hand at her. "Nonsense. The couch will never do."

Rainbow Girl folded her arms. "I won't let you."

"*Uf*, it's *meine haus*. I'll do with it what I like."

The bishop turned to Eli. "What do you say? Will you help me build it?"

"Why doesn't she stay at the big *haus*?" That would be the easier option, and there would be plenty of room for her.

"Because she's staying with me. Now, will you help?"

Rainbow Girl turned to Eli. "Tell him *ne*." Apparently, she didn't intend to stay.

Again, Eli wanted to say *ne* to doing something for the *Englisher* girl who had returned. Since she didn't want the room—and he really had no other choice— he sided with the bishop. "*Ja.* I'll help." Then maybe he could find the girl she once was under her facade.

"Not only one room, but a smaller one across the hall, as well." Bishop Bontrager spun around opposite the first room he'd indicated and thrust out his arms. "No sense wasting this space."

"For what?"

The bishop waved his hand in the air. "No need to get into all that right now. I'd like to go into town tomorrow and purchase the lumber."

This definitely meant Eli would need to put off making progress on his business. "What about your son? Won't he help you?"

"Andrew is being stubborn."

Rainbow Girl planted her hands on her hips. "Would you drop this? He won't agree."

Eli didn't know if she was referring to him or her *vater*. It didn't really matter. He *had* agreed, and the bishop could overrule his son, so, the addition would be built. "I can use *meine vater*'s wagon. What time shall I pick you up?"

Rainbow Girl rolled her eyes. "Don't waste your time."

The bishop turned to his *enkelin*. "It won't be a waste." He swung his gaze to Eli. "I'll check with Andrew and see if he'll allow us to use his wagon without a fuss. It'll be more convenient."

"Seriously?" Rainbow Girl threw her hands up and headed toward the doorway. "Men think they always know what's best." She disappeared inside, still muttering.

Eli frowned. But men did. Even with all that makeup, he could remember how cute she was when she got mad.

Bishop Bontrager clasped him on the shoulder. "Don't worry about her. She'll see the value of it in time."

A part of Eli found a little pleasure in her being upset with him. She had rejected the community and her family, so she had no say in matters. Another part longed to mend this breach. It rankled to have her angry with him when he'd done nothing wrong, but it shouldn't, and that rankled even more.

The bishop held out the tip of the measuring tape. "Take it down to that corner of the *haus* so we can figure out how much lumber to purchase."

Eli wasn't sure this was a *gut* idea, but he was the bishop, so Eli did as instructed.

Andrew Bontrager came around the corner. "What are you doing, *Vater*?"

"Eli is going to help me build another bedroom onto the *haus*."

"What do you need a second bedroom for?"

"I think you know."

Andrew pointed toward the *dawdy haus*'s back doorway. "For her?"

"Ja."

Eli glanced toward the *haus*. Rainbow Girl stood there with her arms crossed. He hadn't seen her return to the opening.

"Why bother? She'll only leave again. Then all the time and materials and work will be for nothing."

So Andrew didn't believe she would stay. Did he want her to leave? Did Eli? *Ne.* He definitely wanted her to stay. Didn't he?

The bishop held his hands out to his sides. "'*We should…be glad; for this thy brother—*' or sister in this case '*—was dead, and is alive again; and was lost, and is found.*' Where is your forgiveness?"

"Forgiveness is for the repentant. Something *she* is not." Andrew spun around and strode away.

Bishop Bontrager gazed toward his *enkelin*. "He'll come around, Dorcas."

"Why's that? Because he *didn't* inherit your stubborn streak?" She disappeared inside.

Chapter Four

The following morning, Dori had slept late—well, late for an Amish. She threw back the blanket and sat up on the couch.

It took some doing, but she'd managed to convince the bishop to stay in his room and let her sleep in the living room. She'd slept more soundly than she had in over a month since being kicked out of Craig's apartment. She had no more worries that anyone would steal her belongings during the night. Sleeping in sweatpants and a T-shirt rather than her jeans and jacket had helped, as well.

The bishop didn't appear to be anywhere in the *haus*. Had he already left with Eli? She pictured Eli's kind face when he'd bought her a sandwich two days ago. Had she missed seeing him this morning?

She heard a sound on the porch, as though something or someone had stepped on a creaky board. With her hand, she pushed aside the blue curtain enough to see out.

Her *mutter* hurried away from the *dawdy haus* across the lawn back to the big *haus*.

What had she been doing here? Had she intended to come for a visit, then changed her mind? *Ne.* She wouldn't defy *Vater.* Then why?

Out of curiosity, Dori opened the front door. On the porch sat a bundle of neatly folded fabrics. She picked up the pile and shut the door.

She spread out the clothes on the couch. *Mutter* had delivered two cape dresses—one royal blue, the other a medium pink—two aprons—one white and one black— and a white *kapp.* In the *kapp* lay several bobby pins. Everything Dori needed to dress the part of an Amish woman. These looked suspiciously like the garments she'd left behind. *Mutter* was welcoming her home even if *Vater* wasn't. *She* wanted Dori to fit in. To look Amish. To stay.

But Dori didn't want any of those things. She had been away for several years and had returned in shame. If she hadn't gotten pregnant and Craig hadn't thrown her out, she would never have come back. Being destitute and desperate had forced her home.

Home?

Was this home? For the time being, because she had no other option. If only Craig would have accepted their baby. No matter how much she needed her Amish family, this would never be home again.

She fingered the pink dress. *Mutter* remembered it had been her favorite color as a girl.

Dori wouldn't feel right wearing Amish clothes. That would give everyone the impression she had come home to stay. Which she hadn't. She was no more Amish than Craig. Or any *Englisher.* She hadn't fitted in before she left and didn't fit in now. Her *vater* and the bishop had repeatedly chastised her for one thing or another, trying to make her into a *gut* Amish woman, but she never could do things quite right, questioned too many of the rules. She'd been a disappointment to everyone. It had been best to leave. For everyone.

Though unwilling to return and no longer Amish, she did need help right now.

She hadn't expected to have a warm welcome, but she hadn't expected *Vater* to scorn her as he had. And she certainly hadn't expected the bishop, of all people, to take her in. Of anyone, she would have expected him to be the toughest on her, but he was the most welcoming. What had caused his attitude change? If he could show her mercy and grace, maybe there was hope that her *vater* would soften toward her, as well. Would Eli too? She hoped so.

She took the pile of Amish clothes and tucked them behind the couch's end table in the corner. She didn't need the bishop pestering her to wear them.

After taking a *gut* long shower, she frowned at her brown roots in the mirror. She wouldn't be touching those up anytime soon.

Overnight, her stomach seemed to have swelled so much that her jeans were no longer big enough to close. She settled for her lime-green sweatpants and an oversize neon orange T-shirt. Definitely not authorized Amish colors, but they fitted over her growing middle.

Now, for breakfast.

A single rinsed bowl with a spoon sat in the bottom of the kitchen sink. It looked as though the bishop had had cold cereal for breakfast. Or had he gone to the big *haus*?

No matter. She opened cupboards and drawers until she had a spoon, bowl and two boxes of cereal. The first, bran flakes with raisins, and the second, sugarcoated corn flakes. His version of sweetening his cereal. She was glad to see he hadn't changed in that respect. She mixed the two in her bowl and poured the milk. She'd actually missed this.

When she was a very little girl, from about age six until she was ten or so, she would sneak across the yard to the *dawdy haus* and eat breakfast with him on Saturday mornings. She laughed to herself. She'd thought no one knew, that it was her and *Grossvater*'s secret, but *Mutter* likely watched her skip across the grass, then pretended to be worried over her absence.

Then things began to change. Kathleen Yoder had defied the church leaders and the bishop by leaving the community and attending college. *Grossvater* had spoken against her actions. He'd pointed a finger in Dori's face and told her to never do anything like that. His anger had scared her, and she stopped her weekly breakfast treks to sit at his table.

Enough of thinking of things lost. She needed to wash her clothes so she could wear something else tomorrow.

Sometime later, noise from behind the *dawdy haus* drew her to the door. She opened it.

In the grass stood a wagon full of lumber as well as three young Amish men with the bishop. One was Eli. She allowed herself a moment to savor Eli's presence, then studied the other two. Who were they? Daniel Burkholder, and the other was… Benjamin Yoder. So the bishop had used his influence to rope in more help. How many more would show up at his request?

Eli hoisted several two-by-fours at once that had to be ten feet long. Smithing had made him quite strong.

The other two young men worked together to carry an equal stack. While the bishop carried smaller items like a bag of nails, hand tools and other lightweight things. Eli set his load in the grass and headed back to the wagon for more. His gaze fell on her, and she smiled. He froze. His eyes widened, as though he'd been caught raiding the kitchen in the middle of the night.

She glanced down at herself. She must look a fright in her brightly colored sweatpants and top…and no makeup. Or had the bishop told him about her condition? She hoped not. She didn't want the tenuous bond between them to be broken. She resisted the urge to place her hands on her rounding belly and leaned a little forward so her baggy T-shirt would camouflage it better. He'd been careful not to mention that the smaller room would be for the baby. She appreciated that. She wasn't ashamed of being pregnant, but for some reason, she didn't want Eli to know. Maybe she would be gone before he ever found out.

This was foolishness. "Don't you need a building permit before you start?" Dori had hoped the bishop would have to wait a couple of weeks before one was issued, giving her a chance to make other arrangements.

The bishop waved a piece of paper in the air. "Got one. Since this is a simple addition with no plumbing, they have a swift process to grant us permits without delay."

Some Amish obtained waivers to exclude parts of construction that went against their community's *Ordnung* but were mandatory in *Englisher* homes, like indoor plumbing, smoke and carbon monoxide detectors. This wasn't new construction, merely a simple addition. But this New Order Amish community had most of the same conveniences as people in the outside world, so there wasn't usually a need to get a waiver, which would take time.

Now, she was going to feel guilty when she left because he'd put in all this money, time, effort and supplies for this project. Probably his plan. A way to shame her into staying. She doubted he could be stopped if he didn't want to be. His son had probably tried. Maybe she could talk to Eli and convince him to delay the work.

Doubtful. She'd seen his resolve solidify when she'd tried to get him to turn the bishop down for this project. He apparently planned to be as stubborn as the bishop. The image of Craig popped into her mind. He was stubborn too. She pushed thoughts of him aside for the time being.

For now, she turned her attention back to the activity outside. She would like to plant herself on the stoop and watch Eli while he worked, but that would make everyone feel awkward.

So she stayed for a minute before closing the door and taking the impressive image of the blacksmith with her.

With Eli fresh on her mind, Dori headed back to the living room. On her way, she checked on the clothes she'd left to dry in the bathroom. They hung over the shower rod and dripped into the tub as well as onto a towel on the floor. They should be fully dry by morning. She would've hung her *Englisher* clothes outside, but that would have drawn unwanted attention to her family. She needed to remain as invisible as possible during her stay.

She opened her backpack on the couch and retrieved her laptop and cell phone as well as their chargers.

Then she unplugged the coffee maker and toaster, and plugged in her devices, stringing the cords over to the table. The phone cord didn't reach, so she slid the table closer to the counter.

The bishop probably never imagined having such electronics in his *haus*. But maybe he should. More and more Amish were forced to have websites for online businesses. With farmland becoming increasingly more scarce to purchase, many had to resort to working for various manufacturers or home-building companies, or starting their own construction business or other ventures. The ones with businesses needed websites to draw customers from outside the community. *Englishers* were nuts for anything Amish made. Foolish people.

She opened her laptop and powered it up. Fortunately, Janis at the shelter, who stole other people's property, never discovered Dori had this. While she waited for her laptop, she switched on her cell phone and turned it into a hot spot to get Wi-Fi. The service would likely be glitchy, but she had unlimited data, and it would be better than nothing. How had she grown up without computers and the internet?

She logged on to her email account. All junk mail. Nothing from Craig. Working to the sound of clunking lumber being stacked and male voices, she turned her efforts to searching for a job. After an hour of filling out online applications, she made herself toast with peanut butter and returned to the table. Needing a break from job hunting, she opened a new browser window and let her fingers hover over the keys. What should she search for?

For fun, she typed in *Eli Hochstetler* and hit Enter.

To her surprise, hundreds of posts came up from various social media platforms. After the first page of results, the rest were obviously not relevant. She found three that seemed like they were referring to *her* Eli. All three raved about his ironwork. She clicked on each one and read. One for an herb chopper, the second for a kitchen knife and the third for a weather vane. Pictures for all three items, but none of Eli directly. His muscled arm wielding a hammer in one, the back of his head in another, his rugged profile in the third. She lingered on that picture the longest. Why were Amish so set against having their picture taken? It was only a picture. And Eli photographed well.

Then she studied the backgrounds of all three pictures. Multiples of similar items like the ones in the posts. It appeared as though Eli Hochstetler had gone into business, making more than just horseshoes. *Gut* for him. He'd always loved pounding on iron. She'd often wondered if he liked it because that was an acceptable way of letting out his aggression. But he never acted angry, like he needed to find a way to disguise the emotion. He genuinely seemed as though he simply enjoyed smithing.

She dug in her backpack and pulled out the door knocker. He had always done *gut* work. He must have a website. She would like to see all the things he'd made. After trying every variation of website names she could think of for him, her efforts yielded nothing. How disappointing.

Eli glanced at the *dawdy haus* again, but since that first glimpse, Rainbow Girl hadn't shown herself. What was she doing inside?

Bishop Bontrager took hold of the horse's harness. "I'm going to go unhitch Nelly and turn her out in the field."

Eli raised up from where he set a bag of powdered cement. "I can do that if you want me to."

"*Danki*, but I can do it." The bishop walked the big draft horse away, pulling the wagon.

Eli turned to the other two and grasped the handle of one of the shovels. "Let's dig a shallow trench for the cinder blocks first." They would form the foundation of the addition. The string lines had already been set out.

Benjamin Yoder took the other shovel.

Daniel Burkholder grabbed the pick. "I can't believe the bishop is letting an outrageous *Englisher* live in his home. And building her a room."

Eli could hardly believe it himself, but that was *not* something to voice out loud. One didn't question the bishop. Besides, the bishop's actions fell under their Amish rules of forgiveness. "Why shouldn't he? She's his *enkelin*."

"She abandoned our faith and is *English* now."

Though Benjamin Yoder didn't say anything, he nodded his agreement with Daniel.

Eli didn't like anyone speaking poorly of her. "She's obviously decided to return." At least he hoped that was what she'd decided.

"Dressed like that? And what about her hair? The bishop can't allow that. Do you think he's okay? He is pretty old."

"Of course, he's fine." But Eli had to wonder about the bishop, as well. In times past, he wouldn't have tolerated her appearance, but now, he seemed fine with her returning as she was. He leaned his shovel against the outside of the *haus*. "I'm going to get a drink of water. Start without me." He charged up the back steps and through the doorway, wiping his dusty boots as he entered. Then he stopped short. He shouldn't barge into a *haus* unannounced with a woman inside. *"Hallo?"*

Rainbow Girl stepped into his field of vision from the kitchen area. *"Hallo."*

His insides did funny things at the sight of her.

"Did you need something?"

He cleared his throat. "I came for a drink of water."

"Come on in." She pulled a glass out of the cupboard, filled it at the sink and handed it to him.

"Danki."

She gifted him with a smile. *"Bitte.* How's it going out there?"

He smiled back. "Fine." He gulped half the glass, then slowed down to sips. No sense rushing.

After a minute, she folded her arms. "Go ahead. Ask your question."

"What?"

"You obviously want to ask me something. What is it? Why do I color my hair all different colors? Why do I dress like this? Why did I leave? What is it?"

She posed all *gut* questions, but not the one he needed an answer to. A question that was no business of his to ask.

"Go ahead. Ask. I don't mind." Very un-Amish, but she'd offered. *Ne*, insisted.

He cleared his throat. "Are you going to stay?"

She stared for a moment, then looked away. Obviously, not the question she'd expected, nor one she wanted to answer.

He'd made her uncomfortable. He never should have

asked. What if she said *ne*? Did he want her to say *ja*? "You don't have to tell me." He didn't want to know anymore.

She pinned him with her steady brown gaze. "I don't know. I don't want to, but I'm sort of in a bind at the moment."

Maybe for the reason she'd been so sad the other day, which had made him feel sympathy for her.

He appreciated her honesty. "Then why does our bishop think you are?"

"He's hoping I do."

His heart tightened. "Why are you giving him false hope?" Why was she giving Eli false hope?

"I'm not. I've told him this is temporary. He won't listen. Maybe you could convince him to stop this foolishness—" she waved her hand toward where the building activity was going on "—before it's too late."

He chuckled. "You don't tell the bishop what to do. *He* tells *you*."

He really should head back outside to help the others. Instead, he filled his glass again and leaned against the counter. He studied her over the rim of his glass. Did he want Rainbow Girl to stay? She'd certainly turned things upside down around here. Turned him upside down. Instead of working in his forge—where he most enjoyed spending time—he was here, and gladly so. He preferred working with iron rather than wood, but today, carpentry strangely held more appeal.

Time to get back to work. He guzzled the rest of his water and set the glass in the sink. *"Danki."* As he turned to leave, something on the table caught his attention. The door knocker he'd made years ago for Dorcas—Rainbow Girl—*ne*, Dorcas, but now Rainbow Girl had it. They were the same person, but not the same. He crossed to the table and picked up his handiwork. "You kept this?"

She came up next to him. "*Ja*. I liked having a reminder of…"

"Of what?" Dare he hope him?

She stared at him. "Of…my life growing up here."

That was probably a better answer. He didn't need to be thinking of her as anything more than a lost *Englisher*.

She pointed to her computer on the table. "I found posts online about a few of your iron pieces you made that *Englishers* bought. They all praised your work."

"I don't care about such things."

"You should. You could sell a lot more of your pieces with reviews like that, but I couldn't find your website."

"I don't have one." He'd hoped to be able to sell enough to make a living off his work. So far, he hadn't and realized he would need a website, but he didn't want to be beholden to her to get it. He wanted to be self-sufficient.

He needed to create more pieces, and now was a perfect time—with the lighter workload with *Vater*'s fields rented out.

Since his *vater*'s heart attack last summer, nine months ago, Eli had been entrusted with more responsibilities around the farm. Fortunately, his *vater* had decided to rent out the fields this year on the recommendation of the community's new doctor, Dr. Kathleen. Eli could have handled running the farm himself with his younger brothers. It wouldn't have been too much for him to manage, but *Vater* thought otherwise, scared after nearly dying.

Though Eli didn't like witnessing *Vater*'s vulnerability, he secretly delighted in the lighter workload. This would give him an opportunity to design more original ironwork pieces in his blacksmith shop behind the barn. He'd consigned a few items in town but hoped to have enough creations to start his own business. Farming was *gut* and honorable work, but he liked making things with his hands, with hot metal and a hammer. He had ideas for new pieces he wanted to create.

If he could figure out how, this was his chance to get his business going. He knew it would take all the time he'd been afforded in lieu of planting and harvesting. He would need to learn all about selling on the internet, creating a website and proving to the church leaders—his *vater* being one of them—that his was a viable business worthy of internet access and use. He wouldn't have another opportunity like this. If he didn't make a go of this by the fall, he would need to give up his dream.

Rainbow Girl broke into his thoughts. "You need to have a website. You could sell a lot more of your work. *Englishers* love buying Amish-made stuff. A website can do that for you."

Ja, he knew he needed a website in order to make money from the *Englishers*. "I plan to hire an *Englisher* to do that for me." So much to do and learn to get started. A bit overwhelming.

"I can do it."

"*Ne*. I'll hire someone." He couldn't be beholden to her.

"That would be a waste of money. There are so many programs out there to help you build a site. And they're easy to use."

He could make his own site? *Ne*. "It would be better if I don't fiddle in *Englisher* things and let an *Englisher* do them."

"So you're going to pay an *Englisher* to monitor your website after it's built and tell you when you have orders? You aren't going to make any money that way. You need to monitor your own site. I can build you a site and teach you how to maintain it."

"*Ne.* I'll hire an *Englisher.*" An *Englisher* who wasn't *her.*

"But you can do this. You'll pick it up fast. I know you will. You always were the smartest boy in class. If I could learn how to do it, then you can."

She thought he was smart? He liked that. He wanted her to help him, but that wouldn't be wise. He couldn't let her do work for him. She wasn't staying. Or at least she didn't know if she was staying. How could she not know? She simply needed to make a choice. The right choice. He wouldn't let her get under his skin to just have her leave again. "*Ne.* I need to get back to work." He headed for the back door.

"Eli, wait."

He turned and resisted the urge to cross over to her. To stand next to her. To stare at her.

She dug a ten-dollar bill from her backpack. "Here. I never had a chance to buy any food with this." She held it out to him.

He waved it away. "Keep it." He strode out the door. She probably needed it more than he did.

Once in the yard again, he picked up the shovel and jabbed it into the ground. The trench would stabilize the concrete blocks of the foundation. But what would stabilize him?

He wished he'd grabbed the pick. Swinging it would

have been similar to the rhythm of swinging his hammer in his forge. An action that helped him think. An action that could replace thoughts of Rainbow Girl. Instead, he was stuck with her image drifting in the front of his mind.

Chapter Five

Midafternoon, Dori sat in the shade of the front porch of the *dawdy haus*. Just about time for her younger siblings to return from school. Which ones were still school-age? John, the youngest at age ten, for sure attended school. Luke and Mark at eleven and thirteen would, as well. Sixteen-year-old Matthew had likely gone off to work with *Vater*. Nearly a man. Ruth, the second oldest, was eighteen now. Where had she spent her day? Inside the big *haus*, having been told not to talk to Dori? And the oldest at twenty-two, Dori was the biggest disappointment to her family.

An open buggy drove into the yard with Ruth at the reins. Mark sat next to her, with Luke and John in the rear seat, jostling each other.

Ruth glanced Dori's way as she drove to the barn and parked. "You boys take care of the buggy and horse. And no dillydallying." She climbed down and crossed the yard to the *dawdy haus*.

Dori squirmed in her chair. She wished she hadn't sat out in the open.

Ruth stopped at the bottom of the two steps. "Dorcas? Is that really you?"

"*Ja.* I go by Dori now." She didn't know what else to say, so she gave her sister a tight smile.

"Dori." Ruth's mouth curved up in a big grin. She set her tote bag on the steps as she climbed them. "You're home."

Dori automatically stood.

Though a bit hesitant, her sister hugged her. "I'm so happy you've returned. I've missed having *meine* sister around."

"I haven't exactly returned. This is only temporary."

"Then why is *Grossvater* building you a room?"

How many times would she have to tell people the room was the bishop's idea? "You know how he can be when he sets his mind to something. I told him I'm here only temporarily."

"Please stay. Do you know what it's like living in a *haus* with all boys? *Mutter* and I are overrun with them."

Dori understood. The *haus* had been pretty boisterous before she left. She had enjoyed time in the kitchen with her *mutter* and sister. "I don't fit in here. And I don't think *Vater* would approve of you talking to me."

"What is he going to do? Shun me? Let him. I've prayed for you to return. *Mutter* wants to come talk to you, but *Vater* forbade her."

"Didn't he forbid you, as well?"

Ruth shrugged. "Not in so many words. He said you were an *Englisher* now, and talking to *Englishers* was not a *gut* idea. Then glared at each one of us. I took his warning as a suggestion."

Oh, dear. Was her sister as defiant as Dori had been? She hoped not.

Had *Vater* told Ruth and the others about the baby? "What did *Vater* tell you about me being here?"

"That you came home because you had no place else to go, and…"

"And what?"

"He doesn't think you're going to stay. He thinks you're too *English* now. But I don't."

Dori couldn't help but to laugh. "You don't think I'm too *English*? Have you looked at me?" She held her hands out to the sides.

"All this on the outside isn't you. It's what's in your heart. And I know in mine that you are still Amish in yours."

Her sweet sister deserved the truth, even if it meant she too would reject Dori. "Ruth, the reason I've come—and it *is* just temporary—is because my boyfriend kicked me out of our apartment."

"How mean. It's *gut* you're not with him anymore."

"That's not all. He kicked me out because…because I'm pregnant. That's why *Vater* won't talk to me."

Ruth's eyes widened. "Oh."

"Craig doesn't want the baby, but I won't get rid of it." Dori caressed her lower abdomen.

A smile slowly took over Ruth's face. "I'm going to be a *tante*."

That was what her sister got out of this? No condemnation? "Don't tell anyone."

"I won't. Does *Grossvater* know?"

"*Ja.* I think that's why he's so set on building rooms for me and the baby in the *dawdy haus*. I wish he wouldn't."

Ruth took hold of one of Dori's hands. "Don't leave. You can't let your baby—*meine* little nephew or niece—grow up in a place where people discard what they don't want. You're staying, that's all there is to it." As stubborn as the bishop, and as willful as her.

Time to change the topic. "Did you pick the boys up after school?"

"*Ne.* I'm the teacher. If they don't behave, I make them walk home."

"I'm happy for you." Her sister was probably a very *gut* teacher. "You always did like school and teaching the farm animals. You would go into the chicken enclosure with your schoolbooks and try to make them learn their letters and numbers."

With an impish smile, Ruth tilted her head. "Even animals could do with a little education."

"You almost had me believing they could count."

"I still say that Claudia Clucker could count." She laughed.

Dori joined her. It felt so *gut* to laugh. How long had it been? Leave it to Ruth to make her forget her troubles if only for a brief moment.

Mark, Luke and John came out of the barn and ran over to the *dawdy haus*. They stopped short of climbing the steps and eyed Dori. Mark spoke for his younger brothers. "Can we go see how the construction is going and help out until supper?"

"Check to see if *Mutter* needs anything first."

The trio ran for the big *haus*.

Dori shook her head. "I can't believe how grown-up you are."

Ruth lifted one shoulder, then gave a mischievous

smile. "Who does *Grossvater* have working on the addition besides Eli Hochstetler?"

"Benjamin Yoder and Daniel Burkholder."

Ruth's eyes widened and gleamed. "I'll have to go see how they're doing." She pranced off the porch.

Dori caught up to her. "Is there something going on between you and Daniel?"

"Me? Why would you say that?"

"Because you lit up at the mention of his name."

Ruth stopped at the side of the *haus*. "There's nothing between me and Daniel."

"But…?"

Ruth bit her bottom lip. "I wouldn't mind if there was. But you can't tell anyone."

"My lips are sealed." Dori enjoyed chatting with her sister. She'd missed moments like this. She hooked her arm with Ruth's. "Let's go see how the men are doing."

In the backyard, all four men wielded hammers, putting the last boards on the wall-stud frames that lay in the grass, ready to be raised into place when the time came. Each one lay on the ground on the side of the wall trench where it would be put up. They'd already dug the trench and poured the footing concrete in the bottom of it.

Ruth spoke up. "*Grossvater*, you'll have three more eager workers here in a minute."

All four hammers stilled, and four heads turned. Daniel's mouth cocked up a tad on one side. Ruth's interest in the young man wasn't one-sided, it seemed.

The bishop put a hand on his lumbar region and straightened. "*Gut*. They can help us lay out the boards for the roof trusses."

Dori had a hard time thinking of the bishop as her

grossvater. He'd seemed very much the bishop before she left. But now he did seem more like a *grossvater*, like *her grossvater*. She turned her attention to Eli, who was focused on her. Her insides wiggled, and it wasn't the baby. She resisted the smile that was tickling her mouth.

The three younger boys ran up, clamoring to help.

The bishop put them to work.

Dori leaned closer to her sister and spoke softly. "So why Daniel and not Benjamin? He's closer to your age."

"Benjamin is nice enough, but he's…he's just not…"

"Daniel?"

Ruth's smile stretched. *"Ja."*

"Well, from the look Daniel gave you, I'd say the interest is mutual."

"You think so?"

"Ja." So what did that say for Eli? And for that matter, herself?

Mutter appeared from around the corner. "I've brought cookies." Her gaze sought out Dori and rested on her.

Dori stared back. She'd missed *Mutter*. She wished she could go up to her and get a hug. She wished she could sit with her on the porch. She wished *Mutter* could tell her what it was like to have a baby and give her advice on how to be a *gut mutter*.

The men and boys grabbed cookies. When the plate was nearly empty, *Mutter* crossed to Dori and Ruth. Three oatmeal-raisin cookies remained. Ruth took one. *Mutter* held the plate out to her eldest daughter.

Dori took a cookie. *"Danki."*

Mutter took the last cookie with a smile and faced

the men. "It is *gut* to have *meine* children together." She stood between her daughters.

Dori knew that *Mutter* was including her, and she welcomed the inclusion. She'd felt like an outsider with Craig ever since she told him she was pregnant two months ago. Truth be told, she'd always felt as though she didn't quite belong in the *English* world, a world she hadn't been raised in. References to TV shows and movies that everyone seemed to have seen. She'd tried to catch up, but there was so much. Some of the shows were so ridiculous, she'd given up. She feared Craig would grow tired of her not quite fitting in and send her away, so she changed her appearance as much as possible to prove to him and others she wasn't Amish.

And prove to herself.

But Craig had sent her away anyway. And she'd ended up at the shelter, where fear ruled her thoughts. But here, she didn't fear for herself or her belongings. Being here served as a sort of comfort that she didn't like. This was not the place for her, so she shouldn't find comfort here.

And yet…

Eli ate his second cookie slowly, not anxious to get back to work. He couldn't seem to take his eyes off Rainbow Girl. Was it any wonder with her brightly colored clothes and hair? Her appearance was designed to attract attention and make people stare. He was no exception, but it was more than her appearance that held him captive.

When she smiled, his insides tumbled about.

He wouldn't mind doing all this work on the *dawdy haus* if she were staying. That would give him hope.

But would she even still be here by the time they completed this project in a week or two? Would all this be for nothing?

Andrew Bontrager and Matthew, his eldest son, arrived home and came around to the rear of the *dawdy haus*, surveying the activity. Andrew shook his head. Matthew glared at his oldest sister and walked away.

Rainbow Girl's *vater* inclined his head toward his wife.

Leah Bontrager didn't turn toward her eldest daughter, but when her lips moved with her whispered words, Eli guessed they were for Rainbow Girl because she nodded. Leah strode around the work area to her husband.

Andrew waved his arm toward Ruth. "Come on, Ruth. Leave the men to their work."

Ruth stepped sideways and hooked her arm with her sister's. "I'll stay out of the way."

Open defiance? What would Andrew do?

Rainbow Girl patted her sister's arm. "Go. I don't want you in trouble with him too."

"Don't worry. *Vater* is all bluster."

Eli was grateful he stood on the side of the construction closest to the girls so he could hear their conversation. How nice of Rainbow Girl to try to protect her sister.

Andrew huffed away with Leah at his side. He allowed his three youngest boys to continue working.

The two remaining ladies sat on the back stoop, chattering. Rainbow Girl seemed happy. He liked seeing her happy. Now, instead of wondering what she was doing, he could glance her way.

Later, when as much work as possible had been completed until the footing concrete dried in the trench, Eli went over to Rainbow Girl. He motioned toward the ragtag bits of construction. "What do you think so far? I know it doesn't look like much now, but in a day or two it'll start resembling a building."

"You know what I think."

Ja, he did. "That you're not staying." He folded his arms. "Well, I think you're wrong." Hoped she was wrong.

Ruth piped up. "I agree with you. She's staying. She just has to."

He liked the way Ruth thought. Between the bishop, Ruth and Rainbow Girl's *mutter*, she wouldn't be able to leave so easily.

With her mouth stretched wide, Ruth rose to her feet. "*Hallo*, Daniel."

His friend gave a nod. "Ruth." After staring for a moment, he turned to Eli. "Benjamin has your horse hitched to your trap." His gaze returned to Ruth.

Eli nodded. "We should go. I'll come back tomorrow to lay the concrete blocks for the foundation."

Rainbow Girl squinted up at him. The sun on her face made her appear to be glowing. "What about your forge? You don't want to neglect your work there."

"If I'm needed, *meine* family knows where to find me, and I'll do some work this evening after supper."

"You work too hard. You should rest. Take tomorrow off."

He knew what she was doing. She was trying to delay progress on the addition. She wouldn't succeed.

He touched the brim of his straw hat. "I'll see you in the morning." He turned and left. He would see her again in about thirteen hours. He mentally shook his head. It wasn't right for him to be thinking about when he would see Rainbow Girl again. He should think of other things. Like what to make this evening in his forge. Perhaps an herb chopper with a rainbow-arch handle. Or a cooking spoon with a rainbow. Would she like a candleholder?

There he went again, letting his thoughts get tangled up around her. He needed to do something drastic to clear her from his head.

After he'd dropped off Daniel and Benjamin at their respective houses, he pulled his two-wheeled trap into the Rosenbergs' yard. Mary was as *gut* as any girl to court. He parked and knocked on the door.

Saul Rosenberg, Mary's *vater*, opened the door. "Eli? What are you doing here? It's almost suppertime."

"I know. I'm on *meine* way home. May I speak to you a moment?" Eli took a step in retreat to indicate he wished to speak privately. No sense in the whole family knowing his business.

"Ja." Saul came out onto the porch.

As he did so, Eli could see Mary in the kitchen with her *mutter*. She glanced up at him from setting the table, and smiled. He smiled back. Mary was a *gut* choice.

Saul closed the door. "What is it?"

"Your daughter Mary. I was thinking…to ask to… maybe court her."

Saul smiled. *"Thinking* to ask? *Maybe?* But you aren't sure?"

Eli didn't reply. He couldn't, because he wasn't sure. "I…"

"Let me save you some trouble. Mary already has an offer to be courted. I'm not sure she's as excited about it as the boy is, but she did say *ja.*"

Unexpected relief swept through Eli.

"If the courtship is broken, I'll let you know."

"Danki." Eli bounded off the porch, into his trap and quickly set Dutch into motion. He shouldn't be this pleased with being turned down. He thought of Rainbow Girl. She didn't need to know about this. Irritation displaced his happiness. He shouldn't be thinking so much of her. Every time he turned around, she dallied in his thoughts. Why did she have to return? Because she was raised here, and this was where she belonged. But he couldn't let her keep him from moving forward with his life.

Once he completed the bishop's addition, he would push all thoughts of Rainbow Girl from his mind. Her wild hair. Her odd clothes. Her sweet smile that made him happy.

He had to admit that he liked thinking about her.

But he shouldn't like it. Shouldn't think about her. He needed to stop. Right now.

Chapter Six

Eli arrived early the next morning alone. He'd told Daniel and Benjamin that he'd lay the concrete foundation blocks by himself since this part could be done in a day. Then the work would have to stop until an inspector came to sign off on the foundation. No sense taking up their time needlessly. He didn't mind spending most of the day here.

He glanced at the rear of the *dawdy haus*. Was Rainbow Girl up? Did she sleep late like a lot of *Englishers*? He hoped he'd get to see her today.

If he didn't have to wait for the inspector at various stages, this project could take a third of the time. After the foundation was inspected, the framing could go up and the electrical wired in. Once those were inspected, the rest of the job would progress without delay.

He combined the mortar and water in a wheelbarrow and set to work on the corners. He hoped to finish this addition by the middle of next week. Not only did he look forward to getting back to his regular routine at his forge, but he also figured that Rainbow Girl couldn't be all that comfortable sleeping on a couch. If she was going to stay, she needed her own space, and the sooner he finished, the sooner she would decide to stay. True, he wouldn't get to see her every day, but she would be in the community, and he could come up with excuses.

Ja. She needed to stay.

When the door opened, he looked up, and his breath caught in his throat.

Rainbow Girl stood in the doorway in the same bright green trousers and orange shirt as yesterday. She held a cup of something steamy. "Aren't the others helping you today?"

How pretty she would look in a cape dress and *kapp* again. He forced air into his lungs. *"Ne.* There's only enough work for one. They'll come to help put up the walls another day." If they were here, he wouldn't get to stay as long or see her as much.

"This is a lot for only one person."

"I can get it done by supper."

"I brought you a cup of coffee."

He set down his trowel and crossed to her. *"Danki."* He took the hot cup.

She smiled at him. *"Bitte.* The bishop and I are going into town."

"Why do you call him bishop instead of *grossvater*?"

She shrugged. "I guess since I was about ten or eleven, he always seemed more like the bishop than a *grossvater*."

He had a hard time imagining what it must be like to have the bishop as your *vater* or *grossvater*. "I need to pick up a few things for *meine mutter*. May I go with the two of you?"

She tilted her head in an adorable way and gave a

winsome smile. "Then how will you finish here by supper?"

He glanced at the blocks all set out for the job to be done. "I'll manage."

"I'm sure the bish— *Meine grossvater* would be happy to have you along."

From somewhere behind her came "*Ja.* Come." The bishop appeared beside her. "We forgot to get the metal electric boxes for the outlets and switches."

"*Ja*, I was thinking about them last night. Would you like me to hitch up a buggy?"

"That would be *gut. Danki.* We'll take mine. It's the smaller enclosed one. Hitch Thunder to it."

"Very *gut.* I'll use up the rest of the mortar I have mixed and get to it." He downed the coffee that was still a bit too hot and handed the cup to Rainbow Girl. *"Danki."* He wouldn't be tasting any more food today.

On the bright side, he'd get to ride into town with Rainbow Girl seated next to him.

And that made him very happy.

Dori hadn't been able to squeeze into any of her regular pants, and she owned no skirts. She hadn't worn dresses or skirts since she'd left the Amish, so the options for her growing belly were limited. That meant settling for her teal yoga pants. They fitted snuggly over her rounded stomach. She topped off the look with a coral-and-pink swirly patterned blouse that hung baggy over her hips, and her black knee boots. Not a great look for job hunting, but better than jeans or sweatpants for interviews. If she even managed to get any.

Sandwiched between the handsome young blacksmith and her *grossvater*, a part of Dori delighted at sitting so close to Eli in the buggy. Another part of her harbored guilt for keeping her secret from him. But he really had no need to know about the baby. She would leave as soon as she could get a job and find a place to live.

About a mile into Goshen, Dori pointed. "Can you drop me off at the coffee shop on the corner?"

"Why?" The bishop gave her his squint-eyed expression when he looked into someone's soul.

What did he see in hers? "I don't think you want to know."

"I do."

She glanced at Eli, who seemed eager to know, as well. "I'm going to apply for a job there, and then use their Wi-Fi to look for other potential jobs."

Grossvater frowned. "You don't need a job."

She took a slow breath. It was a bit maddening. He refused to listen to anything she said. "I do if I'm going to rent a place in town."

"You don't need to do that. I'm building you two rooms."

She looked from the bishop to Eli. "See? He won't listen."

Eli scrunched his eyebrows together. "Two rooms?"

Her stomach flipped. How could she explain the extra space? "He's having you build two, and he wants me to live in one." She didn't need to explain to him who her *grossvater* hoped would occupy the other in a few months' time.

Eli pulled the buggy to a stop at a red light.

"I'll get out here." Dori stepped past her *grossvater* and climbed down before either man could stop her.

"*Danki*. I'll see you in an hour or so." She trotted up onto the sidewalk.

Once the buggy had pulled away, Dori glanced across the street to the sub shop, where Eli had bought her a sandwich. It seemed like so long ago, but it had been only three days. How bleak her life had seemed then. How different it was now. Her life had changed so quickly. From perfect with Craig, to dismal after he kicked her out, to…to nice? Comfortable? Secure? Right now, her life was all of the above, and she was glad of it.

Over an hour later, Dori arrived back at the coffee shop. Eli and the bishop were nowhere in sight, so she went inside. She'd talked to ten different businesses within walking distance, including the coffee shop, and ones she'd applied to online yesterday. She was given one of two answers. She either didn't have ample formal education—eighth grade wasn't enough—or they didn't want to hire someone in her condition. How could so many people tell she was pregnant? Had Eli figured it out as well and was he too polite to say anything?

Today's results had been proof enough that her chances of getting a job were very slim. Because of the numerous people looking for work, the job market was tough, and when the high school students got out for the summer, it would be even harder.

She should have tried harder to get her GED, but she hadn't seen a need while she was living with Craig. And in the Amish world, she never had to worry about that. She knew of a lot of people who'd been looking for work, long before she started. Long before Craig had kicked her out. Long before morning sickness had cost her the waitressing job. People with far more education than she had.

Should she give up on finding work altogether and wait until after the baby was born? If so, she either had to stay with the Amish or return to the homeless shelter. One option was slightly better than the other. But only slightly. How depressing.

This was not how she imagined her life when she left the Amish community. She imagined doing anything she wanted to do, but in reality, a person could do only what their education and resources allowed them. It seemed a lot like the limiting ways of the Amish. Not the total freedom she'd imagined.

She still had the ten dollars from Eli and ordered herself a berry smoothie. She missed having fancy coffees, mochas and lattes, but the caffeine wasn't *gut* for the baby. Sitting, she opened her laptop and quickly connected to the shop's Wi-Fi again. She would do as much as she could until the men showed up.

If she was going to get a job and an apartment, she needed to get her GED. That was how she'd spend her time until the baby arrived.

Before long, Eli strode in and headed her way. "Are you ready?"

Under the table, she slipped her hand to her belly. Had the baby moved in response to Eli's voice? Her heart had certainly reacted to his presence, and a feeling of *ja*-this-is-nice swept through her. "Let me check my email really fast." She clicked the keys.

The conversation from the next table was loud and Dori heard someone say, "There's something you don't see every day. An Amish man with a normal person."

Did they think they couldn't be heard? Dori laughed to herself. *She* was the normal one? Since when had her appearance been considered normal? She glanced up at Eli but couldn't tell if he'd heard them.

He spoke in a hushed voice loud enough for her ears only. "Ignore them."

That made her feel *gut*. He'd been trying to make her feel better. Protective, even. He had no way of knowing that the comment had made her laugh. Regardless, his gesture had been kind and touched her.

Craig would have turned on them and told them to mind their own business, after he'd scolded her for carrying her laptop in an unprotected bag rather than a specially designed padded one.

She closed her laptop and stowed it in her backpack. Before she could pick it up, Eli grabbed it and slung one strap over his shoulder. Sweet again. Was he doing it simply to be nice? Or had he been told she was pregnant?

She grabbed her smoothie, headed out to the buggy and sat between the men again. "Eli, did you get everything your *mutter* needed?"

He tipped his head back against the seat. "Oh, I forgot. It's only a few things. Do you mind if we stop again?"

"Of course not." *Grossvater* waved him on.

Eli parked the buggy at the big-box store. "I won't be long." He jumped down and ran in.

Though she might have liked to have gone in just to spend more time with him, she had the bishop alone. "Did you tell Eli about the baby?"

"*Ne*. That's for you to tell him. But you can't hide this much longer. Our people will want to help you."

"Like *Vater*?"

"Andrew is just hurt. He didn't forbid me to build

the addition to the *dawdy haus* or really try to stop me. He told me I'm being a foolish old man, wasting *meine* time. When you get to *meine* age, the things that were once foolish aren't anymore. I think your *vater* truly hopes you'll stay."

Her *vater* hurt? He was too strong to let anything hurt him and certainly not her or her actions. How would Eli react when he found out about the baby? She wanted to keep it from him as long as possible, because when he did learn of it, he would likely react as her *vater* had.

Eli returned with a plastic shopping bag of items and a box of laundry soap. "*Danki* for waiting."

Once back at *Grossvater*'s *dawdy haus*, Eli went straight to work again after unhitching the horse. *Grossvater* worked alongside him.

On the kitchen table sat a plate of oatmeal cookies covered in plastic, and a note said that a large bowl of potato salad was in the refrigerator. With sandwiches, this would be a tasty lunch.

Dori made lunch-meat sandwiches with all the fixings and mixed up a pitcher of lemonade.

The June day had warmed up nicely but not too hot. Comfortable enough to work outdoors. She set the pitcher and glasses on the floor at the end of the hall, then added the bowl of potato salad with a serving spoon and forks, and returned for the three plates with sandwiches. She carried all of them with one hand and an arm, leaving her other hand free to open the door.

She froze and caught her breath. Eli carried a heavy bag of mortar mix on one shoulder. Had he always been that strong? Or had she simply never noticed? He was so brawny and manly. What would the *English* call him?

A hunk. Amish never thought of the opposite sex in such a manner. Or at least, they never voiced it, but Eli Hochstetler was definitely a hunk. He probably had no idea how physically attractive he was, especially when he smiled. Add to that his kind heart and *gut* nature, and he was practically perfect. Except for the fact he was Amish, through and through.

He stopped next to the wheelbarrow where *Grossvater* stood. *Gut.* She was in time before they mixed more. If she could manage to cease her gawking. "Lunch."

After everyone had dished up their food and poured themselves a glass of lemonade, *Grossvater* said grace for their meal as well as the work ahead of them. Dori settled in the doorway, stealing glances at Eli. *Grossvater* sat on the bottom step, and Eli in the grass that would soon be under her floor.

The first to finish, Eli set his plate on one of the steps. *"Danki."*

Dori didn't want the time with him to be over. "I almost forgot." She sprang to her feet and dashed inside, then returned with the plate of cookies. *"Mutter* left these, as well as the potato salad." She held the plate out to Eli.

He took three and held them up. *"Danki."*

Grossvater took one. *"Ja, danki.* Your *mutter* makes the best cookies."

She liked thinking of him as *Grossvater.* It somehow made him seem kinder and more approachable.

After cleaning up lunch and washing the few dishes, Dori changed into gray sweatpants and a pink T-shirt, then headed outside to see if there was anything she could do. After all, she would be here until at least after the baby was born. She might as well make the best of it. She would start with lending assistance to build her rooms and pursuing her GED. The first allowed her to spend a bit more time with Eli.

Eli carried two concrete blocks over to the side wall of the foundation.

She looked around. "Where's *meine grossvater*?"

He set the blocks down. "He needed to visit a community member."

She strode over to him. "Then *gut* thing I'm here. What can I do?"

His eyebrows knit together. "Do with what?"

"Building the addition." *And spending time with you.*

His eyebrows inched up his forehead, and he laughed. "This is a man's work."

That's right. Amish men built things, and Amish women cooked and cleaned. If she'd stuck to that rule, half the light bulbs in her and Craig's apartment would be out, the bathroom cabinet door would still be leaning against the wall, and the garbage disposal broken and backed up with decaying food particles. It was amazing what she'd learned from online videos. "I'm capable of doing plenty. You lost all that time going into town, and now your one helper has abandoned you."

He shook his head and headed for the block pile again. "Go back inside."

"You think me incapable?" She hurried around in front of him, not wanting to be readily dismissed. "I'll have you know that I've wielded a screwdriver and wrench a time or two."

He laughed. "Neither of which are used in masonry."

"I know that. They were examples to show you I'm capable."

He folded his arms.

Stubborn man.

A manly man.

And handsome.

A hunk.

She folded her arms too. "I'm not leaving. This addition is for me, and I'm going to help. Wouldn't you rather put me to work? Or have me get in your way? The choice is yours."

He huffed out a breath. "Fine. You can mix the mortar." He hefted a bag of dry cement, cut it open across the middle with his trowel and dumped the contents into the wheelbarrow, sending up a cloud of powder.

She waved her hand in front of her face to clear the air.

He added water from the hose, handed her a hoe and walked away. Not one word of instruction.

But what instruction did she really need? *Mix*. She pulled the hoe back and forth to blend the wet and dry ingredients. Not much different than combining the makings for a cake. "How will I know when it's ready?"

"I'll tell you." He grabbed more blocks. With each pair he transferred, he glanced into the wheelbarrow. A couple of times, he added more water.

The mixing turned out to be a lot harder than she'd anticipated. Mortar was heavy, and the process caused her muscles to cry out, but she didn't dare complain. Soon she would have a nice place to live—her own space. And it was a bonus that she got to spend time with Eli. Just the two of them.

A little bit later, after she'd watched his methodology, she knew how to be of further assistance. She could cut his per-block time in half by handing them to him.

While he slapped the mortar in place, she gripped one and heaved. It was all she could do to raise it an inch off the ground. These were heavier than she thought. She didn't want to hurt her back, so she crouched. She still couldn't lift it.

"What are you doing?"

She tilted her head and squinted up at him. "Helping. How much do each of these weigh?"

He shook his head. "Not much. Thirty-five or forty pounds." He grabbed the block she'd been trying to lift and hoisted it with one hand as though it was nothing more than his dinner plate. "Don't try to lift another one of these."

She wanted to protest, but what was the point? They both knew she couldn't, even if she wanted to, so she studied him instead.

The way he applied the mortar in swift motions, never hesitating, mesmerized her. Scoop, splat mortar into place on an already set block, scoop-splat, scoop-swish-swish mortar on the end of the next block and set it in place.

By suppertime, the foundation walls were completed. The room that would be built on top was already welcoming her.

Eli wiped his hands on a rag. "*Danki.* It went much faster with your help."

"And what help would that be? Watching?"

"Mixing the mortar."

"That didn't take much time."

"But it allowed me do other things, so the work went faster."

Her insides danced at his praise. "It did?"

"*Ja.*"

She wasn't sure if that was the truth or if he was merely being nice. Then a smile pulled at her mouth. Of course it was true. She'd never known Eli to lie. But that he admitted it to her was amazing. He could have easily said nothing, leaving her to believe she hadn't made a difference at all.

Dori wasn't the only one who had changed from her Amish roots. Perhaps her influence had set Eli on his own path, cracking the traditions and helping him to soften the rigid ways.

Working beside him had been rewarding. She'd enjoyed the time, and she decided that she would help with the whole addition, whether he approved or not. She could be just as stubborn as any of the men.

What was it about Eli that made her feel happier than she'd been in a long time? And there was something safe in being near him. Both things she definitely wanted to hold on to.

Chapter Seven

The next morning, Dori sat at the table eating a bowl of Oaty-Ohs mixed with Cinna-Apple Rings. She had enjoyed working with Eli yesterday, though her muscles were telling a different story today. She wouldn't see him for a few days, maybe not until next week. It all depended on when the inspector came to look over what had been done on the addition so far.

Grossvater entered through the front door from wherever he'd been. "I have a favor to ask of you."

"What is it, *Grossvater*?"

"Eli's not coming today because the construction has to wait until the foundation is inspected. I had planned to take Nelly to his forge—she's thrown a shoe—but I'm needed on the far side of the district. Are you up to walking Nelly over to Eli's for me?"

"The exercise will do me—us—*gut*." She caressed her stomach. "We'd love to." She would enjoy seeing Eli at his forge, sending a little thrill through her at the prospect. In truth, the prospect of not seeing Eli had saddened her. "Shouldn't I wait for the inspector?" Now that she'd realized that she had to stay, at least until the baby was born, she was anxious for the extra rooms to be finished.

"*Ne*, the inspection card is attached to the back door. Are you sure the walk won't be too much for you?"

"We'll be fine."

"*Danki*. I need to leave. Can you get Nelly all right?"

"*Ja, Grossvater*. I haven't forgotten everything about being Amish." Not that she *was* Amish or ever would be. Despite the fact that she had fully assimilated into the *Englisher* world, that hadn't erased her past. Everything came back to her like an old friend.

His wide grin and the mischievous twinkle in his eyes suggested *Grossvater* might be up to something. He slipped out before she could question him.

Was he trying to get her to interact with the community? Maybe he thought if he got her more involved with the Amish people in the community she would stay, but he was wrong. However, she did like the chance to get out of the *haus*.

Dori had chosen to wear yoga pants that morning. Not only were they comfortable on her growing waistline, but they had a back pocket, which was convenient for carrying her cell phone. She slipped it in there and then headed for the barn. On her way, she glanced toward the big *haus*. *Mutter* was likely in there alone, cleaning up the kitchen.

In the barn, Dori bridled Nelly and walked her outside. How long would it take to get to Eli's?

Mutter met her outside the barn and held up a canvas shopping bag. "Cookies for you and Eli."

"How did you know where I was headed?"

"Your *grossvater* told me. I also packed sandwiches—egg salad. You always liked egg salad. And some cheese, in case you get hungry on your way there or back. I know I had to eat often when I was pregnant with all you children."

Hunger had become Dori's constant companion, but at least now she knew she would have food to eat. The bowl of cold cereal wouldn't last her long. She took the bag from her *mutter*. "*Danki*. But you aren't supposed to be talking to me."

"You aren't shunned, so it's all right."

A technicality. "What about *Vater*?"

"He won't mind."

"Meaning you're not going to tell him." For all the Amish rules, people bent them often enough to suit their needs or wants.

"He saw you working alongside Eli yesterday. He's glad you're home."

Mutter probably just hoped he was glad. "Could have fooled me."

"*Ja*, well, it was a shock—" *Mutter* dipped her head "—seeing you."

Dori *was* quite an odd sight in an Amish community with her colorful hair and *Englisher* clothes.

"I left your Amish clothes on the porch the first morning."

As Dori had suspected, her own clothes had come back to haunt her. "I found them." The ones she'd stuffed safely away in the corner of the living room, where *Grossvater* wouldn't know to ask her about them.

"If you wore them, your *vater* would yield more quickly."

Her *mutter* wanted—*ne*, needed—everyone to be at peace with each other.

"I'll think about it, but I won't make any promises."

A shiver tingled her skin in agitation merely thinking about putting on a cape dress again.

"*Danki*. I can't ask for anything more. You best be on your way, before the *morgen* gets away from you."

Poor *Mutter*. She wanted what she couldn't have. Her family to be whole again and everyone happy. To have one, excluded the other.

Dori headed off down the road toward the Hochstetler farm. An hour later, after she'd eaten half the cheese, she entered the yard.

The clang of Eli's hammer rang through the air.

She walked the horse around to the back of the barn where Eli's forge stood, open like a two-car garage. She stopped a few yards from the large threshold.

He swung his hammer onto red-hot metal. Sparks sprayed up in all directions from the contact point. His actions were smooth and practiced, no wasted motions. Almost as though he worked to some internal rhythm. He looked as though he'd stepped out of a blacksmith calendar. She'd buy that calendar. Especially if all the pictures featured the handsome Eli.

The piece took shape as he worked and worked. An herb chopper. So that was how he fashioned one of those. A table along the rear wall behind the forge fire held many pieces of ironwork. Kitchen knives, cooking utensils, fireplace tools, ax heads, weather vanes and various other items she couldn't identify from this distance.

Nelly whinnied and pawed the ground, evidently not enjoying the view as much as Dori.

Eli looked up, and a smile lit up his face. "Rain—Dor—*Hallo*." He shoved the iron piece he'd been working into the hot coals. "Does Nelly need a shoe?"

Again, her baby responded to Eli's voice, moving around inside her. "How did you know?"

"Usual reason people come unannounced, walking a horse." He ambled over and stroked the draft horse's neck. "How are you doing, Nelly?"

The horse lipped his shoulder.

"Do you know all the horses in the community by name?"

He shrugged. "There are a few new ones I don't. Yet."

"You called me Rain a moment ago. Why?"

His face turned red and not from the hot fire. "Which hoof?" Without waiting for an answer, he went straight to the hind leg and lifted it.

He had to have heard her question, but she would play his game. She pointed at Nelly's leg. "How did you know which one?"

"She had her hind hoof cocked up."

"You certainly know horses."

"Horses are part of *meine* job. They're easy to figure out."

"Easier than people?"

He nodded. "Everything about them conveys something. The different sounds they make. The way they stand, the tilt of their ears, the swish of their tail. Horses have much to communicate."

She'd never thought that much about horses. In her youth, she viewed them as a means to pull buggies and plows. In the *Englisher* world, they were a source of irritation by impeding traffic and leaving smelly things on the road to avoid.

He took the lead rope and walked Nelly over to a post and secured her there. With his tools, he cleaned out the hoof, then set it on a hoof rest and filed it. With various shoe sizes, he measured until he found one that was close and shoved it into his coals with a pair of long tongs. "This will take a few minutes. Do you want a chair?"

She was a bit worn-out from the walk. *"Ja, danki."*

He grabbed a three-legged stool and plopped it down in front of her, well outside the danger zone of getting hit by flying sparks. "You'll be safe here." With the extra long tongs, he moved the metal shoe around in the coals, digging it deeper in the heat.

She instinctively put a hand on her stomach as she sat, then quickly removed it. "So tell me, why did you call me Rain?"

He shook his head. "It was nothing."

"I want to know."

He pulled the shoe out, studied it and shoved it back in. "I used to see you in town every time I went. I didn't know who you were, so I called you…"

"Rain?"

"Rainbow Girl." He pointed toward her head with the long tongs. "On account of your colorful mane."

She ran a hand through her cropped hair. "I kind of like that. You can call me Rainbow Girl. It's a lot better than *Dorcas*."

"Dorcas is a nice name."

"I don't really like it. It doesn't suit me. So either call me Dori or Rainbow Girl. Or just plain Rainbow."

Rather than agreeing, he pulled the shoe from the fire and beat on it, sending sparks into the air again.

She stood and scooted around him to the table with his wares.

He stopped his work. "What are you doing?"

"I want to look at all the pieces you've made."

He put the shoe back into the coals and stood next to her. "Just things I make when I'm caught up on *meine* other work."

She jerked her hand from her stomach again. She needed to stop doing that. Soon enough she would show too much to hide her growing belly with a baggy shirt. She should probably tell him soon.

Besides the pieces she could see from a distance, a six-inch-tall deer sat among various other animals. She picked up an iron frog not much bigger than a real frog. "These are really nice."

"Danki. You can have it." He returned to the horse-shoe.

"Really?"

"Ja. As you can see, I have plenty."

She peered over her shoulder at him and slipped her cell phone out of her back pocket. She took pictures of everything, trying to get as close to each object as she could and still keep it in focus with the limited light. When she finished, she sat down again and inconspicuously snapped a few pictures of Eli. These would look great on his website, him wielding a hammer with sparks flying. Nothing that gave the appearance of him posing, because that would not be fitting.

She smiled. The website he didn't have—her smile widened—but soon would.

Eli struck the iron in an unusual cadence, his normal rhythm off. He couldn't believe Rainbow Girl was here, and he'd been taken aback to have her suddenly standing there. His focus returned to the horseshoe.

Completely misshapen. Ruined.

He tossed it into the water barrel and took another mostly formed shoe from the wall. He wedged it into the fire with the long tongs and worked the bellows. He made shoes ahead of time in various sizes so horses and their owners didn't have to wait so long.

What was Rainbow Girl doing with her phone? Still too much *English*. Would she ever settle back into the Amish way of life? Doubtful. She had said herself that she didn't know if she would stay. But she'd helped him finish the foundation of the addition rather than trying to talk him out of it like before. She almost seemed eager to have the project completed. Was that because she wanted to be rid of him? He hoped not, but when he finished, even if she stayed in their community, he wouldn't see her as often. Only on Church Sundays. If she went at all.

He took his time sizing the shoe and filing Nelly's hoof. He didn't want Rainbow Girl to leave. He cleaned out each hoof.

"Are you almost done?"

Was she so anxious to be away from him? "I want to make sure she has a *gut* fit."

Rainbow Girl held up the cloth bag she'd brought. "Well, when you're done, I have lunch for us."

He nailed the shoe into place, turned Nelly out into the corral, then grabbed a blanket, his tin drinking cup and a jug of water. "The shade on the side of the barn will be more comfortable." He let her walk ahead of him.

He set the jug and cup down, and she did the same with her bag. She took two corners of the blanket and helped him spread it out. They worked well together as they had yesterday, when she'd helped with the foundation, as though they knew what the other was going to do. It made the day's work go faster. With the delay of going into town, he'd accepted he would have to work through supper until dark, or return the next day to finish, therefore holding up the inspection.

He gave her a hand to sit on the blanket, then he sat, as well. The egg salad sandwiches were loaded with lettuce, tomatoes and onions. Just the way he liked them. "Did you make these?"

"*Ne, meine mutter* did."

He'd hoped Rainbow Girl had prepared lunch, then he could compliment her. "Tell her everything was delicious and *danki*."

"I will."

After eating, Eli led Dutch, harnessed to the two-wheeled trap, out of the barn. Rainbow Girl stood some distance away. Eyes closed, face tilted toward the blue sky, one hand on her lower back and the other on her round stomach. She wasn't a horse, so what did *her* stance communicate?

Then his breath got knocked out of him as though a mule had kicked him.

Rainbow Girl couldn't be pregnant!

But it all made sense, her return to the community, and her *vater* being so upset with her instead of welcoming his prodigal daughter home. How could Eli have allowed her to help him with construction? *Gut* thing he'd stopped her from lifting those heavy concrete blocks.

Where was the baby's *vater*? Was he coming for them? He was probably the reason she insisted she wasn't staying. She was using her Amish family. Her *vater* knew, but did the rest of them? Did the bishop? Would he be so welcoming if he did?

Rainbow Girl straightened and turned toward him. She adjusted her shirt, apparently to hide her condition, and walked toward him. "Is everything all right, Eli? You look upset."

"I'm fine." He released the harness and set the brake on the rig. "I'll get Nelly." After striding to the corral, he gripped the top rail and squeezed it as hard as he could, making the rough wood bite into his palms.

He'd thought she might have actually wanted to change her ways, to return to the Amish life, to be the woman *Gott* intended her to be. How could he have let her get under his skin?

Nelly stuck her muzzle over the railing and into his face.

"Did you know?" he asked the sweet mare.

The draft horse stared at him with soulful brown eyes.

"Come on, girl. Time to go home." He walked into the corral and bridled the gentle giant. He no longer wanted to drive Rainbow Girl home or spend time with her, but he couldn't allow her to walk all that way back home. Having lived with the *Englishers* so long and driven everywhere in cars, she'd likely grown soft. He led Nelly out of the corral and toward the buggy. Maybe he'd seen wrong. Maybe the light had played tricks on him. Maybe...

He tied the horse to the rear of the trap.

Rainbow Girl had already climbed in. She should not have done that on her own. What if she slipped and hurt herself or the baby?

He hoisted himself up, took hold of the reins and put the buggy into motion.

"*Danki* for taking *gut* care of Nelly."

"Ja." He glanced repeatedly out of the corner of his eye, trying to confirm if she was pregnant.

After a mile, she said, "Is everything all right?"

Ne, not at all. "Why wouldn't it be?"

"You're really quiet."

His mind wasn't. It was racing with chaotic thoughts and emotions. The drive couldn't end quickly enough for him.

He dropped her off in front of the *dawdy haus.*

"I'll get Nelly so you can be on your way."

"Ne. I'll do it." He drove toward the barn before she could untie the horse.

"Danki for the ride," she called after him.

He waved his hand over his head to let her know he'd heard her. In the barn, he secured Nelly in her stall and hurried back outside.

Bishop Bontrager met up with him at the trap. *"Danki* for taking care of Nelly."

"I'm glad to help."

"The inspector came and signed the card."

"I'll return in the *morgen. Guten tag."* Eli snapped the reins before he could be delayed again.

Rainbow Girl was pregnant. Would she stay until the baby was born? No wonder her *vater* would have nothing to do with her. Eli wanted nothing to do with her either, but it was too late.

He had time to build. He'd given his word freely to the bishop that he'd build the addition. He had a strong back and skilled hands. He gave that too to the bishop, with no resentment.

But Rainbow Girl had wiggled her way into his heart. Without permission. With no recourse on his part. That he did resent, and he would need to excise her from his heart as well as his thoughts.

Strangely, he blamed his own foolishness. Little blame fell on the one who had wronged her family, her community, her *Gott*. He thought of Rainbow Girl and felt a protective need to shield her. Was she shaking his faith? Was she going to be an obstruction between *Gott* and himself? This could not be. He had no intention of following Rainbow Girl into the *Englisher* world. But Rainbow Girl had brought the *Englisher* world to their community in a way that could not be ignored.

But just because *she* returned didn't mean anything for him had changed. He was still in need of a wife. On his way home, he pulled into the Miller farm and asked to speak to Miriam. Her smile made her subsequent refusal seem like a sweet gift.

Her rejection stung, but not like it should. More because of the blow to his ego and less because he cared so much for her that he felt an actual loss. He was more upset he couldn't show Rainbow Girl his life was fulfilling and on track without her.

But it wasn't. It never had been.

And that stung even more.

Chapter Eight

The next day, Dori woke to the sounds of hammers and men's voices outside. She dressed and ate quickly. Since it seemed as though she was going to stay with her *grossvater* for the time being, she exited through the back door, determined to do what she could to make this project go as fast as possible.

Eli, Daniel and Benjamin bustled around the interior of the foundation. They had started early and wasted no time on capping the top of the concrete blocks with wood, and had three floor joists in place already. She'd forgotten how fast Amish men could build things.

She stepped down onto the grass. *"Guten morgen."*

Eli looked up from hoisting a two-by-twelve. He narrowed his eyes at her and dropped the board. "Take a break." He strode to her like a ram toward an intruder.

Dori held her ground and smiled. "How can I help today?"

He gritted his teeth. "Go back inside."

"Ne. I want to do something."

"Ne. Go. Inside."

She planted her hands on her hips. "I'm going to help, whether you approve or not."

He stood in her path. "I won't allow you out here."

Why was he acting like this? He'd let her help him the other day. Was it because there were other men around? Would his manly pride get bruised? "You can't stop me, Eli Hochstetler."

He lowered his voice. "It's not *gut* for the baby."

The blood drained from her face. "How long have you known?"

"Since yesterday. Does the bishop know?"

"Of course. How did you...?"

"Just go inside and don't come out again." He walked away.

She stumbled back into the house and closed the door. Tears spilled down her cheeks. The hurt in his expression wrenched her heart. She should have told him herself, but she'd wanted to revel in the nice friendship they were rekindling. Letting him figure it out on his own had been a grave error in judgment. It had happened right before he'd brought her home. She realized that now. How could she have been so careless? How could she ever make amends?

She slumped into a chair at the table and opened her laptop. Last night, she'd gotten Eli a buddy page connected to another Amish website. Which meant that he wouldn't have to pay for a domain until he was ready. She would show him what his website could be. She would make it up to him for not telling him about the baby. Just because he wouldn't let her do anything further to help build the addition didn't mean she couldn't help him in some other way.

She connected her cell phone to the laptop and downloaded the pictures she'd taken yesterday. Within an hour, she had a basic site ready for content. She did her best to write about each item. Eli could help her fine-tune the descriptions later. All of Craig's instructions about graphics and web design had paid off. She hadn't realized how much she'd learned.

At the end of the day, she had the bare bones of a website built. And the three-man construction team had the skeletal walls of the *dawdy haus* addition up, with the electrical wired in and the floor joists in place. They also had managed to finish the roof, complete with shingles and gutters. Everything ready for the next inspection. Eli wouldn't return for a day or two, and she wanted to show him what she'd accomplished. She stepped out the back door onto the small stoop. Her sister stood talking to Daniel Burkholder. "Eli, may I speak with you a moment?"

He didn't turn to her right away as the other two young men and her sister did, but when he did, the scowl on his face spoke loudly of his irritation.

Well, let him be irritated. He would change his mood when he saw his website. Now he wouldn't have to hire a *Englisher* to build it for him. That would save him money, and Amish were all about frugality.

He huffed out a breath. "What? It's been a long day, and I want to get home."

What he meant was he wanted to get away from her. He probably regretted ever agreeing to help the bishop.

"Would you come here, please? Unless you'd like me to go over there."

He crawled over the foundation and walked between the floor joists to her. "What?"

"Come inside."

"I don't want to. Just tell me what it is."

"I can't. I have to show you." She walked down the hall, hoping he would follow her. And he did. When he caught up to her, she pointed toward her computer. "Look. I made you a website."

He sat and stared at the screen.

"Click around." When he didn't move, she reached in front of him and changed the screen to one of his pieces, a weather vane. She drew in a deep breath. He smelled of wood and smoke. She wanted to lean into the aromas but resisted. If he was angry now, that would upset him even more. "I didn't know quite how to describe the items you make—the correct terminology and all—but you can help me with that. This is merely a temporary site until you can buy a domain name."

He stood. "I told you I didn't want you to do this. Undo it."

His rejection stung. Why wasn't he pleased?

"But this is the best way for you to get orders from *English* customers and make more money. You don't want an *Englisher* in charge of your website. You need to learn this yourself."

He walked back down the hall. "Undo it, I said."

Dori put her hands on her hips. Stubborn man. He could protest all he wanted, but in the end, who wouldn't want a website created for free? Did he realize how much an outsider would charge? A lot. When he cooled down, he'd see that this was a *gut* thing. He would see that she was right. If he still hated what she'd done in a day or two, she would take it down.

Maybe.

She could be stubborn too.

* * *

On Saturday night, Dori sat at her *grossvater*'s table and bowed her head as he said a blessing over the meal she'd cooked. Dried-out chicken with half-raw and half-burnt fried potatoes. It wasn't that she couldn't cook, but her mind kept wandering back to Eli's words when he'd acknowledged that he knew about her baby and his vehement refusal of the website she'd created for him. Something inside her needed him to approve of her work. Approve of her. But he likely never would.

The bishop said, "Amen." He raised his head and picked up his fork.

Dori grabbed hers as well and stabbed a blackened potato chunk. "Sorry about the potatoes."

"They're fine."

They weren't. With the raw and burnt bits aside, the rest of the flavor wasn't bad.

He swallowed a bite of chicken and chased it with a swig of milk. "I have a favor to ask of you."

Dori had a bad feeling about this. "What is it?"

"I want you to come to the big *haus* with me tomorrow morning for family church."

Had she already been here for a week? "I don't think that's a *gut* idea. *Vater* wouldn't like that."

"It will show him you are trying."

But she wasn't. Not really. But she also wasn't actively trying to leave. If she hadn't lost her job, she wouldn't be here. If Craig hadn't kicked her out, she wouldn't be here. If she had been able to find new work, she wouldn't be here. But none of those were likely to change, and life here wasn't as bad as she'd imagined. "I'll think about it." It might actually be pleasant, and she couldn't afford to have *Grossvater* kick her out too.

"And services the other Sundays, as well." He rolled his eyes toward the ceiling.

A reminder that he was providing the roof over her head?

She nodded.

"And would you mind removing the jewelry from your face and ears? It would be distracting for the younger ones."

There it was. Get her to agree to one seemingly benign thing and then ask for more. "Next, you'll want me to wear a cape dress."

"That wouldn't hurt."

She folded her arms on the table. "I'll go tomorrow, and I'll even take out the piercings in *meine* face, but not *meine* ears. And I'm *not* wearing a cape dress."

"What about your hair?"

He was going to push this to see how much she would give.

"It stays the way it is." Brown roots and all. It actually looked pretty awful with it half her natural color and half-multicolored. A few inches longer and someone could mistake it for being intentionally colored on the ends. If she had the money, she would recolor the roots.

Grossvater pressed his lips together.

After a couple of dry, hard-to-swallow bites, Dori had an idea. He wasn't the only one with a wish list. "*Grossvater*, I think you should get internet service and a computer. Before you object, let me explain."

He narrowed his eyes. "I have a feeling I won't like this, but continue."

"So many Amish have websites as a necessity for their businesses to survive. I think it would be a *gut* idea if you had internet and a computer so you could check up on them and monitor their sites." While giving her more reliable service to earn her GED and update Eli's site.

"I don't know how to work a computer."

"I will teach you."

He shook his head. "I don't wish to learn."

Just like Eli.

"One more thing, Dorcas. I want you to take the membership classes."

Changing the subject on her? "I'm not joining church, *Grossvater.*"

"I won't make you. That decision is between you and *Gott.*" He shrugged. "But what would it hurt to sit through the classes? The teacher is quite *gut.*" He gave an impish grin.

The teacher being the bishop sitting across from her.

Two could play at this game. Dori leaned forward. "Here's the deal. I remove the piercings from *meine* face, but not the ones in *meine* ears. No cape dress, but I'll wear less...colorful clothes, black sweatpants and a plain top in a prescribed Amish color. I'll wear a black beanie hat to disguise *meine* hair. I'll attend church on Sundays." She swallowed hard. "And I'll attend the membership classes, *but* I'm not joining."

"Wunderbar." He thought he'd won.

She held up her hand. "I'm not done. I'll do these things in exchange for you getting internet service, a computer and approving a website for Eli." She could be just as stubborn as the men.

He frowned at her.

She held out her hand across the table. "Deal?" As much as she wanted these things for herself, in truth they would help him keep track of what his flock did

with technology and make sure people used it as it had
been approved for each individual. She knew the secrets
of the Amish better than the bishop, and, like *Englishers*, they tried to get away with things, like hiding forbidden technology in their barns or cupboards. Being
the bishop, he wasn't privy to his flock's secret actions.
Most infractions weren't bad or serious, but the internet had the potential for real wickedness. If he knew
all that cyberspace contained, no one would ever gain
approval for a computer again.

He folded his arms. "You have learned some bad
habits living with the *English*."

He hadn't even begun to see all of her "bad habits."

Her hand still hovered in the air between them.

He nodded and, surprisingly, shook her hand. "You
are a tough haggler."

"Danki, Grossvater." Now, if she could just convince
Eli. The following morning, Dori regretted agreeing
to attend the family service. Her *vater*'s disapproving
looks were offset by her *mutter*'s compassionate ones.
Strained silence and awkward glances dominated the
gathering. It was grueling. Worse than Dori had imagined. Worse yet was when the bishop forced her to tell
her brothers that she was pregnant.

Matthew glared at her, while her three youngest
brothers stared wide-eyed.

She wanted to flee. Instead, she distracted herself
by pressing the tip of her tongue against the hole in her
lip. It felt odd to not have the stud there, scraping on
her tooth. She would replace it as soon as she returned
to the *dawdy haus*. She'd promised to remove them for

services but not permanently. She didn't want the holes to close up.

But maybe Eli wouldn't look so disapprovingly on her if she left them out.

Chapter Nine

The inspector arrived late on Tuesday afternoon, so Eli and the others wouldn't resume building until Wednesday. Eli had hoped to complete the room this week. Though he loved working in his forge, he strangely looked forward to this project, which surprised him. He also didn't want to see Rainbow Girl but at the same time did. He'd contemplated several girls he might ask to court, but in the end, he gave up the idea because his heart wasn't in it.

He drove the wagon up next to the corral. "You two get started. I'll take care of the horse and wagon."

Daniel and Benjamin jumped down and headed across the grass.

It would do Eli *gut* to put off seeing her for a few more minutes. Give him a chance to collect his thoughts and prepare himself for her ostentatious appearance. He unhitched the horse. Even mentally preparing himself, Rainbow Girl's appearance startled him every time.

With the horse taken care of, he headed for the construction site.

Rainbow Girl stood in the grass between the floor joists, talking with Daniel and Benjamin.

How had Eli missed her being pregnant? It seemed so obvious now.

Daniel had his arms folded. "I don't think you belong here."

"You're right, but I'm here, for better or for worse."

Where was the bishop? He needed to keep Rainbow Girl out of sight.

Eli marched toward them, climbed over the foundation wall and narrowed his eyes at her. "May I speak with you a moment?"

"Don't worry, I'm not going to do anything dangerous."

He spoke through gritted teeth. "Now." He motioned toward the back door.

She took a slow, deep breath, held it a moment and released it just as slowly. "Okay." She swiveled toward the *haus* and trudged up the steps and inside. Once in the kitchen area, she whirled around. "What? I don't appreciate you ordering me about."

"Too bad. You can't be outside. What if one of them realizes you're expecting?"

"I'm not going to be able to hide it much longer, and it's not going to matter in a few days anyway. *Meine grossvater* has decided to tell the whole church on Sunday." She waved her arm through the air. "He thinks it's best if everyone knows, so they can *help* me."

He didn't want the bishop to do that. Rainbow Girl would be singled out. If the bishop announced this, it would make it real. He wanted to protect her from the ridicule. "If the bishop has decided, then I guess it's done." He turned to head outside again, then swung back. "Please stay in the *haus*."

She tilted her head and pressed her lips together.

A sinking feeling in his gut told him she wasn't likely to obey. "You're a distraction." Mostly to him. "Just stay out of sight of the construction, then."

"I can't make any promises. *Grossvater* told me to see to it that you boys are fed. Can't very well bring you food if I'm not allowed to be seen."

He pressed his lips together. "I'm not a *boy*." Was that how she thought of him? Still the boy from school days?

"Whatever."

In spite of being mildly irritated, he enjoyed this banter, but the sound of plywood sheets being moved on top of the floor joists reminded him that he had a job to do, so he moved to leave again.

"Oh, wait, Eli."

He glanced over his shoulder. "I have a room to finish for you. *Ne*, two rooms."

"*Ja*. But that's not what I wanted to say. It's about that website I made you."

"I told you to undo it."

She paused a moment, biting her bottom lip. "I didn't quite get to that."

He should be irked at her but found he wasn't, which irritated him even more. "Well, do it now."

"Here's the problem." She held up a hand with her fingers splayed. "You already have five orders."

He stared hard at her, trying to process what she'd said. "I what?"

"Five customers have asked to purchase some of your items."

"They have?" He couldn't believe it. "That fast?"

"Ja." She sat at the table and tapped on her computer, then she swiveled it to face him. "An herb chopper—I think that's going to be a *gut* seller for you—an ax head, a weather vane and two animals."

He leaned in toward the screen. "That's too much money. I sell them for less."

"Not anymore. I checked competitors' prices, and these are right in the middle. The *English* will pay these prices and more for Amish-made items. I need to create your online payment account, so you can receive their payments and ship them their orders."

"I don't know how to do that." One of the many things he needed to learn how to do this summer.

"That's what you have me for. I've already told each of them that we are currently having a little problem with our payment system and will notify them as soon as we have the issue resolved."

"We?"

"Unless you'll be doing it, I'll be fixing the issue, so it's kind of a we thing at this point."

Incredible. She'd been home for only a week and a half and already she had orders for him. It had taken him all spring to sell that many pieces by consigning them to various shops around the community and in town. She'd gotten his business going quickly. Gratitude edged out his ire.

"You'll need a checking account to get an online payment system set up. You also need to name your business and purchase the domain name."

This was too much. He didn't understand this computer and website stuff. He didn't want to. He just wanted to make things in his forge. He'd dreaded spending the summer learning how to do all this, but now, he thought, maybe he wouldn't have to. "Would you help me with everything?"

"Of course."

"I'll pay you."

"Let's call it a fair trade for building me half of a *haus*."

He straightened. "Speaking of building a *haus*, I need to get to work."

"We should get all this sorted out soon. You don't want to lose these customers and get any negative feedback."

"I could return after supper."

"You don't need to leave and return. You can eat with us. It'll save a lot of time."

"Ja." He hurried outside, thinking about working alongside Rainbow Girl later. He'd like that. He'd like that a lot.

During the remainder of the afternoon, his mind spent more time on Rainbow Girl and his website than construction.

"Eli, lift your end," Daniel called out.

Eli refocused on the job at hand, but she was never far from his thoughts.

Since no progress could be made on construction earlier that week until after the inspector had come a second time, Dori had taken *Grossvater* into town on Monday to purchase a laptop and get internet service installed. So by Wednesday evening, she had everything in place to help Eli get his payment system set up. This new computer was so much faster than Craig's old castoff.

Grossvater sat in his brown recliner, napping, while

Eli sat in a chair nestled close to hers at the table so he could watch the computer screen while she worked. So close his arm touched hers, sending jolts through her every now and then. She'd imagined what this would be like, but reality turned out to be so much better. She should adjust her position to create a couple of inches between them but enjoyed the innocent contact too much.

Eli fingered the side of the screen. "I can't believe you talked the bishop into purchasing a computer."

"It's so he can keep watch over his flock."

He furrowed his eyebrows at her. "And he believed that?"

"Fine. I wanted better internet, but it's still a *gut* idea for him to keep tabs on what his people are up to."

"Sort of like teaching a cat to swim?"

She shrugged. "Now, watch what I'm doing." Struggling to concentrate on the task at hand and not on the handsome man next to her, she explained her way through the process. "Does all that make sense?"

"Not a word."

"Aren't you learning anything?"

He shrugged this time.

"Then why are you sitting with me?"

"A pretty girl told me I had to. Told me I should learn about computers, but I have no interest when she'll do it for me."

Pretty? He thought she was pretty? "You would rather be in your forge, wouldn't you?"

"Not necessarily."

That answer surprised her. So he sat here because he wanted to be near her and not because he had to. He had a strong enough stubborn streak to have refused her request if he had a mind to. She liked working beside him. "Let's set up your payment system now. Do you have your checking account information?"

Like most Amish, he had a bank account. It was hard to do business with *Englishers* without one. Unless Amish wanted to walk around with bags of cash, they needed safe ways to transfer money to pay for the items they needed—and wanted.

He pulled his checkbook from his back pocket. He'd ended the construction day a little early so he could run home to retrieve it after dropping off Daniel and Benjamin at their homes.

She swiveled the laptop to face him. "Now, do as I tell you."

"I don't think I want to." He pushed the laptop toward her. "Why don't you just do it? It'll be faster. I don't want to click on the wrong thing."

"Because, as a businessman, you need to learn." And she wasn't going to be here forever. He needed to be self-sufficient.

"I never wanted to be a businessman, only a blacksmith."

"If you want to make a living smithing, you need to have some business skills, then you can continue to be a blacksmith."

He gave a playful groan. "Fine. What do I do?"

She moved the laptop in front of him and walked him through, step-by-step, setting up the online system. "You did great. Now, let's get it connected to your temporary site, inform your customers you're ready to receive payments, get you a domain name, transfer your website content to it and market your work on social media."

He stood abruptly and stepped away. "I have to do *all* that? I thought I only had to set up the payment thing. I've had enough for one day. I'll do it tomorrow or the next day."

"You could lose these sales and get negative feed-back, which could damage your chances for future sales." She held her hand out to him. "Sit down. I'll do it for you, and you can watch." The poor man had to be overwhelmed with all there was to take in. She understood. She'd felt the same way when Craig had first tried to teach her about computers. With her new-found knowledge over the past four years, she didn't know how the Amish managed without computers in the modern age.

"I don't care about feedback and all that other stuff."

He did, but he didn't know it yet. All that stuff would allow him to do what he loved. "Sit. I'll talk through it as I do all the *stuff.* You watch."

He took a deep breath and sat. "I thought the com-puter stuff would be…"

"Simpler?"

He nodded. "And less of it. How does anyone know how to do it all?"

"They learn a little at a time, and you can learn it too. I'm sorry for overwhelming you with so much at once."

"I feel as though I'll never have time to work with the iron."

"I'll get you started, then it won't take as much time to keep it up. While I set things up, you be thinking of a name for your business. I chose *Eli's Amish Ironworks*, but you need to choose something you like, and we'll see if we can get you that domain name."

"What about just *Ironworks*? Simple. No extraneous words."

Plain and simple, the Amish way. "It's a little *too* simple. *Englishers* go out of their way to buy Amish-made products, so I think you should consider having *Amish* in the name. It will help you sell more products with no extra effort."

"All right."

"And your first name?"

"Wouldn't that be prideful?"

"Well, you'll want something to distinguish your ironwork from other Amish's. Think about it while we get the rest of it set up."

In the end, he chose *Rainbow Amish Ironworks*.

It gave her a swirl of pleasure inside that he put part of the name he'd given her in the title even if he didn't realize it. She wasn't about to connect those dots for him. He might change his mind.

"I feel as though *meine* head's been run over by a plow."

She laughed out loud. "I imagine it does." She walked him outside.

"Thank you for doing all that computer stuff for me."

"Thank you for building me half of a *haus*."

"Don't thank me yet. We're only half-finished." He hitched up his buggy and drove away.

She leaned against one of the porch's support posts and watched him leave. Why did Eli have to be Amish? Why couldn't he have decided to leave like she did? Why did he have to be so nice? All her questions were answered in her first question. He was Amish through and through. The qualities he maintained by being

Amish were the same ones that made him so attractive—kind, generous, hardworking—but also made him unattainable.

Chapter Ten

Early Thursday morning, Dori strolled along the shoulder of the road. *Grossvater* had set up an appointment with Dr. Kathleen. She didn't know what to expect from the doctor. Having been healthy as a child, she'd seen an *English* doctor only a few times when very young and a couple of times while she lived in the *Englisher* world. Though she liked the idea of an Amish doctor, she also found it a little unnerving. What would Kathleen Yoder be like now? Would she too be more *English* than Amish? When Kathleen had left, it was for a *gut* cause. Dori had left because she didn't want to stay. Didn't want to follow the rules. Would the doctor judge her for her choices? Chastise her for being pregnant and not married?

About a half of a mile into her trek, Eli approached in a two-wheeled trap from the direction she was headed. He pulled to the shoulder. "Where are you off to?"

The baby kicked at the sound of his voice.

"Dr. Kathleen's. *Meine grossvater* thinks I should have the baby checked to see how it's doing."

"And you're going on foot all that way?"

Dori hadn't wanted to, but there wasn't a horse and buggy available to her today. "*Ja*. I don't mind the walk."

"It's too far. I'll give you a ride." He jumped down and looked both ways. "It's safe to cross." He waved her over.

Like she couldn't figure that out for herself. She wouldn't say anything though. She appreciated his thoughtfulness and the ride. As well as the time she would get to spend with him.

He met her in the middle of the two-lane road.

How nice of him to be protective—something Craig had never been—but she could check for traffic and cross a street by herself.

He helped her up and climbed in himself.

The baby squirmed to one side of her belly, as though trying to get closer to Eli.

Once they were at the clinic, he tethered the horse.

"You don't have to come in or stay. I'll have enough energy to walk home since I didn't have to walk here. I don't want to keep you from your work."

"You'll need a ride home. I'll stay." He opened the door and went inside with her.

She doubted any amount of arguing would change his mind, and she would not only appreciate another ride but his company, as well.

Jessica Yoder checked Dori's name off a short list on a pad of paper. Was that the extent of the clinic's check-in procedure? "I'll tell the doctor you're here." She went to the back.

With no one else in the waiting area, Dori sat on the love seat and Eli in a padded armchair.

Dr. Kathleen came out quickly. "Dorcas Bontrager?"

Dori stood. "Call me Dori."

The doctor nodded. "Come on back." She motioned toward an open door, then she spoke to Eli. "Will you be waiting for her?"

"Ja."

"Noah's in his workshop in the barn. You'll probably be happier out there."

"Danki, I would like that." Eli left.

Dori stared at the exam table. No paper covered it. Instead, an actual cloth sheet lay over the flat surface.

When she hesitated, the doctor spoke. "Don't worry. We put on a fresh sheet for each patient."

Dori hopped up and let her legs dangle over the edge.

Dr. Kathleen asked a series of questions about her medical history. The doctor wasn't what Dori had expected. She seemed very Amish, yet she had a medical degree.

As Dori gave her answers, she noted that the doctor wrote everything on paper. "Wouldn't it be faster to put your notes directly into a computer?"

"I wish." The doctor pointed her pen around the room. "All *meine* records here are paper files."

"That must be a pain. You haven't been approved to have a computer." That was wrong. Of anyone, the doctor should have a computer. She would talk to *Grossvater.*

"I have a computer I use for research and communicating with other doctors, but that's it."

"What about your own website?"

"I don't need a website."

"I disagree. *Englisher* doctors can find you and recommend you to their Amish patients."

"I don't want to take anyone's patients."

Sometimes the Amish were too nice for their own *gut*. "You should at least have a patient database. It would make your life as a doctor easier."

"I know. We used them in medical school and hospitals. I'm not as *gut* with a computer as I am with people."

"I can build one for you."

"Really?"

Dori had learned quite a bit from Craig, classes at the public library and various places online. In the *English* world, she felt as though she knew next to nothing about computers, but here, in the Amish community, her knowledge vastly exceeded anyone's.

Eli bade Noah Lambright farewell. He couldn't imagine what was taking Rainbow Girl so long. Had the doctor found something wrong? He hurried inside the clinic.

No one sat in the waiting area. Jessica wasn't at her reception desk. Female voices came from one of the back rooms.

"Hallo?" He leaned to the side to peer toward the voices.

"Come on back," one of them called.

He stepped to the doorway of the doctor's office.

Four women sat in chairs huddled around a laptop: the doctor, Rainbow Girl, Jessica and Deborah Miller.

Jessica glanced up with a smile. "Dori's teaching us how to use the computer. She's going to create a patient database for us. And she's showing Deborah how to search for natural remedies. It's amazing how much information is in one small machine."

Rainbow Girl raised her gaze. "The information isn't

in the computer. It's out there—" she waved her hand carelessly "—in cyberspace. The computer merely finds it for you."

Deborah shook her head. "I still don't understand how information can be out *there* but not really *be* anywhere. It helps me to think of it in a building like a library. Dori has saved us a lot of time."

Saved Eli a lot of time, as well. Because of Rainbow Girl, his business would get a running start far sooner than he could have imagined. She already had the knowledge he had hoped to gain this summer. And she wouldn't be making all the mistakes he inevitably would. Trial and error. Trial and error. That was how he'd honed his smithing skills.

He wished she would decide to stay. If she could see how much he needed her, maybe she would.

Late Saturday afternoon, Dori stood in the middle of her new bedroom. It smelled fresh and clean.

Having spent Thursday afternoon and all day Friday with Daniel and Benjamin covering the inside with drywall and the exterior with siding, Eli worked alone today to put the finishing touches on the addition. He knelt to attach the final electric outlet cover and stood. "All done."

How could one man have so much kindness in him? He never criticized her for her poor choices and worked without complaint for a person he had to feel was undeserving. *"Danki."*

"Bitte. I have a couple of things outside. I'll be right back." He trotted out.

She turned to *Grossvater*, who stood with her. "And *danki* to you too." No one had done anything this nice for her since before she left the Amish community. "I don't know what I would have done without your help."

"'One should not abandon one's own; *Gott* does not abandon His own.'" *Grossvater* liked the German proverbs. There seemed to always be one to fit most any situation.

She walked around the bigger of the two bedrooms, never having had her own before. She'd shared with her sister growing up, then with Craig, then the homeless shelter and lastly *Grossvater*'s living room. Technically, these rooms belonged to *Grossvater*, but they were hers to freely use. She blinked away the excessive water in her eyes. This was nothing to cry over. "Now all I need are a few pieces of furniture, but I'm happy to sleep on the floor to have *meine* own space."

"Ah. Just wait." *Grossvater*'s eyes twinkled like a little boy's.

"For what?"

Voices drifted in through the back door. She peered out of her room to the parade of family members tromping into the *dawdy haus* along with Eli. No one came empty-handed. The only person missing was her oldest brother, Matthew.

Her bed from the big *haus*. A small dresser, a nightstand, sheets, quilts, a floor rug, curtains, as well as the family crib last used when ten-year-old John was a baby. Eli nailed a wrought iron clothing rack with five hooks on it to the wall. He hung a three-hook rack over the door. In a matter of a half an hour, her room, as well as the baby's, was furnished and ready to be occupied.

The tears Dori had held at bay earlier welled up in her eyes now. She didn't deserve any of this.

Mutter sidled up next to her. "I'm so pleased you've come home."

Dori smiled. "This is only temporary."

Vater spoke. "Supper's almost ready in the big *haus*. Everyone, wash up and come inside." His gaze skimmed over Dori as he said *everyone*. "You too, Eli. You've earned it."

Vater was including her in the invitation. She touched his sleeve. "*Danki* for all this."

He didn't look at her but kept his focus straight ahead. "*Bitte*. See to it you haven't put your *grossvater* and the whole family through all of this for nothing." He walked away.

But that was exactly what she planned. She couldn't stay here forever. This could be nothing but temporary.

Her family filed out, but Eli lingered. "Tell me this hasn't been a waste of time."

She knew he wanted her to tell him she was staying, but she couldn't. She wouldn't lie to him. "It's not a waste of anything. I do need a place to live."

"But you still don't plan to stay, do you?"

Unable to bear his scrutiny, she shifted her gaze to the blue-and-red braided rug on the floor.

His boots clunked on the wood floor as he walked away from her.

The following Tuesday, Eli pulled up in his wagon to the bishop's *dawdy haus* to find three buggies out front. Who was visiting him? He parked, set the brake and jumped down. He tethered Dutch and went up to the open door.

Rainbow Girl sat at the table with five people gathered around her, four men standing and a woman sitting in the chair next to her. "I have enough information here. I can create a mock website by tomorrow for you to preview."

Eli stepped inside. "What's going on?"

Rainbow Girl smiled, sending his insides dancing. "I'm helping them with their computers and websites."

"Does the bishop know about this?"

"Of course. Since I was helping him check on everyone's websites, I figured I could do a little work to keep their computers running well and fine-tune their sites."

Each of the people thanked her, then bade her farewell.

She crossed to the kitchen. "Would you like a glass of water?"

"*Ja*, I am thirsty."

She filled two glasses, gave him one and drank half of hers. "I was supposed to go over to your forge today to take pictures of your ironworks for the website. But time got away from me helping all these other people. I'm sorry."

"Not to worry. I brought the pieces to you. They are in *meine* wagon." He followed her outside.

Metal pieces jutted every which way above the edge of the wagon bed. He swung his arm toward his handiwork. "*Meine* inventory."

"You didn't have to do that. This had to be a lot of work, not to mention taking it all back and unpacking it."

He'd been glad to do it to save her some effort. "I thought it would be easier if I brought them to you." Easier for her, but definitely not for him.

"Well, *danki*, but you didn't have to go to all this

trouble." She peeked over the side of the wagon bed. "Is this *everything* you've made?"

"*Ja.* I didn't know if I would need a different inventory number for each item since no two are identical."

"Well, you could give each piece a unique identifying number. Or you could give an inventory number to a type of item with a disclaimer that because these are all handmade, the item received might differ from the item pictured. The second option would be less work for you." Or at least in the beginning, less work for her until he took over the site.

"I know it's more work, but I like the idea of customers being able to choose the exact item they wish to purchase. No disappointments. Which way do you think would be best?"

"Either way would be fine. However, if you number each item individually, I wouldn't recommend putting more than six of a single type of item on the website. Too many choices will overwhelm your customers and might discourage them from clicking that purchase button."

He was the one overwhelmed. Too much to do. Too much to contemplate. Too many decisions. But Rainbow Girl seemed to take this all in stride and knew what needed to be done. "Would you consider helping me with *meine* website a couple of times a week?"

"A *couple*?"

He'd asked too much. "Or just once. Until I get the hang of things." He really needed her help. She'd probably thought that once she'd created his website, she would be done.

She shifted to face him. "You will have regular orders. We should work on them at least three times a week. You don't want people to cancel because their merchandise isn't processed quickly enough."

At least three times? He liked the sound of that. "I could do that. Mondays, Wednesdays and Fridays? I'll come here."

"That sounds *gut*, but not here. I should go to your forge. That's where all your inventory is." Her gaze skimmed over his wagon, and she smiled. "Usually."

"But after everything is numbered and tagged, I would need to bring only new items." He didn't want her trying to walk to his place three days a week. Plus, if she got busy like today, he would be assured of seeing her. "So it's settled. I'll come here." He wanted that little bit of control, and to not have to stand around waiting and wondering when she would arrive.

"Won't that cut into your work time? You won't be able to make as many pieces."

But he'd be with her. That would be time well spent. "I'll have plenty of time to work."

"You are as stubborn as *Grossvater.*"

"Danki." Now, if he could be more stubborn than her about whether she stayed or not.

The next afternoon, Dori relaxed on the front porch of the *dawdy haus* in a rocking chair, grateful to be done staring at the computer screen for a while.

Ruth brought out two glasses of lemonade and sat, as well.

Dori took a long drink. "That hits the spot."

Ruth too took a swallow and licked her lips. "Mmm. I'm glad for summer break."

"That doesn't sound very Amish. I thought all Amish were supposed to love hard work."

"I do love teaching, but I'm as anxious as the children for the school year to end. Tell me about Eli."

Dori's mouth threatened to smile at the mention of his name. "You know who Eli is. He's a blacksmith."

"*Ne.* Tell me about *you* and Eli."

She wished. "There is no *me* and Eli."

Ruth shook her head. "I see the looks between you two. He likes you."

"You are seeing things."

"He built you half of a *haus*." Ruth pointed behind her.

"Because our *grossvater* asked him to. One doesn't say *ne* to the bishop."

"The addition is completed, and still he comes over here. Wasn't he here yesterday? And the day before?"

"I'm helping him with his website and to get the word out online about his business."

"You don't give anyone else in the community as much attention as you give him, or he gives you." Ruth wiggled her eyebrows.

Dori huffed a breath. "Give it a rest, sister."

"Not until you admit you like him back."

"I will admit no such thing. And even if I had any feelings—however small—it wouldn't matter because I'm leaving after the baby is born."

Her sister leaned forward in her chair. "Dori, you can't. You have to stay. You're the only sister I have. Who will I talk to about Daniel?"

"You have plenty of cousins and other women in the community."

Mutter appeared on the porch with a covered plastic bowl, three smaller bowls and forks. "I cut up some fresh fruit. It'll be *gut* for the baby."

"Are you supposed to be here? Won't *Vater* get upset?"

"Since you started the classes to join church, he doesn't mind. I'm so happy you're going to stay."

Would it do any *gut* to contradict her? But she just couldn't let her *mutter* be misled. "*Mutter*, I'm not planning to stay."

Mutter dished them each up a bowlful. "Your *grossvater* had a room built for you."

"Against *meine* wishes." Dori was so grateful for her own space. "It seems no one in this community will believe me when I say I'm not staying." She took a bite of a juicy red strawberry. Sweet and delicious. "Mmm." She took piece after piece as though she were a starving child. She wasn't, of course. She was just pregnant and perpetually hungry.

As Dori popped her last grape into her mouth, Eli drove up in an open two-wheeled trap.

Ruth pointed. "See what I mean?"

Mutter perked up. "Is there something going on between those two?"

Dori spoke before her sister could. *"Ne."* She jumped to her feet and met Eli under the shade of the tree.

He stopped but didn't get out. "I wanted to talk to you about a couple of new items for *meine* website, but I can see that you're busy. I'll come back another time."

Mutter stepped off the porch. "Eli Hochstetler, it's so *gut* to see you. I was talking to your *mutter* after church on Sunday."

He nodded to her. "I don't want to interrupt."

"You aren't interrupting. Is he, Dorcas? Come and join us. Have some fresh fruit." She waved him down. "I won't take *ne* for an answer."

Dori's *mutter* wasn't being very subtle. Had she and her sister planned this? Were they ganging up on her? It wouldn't do any *gut*. Dori wasn't going to change her mind about staying, but no one seemed to want to listen to her. She could no more be Amish than Craig could.

Without further refusal, Eli set the brake and joined them on the porch.

Mutter remained standing. "I have some cookies I baked yesterday. I'll run to the big *haus* and get them." She returned faster than Dori thought possible. Had she actually *run*? Evidently she really wanted Eli to stay.

Dori wasn't going stop her. She liked having Eli around too, but nothing was going to develop between them. Nothing could. Eli saw her as an *Englisher*, and Dori was planning to return to the *Englisher* world as soon as she could. In the meantime, she would enjoy his company. "What are the items you have in mind to add to your inventory?"

He trotted to his buggy and returned with a twelve-inch-tall twisted piece of metal and a short one with two sides. They each had leaves decorating them. "What do you think?"

She studied them a moment and took the taller one. "Paper towel holder, and that one's for napkins." She pointed to the one he still held.

"Right. Do you think people will want to buy these?"

"Of course they will. Maybe even buy them as a set. These are beautiful."

"You can keep those."

Oh, dear. He was giving her gifts now. That couldn't be *gut*. "*Ne*. I don't have a kitchen, but I'll take pictures and upload them to your website." He needed to keep his inventory to sell, and these would definitely fetch a fine price.

"I can make more."

"I appreciate the offer, but you need to keep them." When his countenance faltered, she quickly added, "For now. You're making some regular sales, but you need to keep the momentum going and have constant marketing to make your business thrive. Having a new product like these will help."

"But I want to give back for all the work you're doing for me."

"Have you forgotten about the half of a *haus* you built?" Why didn't he realized the enormity of that? Far more than a little website.

Ruth gave a conspicuous nod to *Mutter*.

As long as neither of them said anything embarrassing, Dori could ignore them.

The pair of them behaved. For the most part. They fawned over him like one might a TV celebrity, asking him questions and being overly interested in his blacksmithing. But it worked for Dori, because she learned much about the humble man Eli had grown into, yet she remained the innocent bystander.

After services on Church Sunday, Ruth hooked her arm around Dori's. "I have a favor to ask you, sister."

Dori sighed. "When you say it like that, I sense I'm not going to like it."

"As you noticed, I'm partial to Daniel Burkholder. Would you ask Eli to have him and Daniel ask *Vater* if they can take you and I for a buggy ride?"

That was a lot of asking and a roundabout way of doing things. But it was the Amish way. It wasn't a *gut* idea for Dori to go on a buggy ride with Eli. She already spent too much time with him, bringing her closer to him. People in the community were likely talking about them. That couldn't be *gut* for Eli. "I can ask Eli to ask Daniel to ask you on a buggy ride."

"You must come too. *Vater* won't let me go alone with a young man. You know how he is."

Ja. When Dori was a teen, she'd sneaked out several times to meet a boy. Usually for a simple walk or to go fishing at a pond. Until she'd left the community. She supposed that sneaking off had led to taking more and more chances until she left altogether. And her leaving probably led to *Vater* being more strict with Ruth. "*Ja,* I'll ask."

"Right now?"

"They're playing horseshoes. I'll wait until he's done."

Her sister's expression turned worried.

Dori had missed her sister. "Fine. I'll ask now."

Ruth beamed. *"Danki."*

Dori nodded as she walked away. She approached Eli near the barn with several other young men, including Daniel. She waited until he threw his last horseshoe. "Eli?"

"Continue without me." Eli strode over to her.

The other men nodded and smiled as though they knew a secret. A secret about her and Eli. They were wrong, of course.

He had that expression that came right before a smile. An expectation. An understated pleasure.

She soaked it in.

"Guten tag." His smile nearly undid her.

She glanced over his shoulder to regain her focus.

"I have a favor to ask of you, but don't read anything into *meine* request."

"All right." His smile dipped below the surface again and lurked, waiting to be released again.

"*Meine* sister wants you and Daniel to ask our *vater* if you can take us on a buggy ride. Ruth is sweet on Daniel."

"I'd be happy to."

Dori was surprised. That hadn't taken any convincing at all. "Do you think Daniel will agree?"

"*Ja.* He's sweet on her, as well. We'll ask your *vater*, then come over to where you and your sister are."

"*Danki.*" She walked back to Ruth, who looked giddy with excitement.

"Well?"

"They are going to ask *Vater.*"

Across the Burkholders' yard, Eli and Daniel stood with *Vater*, who shook his head. The conversation volleyed between them several times. It looked as though Eli was trying to convince *Vater* to let them all go. Finally, *Vater* nodded, and Eli and Daniel headed toward her and her sister.

Dori touched Ruth's arm. "Don't appear too excited. Make him work a little for your affections."

Eli spoke. "I'm afraid we won't be able to take you ladies for a buggy ride today."

Ruth's shoulders slumped.

Daniel spoke. "Since church is at our home, I can't leave. I must stay in case I'm needed, but your *vater* has agreed to let us take you both to the fireworks in a week and a half if you want to—"

"*Ja,*" Ruth chirped.

So much for making him work a little for her affections. Dori stared up at Eli and hesitated a moment longer before answering. "*Ja*. I'd like that too." Her insides did a giddy little dance.

The hint of a smile played at the corners of his mouth.

Chapter Eleven

The following Saturday, Dori pulled on her voluminous gray split-skirt pants. She had outgrown her other clothes in a hurry, even her sweatpants and yoga pants. Eating well was doing both her and her baby well. The stretchy T-shirt knit was the only thing she could still get over her ever-growing belly. She hated these pants almost as much as cape dresses. She didn't know why she had even bothered to pack them when she left, but she was glad she had.

Dori had spent much of the past two weeks evaluating and updating Amish websites, teaching a recalcitrant bishop to use a computer, running virus scans and cleaning up hard drives for community members. No one seemed to understand that these things needed to be done regularly. *Grossvater* was nearly as uncooperative as Eli to learn. All of which had left her little time to create the doctor's database or study for the GED.

Now she was off to Dr. Kathleen's to transfer the database she'd built for her. She'd made it according to the doctor's specifications, and now she needed to in-stall it on the computer at the clinic. "*Grossvater?* May I use your buggy?"

"Are you going to visit Eli?"

"*Ne.*" Though she wouldn't mind seeing him. It was harder to run into him with the addition finished. Fortunately, the arrangement to meet three days a week to update his site and fill orders gave her some regular interaction. "I'm going to the medical clinic."

"But you just saw Kathleen a couple of weeks ago. Is something wrong?"

"*Ne.* I'm not going for a medical visit. I'm installing the database I made for her and see if she likes how it works. There might be other things she may have realized she needs for it to work well for her. These kinds of things are usually a work in progress."

"You know a lot about computers and such."

She supposed she did. She hadn't realized how much she'd learned from Craig. "It's a skill I believe more and more Amish are going to need to learn in this day and age if their businesses are going to survive."

"I don't like all this technology—not one bit—but I suppose you're right. The world is a different place from when I was a boy. We don't have the advantage of isolating ourselves any longer. We are being pulled ever faster into the *Englisher* world."

"We were never truly isolated. The Amish have always been dependent on the *English* to purchase our produce and goods." She cocked her head. "Why are you smiling?"

"You said *we*. '*We* were never truly isolated.' You are still Amish at heart."

Ne, she wasn't. "Don't read anything into that. So

may I use your buggy? I would use *Vater*'s open two-wheeled buggy, but it looks like it might rain."

"*Ja*, for sure it will rain. I don't need *meine* buggy today. I'll have one of the boys hitch it up for you."

"*Danki.*" She went to the bathroom and pulled out her makeup bag. She'd taken to applying her makeup with a lighter touch these days. But as she started today, she halted. Why should she even bother wasting her makeup on people who didn't care about it? Correction, they did care and preferred she didn't wear it at all. So she dropped her eye shadow back into her bag. She would save it for when she returned to the *English* world, to people who cared about such things.

Instead, she experimented with twisting her hair away from her face. When she did so, her brown roots were almost long enough to hide the various colors on the side of her head where her hair hung longer. She tucked in a few bobby pins and attempted the same on the other side. Not nearly as successful. The shorter hair poked out in red spikes all along the roll she'd made, but she stuck in a few bobby pins anyway. Then she twisted the back of her hair and secured it to her head with the remainder of the bobby pins.

She chuckled. She almost looked Amish again. Plain and ugly. She yanked the pins out and shook her hair free. That was better. She may be without makeup and her facial piercings, but she wouldn't give up her fun, colorful hair or her multiple earrings.

After grabbing her backpack with her laptop, she headed out for the barn. Though dark clouds crowded the morning sky, no rain fell yet, but she could feel it coming.

In the barn, her brother Matthew attached the buggy poles to Nelly's harness.

She hadn't seen much of her oldest brother since she'd returned. "*Danki* for hitching the buggy for me."

Finishing, he glared at her and strode away without a word.

"Matthew? Stop."

He halted but didn't turn around.

She watched his shoulders rise slowly and fall as he drew in a long, slow, deep breath. She walked over and around in front of him. "Is something wrong?"

He narrowed his eyes and glowered at her. "Wrong? *You* are what's wrong. I stayed here. I've worked hard for *Vater*. What did you do? You ran off to the *English* world and returned pregnant. You don't deserve to be here. You don't belong here. You left. You're not Amish. And you never will be. Go back to where you came from." He stormed off.

Her brother hated her. A pain twisted in her chest.

She knew her family and friends would likely shun her—but since she hadn't joined church, they hadn't. She never expected anyone to outright hate her. Not like that. Matthew clearly did. That hurt more than she would have expected.

She ached to cry out to *Gott* as she'd done as a child when someone hurt her feelings, but she hadn't spoken to Him in a very long time. He wouldn't be interested in her pain, not after she'd turned her back on Him and her—the Amish people.

She longed to go after her brother and say something to make him not hate her, but everything he'd said was true. She *had* left. She *was* pregnant. And she *didn't* belong.

The problem was, she didn't feel like she belonged anywhere. Not here with the Amish, and not with the *Englishers* either. Oh, she'd faked it while she was out in the world, she'd dressed and played the part, but never truly felt *English*. Now she looked like a confused mess. Not Amish, and not *English*. What was she doing? She should leave, but where would she go? She had no place. As long as she was pregnant, Craig didn't want her. Or their baby. She couldn't return to the shelter. She couldn't live on the streets. Unfortunately, this was the only place that would have her.

She was the prodigal child, and her brother the *gut* child who had stayed behind.

She walked Nelly out of the barn, climbed into the buggy and drove away. By the time she arrived at Dr. Kathleen's, a sprinkling rain tapped lightly on the roof.

Noah Lambright met her outside the clinic. "Go on inside. I'll take care of your horse and buggy."

"Danki." She grabbed her pack and ran for the cover of the porch and knocked on the door.

After a moment, Dr. Kathleen opened the door. "You don't have to knock. When it's unlocked, I'm here and you can simply walk in."

Dori stepped inside. "I wasn't sure, since you aren't normally open on Saturdays."

The doctor closed the door. "I knew you were coming. Deborah Miller is also here doing some research for her *mutter*."

That surprised Dori. "She's allowed to do that?"

"Ja. Her *mutter* has Graves' disease. She's been successful at finding natural remedies that seem to be helping. Her *mutter* is also pregnant and due about the same time as you."

"Really? She's not too old?"

"*Ne.* Her body is still healthy despite her condition."

That shouldn't surprise Dori that an older Amish woman would be pregnant. Amish women had plenty of babies in their later years. *Englishers* would be far more upset at a later-in-life child after having raised a family. "I've finished the database. Sorry to have taken so long."

"Not to worry. I've been without it this long, I'm just excited to have it now."

A very different attitude from the hurry-up *English*. Dori would have been fired by now. "I want you to look at it and see if there are any other features you'd like me to add." She lifted her backpack. "I have a laptop in here." It was *Grossvater*'s new one, but he wasn't about to use it or even open it without Dori twisting his arm.

Dr. Kathleen indicated the table that served as the reception desk. "Deborah's using *meine* computer in the office, so we can look at it out here."

Jessica, the doctor's sister, stood and moved behind the chair. "Do you mind if I watch?"

"Not at all. It sounded like you will be working with the database as much as the doctor." Dori set down her laptop and lifted the lid. While she waited for it to boot up, she took out her cell phone. Still no call or text from Craig, but he hadn't cut off her service. That said something. She set the phone aside, opened the database program from the thumb drive and offered Dr. Kathleen the chair. "I put in a few phantom patient records so you'd have something to look at and click from one record to another." She instructed the doctor about the features.

Dr. Kathleen clicked around for a few minutes. "You

did a great job. This is just what I need. How do we get it onto *meine* computer?"

Dori tapped the red thumb drive sticking out from the side of her laptop. "It's all on here. I just need to plug this into yours, and it'll transfer quickly."

The doctor stood. "Great. Let Jessica use it for a few minutes to see if she thinks of anything to be added. I'll go check to see how much longer Deborah will be."

Though hesitant at first, Jessica warmed up fast to the program.

"I think you're a natural."

"I'm trying to learn about computers. I want to get *meine* GED and take business classes on the computer to get a degree."

Dori perked up. "I'm working on *meine* GED too."

"Would you like to work on our GEDs together? I don't really know what I'm doing."

"I would like that. It will help me, as well."

They arranged for Jessica to come to the bishop's *haus* two days a week so they could study together.

Dr. Kathleen came back out. "She's almost done, so we can move in there and be ready when she is."

With her computer in hand, Dori followed Jessica and the doctor into her office.

Dr. Kathleen indicated the girl behind the desk. "You know Deborah."

"I'm almost done. Let me write down a few of these website addresses. I wish they weren't so long and confusing." Deborah scratched one long convoluted number and letter combination under her previous one.

"There's an easier way to do that." Dori showed her how to bookmark web pages.

"*Danki!* That's so much easier." Deborah added several more.

Why couldn't Eli be as eager to learn this stuff and try on his own? But then, if he did, she wouldn't get to spend nearly as much time with him.

These three women were unique for the Amish. All would increase their computer knowledge before Dori left. She would see to it. It would be her legacy.

Deborah stood. "All done thanks to Dori. *Danki*, Dr. Kathleen. I found some interesting information that I hope helps. I'm going to hurry home before the rain really starts coming down. *Auf Wiedersehen*." Deborah dashed out.

Dori sat behind the desk and plugged in the thumb drive. "You know what this means, don't you?"

Dr. Kathleen took a seat across from the desk. "That I'll be able to organize *meine* patients' files and search them more easily?"

"Besides that. You'll need another computer for Jessica at your front desk."

Jessica beamed.

The doctor held up her hand to her sister. "Don't get too excited. That's not likely to happen. The church leaders were reluctant to approve one. I doubt they'll approve two." Dr. Kathleen stood abruptly. "I'll be back." She ran from the room and into the bathroom.

Dori turned to Jessica. "Is she all right?"

"Morning sickness. She's finally pregnant."

When the doctor returned, she seemed fine, though a bit pale-faced.

"I hear congratulations are in order."

She smiled. "*Danki.* It appears our dear Lord has chosen to bless me with a child after all."

"I'm so happy for you."

"When it hadn't happened right away, people whispered that I was being punished for staying away for so long and becoming a doctor."

Dori frowned. "Do you believe that? That *Gott* was punishing you?"

"*Ne.* I don't believe *Gott* does that. He's a *gut* and kind and loving *Gott*. He waited for His right time. Like sending you back to us. All in *Gott*'s timing."

Dori didn't believe that. The timing had been terrible. She'd lost everything and had nowhere to live. But then, the Amish would say that it had been exactly the right timing.

By the time Dori was ready to leave, the rain fell harder. It ebbed and flowed. Soft, then hard, then soft again.

"Do you want to wait until this lets up?" Dr. Kathleen stood in the open doorway.

Dori looked toward the dark sky. "I don't think it's going to completely let up anytime soon. Maybe not even today at all. I should leave now before it gets any worse. I'll be fine."

"All right." The doctor pulled the short rope of the bell that hung from the porch awning, and a clang rang out.

Her husband appeared in the barn doorway.

Dr. Kathleen pointed to Dori. "Buggy!"

He nodded and disappeared. A few minutes later, he reemerged, holding an umbrella and leading Dori's horse.

Dori dashed from the porch through the open buggy door. *"Danki."* She drove away.

As Nelly trotted down the road, Dori turned her

mind to Eli. Next week, she should go over to his place and take pictures of his work environment to add a bit of depth to the site. Tell the story of how some of the different pieces were made.

Pictures?

Her phone. She didn't remember putting it in her pack.

With one hand holding the reins, she used her other to check the pack's pocket where she normally kept her phone. Nothing. She checked the other pockets. Not there either, so she unzipped her pack and felt around the interior. *Where was it?* She tucked the reins under her arm to hold them while she dug with both hands. No phone.

A car honked.

Dori jerked her attention back to driving. Nelly had wandered into the middle of the two-lane country road. Dori pulled the reins to the side, and the horse moved into her lane again.

Still honking, the car sped up and passed. The boys inside yelled and hooted as they flew by with their music blaring through the open windows. Road water splashed up on the horse as well as the buggy.

Nelly hopped on her forelegs a couple of times and bolted.

The reins pulled out from under Dori's arm. She grappled for the leather strips and managed to grab hold of them. "Whoa!"

Nelly fought the reins at first but then slowed, settling into her previous leisurely walk.

Dori's heart pounded. Didn't motorists know to be cautious when passing an animal? Evidently, teenagers didn't. Probably thought it amusing to spook a horse. As well as its driver.

Nelly favored one of her front hooves.

Dori maneuvered the horse to the shoulder and hauled back on the reins. After setting the brake, she stepped out into the steady but now light rain. She stroked the side of the big draft horse's neck. "Shh. It's all right."

Nelly's hide quivered, and she swung her head toward Dori.

She stroked the leg in question and raised the hoof. The shoe had been thrown.

As a pickup approached from the opposite direction, Nelly nickered, retrieved her leg and pawed the ground. Though the vehicle traveled at a normal speed, the horse was still unnerved.

"It's all right, girl." Dori gripped the harness leather behind the horse's jaw.

The truck slowed a bit as it passed, as though trying to reduce the amount of road splash.

Nelly wasn't having any of it. She tried to rear, but Dori held tight. She needed to keep the horse from getting any more agitated. Nelly jerked her head to free herself.

"*Ne.* Calm down." Life was so much easier with a car. A car didn't get spooked and need to be soothed.

The horse swung her head toward Dori, knocking her off balance. If not for her grip on the harness, Dori would have fallen. Then Nelly wrenched her head the other way, jerking the harness from Dori's grip. She reared and, apparently realizing she was free, lurched forward with the buggy and galloped into a run.

The rear wheel clipped Dori's hip and spun her half-way around.

She lost her footing and slid down the muddy embankment on her backside, causing her wide-legged pants to travel up. At the bottom and in two-foot-high weeds, her ankle hit something hard. A sharp pain shot up her leg. Had she hit a rock or a branch? Either way, it had banged her bone. Wiggling her foot, she assessed that no bones had been broken, but she likely had a cut, a scrape at the very least. As she reached down to feel her ankle, she also straightened her sodden pant legs. She couldn't tell, with all the mud and rain, if there was blood on her ankle, as well.

A wall of bushes and trees stood beyond the weeds. Forward wouldn't be a wise direction, so she rolled to her stomach and clawed her way up the steep embankment. Reaching the halfway point, she slid back down the muddy slope, hitting her other ankle this time but not as hard. Twice more, she made it halfway before slipping to the bottom again. Though pain shot through her first injured ankle, she *had* managed to climb with it, assuring her no bones had been broken but definitely injured.

The sound of a car coming down the road caught her attention.

She hollered and waved her arms, but the bank stood a little too tall for her to be seen.

The motorist drove right on by, completely unaware someone needed help.

Poor frightened Nelly. How far had she run? If the horse and buggy were close, a passerby would eventually stop to investigate. Hopefully sooner rather than later. If Nelly made it all the way home by herself, someone would realize something had gone wrong, but no one would know exactly where to look for Dori. She would just have to wait. Someone would eventually find her.

She turned her thoughts heavenward. Gott? *Please, help me get out of this mess.*

What was she praying to Him for? He hadn't listened to her prayers in the past. But it couldn't hurt, could it?

A moment later, the rain increased to a torrent.

With closed eyes, she tilted her head toward the sky. "Seriously!" Wasn't her life bad enough? She rolled to her back and leaned against the steep bank. At this point, she couldn't get any wetter, but the heavy rain would wash off some of the mud. She could at least be grateful for that.

She didn't know how long she leaned there with her ankle throbbing while the rain washed her face. A stream of water trickled over her feet.

How long before the heavy rain rose in the ditch, turning the stream into a rushing creek?

She wrapped her arms around her protruding belly. "Don't worry, baby, I'll protect you. *Gott*, please make the rain stop. And please, have someone come by and notice I'm here. Eli would be nice to send *meine* way."

But what were the chances he would happen to be out in the rain and happen to find her at the bottom of a ditch?

None.

Chapter Twelve

Eli swung his hammer down again and again on the red-hot piece of iron. This would be a rattle for Rainbow Girl's baby. He thought a lot about Rainbow Girl lately.

With the addition finished, he'd feared not seeing her, but he had been surprised she'd insisted upon working together on his business website and orders *three* days a week. He'd hoped for one day a week, tried for two, but she'd said they needed to meet *at least* three days a week or his online orders would suffer.

He was fortunate indeed. Her assistance allowed him to focus on making items to sell. He shook his head. He had to admit he'd been more focused on Rainbow Girl lately than his ironwork.

Eli dunked the rattle into his pail of water and set it aside to cool, then put out his forge fire. Though he usually liked working on cool, rainy days, and it wasn't one of his scheduled times, he wanted to see Rainbow Girl. Only to get her opinion on the marketability of his latest creation. Once she had taken photographs of it, he would give it to her as a gift. He also wanted to fine-tune some of his product descriptions and check on more orders. She kept trying to get him to buy a computer so he could manage all this himself, but he preferred to have her do it. Not only was that easier and gave him more time to create, but he got to spend time with her.

He hitched Dutch to a small open-air buggy with a cloth top. He didn't want to get drenched before he arrived, but he also didn't want to be closed in.

Once at the bishop's, he parked in front. He would wait until he knew if it would be all right to visit before unhitching Dutch and putting him in the barn. He bound up the steps and knocked.

Bishop Bontrager opened the door. "Eli, come in, come in."

Eli stepped inside. "I came to see Dorcas. About *meine* website." He didn't want the bishop to think there was anything more to his visit than that. Because there wasn't.

"She's not here. Went to Noah and Kathleen's to do something with a computer for the doctor." He glanced at the clock on the coffee maker. "I thought she would've returned by now. Said she wouldn't be gone long."

Eli's insides twisted. "Do you think she's all right?"

"I'm sure she is, but it wouldn't hurt to call. Our telephone's in the barn."

"I'll call. You stay here." Eli could move faster alone, and the old man didn't need to be out in the rain. He ran to the barn and found the community's typed directory in a wooden wall pocket by the phone. The doctor's number had been handwritten on the front. He dialed.

Noah answered.

"Dorcas Bontrager came to work on the doctor's computer. Is she still there?"

"*Ne*. She left a few hours ago. Is something wrong?"

Eli's insides wrenched harder into a painful knot. "I don't think so. Did she say if she planned to go anywhere from your place besides home?"

Noah made Eli wait while he asked the doctor. "*Ne*. Kathleen understood she was heading home. She left before the rain had gotten harder. Is she not there?"

"*Ne*. But I'm sure she's fine. She probably stopped to visit a neighbor. *Danki*." But Eli had a bad feeling. Rainbow Girl didn't socialize with others in the community except to work on their websites. Their people were still wary of her. Had she run away from the community again? Or had something happened to her? Either way, he needed to find her. He returned to the *dawdy haus*. "She's not there. She left hours ago. I'm going out to look for her."

The bishop headed out the door with him. "I'll send Andrew and Matthew in search of her as well, and have Leah call the neighbors."

Eli nodded as he climbed in his buggy. "I'll retrace the direct route between here and the doctor's. Have them check the alternate routes." He drove away at a faster clip than normal.

He arrived at the doctor's with no sight of her, here or on the road. Dr. Kathleen had been on the phone, calling neighbor after neighbor since he'd telephoned. No one knew Rainbow Girl's whereabouts.

That likely meant she'd gone to town since no one had seen her. Had she left them again? Left him. Though he wanted to go find her, he didn't want to know for sure that she'd left. He wanted to return to his forge and forget all about her. Pound the baby rattle into a lump.

How would he figure out his website and manage his orders? He needed her. He would find her.

But when he pulled out onto the road, he headed back the way he'd come at a more normal pace this time. He didn't want to return without her, but he couldn't make himself head toward town and her face-to-face rejection.

About a third of the way, something in the road caught his attention. He stopped, got out in the rain and picked it up. A horseshoe. One he had fashioned. Had this come off Nelly? If so, Rainbow Girl had been heading home rather than into town. His spirits lifted, then crashed again. So where was she?

Shaking off the rain, he climbed back into his buggy and drove at a faster pace. Maybe she had arrived at the bishop's, and he'd somehow missed her.

About another mile down the road, he noticed a draft horse and buggy under some trees at the edge of a field. Not just any horse. Nelly. Maybe she had driven the horse there to wait out the storm. He hurried to the clump of trees. He jumped from his rig and opened the door of hers. Rainbow Girl wasn't inside, but her pack sat on the floor.

He scanned the vicinity. No Rainbow Girl. "Rainbow? Dori!" The nearest Amish *haus* wasn't even in sight. He knew which direction, but did she?

He lifted Nelly's front hoof that she held cocked. The shoe was missing. He unhitched the horse and secured her to a tree. "I'll return for you." He climbed aboard his buggy, intending to drive to the nearest *haus*. Instead, he headed back to where he'd found the horseshoe. He got out and looked up the road and down. Where would she have gone? Rain pelted him and ran off his hat. Was she out in this?

"Rainbow!" He listened. "Dori!" He didn't know what to call her.

If Nelly threw a shoe here and ended up a mile away, where had Rainbow Girl gone? He pulled the reins out in front of Dutch, turned him and walked down the side of the road.

She had been headed in this direction. Nelly's shoe had come off—for some reason. Something must have happened, because he'd checked her shoes not that long ago. One wouldn't have simply *fallen* off. Had she spooked?

"Rainbow! Dori!"

He heard a muffled voice and stopped the horse. "Rainbow?"

"I'm here."

The voice came from up ahead.

"Where?" He couldn't see her on either side of the road.

"The ditch."

He leaned over and saw her twenty-five yards up the road. He jogged, bringing the horse with him. Taking the tether weight from the floor of the buggy, he secured Dutch. It wouldn't do him any *gut* to have his horse wander off or spook and bolt.

"Are you all right? Are you hurt?"

Waterlogged and mud caked, she stood at the bottom of a ten-foot or so incline, staring up at him, with one hand on the muddy side of the embankment, the other on her stomach. "Wet and cold mostly. Other than that, I'm fine."

Was she really? Or merely telling him what he wanted to hear? "Is the baby all right?"

She sucked in a breath. "*Ja.* It's been kicking me. Gave me a real wallop at the sound of your voice."

That idea made him smile. Certainly the baby didn't know *his* voice, did it? "I'll get you two out of there." He moved closer to the edge.

She held up her hand. "What are you doing?"

"I'm coming down for you."

"*Ne!* It's too slippery to climb up. Why do you think I'm still down here? We don't want to both be stuck."

Just because she couldn't climb out, didn't mean he couldn't. "I can't reach you." Even prone on the ground, he doubted he could. Why hadn't he thought to bring a rope? Because he never imagined she'd be at the bottom of a deep ditch and he'd need one.

"Go get help."

Leave her? That didn't sit well with him. "I can't leave you down there."

"I'm not going anywhere. I promise to still be here when you return."

He would *not* abandon her. He would think of something else. "To your left a few feet, I can see a fallen tree branch. Do you think you can reach it?"

She looked. "I think so."

"Point one end of it up the bank for me to reach."

She turned and leaned for it, then sucked in a breath.

"What's wrong?" She wasn't going into labor, was she? She *was* a little over seven months pregnant. "Is it the baby?"

She shook her head. "I hurt *meine* ankle when I slid down here. I'll be fine." She grabbed a twig of the bigger branch and pulled the whole thing toward her.

Hopefully, it would be large enough and strong enough to use to pull her up. He needn't have worried. As she pulled the branch and maneuvered one end up the bank, it kept coming. Grunting and groaning, she eventually hoisted the thick end far enough for him to grab. "Let go of it." When she did, he pulled it all the way up.

"What about me? I thought you were going to hold it so I could climb up it."

"I am, but there are too many offshoots. I'm going to break off some of the smaller ones to make it easier to hold on to." Using his boot and leaning the branch against the buggy, he stomped off branch after branch but left a larger one near the base. He fed that end down the hill. "Put your arm between the larger branch and the one that shoots off from it."

"Why?"

"In case your hands slip, you won't fall." Her wet, muddy hands were small compared to his and not as strong. She also had to be tired from her ordeal.

"What if your hands slip?"

"They won't." He wouldn't let them. "Hold on and climb with your feet. I'll do most of the work."

She got into position as he'd instructed.

"*Gott*, please let her hold on tight and don't let the branch break." Hand over hand he hauled up the hunk of wood and Rainbow Girl along with it.

Halfway, her feet slipped from under her.

The branch slid a few inches in his grip, and he sucked in a breath. That definitely tore some flesh. "Are you all right?"

"*Ja*. Don't let go."

"I won't."

She got her feet back under her. "That seems to be the same place I kept slipping on *meine* own. You were right about having the offshoot under *meine* arm."

He'd been glad for it, as well. *Gott* had supplied what they needed. He hauled the branch up faster this time. He wanted to get her to safety as quickly as possible. When she was nearly at the top, his next reach latched onto her wrist, then her other wrist. He hefted her forward and into his arms. She was safe.

Her arms wrapped around him. "*Danki*. I didn't know how I was going to get out of there."

"You're safe." He searched her face to see if she was truly all right. He wiped rain and mud from it, then caressed her cheek.

As though some invisible force pushed him forward, he leaned closer. He pressed his lips to hers. Soft and sweet. Or had she kissed him? He couldn't tell. All he knew was he never wanted to let her go.

But he must and did. "Are you sure you're not hurt?"

"Only *meine* ankle." She held her foot out. A gash cut into her flesh.

He lifted her into his arms, and she sucked in a breath. "What is it?"

"*Meine* hip hurts too."

"What happened to your hip?"

"Nelly spooked and lost a shoe. I stopped to check her. When she bolted, the rear wheel clipped *meine* hip. It's only a bump. I'll be fine."

He leaned forward to set her in his buggy.

Her grip tightened around his neck, and her tone was alarmed. "What are you doing?"

"Setting you in the buggy."

"You can't. I'm all muddy."

"I'm aware of that." He was muddy now too from holding her. "I can easily clean the buggy. Now, let go of me so I can look at your injury." Not that he really wanted her to release him.

With a heavy sigh, she freed him.

He set her on the seat and assessed her ankle. "This doesn't look too deep, but it bled and is full of mud. I'm taking you back to the doctor."

"You don't have to do that. I can clean it and put a bandage on it when I get home. It'll be fine."

"This could get infected." He rounded the buggy and climbed in.

"It'll heal. We need to find Nelly."

"She's fine, which is more than I can say for you." He turned Dutch around and headed for the clinic. "Think of the baby. Are you sure it's all right?"

"The baby's fine. Nelly threw a shoe somewhere around here. Maybe we can find it."

Amazing. She'd just been through a harrowing experience, and she was thinking of the horse. He pushed the horseshoe on the floor of the buggy with his boot. "Found it. That's why I was walking Dutch rather than driving, and the reason I could hear you when you called back to me."

"That was lucky."

"That was *Gott*."

During the whole drive, he could think of nothing but Rainbow Girl's well-being, the baby and…that kiss.

He shouldn't have done it but longed to do it again.

Dripping wet, Dori hooked her arms around Eli's neck as he carried her into the clinic. She didn't need him to carry her, but she liked being in his arms. She couldn't believe they'd kissed. It had sort of been a mutual meeting in the middle. Nice and sweet, but she knew he hadn't meant to do it. A *gut* Amish wouldn't kiss someone until they were at least engaged. Most didn't kiss until the wedding day.

Dr. Kathleen rushed over. "You found her. Bring her in here and set her on the table." She motioned toward one of the back rooms.

Dori swung her legs. "Don't you dare put me on that clean white sheet." She didn't want to get it all muddy. The black buggy seat had been bad enough.

"Would you stop worrying about a little dirt? You are more important than getting something dirty."

But someone would have to clean it up. "I can stand. Please let me."

The doctor gave him a nod, and he finally relented. "She has a cut on her ankle, and her hip's bruised. And make sure the baby's all right. She fell into a ditch."

Dori liked that he cared enough to not leave anything to chance.

Dr. Kathleen removed a washcloth and two towels from a chest of drawers. "I'll check her thoroughly. There are a lot of people out searching for her. Would you make a few calls and spread the message that she's been found and is well?"

He turned to leave but stopped at the doctor's voice. "In a lower cupboard in the kitchen are some extra towels to dry off with."

"*Danki*, Dr. Kathleen." Then he left.

The doctor set the towels on the dresser next to a plain white ceramic pitcher and basin. "I didn't think we needed him hovering. It's *gut* if he has something to do." She poured water from a pitcher into the basin. "Your ankle seems to have stopped bleeding, so if you're all right to stand, you can wash up here. I'll get you something clean to wear."

Dori limped to where she could wash off some of the mud. Her thin knit pants, soggy and muddy, clung to her legs. *"Danki."*

The doctor opened a cabinet door behind Dori and closed it. "There are dry clothes on the table. If you're all right alone for a few moments, I'll retrieve more water. What you have will get dirty fast."

"I appreciate that. I'm fine." Once alone, she washed her face and hands, and did her best to get the mud from her arms.

Dr. Kathleen returned and swapped out a clean basin and pitcher and took away the dirty ones.

After washing up as best as she could, Dori removed her clothes and put them in a muddy pile near the door. She unfolded the clothes the doctor had left for her. A lavender cape dress. Of course. What else would an Amish woman have to offer? Dori didn't relish putting it on, but it was better than her filthy, sodden clothes. She never imagined wearing one of these again, but the dry dress felt *gut* against her cold, damp skin.

The doctor knocked on the door. "May I come in?" *"Ja."*

Dr. Kathleen entered with a smile. *"Wunderbar.* If you'll sit on the exam table, I'll see how you and the little one are doing."

Dori hopped up with her legs dangling over the edge. "I didn't actually *fall* into the ditch. I slid down the embankment on *meine* backside."

"Then the baby should be fine, but let's check to make sure." The doctor put her stethoscope on Dori's belly. "The heartbeat sounds strong." She pressed on various places on Dori's stomach. "Any pain?"

Dori shook her head.

After Dr. Kathleen seemed satisfied that the baby had escaped unscathed, she moved on to cleaning the cut on Dori's ankle and stitching it up. "Eli was very concerned about you."

She had noticed. "He seemed as relieved to have me out of the ditch as I was to be out. And he kept asking about the baby."

"I think he cares for you both."

"Not likely. The prodigal child and all, returning from the big, bad world. He needs me to manage his website. Nothing more." But that kiss did make her wonder.

"I think there's more than that."

"I'm not even planning to stay. He knows that, and *meine grossvater* knows that. Once the baby is born, I'm getting a job and finding an apartment."

"You could do worse than remaining with the Amish. Is it really so bad here?"

Dori knew that there were worse fates, but she didn't want this life. If Craig would take her back, she would be gone already. Never would have come.

After Dr. Kathleen finished examining and patching Dori up, they both went out into the reception area.

Eli's instant smile did funny things to Dori's insides that had nothing to do with the baby moving.

He shoved away from the counter he'd been leaning against. "How's the baby? Is it all right? It's not hurt, is it?"

The baby responded to his voice as it usually did. As it had when he'd pulled her out of the ditch.

The doctor gave Dori a knowing look. "The baby's fine, as is the *mutter*-to-be. The heartbeat is strong. From the bruising, the buggy hit only the outside of her hip, so no risk to the little one." She addressed Dori again. "I want to see you in a couple of days to check on your ankle, and also next week to remove the stitches. If you have any concerns, call anytime of the day or night."

Nodding, Dori limped to the reception desk. "I will. I think I left *meine* phone here." She picked it up from where she'd set it earlier. "If I'd had this, I could have called for help right away." But then, Eli might not have been the one to find her. And he never would have kissed her.

Dr. Kathleen handed Dori a pill bottle. "Take these for the pain."

Eli pointed at it. "Are those safe for the baby?"

The doctor shot Dori a quick, sideways glance. "I wouldn't give her anything that wasn't. She should rest for a few days and stay off her ankle as much as possible."

"I'll make sure she does." He scooped Dori up into his arms.

Dori caught her breath. "What are you doing?"

"Carrying you to the buggy."

"I can walk."

"The doctor said you're supposed to stay off your ankle."

The doctor opened the door for Eli. She was right about one thing. Eli really was worried about her and the baby, but that didn't mean he cared for her.

The rain had slowed to a drizzle.

He placed her gingerly into his buggy. "Are you comfortable?"

"Ja." How sweet of him to be so careful. "You cleaned the seat."

"I told you it would be all right."

Dr. Kathleen brought out a quilt. "Keep her warm."

The rain had put a chill in the air, and Dori's hair still hung in colorful wet tendrils.

With the quilt tucked around her, Eli drove off.

On the way, Dori spotted Nelly and pointed. "There she is."

"I'll return for her later."

"She's cold and wet and scared. Let's get her now."

Though he fussed and said the horse could wait, Eli guided the buggy off the road to where Nelly waited under the protection of the trees. He got out. "Wait here. I'll tie her to the back of *meine* buggy."

Once he had secured Nelly, Dori asked, "Would you get *meine* backpack with the computer in it, if it's even still there?"

Eli retrieved it without question.

Dori unzipped it. *Grossvater*'s laptop sat inside. She doubted she would be able to talk him into purchasing another one if it had been stolen.

Standing outside the buggy, Eli asked, "Anything else?"

"Ne."

With everything set, he climbed in again.

"Danki for searching for me and finding me." *And for that kiss*, she thought. Though it had likely just been a reaction to the situation, she would treasure it.

* * *

After supper, Eli worked in his forge. Two thoughts swam around and around in his head. Rainbow Girl could have been seriously hurt or died.

He also couldn't shake that kiss. He shouldn't have done that. The community frowned upon unmarried people kissing. But the feel of her lips on his had been wonderful. He wanted to kiss her again, but he couldn't. He wouldn't. He shouldn't.

Vater came around the corner and into the forge. "It's getting late."

Eli looked past his *vater* into the darkness. He must have been out here for hours for it to be so late. Where had the time gone? He certainly didn't have much to show for the time spent, a misshapen piece of iron and a dying fire. "I'll finish up here and be in shortly."

"You did well today in finding the bishop's *enkelin*. It won't go unnoticed by him."

The bishop had been very appreciative. The whole family had. "I did what any of us would do."

"For you, I think it was different. Watch your heart, son. Dorcas Bontrager might have returned, but she's not one of us."

He knew that, but it didn't stop the feelings growing inside him.

She'd looked so...so... Amish in that cape dress. Except for her colorful hair hanging down, she appeared every bit as Amish as anyone else.

She could be Amish again. If she wanted to be.

But she didn't want to be.

What could he say or do to convince her to stay and become Amish? "Maybe if I talked to her, I could persuade her to stay."

Vater put his hand on Eli's shoulder. "She lived in the *Englisher* world for a long time. It's hard for a person to come back from that. Don't get your hopes up, *sohn*."

Vater was right, but it was too late. Eli's hopes had already soared.

"Even if she did return to our Amish ways, how could you trust that she would stay? If she left once, she will likely leave again."

"But she would know that the outside world hadn't worked for her. She went out there to test it, and it had failed her. I— We won't fail her."

"Some people can't see that this life is the best life they can have. They always think that there is something better someplace else."

Dr. Kathleen had been out in the world far longer than Rainbow Girl had been, and she'd returned.

"I will pray for *Gott* to change her heart." And if He didn't change her heart, then He needed to change Eli's.

Chapter Thirteen

Dori had enjoyed working with Dr. Kathleen and her sister, Jessica, creating a website and database for them. Then she'd created a website for the doctor's husband, Noah, and his woodworking business. Then, as she'd gone through the websites of the different community members for her *grossvater* to review, she contacted the ones she felt she could help improve their sites.

People paid her, and she'd saved up quite a nice little nest egg. Enough to move into a small apartment in town. But then, she wouldn't have this website work with the Amish, and her baby was due in just under two months. It would be best if she stayed put until after the baby came.

Dori had outgrown even her wide-legged, split-skirt pants. She dug out the cape dresses from behind the living room end table. She didn't really have anything else to wear at this point. Maybe she should go into town to see what she could find at a thrift store. Did she really want to spend her money on clothes she would wear for only a couple of months? Clothes that would stand out among the Amish? Clothes she didn't really want?

Ne. It would take away from being able to rent an apartment.

She put on the rosy pink cape dress. She wasn't sure how to make it hang right over her growing belly, even though the gathered skirt had plenty of fabric. She fastened it the best she could and hiked across the yard to the big *haus* and knocked. Strange to knock on the door of the home she grew up in.

Mutter came around the side of the *haus*. "*Guten morgen*, Dorcas."

"*Mutter*, can you help me get this to fit right?"

Mutter's smile stretched wide. "*Ja.* Come inside." She made quick work of moving buttons and adjusting things, and soon the dress fitted *wunderbar.* "Bring me the other dress, and I can alter it, as well."

"You don't have to do that."

"I want to." *Mutter* glanced at Dori's belly.

Dori held out her hand. "Would you like to feel your grandchild move?"

"*Ja.*"

Dori placed her *mutter*'s hand on her stomach where she'd last felt the baby move. As though the child inside knew its *grossmutter* was there, it gave a high five.

Mutter sucked in a breath. "It's a strong one."

"*Ja.* Sometimes so strong it wakes me up at night or knocks the wind out of *meine* lungs." Dori was glad to be able to share this with her *mutter.* This experience would have been so different if she was still with Craig. And not for the better. She rarely thought of him anymore.

In the early evening of the Fourth of July, Dori sat on the porch of the big *haus* with Ruth. Crickets chirped in the distance. Though she wore her pink cape dress, she hadn't put her hair up nor put on a *kapp*. She studied her sister from the side.

Ruth, the perfect picture of what an Amish woman should be and look like, twisted one hand in the other, shifted her feet about and leaned forward on the bench, then back.

Dori suspected if she said boo, her sister would shoot straight up into the air, but she dared not try it. Ruth didn't need to be any more agitated. Had Dori been like this when she was younger? She'd felt giddy around Craig, but that was a long time ago. Now her giddiness came from a different source. "You're going to wear yourself out. You're wearing me out just watching you."

"I'm sorry. I'm just excited about tonight."

Though a struggle, Dori managed to keep her emotions under control.

An open buggy came up the road.

Her sister stood up. "That must be them." She peered into the *haus* through the screen door. "They're here, *Vater*." She sat back down.

The buggy pulled into the yard with Eli at the reins. Dori replayed their shared kiss the week before. Warm soft lips on hers, and strong arms around her. She'd felt safe with him. Dori's pulse quickened. The closer he came, the more her own delight wound up. If she wasn't careful, she might start twisting her hands together and shuffling her feet. Would they kiss again tonight? With fireworks shooting off overhead? She hoped so.

When the buggy stopped, both men got out.

Vater stepped forward. "You girls stay here." He went down off the porch. "I expect you boys to have *meine* daughters home at a reasonable time."

Dori lowered her head. How embarrassing.

Though Daniel looked apprehensive, Eli didn't flinch. "We're meeting up with several others, so we'll be part of a larger group. Fireworks don't start until dark. We'll return as soon as they're over."

Vater nodded. "*Gut.* I am trusting *meine* daughters with you two."

Dori wanted to spare them all some humiliation and grabbed her sister's arm. "Come on." She escorted Ruth off the porch. "We'll be fine, *Vater.*"

Vater narrowed his eyes at her. "You behave."

"I will." What more trouble could she get into? She was already pregnant.

Daniel helped Ruth into the back seat and sat beside her.

Dori thrilled in anticipation of sitting next to Eli.

He took Dori's hand and assisted her into the front. "Be careful. Watch your step. Don't slip."

"I'm fine." Her accident last week rattled him more than it had her. Though her hip and ankle were both still sore, she and her baby were fine. She settled on the seat near the middle so he'd have to sit close to her.

But he managed to sit on the far edge of the seat so as not to have his arm brush against hers. Leaning forward with his elbows resting on his legs, he snapped the reins and clicked his tongue. The horse obeyed.

She wanted to calm his fears. "I really am fine. I went to the doctor's yesterday, and she said we are both doing well." She put her hand on her belly.

"I know."

Then what had him in a mood? Wait a minute. He knew? How? "What do you mean you know?"

"I stopped by the clinic and asked her if it was safe for you to be out tonight."

She wasn't sure whether to be offended by his intrusion or delighted he cared enough to ask. "So if she'd said I shouldn't go, you would have canceled?"

He swung his head sideways, and looked at her for the first time. "You wouldn't want to risk the baby, would you?"

"*Ne*, but…"

"Would you have still come if she'd said it would put the baby at risk?"

She didn't want to answer but did. *"Ne."* But she would have considered it to be near Eli.

"That wasn't a very convincing answer. Are fireworks more important than your baby's well-being?"

This conversation had gotten off track fast. "Of course, *meine* baby's more important." She wouldn't intentionally do anything that could harm her baby, but that didn't mean the thought of being near him didn't cross her mind. "I only wanted to assure you we were fine."

"If I thought I had any chance at talking you out of going tonight, I would have tried." He faced forward again.

That stung. "Why? Because you don't think I should go?"

"You should be resting for your sake and the baby's."

She wished she hadn't brought it up. Time to steer this conversation in a different direction. "I added those new items you made to your website. You have two more orders. I'll come over in the morning with the invoices, and we can box them up and take them into town to ship out."

"*Ne.* I'll come to the bishop's in the afternoon. You sleep in."

She did like the idea of sleeping in but didn't like being told what to do. She needed to let her emotions cool off before she spoiled the evening altogether. "Sleeping in will be nice." Not that she actually could with an active baby kicking her insides.

Eli did not want to be here beside Rainbow Girl. *Ne,* it wasn't that he didn't want to be beside her, it was that he wanted to keep her safe. He could do that better back at the *dawdy haus* or his forge. The images of her in the ditch still haunted him. He couldn't shake them, and he still bore the wounds in his palms where the slipping branch dug in and cut his flesh. Not bad, but still tender. How could she be so cavalier with her safety?

She looked so Amish in the cape dress, even with her colorful hair down, and he wanted to wrap her in his arms and protect her from everything. He wanted to keep her safe and close. He wanted to kiss her again.

Eli pulled the buggy to a stop in the meadow near a couple of other early arrivers. He helped Rainbow Girl out of the buggy, but he made sure not to remind her to be careful. He would just see to it she didn't slip.

With the basket of food packed by his *mutter* and a quilt to put on the grass, he led the way to a spot in the shade of an oak tree. He set the basket down and refused help from either of the girls and had Daniel help him spread the quilt on the ground.

Before even sitting on the blanket, Ruth spoke to her sister. "You want to go for a walk around the pond while we wait?"

"That would be nice."

Both girls turned to Eli and Daniel, but it was Rainbow Girl who spoke. "What about you two?"

Daniel smiled. "Sounds *gut*."

It would be better if Eli didn't go. The more he was around Rainbow Girl, the more he wanted to kiss her. This was definitely not the place for that. "I'll stay here and keep an eye on our things." Not that anyone would bother their stuff. He lowered himself to the quilt to deter anyone from trying to coax him otherwise.

Rainbow Girl's expression changed. "I'm a little tired. I think I'll stay here, as well. You two have fun."

Daniel and Ruth left without a fuss.

Rainbow Girl stepped to the edge of the quilt. "It'll be *gut* to rest."

Eli jumped to his feet and offered her a hand to help her sit safely. He couldn't tell if she was allowing the other couple to have a little time to themselves, or if she wanted to be alone with him. Well, not exactly alone in a meadow full of other Amish. "I think resting is wise." He sat again on the far side of the quilt.

"I think I've figured it out. Figured *you* out."

He quirked an eyebrow, not knowing what she was talking about. "What's that?"

"Last week, when you pulled me out of that ditch."

He pushed aside the image of her down there all muddy. "It's over with. No sense dwelling on it." He certainly didn't want to.

"But I think you're bothered by it."

"Of course I'm bothered. Who wouldn't be? You could have been seriously injured or worse. It had to be very scary for you."

"Not as much as I would have thought. It was strange. I never felt as though *meine* life was ever in any real jeopardy. *Ja*, I wondered how long I'd be stuck and how high the water trickling over *meine* feet would get, but not any real danger."

"Because *Gott* was with you."

A short laugh burst from her. "*Gott?* I doubt He bothers with me."

Eli smiled. That meant she still believed in Him. That was *gut*. "He does *bother* with you. With all of us."

She shook her head. "I didn't start this conversation to talk about Him. I wanted to talk about something else. About our kiss."

"Shh." He glanced around at the nearest Amish. "Someone might hear you."

"So? It's not a crime to kiss."

"Our people wouldn't approve. And what if your *vater* found out? He wouldn't be happy. You heard what he said when we left this evening."

"It was just a kiss."

"*Ne*. It was a *kiss*. Not something to take lightly."

She tilted her head. "A kiss doesn't have to mean anything."

Doesn't have to mean anything? It had meant a great deal to him. Had it meant nothing to her? "I think a kiss always means something."

With narrowed eyes, she studied him for a moment. "Always?"

"Always. How can something so intimate not be?"

She continued to stare at him for a while. "So if a kiss *always* means something, what did it mean to you?"

Ne, this wasn't *gut*. He didn't want to talk about this. "I don't know. I wasn't thinking. Now, stop talking about it before someone hears you."

She shifted to face him. "Someone once told me that

a kiss *always* means something, so I'll tell you what it meant to me."

Was she throwing his words back at him? "I don't want to know." But that wasn't true. He did.

"It meant that we weren't strangers. That even though I'm not technically Amish, I'm not completely cast aside."

She'd ignored his request, but it pleased him to know their kiss hadn't meant nothing to her as she had implied.

She chattered on. "I've told you. Now it's your turn."

He shook his head. He wasn't about to say any more than he already had.

She lowered her voice. "Would you like me to tell this growing crowd what we've done?"

He straightened. "You wouldn't. Your *vater* and your *grossvater* would never let you leave the *haus* again." Nor allow him to see her.

"Wouldn't I?"

He had no doubt that she would. "As I said, I wasn't thinking. I was so grateful that you were all right, but that's no excuse. I still shouldn't have done that." But he was glad he had.

All this talk made him want to kiss her again. He should have gone on that walk around the pond.

When the last fireworks faded overhead, Dori wished for more so this night would never end. The fireworks had seemed more brilliant and spectacular this year, but she didn't know why. There hadn't been anything new from years past. She just kept thinking how nice it was to share them with Eli.

People all around the meadow rose, folded up their

quilts and blankets and headed for their buggies, like birds being scattered by a predator. Even Daniel and Ruth got to their feet. Eli did not.

Daniel shifted from foot to foot. "Shouldn't we get the buggy? I don't want to make Andrew or the bishop angry by not getting the girls home promptly."

Eli waved a hand toward the cluster of buggies. "Everyone's crowding around. There's not enough room for everyone to leave at the same time. Once some are on their way, there will be more room to maneuver. Do you really want to be bunched up on the road behind several other buggies?"

Dori had to hand it to Eli, he was thinking ahead. She certainly didn't mind spending a little extra time with the blacksmith.

Daniel stared at all the people swarming around the buggies. "I suppose you're right." After a couple of minutes, he spoke again. "I'm going over to check on the horse, to be ready when things clear out."

He headed off.

Ruth caught up to him. "I'll go with you, Daniel."

Dori chuckled. "Does *meine vater* scare him that much?"

"That and the man behind your *vater*." Eli stood and held out a hand to her.

She placed hers in his larger one, strong and warm. "What man?"

He pulled her to her feet with little effort on her part. "The bishop."

My, Eli *was* strong. "He's not scary." Less so since she'd returned a little over a month ago.

Holding her hand longer than necessary, he gazed

down at her a moment before answering. "He's the bishop, therefore he's scary to a lot of people."

"You're not afraid of him, are you?" Would Eli try to kiss her again? No one was around or looking. They were all busy trying to leave.

"I try not to put myself in situations that would cause him to look crossly in *meine* direction."

Situations like this?

He continued without a clue as to her thoughts. "Follow the rules, and there's no need to worry."

She liked Eli's self-confidence. Part of the reason she'd left the community was the bishop's anger toward her. The more he stated his disappointment in her, the more rules she broke, the more displeased he was. On and on it went until she couldn't take it any longer, and finally left. But he had changed in her absence.

"We should head over to the buggy now." Eli released her hand and picked up the quilt.

Her hand felt empty and cold without him holding it. When she took a step, a pain shot through her injured hip, and she gasped.

Eli dropped the blanket and took her elbow. "What's wrong? Is the baby coming already?"

"*Ne. Meine* bruised hip is sore and stiff from sitting on the ground. I'm fine."

"Are you sure?"

"*Ja.* I'm sure. Go on ahead. I'll take it slow until it loosens up."

"I'll walk with you."

He didn't have to do so, but she was glad he did.

By the time they reached the buggy, half of the crowd had already cleared out, making it easier to get around the vehicle. Some of the buggies formed a line leading to the road, while others trotted their horse down the road in one direction or the other. Daniel had theirs all ready. "Do you want me to drive this time?"

Eli shook his head. "I'll drive."

Once everyone had climbed aboard and was seated in the same place as before, Eli set the horse into motion. Even with waiting, they weren't the last buggy to leave the meadow.

Dori leaned back to relieve the pressure on her lungs from the baby and to make it easier to breathe.

Eli glanced at her sideways. "Are you all right? Is your hip all right? Do you need me to stop?"

"I'm fine."

The baby within shifted to the side of her belly where Eli sat as though it was trying to get closer to him. Dori couldn't blame the little one. If Dori could figure out how, she would scoot closer, as well.

The buggy wheel dipped into a pothole, rocking the vehicle almost violently. Dori grabbed the side of the seat, then found herself pressed against Eli's side.

His arm wrapped securely around her shoulders. "Are you all right?"

"I'm fine." Better now with him closer.

"Sorry about that. I didn't see the hole in the dark."

"It couldn't be helped." Afraid he might remove his arm and pull away, she leaned her head against his shoulder.

He released the pressure around her as though he might pull his arm away, but he couldn't without drawing attention to where he'd placed his arm. It relaxed back into place.

The swaying of the buggy lulled Dori and caused her eyelids to grow heavy.

What seemed like a moment later, his hand and arm jiggled her awake. "We're almost there."

Dori looked ahead and could see her family home.

Eli removed his arm from around her and turned in the seat to the couple in the back. "We're here."

Daniel and Ruth straightened and shifted apart.

As Eli faced front again, he scooted a couple of inches away from Dori.

Instinctively, Dori did so too. She smiled to herself. Had her parents as well Eli's and Daniel's parents done the very same thing when they were courting? Not that Eli was courting Dori, because he wasn't, but the situation would have been similar.

Vater and *Mutter* sat on the porch of the big *haus* with *Grossvater*. Sentries waiting for the wanderers to return.

A reminder of what she didn't like about the Amish, and the reasons why she wasn't staying. She needed to stop thinking of Eli the way she had been this past week and to stop dreaming about another kiss from him. No *gut* could come of it.

Dori shook her head. "They all came out to see that we behaved."

Eli chuckled beside her as he turned into the driveway and stopped in front of the big *haus*.

Daniel helped Ruth down from the buggy.

Eli gripped Dori's hand firmly. Was it because he wanted to hold her hand? Or because he feared she might fall?

As she climbed down, her foot caught on the step, and she stumbled forward into his arms.

His embrace held her securely on her feet.

Gazing up at him, she longed for him to kiss her

good-night. If there wasn't an audience, would he? *Ne*. If he did, it would have to *mean* something, and for him, it couldn't. Not as long as she wasn't Amish.

She would never become Amish.

Chapter Fourteen

The summer sped past, and now, on the last day of August, Eli sat in a chair next to Rainbow Girl at the computer in the bishop's *haus*. She was updating his website. Again. She seemed to do it every time they met. He received orders for his products regularly, thanks to her, and he was making *gut* money.

Eli tapped a price on the screen. "You are still charging people too much."

"*Ne*. These are market-value prices. You could probably charge even more, and *Englishers* would pay it."

"*Ne*." He shook his head. "You have the prices too high as it is. It doesn't cost me that much to make them."

"That's what they're worth. You have a unique skill. You make intricate, beautiful pieces and don't understand their value to the outside world. Your time and expertise are very valuable."

He harrumphed. Though he liked earning the prices she put on his work, he didn't want to cheat people.

"When are you going to get your own computer?" She tapped on the keys. "The church leaders have approved one for you."

He didn't want his own computer. He liked working with her. "Why should I get a computer? You would be the one to have to run it for me anyway."

"You could learn."

"I don't want to learn. I only want to make things out of hot iron." If it weren't for spending time with her, he wouldn't be doing any of this.

She drew in a quick, soft breath as she had done every few minutes for the past hour and a half.

"Are you all right?"

Nodding, she released the air in her lungs. "I'm fine. These are what people tell me are practice contractions. Braxton Hicks."

His breath caught in his throat, and his insides galloped like a runaway horse. "Is the baby coming? Now?"

"Ne, ne." She pushed her chair away from the table and stood. "I'll be right back." When she reached the hallway, she gripped the wall and bent over, sucking in air between her teeth.

Eli jumped up and hurried to her side. "You aren't all right, are you?"

She didn't answer but shook her head, then contradicted that action with a nod.

Was that a *ja* or *ne*? "I don't know what that means. Tell me what to do."

A moment later, she straightened and breathed normally. "I think that might have been more than practice. It was a lot stronger than the others."

"What do you mean?"

"I think I'm in labor."

"The baby's coming?" Eli jerked his head about, looking around. "Where's the bishop?"

"Out visiting, but he wouldn't be much *gut*. Go to the big *haus* and tell *meine mutter*."

"All right." He dashed for the door.

"Eli?" Rainbow Girl's strained voice stopped him in his tracks.

He swung around. "What?"

"Would you bring me a chair?"

He brought her one of the straight-backed ones from the table. "Maybe I shouldn't leave you."

"Unless you plan to deliver this baby, get *Mutter*. Now."

He swallowed hard and ran out the door. He pounded on the door of the big *haus*. When no answer came, he let himself in. *"Hallo?"* Nobody replied, and a quick search yielded an empty *haus*.

He ran back to the *dawdy haus*.

Rainbow Girl still sat in the chair at the entrance to the hall.

"Your *mutter* wasn't there. No one was." That meant there were two lives in his hands, Rainbow Girl's and her baby's. "I don't know how to help you. What should I do? I can go get someone else."

She shook her head. "That would take too long. Go hitch up a buggy and drive me to the clinic."

He breathed easier. He wasn't going to have to… *Don't think about it.*

He'd never hitched up a buggy so fast. He pulled it to the front of the *dawdy haus* and ran inside.

Rainbow Girl stood with her hands braced on the table, breathing erratically and moaning.

"Please don't have the baby right now."

Rainbow Girl shook her head, and her breathing

steadied. "I'm fine. Just get me to the doctor's." She took a step and faltered.

This would be too slow. Eli scooped her up into his arms. "How many pains have you had while I was getting the buggy?"

"Just that one."

Gut. There was still time.

He carried Rainbow Girl to the waiting buggy. After placing her on the seat, he climbed in and set the horse into motion. When the vehicle jerked forward, she sucked in a breath.

"What is it? What's wrong?"

She spoke through gritted teeth. "Too bumpy."

"I can't help that. Do you want me to stop?"

"*Ne.* Just keep going. Get me there as fast as you can."

He urged Dutch to pull the buggy as quickly as he could.

A few minutes down the road, Rainbow Girl straightened. "Go back. I left *meine* phone on the table."

"*Ne.*"

"But we should call ahead to the clinic and let them know we're coming."

She was thinking like the *English.*

"*Ne.*" He couldn't risk her having the baby in the buggy. That would be bad. "The doctor will understand us coming unannounced."

Rainbow Girl gripped his arm. "Eli?"

"*Ja.*"

"I'm scared."

He was too, more than he could have imagined. "Everything will be all right." As long as they arrived in time.

"Danki."

He prayed the whole way while keeping one eye on Rainbow Girl. It seemed like forever before the clinic came into view. *Please, let the doctor be there.* A buggy sat out front. *Gut.* That likely meant that she had a patient and was there. He hauled back on the reins until the horse stopped. He set the brake and scooped Rainbow Girl up into his arms again.

"I can walk." She sucked in a breath between her teeth.

"This is faster." The sooner he could turn her over to someone else's care—someone who knew what to do—the better for both of them, *ne*, all three of them. But he rather liked having her in his arms.

Rainbow Girl turned the knob, and he pushed the door open with his foot.

The Miller family crowded the waiting area.

Moaning came from one of the rear rooms.

A loud female voice called from the same vicinity, "I can't see any other patients right now. You'll have to come back tomorrow."

Eli glanced from one wide-eyed Miller face to another. He spoke to them. "We can't. She's having a baby."

Deborah Miller wove between her family members and trotted to the back.

Young, almond-eyed Sarah Miller, the youngest, stood next to Eli and stared up at him. *"Mutter* is having our baby now."

"Oh, dear." What would that mean for Rainbow Girl? Rainbow Girl patted his hand. "Set me down."

Before he could, Dr. Kathleen came out. "Busy day. Bring her into *meine* office."

Eli followed the doctor.

"Have her sit in a chair until *meine* husband can pull down the extra bed."

Eli gingerly lowered Rainbow Girl to her feet. "I can do that."

"That would be *gut*. I'll send *meine* sister in to help you." The doctor smiled at the *mutter*-to-be. "How far apart are your contractions?"

"A few minutes or so."

"They come about every seven or eight minutes." He'd been timing them on the ride here. "They're getting closer all the time."

Both women stared at him for a moment.

"What?" When his youngest sister was on the way, it had been Eli's job to time the contractions while his *vater* went for the midwife.

The doctor nodded. "I'll return in a few minutes. I'll send Jessica in. Keep timing her contractions." She left.

A moment later, Jessica entered and walked to Rainbow Girl. "We need to move you to the end of the desk beside the bookcase to make room for the bed. Let me know when the next contraction ends?"

Rainbow Girl nodded.

"She's about to start one." It had been nearly seven minutes since the last one.

Rainbow Girl pinned him with a stare. "How do you know?"

"I have a *gut* sense of time." He held up his wrist. "And a watch."

Rainbow Girl sucked in a breath. "He's right." She moaned.

Eli couldn't wait, grabbing the back of her chair and

pulling it along with her into place. "Why does she need to be over here?"

Jessica moved across the room and pointed toward the top of the paneled wall. "There are wooden catches on each side that need to be turned vertical. Then the Murphy bed can be lowered."

He twisted the catches and lowered the bed.

Jessica held up an index finger. "Oops! Let me go grab some bed linens and a pillow." She did and had the bed made in a snap.

After Rainbow Girl's next contraction, Eli carried her, against her protests, to the bed and set her on it.

"You know I can still walk."

"Not when one of those pains hits you. It's faster if I carry you, then you don't risk falling." He pointed toward the door. "I'll wait out there."

Jessica stood in his way. "Stay with her until Dr. Kathleen comes in. It's best if she's not alone." She skittered out of the room.

He stared after her. He didn't want to stay. He didn't know what to do. With the Murphy bed down, there wasn't much space to move around, so he sat on the edge of the desk and watched for signs of the onset of another pain.

"Stop staring at me."

He couldn't. "I don't know what else to do."

"Talk to me."

"What do you want me to say?"

"I don't care. Talk about your family. Tell me a story. Why you like being a blacksmith. Anything."

"We needed a blacksmith in our community. Ours had passed away, and I don't care so much for farming. Don't tell anyone."

She smiled at that, and he continued to tell her about how he got started, learning from a neighboring community's blacksmith.

Dr. Kathleen came in, and he stood.

She pointed toward the door. "You can wait in the other room."

Finally. He escaped as quickly as possible before the doctor changed her mind.

The Miller family occupied all the seats. Eli would rather stand anyway.

Deborah Miller also stood. "*Meine vater* and Amos are in the barn with Noah Lambright. You could go join them if you like."

He would love to retreat with the other men. "I'll do that after the doctor tells me how she's doing."

It seemed like forever before Dr. Kathleen emerged. He checked his watch. Had it been only a few minutes? He crossed to her. "How is she?"

"She's doing fine. It will be a little while yet. Why don't you go sit with her?"

"Me?"

She patted his arm. "She'll be less scared if she's not alone."

But *he* wouldn't. "Why not one of these women?"

"Because she asked for you." The doctor walked into the first room with her other *mutter* in labor.

Eli took a deep breath and entered the one with Rainbow Girl in it. He smiled. "How are you?"

"Apparently, I haven't had nearly enough of these pains that feel as though I'm being ripped in half. It might be a while yet before the baby comes. *And* the pains will probably get a lot worse. How is that possible? I already feel like I'm going to die with each one."

He did *not* want to see her in any more pain. He cocked his thumb toward the door. "There are several women out there. I'm sure any of them would be happy to come in here with you. You'd probably be more comfortable with one of them."

"If you don't mind, I'd like you to stay with me."

He did mind. "Of course, I'll stay. Whatever you want." He sat on the edge of the desk again.

"I don't really know those women. I mean I know them, but I don't really *know* them." She sucked in a breath between her teeth.

He fell to his knees beside the bed and took her hand. "Squeeze it as hard as you like. I can take it."

She did.

And it actually hurt.

Two hours later, Teresa Miller in the next room had a baby boy named Micah. After seven girls, Bartholomew Miller finally had a son. He must be more than pleased.

Four hours after that, Eli continued to pace in the waiting area. As it had turned out, the rush to get to the clinic hadn't needed to be so rushed after all. Rainbow Girl had been offered the chance to go to the hospital in Goshen, but she turned it down as long as she had Dr. Kathleen. Rainbow Girl screamed in pain every minute or two, but fortunately her parents were there. Her *mutter* at her side and her *vater* pacing with Eli in the waiting area. They glanced at one another every third pass or so. The bishop sat in an overstuffed armchair, head back, eyes closed. How could he be so relaxed?

It seemed like forever had passed before a cry finally heralded the birth of the second baby that day.

Eli's breath released in a rush of relief.

When Rainbow Girl's *vater* was invited to go in and

see his daughter and grandchild, Eli slumped onto the love seat, completely worn-out. How could he be this exhausted? He hadn't done anything. Rainbow Girl had to be utterly spent. How had she done this all day?

He didn't know how long he'd sat there before the doctor came out. He stood. "How is she?"

The bishop stood, as well.

She nodded. "*Mutter* and daughter are doing fine."

"And what about the baby? Is it a boy or girl?"

She smiled with a hint of a laugh behind it. "A girl."

Eli smiled back. "A little girl."

"Would you like to go in and see them?"

Ja, he would but was tentative. "I don't want to bother anyone."

"Let me ask." She disappeared and returned quickly. "She wants you to come in."

The bishop patted his arm. "Tell Andrew and Leah that I'm heading home and will let the other children know." He left.

Eli followed the doctor into the room and told them the bishop had gone home.

Her *mutter* sat in a chair beside the bed, and her *vater* stood behind her *mutter*, gazing down at his daughter and *enkelin*. He seemed pleased.

Though Rainbow Girl wore a huge smile, the dark circles under her slowly drooping eyes spoke of her exhaustion. "Meet *meine* daughter, Tabitha."

"That's a beautiful name for a beautiful baby girl."

"Would you like to hold her?"

"Me? *Ne*. I don't think that's a *gut* idea."

Leah Bontrager stood and motioned him over. "Sit. It will be all right."

Eli looked to Andrew Bontrager. When the older man

gave him a nod, Eli sat. Rainbow Girl handed over the sleeping bundle. He gazed upon her tiny, scrunched-up face and instantly fell in love with the little one. He would do anything to protect her.

And her *mutter*.

Rainbow Girl.

Now she had to stay and join church. She just had to. What would he do if she left?

Dori regarded Eli holding Tabitha in the chair next to the bed. The big, strapping, muscle-bound blacksmith holding a tiny, helpless newborn. She trusted him completely with her daughter. She suddenly realized that she should tell Craig that he had a daughter. But would he even care? The man sitting here next to her cared more for her daughter than the little one's own *vater*. "*Danki* for looking after me and Tabitha."

"I didn't do anything. The doctor did everything."

"You kept us safe and got us here." She had never felt more secure than with him.

He gave a crooked smile. "Turns out, there wasn't such a rush to get you here after all. Sorry about all the bumps in the road."

"Couldn't be helped. Getting us here gave us both peace of mind."

He returned his gaze to the bundle in his arms. "She's perfect." He spoke like a proud *vater*.

But Dori knew that could never be.

Dr. Kathleen came to the doorway. "With two new *mutters* and babies to look after, we've made up beds in the big *haus*. I would like to get both of you over there as soon as possible. Ladies have come and fixed a *wunderbar* supper. It will be easier to care for you there overnight."

Dori turned from Eli and her daughter to the doctor. "I don't want to inconvenience you. I can go home."

The doctor shook her head. "That's not a *gut* idea. You seem fine, but I should keep an eye on your baby at least overnight. Things can develop quickly with these little ones. The beds in the big *haus* are more comfortable, and I'll be closer." She held up her hand. "I'll hear no further arguments. The Millers are helping Teresa and Micah over there right now."

Staying at Dr. Kathleen's *haus* eased Dori's concerns. She wasn't sure how to care for her new baby yet, though *Mutter* would help.

The doctor pointed to Eli. "Hand the baby to Leah. I need you to help Dori across the yard. She needs someone to support her."

Dori liked the idea of holding on to Eli for support. He *was* strong.

He turned Tabitha over to her *grossmutter,* scooped Dori up into his arms and stood. "Lead the way."

The doctor laughed.

Dori hooked her arms around his neck. She didn't mind being in his arms.

The whole parade of them marched toward the big *haus.*

Once upstairs, Eli deposited her on a big, comfortable bed. Much better than the thin mattress of the Murphy bed.

After a tasty supper of chicken and dumplings, everyone left, except a couple of members of the Miller family, Dori's *mutter* and Eli. He decided to stay for a little longer.

She fed Tabitha and stopped resisting her heavy eyelids. It had been a long day.

Dori woke to a baby crying in the distance and the dawning light drifting in through the open curtains. Where was Tabitha? Dori glanced around. Where was she? This was not the *dawdy haus*, but the doctor's home.

Dori's *mutter* lay curled on the bed next to her. But where was her baby?

She turned her head to the other side.

Eli sat on the floor with his head leaning against the wall, asleep. Cradled in his crossed legs, Tabitha lay snuggled up and sleeping too. One gigantic hand on the top of her little head, and the other hooked around her blanketed legs. She breathed a sigh of relief. The crying baby was not hers.

Mutter rose up on one elbow and moved a stray strand of hair from Dori's face. She indicated the sleeping giant and whispered, "He was up walking her during the night. He'll make a *gut vater.*"

Was her *mutter* hinting? Eli would make a *gut vater*, but he could never be Tabitha's. He deserved someone better than Dori. A *gut* Amish wife. A wife who would give him his own children and not those of another man. Worse, an *English* man.

For now, she would be content to watch the two sleep. Soon enough this tranquil atmosphere would be shattered. First by a baby crying, then by Dori's leaving.

Chapter Fifteen

Two weeks after Tabitha's birth, Dori traveled into town with Eli, who had orders he needed to ship. Since her daughter's arrival, he spent a lot of time at *Grossvater*'s *haus* and stopped by every day, even if only for a few minutes. He spent a lot of time with Tabitha. And even more time with Dori. There was always some excuse or other for coming to the *haus*. She didn't care what the reason. She enjoyed his company.

Dori's hair had grown out and looked terrible. She planned to buy hair dye today and make it all one color. She hadn't decided which one yet. Maybe she would choose pink for the whole thing in honor of having a daughter.

Eli stopped in the drugstore parking lot. "Would you like me to go in with you?"

Dori gazed down at her daughter in her arms. "She's asleep. I hate to disturb her."

"I'll take her." He set the brake, got out and came around to her side of the vehicle.

"You really want to?"

"Ja." He held out his arms. It was such a change from

two weeks ago, on the day of her birth. He'd been terrified to hold her, but he had quickly gotten over that.

She placed her daughter in the safety of his strong arms. "I won't be long." Now he looked comfortable and at ease holding a baby. It warmed Dori's heart. *"Danki."*

Though she didn't want to part from either of them, she dashed inside the drugstore and surveyed the options. No pink, purple, blue, orange or green. This wasn't the kind of store to carry such colors.

She wouldn't be Rainbow Girl much longer. That saddened her. Eli had given her that affectionate name. She didn't want to lose her fun hair colors. She wanted to be Rainbow Girl. Eli's Rainbow Girl. But she couldn't. As long as she remained Rainbow Girl, she could never hope to be Eli's.

She studied the options and picked up a box that was close to her natural color. That would be something different. If she couldn't have an unusual color, she might as well go back to her natural one.

Grossvater had been so kind to her, and her *vater* even started speaking to her again. It would be nice to give something back to all of them, her *grossvater*, her parents, her family, the whole community. To Eli. She could always color it different colors again later— after she left—but for now, she needed to stay with the Amish. She couldn't bear to be parted from her little girl.

She purchased the hair color and headed outside to meet up with Eli. He seemed to love little Tabitha, and loved holding her as much as Dori did. He would make someone a *gut* husband and *vater* someday. At the thought of him married to someone else, a pang twisted inside her. Hopefully, she wouldn't be around to witness that.

She headed across the parking lot toward the buggy. "Dori?"

She recognized that voice and spun around. "Craig?" She couldn't believe, after all these months, she was finally seeing him again.

"I see you've had the baby. Or did you…?"

Have an abortion? "I told you, I would never do that. I had the baby. Two weeks ago."

He took her hands in his. "Great. Then you're coming home?"

"You want us back?" She'd dreamed of this, but she hadn't truly expected it. He'd changed his mind after all.

"Just you. Leave the kid with the Amish people."

Leave her child? How could he ask that? "If you could just—"

"Don't say it. I don't want to see it. I don't want to know." He squeezed her hands. "It hasn't been right without you. I've missed you so much. I haven't eaten well. I don't sleep. I feel lost without you."

Part of her wanted to fall into his arms and leave *everything* else behind. When she thought of only him, she imagined she could. "If you missed me so much, why didn't you come for me?"

He shrugged one shoulder. "I didn't know how to find you."

Didn't know how? "You could have asked *any* Amish person where the Bontragers lived, and they could have told you."

He scrunched up his face. "I don't want to talk to *those* people."

She couldn't believe him and pulled her hands free. "*I'm* one of *those* people."

He held out his hands. "But you're different."

"Not that different." Not as different as she'd thought.

"Wearing their clothes doesn't make you Amish. Even with your hair pulled back and under that funny hat, I can tell you still have it all different colors. That's how I could tell it was you. It lets me know you aren't one of them."

She had taken to wearing the more comfortable cape dresses since her experience in the ditch, and since Tabitha's birth, putting her hair up in a *kapp* was easier. The weight of the hair color in her bag grounded her in this moment. She wouldn't have rainbow hair much longer.

"Stop hiding with those people and come home. Dori, I love you. I don't want to live without you."

He was right. She had been hiding with the Amish, but no more. "But you don't want our child?"

"How can I? I don't even know it."

It? Anger boiled inside her. "Our child is not an *it*. Do you even want to know if you have a son or a daughter?"

He held his hands out to his sides. "I can't afford to. *I* don't have a child. I don't make enough to support three people right now. Later, when we can buy a house, then we can have a kid."

"What about the one we already have? Do we somehow forget that one?" She couldn't.

"Obviously, *you* can't do that. We can leave it with your Amish relatives, and when we get a house, we'll go and get it."

It? He acted like their daughter was a piece of furniture. "And how long would that be?"

"Two, maybe three years. Five tops. It will walk and talk by then, and no diapers." He gave a triumphant smile.

"You expect me to give up my child for *five* years?" Five days would be a challenge.

"You make it sound like we'd be leaving it on the side of the road. The Amish people would take care of it."

"It, it, it. Our— My child is not an it. *Auf Wiedersehen.*"

"I don't know what that means."

"*Gut* bye." She turned to leave.

"Can't we at least talk about this?"

She faced him again. "Unless there is any chance of you changing your mind, there's no point, because I'm not changing mine."

He took her hands again. "Why do you have to be so rigid? I'm sure we can come to some sort of compromise."

Compromise? That gave her hope. Was he really willing to compromise?

In the shade of a tree, Eli cradled Tabitha in his arms. The man talking to Rainbow Girl must be her old boyfriend, Tabitha's *vater*. He'd seen the joy on Rainbow Girl's face when she first saw the man, and he'd taken her hands in his. And now she wore a smile of what looked like contentment.

She'd said Tabitha's *vater* didn't want her. Did he want her now? Eli didn't want to give the little bundle up. She'd climbed into his heart from her first breath in this world. Before that, when her *mutter* had stolen his heart.

Would Rainbow Girl leave? He didn't know how he

would go on if she did. And she would take his Tabitha with her. He didn't want to lose this little one. Or her *mutter*.

Rainbow Girl strode away from the man and marched up to Eli. She stretched out her arms and spoke in English instead of *Deutsch*. "Give me my daughter."

Why? Was she going to leave with that man right now? He pulled his Rainbow Baby closer and spoke softly in *Deutsch*. "I'll hold her." He walked off toward the buggy.

She trotted to catch up. "Seriously? You're not going to give her to me."

She seemed too upset to hold one so helpless. "I don't mind holding her."

"You realize she's *meine* daughter, don't you?"

One of the many reasons he loved Tabitha so much. How could a *vater* not love her and want her?

At the buggy, he opened the door for Rainbow Girl. She climbed in and held out her arms. Instead of handing over Tabitha, he closed the door, walked around the buggy and climbed in the other side.

Rainbow Girl once again held out her arms. "I'll take her now. You can't drive while holding her."

He was sure he could, but it might not be the safest for his little one. "I'm not driving."

"What do you mean?"

He settled in the seat. "*Meine* hands are full." He looked at Rainbow Girl and nodded toward the reins.

She touched her chest with her fingertips. "You want me to drive?"

"Well, I obviously can't."

She huffed a laugh. "Are all men so stubborn?" She

gathered up the reins, backed the horse up and set the buggy into motion.

He didn't know how much longer he would have his Tabitha and her *mutter* in his life. Rainbow Girl clearly still had feelings for the *Englisher*. The pain of that hit him in the center of his chest. How would he manage without them? Without her?

Once at the bishop's *haus*, Rainbow Girl fed Tabitha and put her in the crib.

Eli pointed to the computer. "Teach me how to work *meine* website."

"I thought you didn't want to learn. You didn't want to mess with *Englisher* things."

"I've changed *meine* mind. Teach me." If she was going to leave, he needed to master it like he'd done with blacksmithing. Why hadn't he learned his website from the start like she'd tried to make him do repeatedly? He'd actually acquired quite a bit of knowledge sitting next to her the past three months, but not enough to take care of it solo.

"Right now?"

"Ja." He'd wanted her to think he couldn't do it himself so he could spend more time with her, and she would realize she needed to stay in their Amish community. Because, if he needed her to tend to his site, she would be around him and he would get to see her often. He would always have an excuse to come see her. He could keep her close. But he couldn't any longer. She would leave. Leave him behind. Again. "Teach me before you leave."

"What? I'm not leaving."

But she was. Why was she lying? "From the day you

arrived, you insisted that you weren't staying. I need to learn how to work the website before you go."

"What brought this up all of a sudden?"

Though he didn't want to talk about him, he seemed to have little choice. "I saw you with that man."

She squinted. "What man?"

"The *Englisher* in town."

"Craig?"

"Is that his name? Is he Tabitha's *vater*?"

She took a deep breath. "*Ja*. He's her *vater*, but that doesn't mean I'm leaving."

"*Ja*. It does. I tried to deny you would leave, but I saw you with him. I saw how happy you were to see him. He was happy to see you too. He wants you back, doesn't he?"

"Well, *ja*, but…"

He'd thought it had hurt the first time she left, and he hadn't been in love with her then. Not really. Now would be a hundred times worse, because she would take Tabitha along with his heart. "But what? If he would take your daughter, would you return to him?"

She stared at him for a long moment. "He doesn't want Tabitha, so it doesn't matter."

"So if he wants you but not her, what does he expect you to do with your daughter?" When she didn't answer, he prodded. "What? Tell me."

"Leave her here with the Amish."

"You would do that?"

"*Ne*. I could never leave her behind."

"But if he wanted her?"

"He doesn't. You don't have to worry about me leaving. I'm staying for now."

"Because you have to? Why don't you leave her and

go back to that man?" He waved a hand in the air. "I'll take care of Tabitha and raise her."

"You?" she chuffed out.

"Why not me?"

"Well, for one, you're a man. Two, *meine mutter* would fight you for her and likely win. Three, I'm not giving her up. Not for Craig. And not for you."

But if the *Englisher* wanted Tabitha, Rainbow Girl would return to him and be packing right now. He'd seen it on her face when she first saw him. Eli needed to get away from her and stormed off out the front door.

"What about your website?"

He didn't stop.

Each step Eli took away from Dori twisted her heart more painfully. "Eli, wait." She hurried to catch up to him and planted herself in his path. "I'm not going back to him."

He stared hard at her for a long moment. "I want to believe that."

"But?"

"I can't. I saw you with him. You still love him. Have you merely been toying with *meine* affections?"

She'd thought she still loved Craig but realized it was more of a pattern of thoughts at this point. There were no real feelings behind them anymore.

When Craig had suggested she leave Tabitha behind and return to him without her, she knew she could never go back to Craig. An invisible weight she hadn't known she carried fell away. A tether snapped. She'd broken free of him and what she'd had with him. In truth, it had been empty and meaningless. What she thought she had with him, she actually *did* have with Eli. Or at least *had*.

"I don't love him anymore. I don't know if I ever really did. I had silly notions of the outside world, and I thought Craig fulfilled those. But they were all empty." She took his hand. "Everything I want is right here."

He pulled free. "*Ne.* It's not. You want him and the *Englisher* world. I will *never* be able to trust you." He walked away.

She hurried to catch up to him. "*Ne.* Don't say that."

Tabitha's wail cut through the air.

"Go take care of your daughter." He walked away.

She wanted to follow, but her daughter needed her. She didn't want Eli to leave. She might never get him back, but if she didn't tend to her daughter, Eli wouldn't see her as a *gut mutter.* She hated having to choose between them, but there was only one choice. She turned back toward the *dawdy haus.*

After feeding, changing and getting Tabitha to sleep, Dori took the hair color she'd purchased in town to the bathroom and stood in front of the mirror. With her hair up and her *kapp* on, she looked Amish. Her roots had grown long enough that when she twisted the front, pulled everything back and secured it on the back of her head, her brown roots covered half of it. What wasn't covered, her *kapp* disguised. She removed it now and took out the bobby pins.

Her hair looked awful in all its contrasting colors and kinking in different directions. It was as though it didn't know what to do or be. Should it be up or down? So it stuck out all over. Should it be Amish or *English*? Both, with neither truly winning the battle. A confused mess. Just like her.

Eli's words echoed in her mind. *I will* never *be able to trust you.* That couldn't be true. But Eli believed it. Would she ever be able to change his mind? Not like this.

After brushing through her hair, she took the dye and a towel to the kitchen sink. This was the closest shade she could find to her natural one. Hopefully, it would cover the various colors.

When she was finished and her hair mostly dry, *Grossvater* came inside. "Your hair."

"What do you think?"

He smiled. "It looks *wunderbar*."

The dye had covered most of the colors while others gave it a strange shade. "Once I put it up and cover it with *meine kapp*, no one should be able to tell."

"You will look like a proper Amish, then."

Did she want to? For Eli? Would *he* view her as a proper Amish woman?

The next day, the Saturday before Joining Sunday, Eli beat on the piece of hot steel on his anvil, bending it around and around and folding it over on itself. Another one ruined. He doused it in the barrel of water, then tossed it onto the pile with the other carnage from his foul mood. It clanged and clattered as it settled into place.

As he reached for another iron rod, he froze.

Rainbow Girl stood at the entrance to his blacksmith workshop with Tabitha swaddled in her arms. What was she doing here?

"*Hallo*, Eli."

He resisted the urge to go to her and gave her a curt nod instead. "Do you have a horse who needs shoeing?"

"*Ne*. I— We came to see you."

Like iron being drawn to a magnet, he gravitated to

her and Tabitha. He scooped Rainbow Baby up into his arms. This was where his little one belonged, but she would be taken away from him all too soon. He handed her over. "Why have you come?"

Rainbow Girl removed her *kapp*.

"What are you doing? You aren't supposed to do that."

She turned around. "See? I dyed *meine* hair back to its natural color."

A *gut* start, but anyone could appear Amish on the outside. "Why are you showing me?"

"So you could see that I'm becoming Amish. I can join church tomorrow."

Unless she didn't. She'd said *can*, not that she *was* going to.

"You think that changing your hair makes you Amish? It takes a lot more than that. It's not what's on the outside, it's what's in your heart. And your heart is *English*. Go back to where you belong and leave us be."

"I want to show you that you can trust me."

"*Ne.* Every time I do, you crush *meine* heart under your foot."

"When have I ever done that?"

"I've liked you since we were twelve. You went wild on *Rumspringa*, but I thought you would settle down like most Amish youths do. Instead, you left the community. I kept waiting for you to return, a few months passed, then a year, but you didn't come back. Then one day, I realized I no longer expected you to return."

"But I did."

"Only because you were forced to. And you've never really returned in your heart." He thumped his chest with his fingertips. "You keep looking over your shoulder to the *Englisher* world. Why don't you go back to Tabitha's *vater*?"

"How many times do I have to tell you that he doesn't want her, and I don't love him?"

Until she believed it herself. "You don't want the Amish life. Leave your baby with us. Go back to your *English* life. Everyone wins."

"But I don't want to leave her."

"Think of what's best for your daughter. She will have so much love here." He wanted to beg Rainbow Girl to stay, but unless she *wanted* to, she wouldn't stay for long.

Back at the *dawdy haus*, Dori paced in her bedroom while *Mutter* softly sang a hymn to Tabitha in the other room.

Eli had been right. Dori did keep looking back to the *English* world. Which one did she want to belong to? The Amish one that had taken her in and cared for her and her baby when they needed help most? Or the *English* one, where her baby's *vater* was? Craig would welcome her if she left Tabitha behind. Her baby would be well cared for and loved. She would have a *gut* life. Didn't her daughter deserve that?

If Eli hadn't been so hurt and upset about her talking to Craig and was willing to give her a chance, she would stay. If he asked her to, she would stay. She would join church.

But if Craig would welcome and love their daughter, she would return to the *English* world. So where she ended up depended on a man? Which man would love her?

That wasn't right. A decision like this should be

made by what she wanted. Did she want Craig? Or Eli? *Ne.* Did she want an *English* life with or without Craig? Or did she want an Amish life, with or without Eli?

She wanted security. Could either man give her that?

Maybe she *should* leave Tabitha behind so her daughter could have a *gut* life, a better life without Dori, and walk away from them all. Start over in a different town. Away from the Amish and away from Craig.

She fingered the door knocker. The thing that had tied her two worlds together. The thing that had kept an open door in her mind to the Amish world.

She sat on her bed and counted the money earned from helping so many Amish with their websites and computers. She hadn't done anything special, ran a few programs to get rid of viruses and malware and defragged their hard drives. But each person had paid her a fee. She had enough to rent a small apartment. Her biggest obstacle would be to find a job.

When she left, she would no longer have regular income from computer work. No Amish would be allowed to come to her for help. She would need other means to support her and her baby. Work that would pay enough for living expenses as well as childcare. How would she ever be able to afford that? She wouldn't. So she either needed to resign her fate to remaining with the Amish for the next eighteen years, or leave Tabitha here until she could provide for her. Dori disliked both options. But as Eli had said, she needed to think of what was best for her daughter above all else. She had her GED now, so she should have better success finding a job.

She left her room and stopped at the end of the hall before entering the living room.

Mutter sat in the rocking chair, singing as she gazed at Tabitha.

Dori's eyes watered at the scene. "You'll always look after her, won't you?"

"Of course. Both of you." *Mutter*'s expression changed from happy to worried. "Why do you ask this? You will take care of your daughter."

Dori wanted to but couldn't see how. "I don't think I can stay."

"Ne." Tears filled *Mutter*'s eyes. "You can't leave again. It will break your *vater*'s heart. It will break *meine* heart."

"I don't fit in here." Just when she thought she and Eli might have a chance, Craig had spoiled it, but she couldn't blame Eli after the life she'd lived outside the community.

"What about your daughter?"

That hurt most of all. "I can't take care of her out there. I'll come back for her."

"Ne. This is wrong."

Everything about her life the past few years had been wrong. Everything except Tabitha.

"You aren't leaving right now, are you?"

"Ne." She needed to make a few plans. "But soon. Don't tell anyone."

"How can I not? Your *vater* should be told, as well as your *grossvater*."

"Ne. You can't tell them. Promise you won't tell anyone. Promise right now, or I'll take Tabitha this minute and walk out the door. You'll never see either of us again."

Mutter gasped. "I don't like this one bit."

"But you won't say anything?"

"I will keep your secret."

Dori had told Eli she could never leave her daughter behind, but here she was planning to do just that. But not forever. Only until she could make a *gut* life for her, so she could take care of her the way she needed.

Chapter Sixteen

At church the next day, with her plans set, Dori wanted the service to be over quickly. Wanted this whole day to be over so she could leave. Leave this world behind her—for *gut* this time. Except to return for Tabitha. But if she couldn't find work that could support them both, her daughter would be better off remaining here.

She shook her head. She couldn't think that way. Tabitha might be better off staying here, but Dori wouldn't be better off without her. In order to provide for her daughter, Dori needed to find a *gut*-paying job and get settled in a place, then she could return for her little girl. But even when she had all that and came back for her, how much would she really see of her daughter if she had to pay for someone else to look after her all day.

As the rest of the family headed toward the *haus*, *Vater* asked Dori to remain. "Your *mutter* said I should speak to you."

"She did? About what?" *Mutter* wasn't supposed to tell anyone about her plans to leave.

"I assume about your decision today."

So *Mutter* hadn't told him of her plans.

"Make the right one, and all will be well." *Vater* strode off.

She wished she knew what that was.

Eli stood off in the distance but ducked away when she made eye contact.

Inside, Dori sat between her sister and her *mutter*, who held Tabitha. Decision Sunday had come, and she had made hers. She would start over someplace new.

Service was at the Hochstetlers'. Eli's family's home. She wished it could have been someplace different. It had been hard seeing him. If she could have skipped church without raising suspicions, she would have. But she needed to keep up a front so she could escape unnoticed.

The bishop spoke of the importance of joining church. It had to be of one's own free will, but families put much pressure on their children to join. Joining for Dori would be wrong, because she would do it to show Eli he could trust her. That was the wrong reason. Besides, he hadn't even been able to look at her this morning.

What was the right reason? Because she wanted to be Amish? What did it mean to *be* Amish? What did it really mean to join church?

The bishop continued with his sermon. "If you feel *Gott* calling to your heart, you are ready to join church."

She'd heard this every year growing up. She'd never paid it much attention because it didn't pertain to her. And again this year, it had no bearing on her future. She would leave as soon as she could make the arrangements. Maybe as soon as Monday or Tuesday. She had her money as well as her GED. Which direction did she want to go? West. Fewer Amish.

She didn't want to leave Eli. She didn't want to leave Tabitha. She didn't want to leave *Gott*.

Gott? What did He have to do with this decision? Then she realized—everything. *Gott* was the reason to stay. *Gott* was the reason to join church. Her whole life, she'd viewed the Amish life by what others expected of her. *Gott* was the reason for everything. His was the only expectation that mattered. She finally understood what it meant to be Amish. It wasn't about what she wore or what she did or even following the *Ordnung*. It was about belonging to *Gott*, being loved and cherished by Him. For the first time in her life, she truly wanted to be Amish. To belong to *Gott*.

"Who among you will come forward to join?"

Dori's insides leaped up, but she forced her body to remain seated. She wanted to stand but didn't feel worthy. She hadn't understood what it meant to be Amish or to join church, but now she did. She wished she could go back and retake the classes to view everything her *grossvater* had said in light of her revelation that *Gott* should be the center of everything. Everything she did, thought or became. He was the reason for life.

For the first time that morning, Dori focused on *Grossvater*. He stared at her with a sad expression. He'd hoped she would join and wore his disappointment clearly on his face. She would wait until next year, when she could take the joining classes again to really understand and learn about *Gott*.

Instead, she obeyed the still-quiet voice in her heart and rose to her feet. This was why she'd twisted her hair up and put it under a *kapp*. The reason she'd removed all of her earrings. She'd obeyed that little voice inside her that had told her to do those things. It hadn't been her rebellious side as she had thought, telling her to fool everyone into thinking she'd decided to stay when she hadn't. It had been *Gott* preparing her, making her ready.

Mutter sucked in a soft breath.

Giving a nod, Dori walked to the front and knelt with the others.

Grossvater had never worn such a huge smile.

She sought out Eli. When she found him, his scowl told her all she needed to know. He didn't approve of her being up there. He didn't think she was *gut* enough. He didn't think she was Amish enough.

Gott didn't ask her to be *gut* enough or Amish enough. He wanted her to be obedient to Him. He wanted her to join church, so she would do it for Him.

She prayed Eli would come around.

When the service ended, Dori stood and turned around, anxious to talk to Eli. But he was gone.

Mutter bounced a fussy Tabitha in her arms. "I think she's hungry."

Dori took her daughter and held her close. "I'll find a room to feed her in." Eli would have to wait.

While Dori fed her little one, *Mutter* brought in a plate of food.

Once Tabitha had a full tummy and a clean diaper, Dori headed outside. She searched the crowd for Eli but couldn't spot him, so she crossed to her *vater* and oldest brother. "Have you seen Eli? I can't spot him."

"I haven't seen him." Her *vater* gave her a big smile. "But while I have you here, I wanted to tell you how happy you've made me today. When you left, you broke *meine* heart, but today you have made everything right."

Matthew grunted.

Vater faced him. "Do you have something to say, *sohn*?"

With a scowl, he shook his head.

"Your sister was lost and now is found. We must rejoice in her return."

Her brother straightened and poked his finger in her direction. "She doesn't belong here and should leave." He stormed off.

"Matthew, come back here and apologize to your sister."

He took off in a run.

Her leaving and behavior had hurt him more than Dori could have imagined. She'd hurt many people when she left. Hadn't a clue so many people had cared.

Vater swung his gaze to her. "He will come around. Give him time."

She wasn't as sure. "I understand. I made bad choices. There will be consequences. Even so, I wouldn't want to be anyplace else."

"I'm glad to hear that."

"I need to speak to Eli. I'm going to go find him." As she walked off, she hoped he wasn't as hurt as her brother, but it didn't matter. She would earn back his trust if it took the rest of her life.

After church, Eli had escaped the crowd and now paced in the limited space of his forge. He grasped a foot-long iron rod. He couldn't work on a Sunday, and that frustrated him, but at least holding the cold metal helped calm him.

His heart had soared when Rainbow— Dori— *She* had gone up front to join. But why if she planned to leave? Had she done so for him, to prove he could trust her?

That wasn't necessary. He'd decided last night that it would hurt too much if she left again, and he would try his best to talk her into staying. But now that she'd joined, he feared it was for the wrong reasons. That would be worse than her leaving. He would never be certain she would stay. Each morning when he woke, he would wonder if she'd be gone.

He'd been selfish. *Gott* should be the reason she joined. Not him.

How could he be certain of her motives? If he asked her, that would be the same as accusing her of tainted motives. If he didn't, he would never know.

"Eli?"

He jumped at the sound of her voice and spun around. "Rain— Dor— Um." He frowned. "What are you doing here?"

"We came to see what you were up to. You aren't working on a Sunday, are you?"

She hadn't understood his question.

"*Ne.* I'm not working." He tapped the hunk of metal on his anvil. "I didn't mean what are you doing in *meine* forge. What are you doing here in the community? Here at church? Why bother coming?" He tossed the rod into the pile of scraps.

The clattering it made startled Tabitha, and she let out a whimper, then a cry.

He hurried over. "I'm sorry, *liebling.* I didn't think. Shh, little one. It's all right." He put his large calloused hand on her head.

Tabitha calmed right down and turned toward his voice.

Rainbow Girl gazed up at him. "You have a way with her."

He kept his gaze focused on the babe. "I didn't do anything special."

"You didn't have to. She likes you being around." She shifted Tabitha in her arms. "You're missing out on the food. Are you coming back to the gathering?"

He removed his hand from the baby's head and shook his own. "I'm not…" He couldn't say he wasn't hungry, because that would be a lie. "I'll be out in a little bit." He stepped away.

Tabitha's head cocked in his direction.

"She always tries to find you when she hears you. Always responds to your voice. Somehow she's known from the start that you are a man to be trusted."

"Really?" He liked the idea and hoped her *mutter* trusted him, as well. He came forward again and held out his arms. "May I hold her?"

Rainbow Girl tilted her head. "You're asking?"

"Of course."

She smiled at him, and his insides went fuzzy. "Do you realize this is the first time you've asked to hold her?"

"I've held her many times." The more he spoke, the more Tabitha craned her head toward him.

"Each one of those times, I've either asked you, handed her to you or you've simply taken her out of *meine* arms."

"I have? I didn't realize. I'm sorry."

"Don't be sorry. Tabitha really likes you, and you are very comfortable holding her. Not all men are."

She stepped closer and transferred the precious, little bundle into his arms.

Tabitha gazed up at him and one corner of her mouth pulled up into a smile, and a dimple showed on her right cheek. "She looks like you."

"Shall we go out and eat?"

He handed Tabitha back. "I have stuff to do in here." He spread his hands to indicate his workshop and forge.

"On Sunday?"

"Ne." He couldn't go on like this, not knowing her motive. *Gut* or bad, he needed to ask. He rubbed the back of his neck with his hand. "I was confused when you went up front and joined church. If you plan to leave, why join church? Why make everyone believe you're going to stay? Why get everyone's hopes up?" Why get his hopes up?

"I joined because I wanted to. I didn't know I wanted to until today. I *am* going to stay. I didn't want to when I came. Not from the beginning. I always planned to leave."

"So what are you saying? Are you keeping your options open?"

"Ne. I realized that this is where I belong. This, our community, is where I want to be. Here, standing in your forge with you, is where I want to be."

"So you're not going to leave?"

When she shook her head, his shoulders relaxed.

"I will be honest with you. Last night, I was. If I'd had someplace to go to, I would have. Since I didn't, I came to church one last time."

"So what made you decide to join if you were practically out the door?"

"I went back and forth on that decision. I realized

Gott is the reason for everything. I kept thinking *meine* decision was between Craig or you. That whichever one of you wanted me, that's where I would be happy, but I realized it wasn't a choice between the two of you. Not even a choice between worlds, *English* or Amish, with or without either of you. It was to choose *Gott* or not. *Gott* is the reason for everything. I'm staying."

His hope soared. She'd chosen for the right reason.

"I can't tell you how happy that makes me."

"I know I've hurt you, but I want to prove to you that you can trust me. No matter how long that takes."

He didn't need any time. He trusted *Gott*, and that was what mattered. "From the start, I felt as though *Gott* brought you back for me. I didn't know if I could handle you leaving again. It was hard enough the first time when..."

"When what?"

He gazed straight into her eyes. "When I didn't care as much for you. But now..."

She took a step closer and tilted her head to look up at him. "But now what?"

"But now I care for you both. I want to be Tabitha's *vater*. Will you allow that?"

She gifted him with a smile. "What are you asking?"

Hadn't he been clear? "I love her as *meine* own. I will take *gut* care of her. What do you say?"

"And what about me?"

"You? You're her *mutter*."

Her smile didn't waver, as though she knew something he didn't. "But you want me to give *meine* daughter to you?"

"Ne— Ja— Ne." Now he understood. He hadn't asked her to be his wife, only asked if he could have

her daughter. "Let me start over. Rain— Dor— I don't know what to call you anymore. You don't like *Dorcas*. You're no longer Rainbow Girl. Are you going to expect everyone to call you by your *Englisher* name, Dori?"

"Dori was *meine Englisher* name, but it doesn't suit me now that I'm Amish."

He liked the sound of that. She was Amish. "You could go by *Dorcas* again."

She scrunched up her nose. "*Dorcas* doesn't suit me either. I need something different for this new phase of *meine* life."

He smiled. "How about Dee Dee? Dorcas, Dori, *Dee Dee*."

"I like that."

He put one hand on her shoulder and the other on Tabitha's head. "I don't want to lose either one of you. Dee Dee Bontrager, would you and your daughter become *meine* family—*meine* wife and daughter?"

"*Ja.* I— We would love to."

He cupped her face in his hands, leaned over his Rainbow Baby in her arms and kissed her.

For all her protests to the contrary, she—Dee Dee Bontrager, soon to be Hochstetler—had become Amish after all.

Epilogue

Early August,
Five Years Later

Dee Dee Hochstetler stood in her kitchen with her sister, Ruth Burkholder. She set empty glasses on a wooden serving tray along with the heaping plate of oatmeal cookies. Having been hunched over the table, Dee Dee jerked straight up and sucked in a breath. She placed a hand on her protruding belly. "Hey in there, settle down."

Ruth rushed to her side. "You aren't going into labor, are you?"

Dee Dee shook her head. "*Ne.* This one's just over-active. Doesn't give me a moment's peace."

"*Gut.* Because it's *meine* turn." Ruth picked up the pitchers of lemonade and iced tea. "You already have three little ones. I want to have *meine* baby before you have another one."

Like herself, Ruth was very pregnant.

Dee Dee lifted the tray. "You're welcome to have yours first. I want a chance to meet *meine* niece or nephew before this active one keeps me too busy." She exited out her kitchen door and held the screen open with her elbow for Ruth.

Eli hurried over in spite of having five-year-old Tabitha clinging to his back, three-and-a-half-year-old Sarah seated on one foot, holding on to his leg, and nearly two-year-old Evie sitting on the other. "Let me take that." He snatched the tray from her, and the glasses clinked.

"You're a bit occupied." Dee Dee loved seeing Eli playing with their daughters.

He glanced over his shoulder at one giggly girl, then at the two others on his feet. "*Ne.* They're no problem."

Dee Dee caressed her stomach. She hoped this one was a son for Eli. She never complained about having all girls so far, but she knew he longed for a son. Most men did. She'd worried when Sarah was born that he might favor his own daughter over Tabitha, but he showed no hint of that. Craig had eagerly signed away his parental rights, and Eli had officially adopted her.

With the girls still on each of his feet, Eli lumbered along toward the quilt stretched over a frame in the yard with the other three women around it, two as pregnant as Dee Dee and her sister.

Daniel Burkholder came over and relieved his wife of the beverage pitchers.

Dee Dee loved her life with Eli on their little farm. It had no crop fields, just a livestock pasture and a kitchen garden. Eli's ironwork business was thriving better than they'd ever dreamed of. Dee Dee took care of the business end of things so Eli could freely work in his blacksmith shop, creating beautiful and useful things.

Dr. Kathleen's and Deborah's husbands played in the yard with their three children.

Eli and Daniel made sure each of the four pregnant women as well as the bride-to-be had something to drink and a cookie before feeding the children and themselves.

Lowering her very pregnant body onto the chair in the circle, Dee Dee let out a huge sigh.

"You all right?" Dr. Kathleen asked.

"I'm fine. A part of me can't wait for this baby to be born so I can breathe and move around again."

"And the other part?" Deborah Burkholder asked.

"Wants it to stay in there forever. Once I have this little one in *meine* arms, I'm going to be too busy to do anything else, including sleep."

Deborah put her hand on her large belly. "I can't wait for mine to be born. I hope it's a girl this time."

It was going to be a race to see which of four out of five women around the quilt would give birth first. Dee Dee was pregnant with her fourth child, Dr. Kathleen Lambright with her third, Deborah Burkholder with number two and Dee Dee's sister, Ruth, pregnant with number one. All due imminently. It was anyone's guess who would go into labor first. Everyone secretly hoped Dr. Kathleen would be the last so she could deliver all their babies before she was unavailable.

Dee Dee gazed at the four ladies around the circle and felt a kindred spirit with them. Each had stepped sideways out of the traditional Amish mold. Dee Dee's sister, Ruth, had started an Amish blog to give the outside world an accurate view of the Amish people. Deborah Burkholder had been a model and earned a higher education degree in nutrition and homeopathic remedies. Kathleen Lambright had become a doctor, and her sister, Jessica, had earned her degree in business. Together, Jessica and Dee Dee helped other Amish make their businesses more effective. No more need to go outside their community for computer help.

Today, it was Jessica's quilt that had brought this group of rogue Amish women to Dee Dee's home. They were stitching the layers of her star quilt together for her upcoming wedding this fall.

Ruth gasped and dropped her lemonade in the grass.

Dee Dee reached for the toppled glass. "Don't worry. It didn't break." She patted her sister's arm.

Ruth's face had lost all its color.

"What's wrong?"

"How do I know if *meine* water broke?"

"Trust me, you'll know."

"Then I think it just did."

Dee Dee shifted her gaze across the circle. "Dr. Kathleen, it's time."

The doctor stood. "Let's get you inside the house."

"Not me. Ruth. Her water broke."

"Daniel!" the doctor called.

He rushed over.

"Help your wife into the house. Your child is on the way."

Dee Dee was relieved to turn her sister over to others. She put a hand on her aching back.

Eli with the three girls came up to her. "Are you all right? You're not in labor, are you?"

"I'm fine." But if the pain lanced across her back and wrapping around to her stomach was any indication, she was. Right now, she needed to focus on her sister.

By the end of the day, four baby boys had been born.

Dee Dee had managed to wait until after Ruth gave birth to have hers. The work and excitement had put Dr. Kathleen into labor with Deborah close on her heels. An influx of other women from the community left none of them without plenty of help. Each new *mutter* had been taken to her own house. Dee Dee's home sat quiet at one in the morning. She would cherish this rare moment of silence. She had nestled herself in the living room recliner to feed baby Abel, who now slept in her arms.

Eli came into the dimly lit room and knelt beside her. "How's he doing?"

"Great. He ate well. Are you happy to have a son?" Dee Dee knew she was.

"I am, but I wouldn't have minded to have another daughter. I love *meine* girls. All of them." He leaned forward and kissed Dee Dee on the mouth. "Let me take him. You go get some sleep." He scooped the little one into his big, strong arms.

She had the life she had always wanted. She stood, tiptoed and kissed her marvelous husband. *Gott* had blessed her in spite of her prodigal ways.

* * * * *

THE AMISH BAKER

Marie E. Bast

My husband and sons,
you three are the joy of my life.

In loving memory of Lois Walline, my mom,
and Blanche Browning, my aunt, the two best cooks
and bakers I have ever known. I miss you dearly.

Also, to Melissa, my editor and wizard in disguise,
for believing in me, and Scribes202,
my critique partners.

For I know the thoughts that I think toward you,
saith the Lord, thoughts of peace, and not of evil,
to give you an expected end.
—*Jeremiah* 29:11

Chapter One

Washington County, Iowa

Sarah Gingerich stomped into her Amish Sweet Delights bakery an hour earlier than her usual arrival time of 4:00 a.m. Who could sleep a wink after what Bishop Yoder had said to her yesterday? She slid the dead bolt closed. *He had his nerve.*

Straightening her shoulders, she shook off the indignant words. *Gelassenheit*—calm down and let it go.

She scooted to the pantry for flour, mixed the bread dough, tossed it on a floured board and began kneading. After folding the soft mass over, she floured and kneaded again.

As she punched the dough a little harder than necessary, the bishop's words came rushing back to her. Heat rose from her neck to her ears, burning her now as it had when he had said them. She couldn't believe that during his preaching on the rewards of being a wife and mother, he had stared straight at her the entire time. Later, he called her aside and mentioned it was time she stopped mourning Samuel and remarried. Why would he say such a thing?

Maybe it was just a casual comment, or maybe the bishop thought he was looking out for her best interest. That's all. She steered her hands back to kneading and mentally put a circle around her bad thoughts and tossed them away.

Tears pressed at the corners of her eyes. They caught on her lashes, and she batted them away. She had her *daed*'s bakery and the apartment upstairs; she didn't need an *ehemann* for support. Sarah plopped the dough in a bowl, covered it and pushed it to the side. Then she grabbed more ingredients, stirred up several batches of yeast rolls and set them to rise.

While the yeast worked, she stirred up a spice cake and shoved it into the oven. When the cake tested done, she pulled it out and popped the bread and rolls in to bake. She set the timer and started on the pies and cookies.

When the first batch of baked goods had cooled, she carted the pastries to the front of the shop and placed them in the display case. A job Hannah Ropp, her friend and assistant, usually performed. Hannah loved to decorate the shelves with rows of cookies and cupcakes in cute patterns—maybe in a heart shape.

Where is Hannah? She's usually here by now.

Sarah set the goodies the *kinner* liked on the bottom shelf. Treats adults normally selected took over the middle shelf. The best sellers, breads and rolls claimed the prize spot on the top shelf.

Without Hannah, she didn't have time to arrange the shelves neatly. Her eyes roamed over the display. Not as *gut* a job as her friend would have done, but good enough for now.

The bakery's cell phone, which the *Ordnung* allowed for business, jingled and lit up with Hannah's name. She touched the screen. "Where are you?"

"I figured you'd forget. I have a doctor's appointment this morning and will be in around noon."

"I'm sorry. I did forget." Tension laced her voice.

"Oh, no. Is something wrong?"

"I wanted to tell you what Bishop Yoder said to me yesterday."

"What did he say?" Hannah asked, her voice steeped in concern.

"He told me it's time to get remarried." Sarah blurted into the phone. "I'm happy. I don't want an *ehemann*."

"*Ach!* I told you that I heard the bishop had a habit of pressuring some of the widows into remarrying. Now do you believe me?"

"Hannah, that's gossiping and a sin." Sarah shook her head.

"It's only a sin if it's not true. This is true."

"Shame on you, Hannah Ropp. You're looking for loopholes in the Bible."

"*Jah, jah.* Gotta go. Hang on 'til I get there, and we'll talk about it."

"Don't hurry. I'm managing." Sarah hit the end button.

She grabbed a wet dishcloth and started wiping off the crumbs she'd spilled on the counter. As her hand zipped across the Formica, it bumped the walnut papa and mama bears Samuel had carved, knocking them over with a bang. Sarah jerked her hand back.

Slowly, she picked each one up—holding her

breath—and surveyed for damage before setting it upright. She heaved a long sigh.

Both fine.

The bears were one of the few things she had left to remind her of Samuel. They brought her comfort and served as a good form of advertisement for the Amish artisans in the area. Many *Englischers* had admired the walnut carvings and asked for directions to the woodcraft shop.

The bishop's words flitted through her mind again. Working fourteen hours a day in the bakery gave her little time to care for a family. Would an *ehemann* allow her to keep the shop? The bakery was her life. It was all she had. She couldn't give it up. Not to mention, she had an obligation to the town—Kalona—and to her customers.

When Samuel had died three years ago, she had stumbled through those first few weeks as if she were groping her way around a dark house without a lantern. Nothing made sense, she couldn't make a decision and she had no desire to bake. She had promised to *liebe*, honor and cherish Samuel "'til death do us part," but she'd figured that meant after fifty years of marriage and seven *kinner*.

Her heart had shattered as if it were a crystal dropped upon the floor. Hannah had helped her plow through the sorrow of Samuel's death.

But life had had no meaning after Samuel died until she returned to the bakery and continued with her cookbook that she would dedicate to her parents and the bakery they loved. Some of their recipes mingled in with her recipes.

Nein. She couldn't give up the bakery. She wouldn't. The bishop couldn't make her remarry.

Could he?

She didn't believe Hannah's gossip. Surely the bishop was only matchmaking those who wanted a spouse.

After grabbing a set of pot holders, she opened the oven door to a steamy whiff of white bread, mingled with the aroma of fresh cinnamon rolls and buttered buns. She set the pans on racks to cool. Pivoting, she glanced at the clock.

Ach. Almost time to unlock the front door.

Sarah pulled out the medium-roast and the decaf beans and started the coffee. While it brewed, she wrote the daily special on the chalkboard, then scooted to the front door, pulled the dead bolt back and flipped the sign to Open.

She puttered around the shop, setting out foam cups and filling the napkin holders. When the doorbell jingled, she stashed the napkin bags behind the counter and looked up into the face of an Amish man she'd never seen before. Judging from his trimmed beard and hair, he was New Order Amish. In her Old Order community, men didn't trim their beards.

"Welkum." Sarah whisked out her best smile.

"Danki." His voice was as quiet as his footfalls. Glancing at the pastries, he smiled and shook his head as if the decision were too much for this early in the morning.

"Can I help you?" Sarah's gaze locked with his sage-green eyes, which were set against sun-bronzed skin. A handsome face for sure and for certain. *Ach.* She stared. He'd think her a forward woman. Her cheeks heated like roasting marshmallows and she glanced away.

He removed his straw hat and twirled it around in his hands as he studied the rolls, cookies and pies. Each received a generous amount of time.

"*Gut morgen.* I'm Caleb Brenneman. How do you do?"

Sarah's stomach tickled as he looked at her. "Fine, *danki.* I'm Sarah Gingerich. I own the bakery."

"Nice to meet you. I'll have a cinnamon roll and a cup of that *gut*-smelling coffee."

She handed him the roll and coffee, then gestured to the five tables and chairs by the windows. "Feel free to have a seat."

After serving the others who'd trailed into the bakery behind Caleb, Sarah refilled the display case but sensed the newcomer's eyes watching her work. Did he know her? She couldn't place him. Because of the bakery, she was acquainted with most of the Plain community around Kalona, at least by sight. Still, the Amish were scattered in seven counties in Iowa, so there were plenty she hadn't met.

She glanced his way at the exact moment when he looked at her. *Ach–caught!* A smile brewed deep in her chest and crept onto her lips. "Do you live around here, Caleb?"

"I bought a farm north of town."

"You're from Iowa then?"

"I grew up here. When I met my *frau,* I moved to Seymour, Missouri. After Martha got cancer, I moved her and our family back, so she could have treatment in Iowa City, and we'd be closer to my *bruder* Peter and his family."

The doorbell jingled and Sarah reluctantly peeled

her eyes away from Caleb and focused on her customer. "*Gut* mornin'."

"Morning, Sarah." Mrs. Wallin smiled as she entered the bakery. "Just a loaf of white bread today."

Caleb finished his cinnamon roll and coffee, tossed his cup in the wastebasket next to the counter and tipped his hat to Sarah. "Have a *gut* day."

Sarah gave a nod. "You, too." As she was bagging the white bread for Mrs. Wallin, she peered up and caught his wink, and had to steady her hands.

Her pulse jumped. Her mind raced in a hundred different directions, but only for a few seconds. What was she thinking? She didn't want to remarry. The bakery was her life.

Caleb strode toward his buggy, his heart pounding like a blacksmith's hammer. Sarah's chocolate-brown hair and cinnamon-brown eyes had stolen his attention. He'd tried to refocus but couldn't keep his eyes from following her. He could have sat in the bakery all day, staring at her as she worked.

Still, it was unmistakable with her navy blue dress and the shape of her prayer *kapp*. She was Old Order Amish. If she were single, where could the relationship go? He enjoyed the liberties his church allowed— shorter beard and hair, Sunday school and Bible study. The Old Order wanted only the church to interpret Scriptures, while New Order encouraged small group study.

His church even believed in church outreach and helping the non-Amish. They also permitted electric conveniences, such as the tractor, mechanical milker and refrigerator, rototiller, lawn mower, chainsaw and propane gas. Without grown *sohns* to help Caleb, he needed such things on the farm.

He must chase thoughts of the beautiful baker out of his head. A relationship between Old Order and New Order would never work. *Jah*, he must forget about Sarah with the cinnamon-brown eyes and concentrate on his farming and crops.

Caleb climbed into his buggy and tapped the leather straps against Snowball's back. "Giddyap, slowpoke. I have chores waiting at home."

As the horse trotted along, Caleb gawked at his neighbors' fields and mentally compared theirs to his. *Jah*, his looked *gut*, maybe better.

Caleb parked the buggy by the barn, stepped down and welcomed the cool breeze that swept across his face. He pulled his hat off, swiped a hand over his brow and then plopped his hat back on his head.

His mind steered his hands back to the job at hand. As he unhitched the horse and walked him to his stall, Caleb tried to push Sarah's image from his head. What was wrong with him? He was acting like a sixteen-year-old *bu* who was getting ready to court.

This was nonsense. Martha had died only a year ago; it wasn't time to start thinking about getting another *frau*.

Nein. Nein. Too soon.

Sarah glanced up as Melinda Miller maneuvered her shopping bags through the bakery doorway. "Congratulations on your *sohn*. I have a *boppli* gift for little Abraham's *mamm* and *daed* to enjoy." Sarah scooted to the kitchen, snatched the gift box off a table, returned to the front and handed the box to the new *mamm*. "I was going to drop it by after work today, but you saved me the trip."

Melinda lifted the cover enough to peek in. "It's a cookie shaped like a little buggy with a *boppli* in it. It looks delicious. *Danki*, Sarah." She leaned over the counter, her face beaming like that of a five-year-old girl with a new dress. "A dozen maple-pecan rolls. Motherhood is *wunderbaar*. Too bad you and Samuel never had *kinner*."

The words slammed into Sarah, wrapped around her scarred heart and squeezed. She and Samuel had wanted a *kind*, a child. Concealing the ache in her chest with a smile barely there, she worked swiftly to bag the order and hand it to Melinda. She took the money, slipped it into the drawer and then slumped a hip against the counter to help ease the pain.

"*Danki*, Sarah. I'll see you next week." Melinda opened the door carefully, trying not to bump her baked goods while guiding her shopping bags.

Alvin Studer held the door for Melinda. When she was through, he entered.

He walked by the display case, slowly checking out the sweets. "You're a *gut* cook, Sarah."

"*Danki*, Alvin, but you mean baker."

"What?" He looked up, his eyes full of puzzlement.

"Never mind." She waited for his order as he paced the floor, looking at breads and rolls, then stealing glances at her. He bent his tall, lanky frame closer to the display case and peered inside. His long face twisted with indecision.

Sarah's mind wandered back to Caleb Brenneman. Remembering his handsome face pulled a smile across her mouth as she fought to push it away. Most Amish men didn't come into the bakery, so she'd probably never see him again. That was *gut*—she'd forget about him in a few days.

"Have you made a selection yet, Alvin?"

He stepped to the counter and gave her a smile while his eyes roved over her. "A loaf of cinnamon-raisin bread." He hesitated. "Would you like to go for a buggy ride with me Saturday night, Sarah?"

Stunned, she stepped back. She didn't want to go for a ride with Alvin, or any other man. She had her life. It was comfortable, and she liked things as they were. But with Alvin, she'd heard he had hit his last *frau*, so the answer was an emphatic *nein*. Yet the idea of courting anyone who wasn't Samuel frightened her.

How should she answer Alvin? She hated to be rude, though she wanted no misunderstanding in how she felt. "*Danki*, Alvin, but my shop requires all my time. When I'm not out front, I'm in the back, baking. I have no free time to squeeze in a buggy ride. Sorry, but that's the life of a baker."

His eyes turned dark and mean. His expression hinted that he wanted to say something but didn't.

She drew in a ragged breath. Her hands fumbled as she plucked the bread from the shelf, almost dropping it. She shoved the loaf in a sack and set it on the counter. "*Danki*, Alvin."

He stared at her. The doorbell jingled twice as the stout Bertha Bontrager bumped the door with her hip as she entered. Alvin didn't flinch at the noise.

Sarah blew out the breath she was holding. "Afternoon, Bertha. What can I do for you today?"

"The bishop said you'd be receptive to my invitation," Alvin whispered as he tossed Sarah a cold look and laid a five-dollar bill on the counter. "Keep the change. I'll see you next time." He grabbed his sack and stomped out the door.

Sarah was stunned and winced as a shiver ran up her spine.

Sarah took advantage of the lull in business after the lunch hour and wiped down the counter. The door opened and Hannah whooshed in like a butterfly.

"*Hullo.* Sorry I'm late. My appointment took longer than I thought it would."

"Don't worry. I managed just fine."

Hannah hurried to the sink and washed her hands while Sarah loaded a tray with cookies. "Have you baked the afternoon order yet?"

"*Nein.* I've been too busy."

Hannah disappeared through the kitchen doorway. "I'll start it."

After the bell tinkled, a cool breeze swept over Sarah. She glanced up from cleaning the display case and froze as Bishop Yoder approached the counter.

"Do you have a cup of coffee and a slice of banana bread left? I'd like to sit and rest a spell."

"*Jah*, but it's the last cup of coffee in the pot so it's free. Sit. I'll bring it to the table."

Her stomach roiled at the bishop's presence. She poured the strong brew and laid a slice of banana bread on a plate. She drew a deep breath. He very seldom came into her bakery. His *frau* was one of the best cooks in the community. She carried a tray with his coffee and banana bread to the table and set it down in front of him. "Enjoy, Bishop Yoder."

"*Danki*, Sarah. Please sit and join me."

Her feet itched to move away. "Only for a minute—I have to start cleaning the display case for closing."

"This will only take a minute." He took a bite of the banana bread, then a sip of coffee. "This bread is very *gut*."

She pulled a wooden chair away from the table and sat.

"I believe Alvin Studer came into the bakery and asked you to join him for a buggy ride. He is a *gut* man and his six *kinner* need a *mamm*."

A shiver ran up her spine as she averted her eyes from the bishop's face. "*Jah*. He did ask. I was busy and didn't have time to talk with him." It was only a little white lie.

"Sarah, it's *Gott*'s will that you remarry. Each person in our church must lose the desire for self and think of the community. That is what we believe. *Jah*, it's time for you to sell the bakery. It's Satan's lie that makes you think that a career outside the home is fulfilling. Alvin needs a *frau* and *mamm* for his *kinner*." His eyes pierced hers like the tiny, sharp point on a straight pin.

The bishop was matchmaking her!

Chapter Two

Plop…plop.

Caleb stopped and listened.

Plop. The sound cut through the still afternoon. He turned his head in the direction of the pond but couldn't see past the grove of maple trees. Maybe an animal skittered over the water. He trained his concentration back to the job at hand.

Plop…plop.

Caleb listened. *Jah*, definitely coming from the pond. Surely Jacob hadn't skipped school again to go fishing.

He laid his fence-mending tools on the ground and raced across the field. His long strides carried him quickly to the shade of the trees. Scanning the perimeter of the pond, his eyes came to rest on his six-year-old *sohn* reclining on the grass.

Caleb walked to within ten feet of the *bu*. "Jacob, what are you doing?"

Jacob sprang to his feet, almost losing his balance as he teetered on the edge of the pond. He stepped back and whirled around. "I'm th-throwing r-rocks in the water." His head hung, but his brooding gray eyes peered up.

"Again, you skipped school. Are your chores done?" Caleb's intent gaze froze Jacob to the spot.

Jacob shrugged his shoulders. *"Nein."*

"Work on the farm takes priority over playing." Caleb furrowed his brow. "You know chores always come first. Milk cows need to maintain a strict schedule."

"I-I'm sorry," Jacob whispered, almost too low for Caleb to hear.

"What has gotten into you?"

Jacob shrugged again with a blank face.

"Go and unhook the gate and let it swing open so the cows can come in from the pasture for milking. Then feed the chickens. After chores, go to the house and get on your knees and ask *Gott* to forgive your laziness." Caleb turned and walked back to the fence but glanced over his shoulder to make sure Jacob headed toward the barnyard. Caleb shook his head as he watched the *bu* kick a stone in his path.

"Jacob, don't take your anger out on the earth. Anger is a sinful thing. In prayer today, tell the Lord your transgression. Go, sit in silence and talk to Him about what you have done. We'll discuss an extra chore for your punishment."

Caleb watched as Jacob trudged to the barnyard with his shoulders slumped. He would leave the *bu* alone for a while to think about what he'd done.

His wife's death had been hardest on his *sohn*. Jacob had cried for hours after the cancer took his *mamm*. Martha's caring ways had woven a strong bond between her and the *bu*.

Caleb returned to the pasture. Holding a piece of wire fencing, he stretched it tight around the wood post, pulled the hammer out of his belt and drove a staple over the wire to secure it. He walked down the fence line, found another piece of loose fencing and fixed it. Mr. Warner, on the farm next door, didn't much care for Caleb's cows trampling down his corn.

He took a step back, removed his hat and wiped trickles of perspiration from his brow while he surveyed the work. After smacking the hat against his thigh to remove dust and moisture from it, he plopped it back on.

For a small *bu*, Jacob gave Caleb more problems than this old fence. *Jacob, Jacob, Jacob, how do I get through to you?*

He looked up toward heaven. *Lord, what do I do with him?*

Caleb had consulted the bishop about Jacob's sadness after his *mamm* had died. "Time will cover the wound," the bishop had said, "like a healing salve."

Martha had passed over a year ago, but the salve hadn't eased Jacob's pain. At least, not yet.

Like Jacob, Caleb had thought about Martha a lot at first. He'd missed her terribly. Yet ever since the encounter with the pretty baker, he couldn't erase the memory of Sarah's smile, her chocolate-brown hair or those cinnamon-brown eyes. They started pushing the memories of Martha into a secret spot in his mind. Was it right to let new memories replace those he had of Martha? He touched his hand to his stomach, where Sarah's nearness had stirred him. For sure and for certain, she was an attractive woman.

Was it too soon to remarry? Jah, his *kinner* needed a *mamm*, but a woman as nice-looking as Sarah must have an *ehemann*. Guilt prickled the back of his neck, and he shook Sarah's image from his mind.

He grabbed his fence-mending tools, carted them back to the barn and hung each one on a hook. Then he pulled off his gloves, straightened them out and laid them flat on the bench. When he walked past the milking floor, he saw that Mary had already led the Holsteins to the stanchions and had started applying the iodine mixture to the cows' udders. Jacob sat off to the side, watching and learning. Caleb smiled. In a couple of years, the *bu* could take over that chore.

It'd be nice to have his *sohn* work alongside him. Someday, Jacob would own the farm, unless Caleb remarried and had another *sohn*. Then the youngest *bu* would inherit the farm, according to Amish custom, and he'd give his older *bu*, Jacob, money to start his own business. Mary would find some young *bu* to marry, and he'd have his own farm or business to take care of Mary and their family.

Caleb followed Mary and wiped the cow's udders with an alcohol wipe. When he was finished with the disinfecting, he attached the vacuum line and started the milking process.

Glancing at Jacob sitting quietly and wearing a sorrowful face, Caleb racked his brain for a way to help the *bu* deal with grieving and his feelings of emptiness and loneliness. Sometimes he wished Jacob were more like Mary.

At thirteen, she was strong willed and self-sufficient. From an early age, Mary did for herself. Her independent way seemed to help her deal with her mother's death and grieving the loss.

Jah, for sure and for certain, *Gott* had blessed Mary

with a tenacious personality and a thriving business making jellies, candies and crafts the *Englisch* liked.

Nein. Jacob wasn't as tough as Mary. He was the sensitive one.

Caleb had a surprise for Jacob tomorrow. One that just might ease his pain for at least a little while.

Caleb settled on the seat and watched his *sohn* mosey toward the buggy. Jacob climbed in and plopped down beside his *daed*. Caleb shook the reins. "Giddyap, Snowball."

"Why do we have to go to Kalona, Daed?" His lips set in a pout.

"We are going to drop off some of Mary's pillow covers, pot holders and *boppli* blankets at a consignment shop."

"Why can't Mary go instead of me?"

"She is busy with the housework, cooking, laundry and making things to sell."

"I don't want to go."

Caleb looked at the *bu* a moment, trying to figure out what would make Jacob happy. Most *kinner* would enjoy a trip to town. "You will go and help. Not another word about it."

A few minutes later, he glanced at his *sohn*. Jacob held his back straight as a stick, staring straight ahead. What could he possibly do for the *bu* to take the stiffness and hurt out of his heart?

Caleb gave up on conversation and instead rubbernecked at his neighbors' fields the whole three miles to Kalona. *Jah*, his fields looked as *gut* as these.

Their errands didn't take long, as Snowball trotted them around town. Caleb hadn't eaten much for breakfast, so a roll and cup of coffee would sure be *gut* right about now. He stopped the buggy one shop down from the bakery.

"Where are we going now?" Jacob looked from one side of the street to the other.

"You'll see. It's a surprise." Caleb walked beside Jacob and ushered him to the Amish Sweet Delights bakery, opened the door and motioned for Jacob to enter. As his *sohn* passed, Caleb detected a trace of a smile.

Caleb leaned down by Jacob's ear and whispered, "You can order anything in the case. Ask for a glass of milk, too. We'll sit a minute and refresh ourselves."

Two customers stood in front of them. The man at the counter was an *Englischer*, clean-shaven and wearing brown trousers and a matching shirt—the same kind of clothing that Caleb had seen on deliverymen. His stomach tightened as he overheard the man tell Sarah how nice she looked today.

She didn't appear to hear him. "Who's next?"

The woman in front of Caleb took her turn at the counter. The bakery door behind Caleb opened, and two young Amish *buwe*, Noah and Matthew, entered and stood in line behind them. The *buwe* tapped Jacob on the shoulders, letting him know they were back there. They talked and laughed, trying to coax Jacob into a conversation.

The woman in front paid, picked up her sack and left.

"We're next, Jacob." Caleb stepped forward as the *buwe* joked and teased Jacob about a girl in school. He glanced back over his shoulder. "Jacob, it is our turn to order."

"*Nein*, I don't like her." Jacob spouted the words at

his friend and gave Matthew a shove. Jacob whirled back around, stepped on a broken cookie or something on the floor and lunged forward. His arms flung out as he slid across the counter, hitting the walnut bears and sending them sailing through the air. They banged on a table, bounced off and smashed against the wall.

Jacob's eyes widened and his mouth gaped as he stumbled back away from the counter. Caleb caught him and steadied Jacob until he regained his balance.

Everyone at the tables stopped talking and stared at the commotion. The men at the table where the broken bears lay shoved their chairs away from the pieces.

Stunned, Caleb wasn't sure what to do. He looked from the bears to Sarah. She shrieked and ran to retrieve the fragments. Tears clouded her eyes, threatening to spill over as she hugged the pieces to her chest and walked back to the counter.

Caleb placed a hand on Jacob's shoulder. "Jacob, you have broken them."

"I'm sorry. I didn't mean to do that."

Sarah laid the pieces behind the counter, straightened and looked at Jacob. "I know you didn't. They shouldn't have sat there. It's my fault."

Caleb removed his wide-brimmed straw hat from his head. "Sarah, I can take the pieces and make you a new set. They won't match exactly, but it'll be close and most won't tell the difference."

She swallowed hard and shook her head. "No, that's not necessary. It wouldn't be quite the same. These were the last things my husband made me before he passed away." Her voice caught in her throat.

Caleb glanced over his shoulder at every pair of eyes in the bakery boring a hole through his back. His cheeks burned, and he sucked in a deep breath. "Jacob must pay for the damage he caused."

"*Nein*, Caleb, it's not necessary." She placed an index finger at the corner of her eye and blotted a tear that had escaped.

"Jacob will be here early Saturday morning to help you in the shop. He can clean the tables, the chairs and the floor, and help fetch supplies. Whatever you need him to do, for as long as you need him, until he pays off the debt. He must make amends."

Sarah looked at Jacob, a small-framed *bu*, maybe six or seven years old, with a tuft of blond hair poking out from under his hat. "Do you want to help me?" she asked, softening her voice.

He nodded. His sulking brown eyes resembled those of a scolded puppy and tugged at the edges of her heart.

"*Gut.* I'd appreciate that." She let a smile pluck at the corners of her mouth.

"We'll take three cinnamon rolls to go, please." Caleb plopped his hat on his head. "Again, we are very sorry." The red flush in his cheeks deepened, but Sarah pretended not to notice.

Sarah handed the order to him over the counter. Caleb's hand glided over hers as he grasped the sack, sending an unexpected rush through her. The warmth jabbed at her heart as though a tiny arrow had pierced it. She jerked back in response. She hadn't felt the touch of a man's hand in a long time.

The sensation had startled her. Or maybe it was her reaction that had startled her.

She'd enjoy getting to know Jacob and most assuredly his papa, too.

Chapter Three

The scent of lilacs and freshly cut grass saturated the morning breeze. Caleb inhaled a deep whiff and watched as Jacob climbed into the buggy and sat next to him. Jacob's face looked like that of a shunned man. "Jacob, doing a little work to repay a debt can't be as bad as all that."

Jacob shrugged.

Caleb shook the reins. "Giddyap, Snowball." The horse trotted down the drive, past the vegetable garden and out the gate between the white picket fences surrounding the barnyard. Snowball turned right toward Kalona without any coaxing.

"Please be helpful to Sarah." Caleb flashed his warning face at Jacob.

He nodded. "I will. How long do I have to stay and help her?"

Jacob looked deep in thought, worrying his bottom lip. Caleb regretted his prior words. He knew the *bu* wanted to make amends.

At times Jacob seemed to have a rebellious nature, but Caleb had to trust his *sohn*. "We'll see how much work she has for you to do. Maybe a couple of hours. You can let me know if you get tired."

"Okay."

"But you understand why you must help her, *jah*?"

Jacob put a hand up to shade the sun from his eyes. "I'm working to pay for the cost of the bears I broke."

"Not just that, but the pain and suffering you have caused her. They were the last gift her *ehemann* had given her before he died. Now they're broken. Your helping is just a respectful way of saying you're sorry."

"I'm really sorry I did that."

"I know you are."

They rode in silence but Caleb sensed something different about Jacob. His voice wasn't as cold and distant as it was when they had driven to Kalona last week. He had an obligation now to a very nice woman, and it appeared he accepted the responsibility.

Glancing at the chaos in the bakery's kitchen—containers covering the table, sugar spilled on the counter and pans strewn about—Sarah felt daunted by the mess before her. She brushed the flour from her hands as she checked the time… Running late. Why had she given Hannah the day off? The special order, along with her regular baking, swamped her with work.

Sarah made the last loaf of bread and set it to rise. She grabbed a wet cloth and tidied up her work area. After pushing the utensils to the side, she scooted to the pantry and lugged enough ingredients to the table for six dozen sugar cookies.

Jacob would arrive soon, and she didn't have time to talk or show him what to do. She barely had enough time to get ready to open.

What had she gotten herself into by accepting Caleb's offer for the small *bu* to help…and on a Saturday? Sarah hurried to the front and unlocked the door for Jacob but left the sign on the window turned to Closed.

She'd dirtied almost every pan in the bakery, so maybe Jacob could wash dishes. When he finished with that, they'd figure it out. She'd been meaning to hire extra help but hadn't had time to advertise or interview.

She glanced at the dirty pans in the sink. It would save time if she had clean cookie sheets. She could fetch the spares she'd stored on the top shelf of the built in cupboard. They were reserved for large orders, like a wedding, but an emergency should warrant the hassle it took to get them down.

Sarah opened the cupboard doors, pulled the step stool over and climbed up. She wasn't quite tall enough for her fingers to touch the shelf next to the ceiling. She stretched. Almost there…but not quite.

Sarah braced a hand on the cupboard and rose to her tiptoes. The pans remained a couple of inches from her grasp. If she stood on the stool's back support, it would give her the boost she needed. She stepped onto the vinyl-covered back and reached for the pans. The stool rocked this way and that way. She flung her arms out, trying to grab hold of the shelf, but missed. She reached for the cupboard door to steady her footing. The stool wiggled, toppled to the right and tossed her straight into a pair of waiting arms and a hard chest.

Arms flailing, she screamed and clutched at his shirt. Her heart galloped against her ribs while she tried to calm down. She gulped a breath.

He dipped his head and his beard tickled her face. Sarah peered up into sage-green eyes and a beaming smile that reached all the way to the corners of his eyes. For once, her brain and tongue failed her simultaneously.

"You could have gotten hurt." Caleb raised his brow, as if waiting for her reply.

A heavy sigh escaped her lips. "*Danki.* You can put me down now." His nearness had created a wild thumping in her chest. When her feet touched the floor, she drew a deep breath and glanced up into his face.

His eyes locked with hers. "Can I trust you to stay on your feet this time?"

She nodded and pulled away from his gaze, trying to calm her runaway heart and snag back her fraying nerves. "Of course. *Danki* for your concern and your help."

Stepping back to regain her composure, she straightened her dress. Then she placed her hands on her prayer *kapp* to make sure it was still secure. She moved it slightly and felt confident of its placement.

Sarah relaxed her shoulders. "Hannah asked for the day off, which has left me to do all the baking, including an extra order for an *Englisch* woman." She turned to Jacob. "What I'd really appreciate right now, if you don't mind, is for you to wash some cookie sheets."

"We'll hang our hats and Jacob will get started." Caleb motioned to Jacob and pointed to the rack by the back door.

Jacob stared at the heap of pans in the sink. Then plunked his hat on a hook, rolled up his sleeves and went to work. Sarah grabbed a towel from the drawer, wrapped it around Jacob's waist and tied it. "This will help protect your clothing."

Caleb raised an eyebrow in a questioning look. "I have some errands to run later. I'll wait out front for a little while to see if you have anything you need me to do, like reaching for something."

"*Danki* for the thought, but I won't be getting on the stool again."

"I didn't mean just that. I could carry a heavy flour sack and refill the bin." The look on his face appeared to be dead serious, except his twitching lips betrayed a suppressed grin.

She flashed him a wry smile. "*Danki,* but we're good for now."

Sarah stole a peek at his back as Caleb returned to the front of the bakery. She touched her hand to her heart and blew out a long breath. How was she ever going to get through the day with him only a few feet away? She clutched the rolling pin to steady her hands.

After she finished the baking, she loaded the cart with cooled pastries, pushed it to the front and transferred them to the display case. Her cheeks warmed as she sensed Caleb's eyes following her every move. "Would you like a cup of coffee and a roll?"

While he ate and read the Amish newspaper, *The Budget*, she continued her morning preparations. When the first customers arrived, Caleb threw his cup away and left to run his errands.

Sarah peered through the doorway at Jacob washing pans and a lump wedged in her throat. It was nice of him to help, even if it was his *daed*'s idea. The pan he was scrubbing looked shiny and clean. He was a hard worker and eager to please. "Customers have come in, so I'll be out front most of the time."

Jacob nodded. "Okay."

While she waited on customers, Jacob pushed the cart out front with sheets of cooled cookies and rolls to replenish the display case. He wiped off the tables, greeted the customers and took dirty dishes to the kitchen without her asking.

When the noontime crowd had disappeared, Sarah was famished. "Now is our slow period, Jacob. How about a peanut butter sandwich and cookie?"

"Okay."

Sarah laid the sandwiches and cookies on plates while Jacob poured himself a glass of milk. They sat at a table by the window and ate in silence as they watched people walk by. She'd often wondered what it would have been like to have a *kind*. At night she sometimes dreamed about one, then woke drenched in tears. Jacob seemed like the perfect little *bu*. He was helpful, sweet and friendly to her customers. It had only been one day but he had already burrowed into her heart, and she didn't want to let him go. Ever.

She swallowed hard. That was a selfish thing to think. *Forgive me, Lord.*

"*Danki*, Jacob, for spending the day. You are a *gut* worker, and I really appreciate your help. In fact, I was so busy that I couldn't have done it without you."

"I'll come back next Saturday."

"You don't have to do that. I'm sure one day's worth of work is enough to pay for the walnut bears."

The doorbell jingled.

"But I *want* to help you." He glanced up at her, his eyes stealing her heart.

She scooted her chair back so she could go wait on the customer. "I can't ask your *daed* to bring you to town again. That would be an imposition. He must be busy and probably needs you at home."

"Please let me help?"

Caleb stepped closer to the table. "You want to what?"

Sarah jerked her head around, surprised to hear Caleb's voice.

"I want to work at the bakery another day to pay my obligation."

"Okay, I'll bring you to Kalona next Saturday."

"Caleb, I hate to ask you to do that. Jacob was here all morning and worked hard. It's unfair to ask him to come another day."

He looked at Jacob and then at Sarah. "This is the most enthusiastic I've seen him in a year. I have some business in town, so it's no imposition."

She mulled over his offer for a minute. "*Danki*, Caleb."

Jacob flashed her a smile, grabbed his hat and followed his *daed* out the door.

Her heart thrived on the small *bu* and already ached for him. Saturday, she'd get to see them both again.

Caleb turned Snowball into the driveway and headed toward the barn. He couldn't understand the change in the *bu*. Jacob had whistled almost the whole way home.

"Daed, I liked working at the bakery. Sarah said I did a *gut* job." When the buggy stopped, Jacob hopped out. "I'll start chores."

He stared after his *sohn*. What had gotten into him? Perhaps he had eaten too many cookies today and the sugar was giving him a burst of energy.

While he led Snowball to a stall, an image of Sarah

fought its way back into his mind. He tried to forget about her smile, about how her small frame had felt in his arms, about how her hair had smelled of peach blossoms. But he couldn't do it.

He couldn't stop thinking about her.

She was a widow. Did she mention that so he'd know? *Nein*. He was sure that was not possible. She only mentioned it because her *ehemann* had made her the bears. Yet a small part of him wanted to think that she wanted him to know.

All week long, Jacob stayed in a *gut* mood. He did all his chores on time and without one complaint. He cleaned his room without Caleb having to ask. In fact, he never saw the *bu* sitting once, only at mealtime and in the evenings. Amazing!

At 5:00 a.m. on Saturday morning, Caleb knocked on Jacob's bedroom door to wake him for chores, and he was surprised to find him dressed and ready to help with the milking. Usually he had to pry the *bu* out of bed. Evidently Jacob was smitten with something at the bakery. Caleb ran a hand through his hair. But what?

The work? Hard to believe.

Sarah? He wouldn't be interested in girls at his age. Yet he did believe Jacob still missed his *mamm*. Sarah had praised the *bu* for doing a *gut* job, as Martha often had. Maybe he needed to do that more, as well.

Jacob helped hitch Snowball to the buggy, then was the first one to hop in the buggy. The closer Snowball got to town, the faster he trotted and the faster he got his treat of oats.

Caleb's heart rate also increased the closer they got to Kalona. He rubbed his sweaty palms across his thighs. It was too soon for him to think about a *frau*.

* * *

Sarah couldn't resist a smile when the bakery door opened. "*Gut* mornin', Jacob. Ready to work again?"

He nodded. "Daed had errands to do and will stop back later."

"*Gut.*" Sarah swiped her hands together to dust the flour off and gave him a pat on the shoulder. "This is Hannah Ropp. She works with me in the bakery."

"Nice to meet you, Jacob." Hannah smiled. "So, you're going to spend your Saturday with us? *Datt* is *wunderbaar*. We can certainly use the help around here."

"Nice to meet you, Hannah." He hung his hat, rolled up his sleeves and dug in to the dirty pans stacked in the sink.

"A man of few words—I like *datt*," Hannah teased.

Sarah finished making the apple pie, sprinkled the top with cinnamon and sugar and then set it in the oven beside the other three pies. She glanced at Jacob, who was busy scrubbing the jelly roll pan. "Jacob, what would you like to do when you grow up? Farm like your *daed*?"

"Be a baker like you."

Sarah paused. She hadn't expected that. "*Jah?*" She turned toward Jacob. "You could come and work with Hannah and me. We'd like that, wouldn't we, Hannah?"

"Of course we would." She laughed.

"My *daed* was a baker, Jacob. This was his bakery. I worked here every day after school, helping him." Sarah finished kneading the dough, set the mound of wheat bread into a pan, covered it and set it off to the side to rise.

"After Mamm died, the bakery was the place Daed,

my brother Turner and I worked together as a family. After Daed and my husband, Samuel, died, the bakery, Hannah and our customers became my family. Turner took over Daed's woodworking shop. Now he's too busy to stop by much."

"I didn't think I'd seen Turner in here lately." Hannah tossed her a curious look.

"*Jah.* He usually stopped in for a roll and coffee a couple of times a week, but not lately. Maybe he had extra woodworking orders with summer and the *Englischers'* wedding season close."

Jacob finished washing pans, swept the floors and then trotted to the front and wiped off tables. He laughed with Sarah and Hannah when a lull in customers permitted it.

Sarah snatched little glances of Jacob as he worked. He was a *wunderbaar* little *bu*, and she enjoyed his company. "Jacob, did your *mamm* bake you cookies?"

"*Jah*, Mamm was a *gut* baker. She made all kinds of cookies and pies. On my birthday, she'd make me a cake. She made a quilt for my bed. It had squares on it and each one had a different-shaped leaf made out of autumn-colored fabric. When I was sick one time, she sat up all night beside my bed." His voice cracked and he wiped a tear from his cheek.

Sarah's heart wept as she sensed Jacob missed his *mamm* and craved the attention of a mother figure. She had experienced that before when other *kinner* in her church had lost a parent. Perhaps she could fill the void for Jacob in some way.

Maybe his *daed* didn't see Jacob's need to confide in a woman. On the other hand, maybe he did and that was the reason why he agreed to bring Jacob to work with her in the bakery.

Late morning, Caleb pushed open the bakery door, and Sarah met him at the counter. "Would you like a cookie and a cup of coffee before you head home?"

"*Datt* would be nice. Would you sit with me at a table for a few minutes?"

"*Jah.* I have a little time. Especially now since I have two good workers in the bakery." She said it in a voice a bit louder than normal and glanced over her shoulder at Jacob to see if he had heard.

She caught the little smile pulling at the corners of Jacob's mouth as he tried to hold it back.

Her heart stuttered at Caleb's nearness. She handed him a cookie on a plate, poured two cups of coffee and then followed him to a table. When she sat, her gaze met his. His sage-green eyes held hers as tightly as his two strong arms had last Saturday. A rush of warmth flooded her cheeks as she remembered that moment.

"I hope Jacob helped some. He's a small *bu* and has his limitations."

"Jacob is a fabulous worker. He washed pans, mopped the floor, cleaned tables, loaded trays on the cart and pushed it out front. He's a great help and strong, too. Does he do a lot of work at home?"

"His sister, Mary, who's thirteen, does the house-work. Jacob works outside, mostly in the garden. When he gets older, he'll farm with me."

"I see. Is that what he wants to do?"

"What boy doesn't want to work alongside his *daed*?" Caleb's smile reflected a fatherly elation.

"*Jah*, indeed, but sometimes *kinner* want to go their own way and try something new."

Brushing off the temptation to enlighten him that Jacob preferred the bakery to farming, she sipped her coffee and held her tongue. It wasn't her place to do so, and besides Jacob could change his mind. It might just be a novelty for him to work in a bakery. Something different than cleaning a dirty barn.

Jacob and Hannah both let out a laugh.

"I haven't heard him laugh since his *mamm* died. It's doing him *gut* to come and work here."

"Hannah and I enjoyed having him." She turned and faced the kitchen. "Jacob, your *daed* is here for you."

Jacob strolled to the front of the bakery and stopped at the end of the table.

"I heard you worked hard for Sarah. Are you ready to go home?" Caleb stood and picked up his hat.

Jacob's eyes sparkled. "*Nein*. I'd like to stay and live with Sarah at the bakery and work for her. She asked me to."

Shocked, Sarah looked at Caleb's face. His eyes widened and his mouth gaped. She turned her gaze back to Jacob. Had she heard him correctly?

She stood and faced Caleb to explain. But his complexion had turned ashen and his hat slipped from his hands and dropped to the floor.

Chapter Four

Still reeling from Jacob's announcement that he wanted to live with her, Sarah pressed a hand to her chest. Without saying a word, Caleb retrieved his hat from the floor. He straightened and glanced at her, his eyes dewy like the forest during a heavy mist.

The bell jingled as the bakery door pushed open and an elderly couple entered. Hannah rushed to greet the customers, nodding to Sarah and indicating she had this. Sarah blew out a breath. She didn't want to delay this conversation.

Caleb's skin above his whiskered cheeks had turned cherry-red. His six-foot stature seemed shorter as his shoulders slumped with the weight of his *sohn*'s brutal words. The man's eyes reflected his world crumbling like a day-old cookie.

Sarah drew a sharp breath and prepared to deal with what she had started. "Let's sit a minute."

Since the tables were empty, she motioned toward the corner table so customers wouldn't overhear their conversation. It also gave her a second longer to decide how to explain this misunderstanding to Caleb. He probably believed she had meddled in his life.

The late-afternoon sun and heat streamed through the window, intensifying her discomfort. She blotted the moisture clinging to her neck with her hand as the guys slid behind the table.

Sarah leaned behind Jacob and pulled the cord on the blind, her mind racing about how to approach the subject. She scooted out the chair directly opposite from Caleb and sat.

How was she going to explain that his *sohn* would rather work in the bakery than on the farm? Not something an Amish man wanted to hear, or probably any man, if he had his heart set on it. She swiped her palms on her apron as she directed her attention across the table.

Caleb glanced down and raised his forearms to the table with his calloused, weathered-roughened hands outstretched in front of him. He sucked in a loud breath and cut his eyes to his *bu*.

Jacob sat next to Caleb, acting as if he were unaware of the impact his words had had on his *daed*. The *bu*'s small body scooted up next to the table, with only the tops of his shoulders and head visible above the table.

"Sweetie." Sarah looked at Jacob and whispered. "When we talked about you working in the bakery, I meant when you had grown and finished school."

"But you said you worked in your *daed*'s bakery every day after school and liked it because you were in a family. I want to be part of a family, too." His tiny voice started to tremble.

"I'm sorry that you misunderstood."

Sarah raised her eyes to Caleb, imploring his help.

She realized Jacob was desperately seeking what he'd lost, and her heart was breaking for him.

Caleb remained silent. By the pitiful look on his face, it was as if his *sohn* had asked for a divorce from his family.

Jacob's words sliced through Caleb's heart like a steel blade, then plunged to the very depth of his soul.

A shiver coursed through his body. After Martha's death, he'd stayed late in the fields and lingered cleaning tools so exhaustion would consume him at bedtime. That helped Caleb deal with the grief. But without giving it a thought, he'd let his *kinner* struggle with their *mamm*'s death on their own. What had he been thinking? Then he'd scolded Jacob when he relaxed by the pond. Instead, he should have taken a few minutes to lie with the *bu* in the grass.

He reached over, enfolded Jacob's hand into his and squeezed gently. "Jacob, we can't ask Sarah to let you live with her. She is busy with her bakery and probably doesn't have an extra bedroom in her apartment."

"But Daed, I could help her and sleep in her bakery."

"*Nein*, that won't work, Jacob. You can't sleep in the bakery. When she needs help, I will drive you into town to help her. I know Sarah is your friend and you would like to spend more time with her. What would you say if we invited her out to our farm for dinner next Sunday?"

His face glowed. "*Jah*, okay."

"Sarah. If you are available for dinner, Jacob and I would be honored to drive into Kalona and escort you to our home."

"*Jah*, I would like *datt*." She turned toward Jacob.

"When I come to your house, I'll scrub *your* sink full of pans."

Jacob laughed. "Okay, but I'll help you."

"*Datt* sounds *gut*. Go tell Hannah I said for her to bag some cookies for you to take home." Jacob ran to the back of the bakery.

"Caleb, I'm so sorry. Jacob and I were having a casual conversation as we worked. I told him about working with my family in the bakery after school. I didn't realize he took it a different way. What I didn't tell Jacob was my *daed* was very strict and my *bruder* and I worked hard from a very early age. But I liked helping in the bakery and didn't mind."

"I understand. Jacob's *mamm* died a year ago, and he still misses her. Martha's death had a devastating impact on the *bu*, and I failed to notice it. I stay in the fields too late and don't spend enough time with the *kinner*. That'll change." He stood, retrieved his hat from the peg and nodded to Sarah as he headed for the door.

Jacob dragged his feet as he made his way to the front of the bakery, a smile touching the corners of the *bu*'s mouth as he said goodbye to Sarah, but it disappeared and was replaced by a sadness that Caleb worried wouldn't go away.

Caleb followed Jacob into the house, hurrying to catch up. For a six-year-old, he could surely outrun his *daed*.

Jacob held the sack up. "Mary, I have some cookies from the bakery. We can share."

Mary shrugged at her brother, rolled her eyes, then finished making a pie and placed it in the oven.

"Guess what, Mary? Sarah is coming to dinner next Sunday, and we get to cook for her!"

Mary stopped and glared at Jacob. "Is that so? Am I the one who will be cooking dinner?"

Caleb cleared his throat. "We will all make dinner together for our guest. It doesn't have to be anything fancy."

"You mean *your* guest." She shoved the laundry basket of clothes she'd been folding to the corner. Then grabbed the pot holders and pulled the cornbread out of the oven.

The assault of ammonia and floor cleaner tipped Caleb off to how hard Mary had been working since they took off for town. The house was clean, the table set for dinner, and the steamy whiff of ham and candied sweet potatoes smelled *gut*.

He hadn't noticed before, but Mary's feelings were sensitive, too. She'd had a deep attachment to her *mamm*, and bringing another woman into her home was going to meet with resistance, no doubt.

Mary was a thirteen-year-old going on thirty. She never complained; she just did what had to be done. Caleb moved out of her way as she dished up dinner in silence. He hung his hat on a peg by the door and dragged his hand through his hair to smooth it down. Apparently neither Jacob nor Mary was happy. Their lives had fallen apart since Martha's death, and it was all his fault.

He had to give his *kinner* a loving home. Martha would have been disappointed in his behavior. He treated Mary and Jacob like adults. He needed to let them be *kinner*. Maybe he could hire someone occasionally to help with the household chores.

The next morning Caleb tried to help Mary whenever he could. He made Jacob pick up more responsibility around the house, as well. The week passed with little complaining or talking of any kind from Mary. She said what was necessary and not a word more.

On Saturday Caleb watched as Jacob helped make sugar cookies. He dusted the table with flour, as Mary did. Rolled out his dough and used a round cookie cutter to stamp out shapes. Caleb walked over to survey the work, his shoes crunching over the sugarcoated wood flooring.

"When I grow up, Mary, I'm going to work with Sarah in her bakery." Jacob slid a spatula under the dough and set each cookie on a baking sheet.

Mary glanced at Jacob and rolled her eyes.

Caleb prayed Sunday dinner would go off without any problems.

On Sunday Caleb peeled and cut potatoes and carrots while Mary prepared the roast. When everything was almost ready, he and Jacob hitched Snowball and rode to Kalona to fetch Sarah. The whole way there, Jacob made plans for Sarah's visit.

Yet a slight uneasiness bubbled in Caleb's belly. Mary had offered no conversation while they worked in the kitchen this morning. Was she still brooding about cooking for their guest?

When they pulled up, Sarah was ready in front of the bakery. Caleb walked her to the buggy. Just as she stepped up to the carriage, she jerked her head at the sound of wheels and horses' hooves pounding the paved road as a buggy approached.

"*Ach.* Melinda Miller." She gave her a wave, then

accepted Caleb's help to step up. "She'll be sure to tell everyone she saw me getting into your buggy."

Caleb waved his hand in a dismissive manner. "It's Visiting Sunday, and you're going visiting."

"*Jah*, that's true," she reasoned.

When he pulled into his driveway, Sarah's gaze bounced from the gardens to the fields. "It's a lovely farm, Caleb."

"*Danki.*" He helped her out of the buggy and escorted her up the porch steps.

Jacob grabbed her hand. "I'll show you my room."

Sarah turned and gave Caleb a shrug. "Guess I have a tour guide with an itinerary for the day."

"Slow down, Jacob. Show Sarah your room while I unhitch Snowball. Then we must eat before anything else. Mary will have dinner ready." Caleb's stomach had been rumbling for the past hour, and he didn't want Mary's hard work on dinner to go to waste. He hurried to unhook Snowball, walked the horse to his stall and then hurried back to the *haus*.

Caleb hung his hat on the hook, washed his hands and, while Mary poured the cold milk, he carried the food to the table. "Jacob and Sarah. Time to eat."

Jacob led his guest to the table and pulled out a chair. "This is where you sit."

"*Danki.*" Sarah made herself comfortable.

Caleb motioned to Mary. "This is my *tochter*, Mary." Then he turned to Sarah. "This is Sarah Gingerich from the Amish Sweet Delights bakery."

Mary gave Sarah a slight nod.

Sarah reached out to shake Mary's hand, but Mary stepped back. "Sorry, my hand may have grease on it from the roast. I wouldn't want you to get any on your hands or your dress."

"Mary. Please wash your hands." Caleb tossed her a warning look. He knew Mary's stubborn nature. She wouldn't warm up to Sarah until she was ready, but he wouldn't stand for her offensive behavior.

She washed her hands at the sink, came back and offered a hand to Sarah. "*Hullo*, Sarah. *Welkum*." Mary's words hit their destination like icy pellets.

Caleb exhaled. It was going to be a long afternoon. "Shall we all join hands for prayer?" He said the blessing, then passed the serving platter around the table.

"*Ach*. New Order Amish pray aloud at the table. We do not." Sarah gasped.

"*Jah*. On the off-Sundays when the church doesn't have preaching, the New Order Amish have open Bible study and Sunday school to deepen our personal relationship with *Gott* and our assurance of salvation."

"*Ach*. Old Order still clings to the adage that only the church interprets scripture, and beyond living a godly life and working hard, we can only have hope of our salvation." Sarah took a bite of food and turned to Mary. "Mmm, this roast is delicious."

"*Danki*."

"Did your *mamm* teach you how to cook?"

"Of course."

The heat from Mary's rude words burned on Caleb's cheeks. He'd hoped Mary would like Sarah. *Apparently that's not going to happen.* "Sarah, Jacob and I have a little surprise for you after dinner."

"I like surprises. That sounds like fun."

When they were finished eating, Sarah jumped up, began clearing the table and carrying the dishes to the sink. Caleb helped Sarah while Mary put the condiments and leftover food away, then joined Sarah at the sink.

"Sit, Caleb, finish your coffee. You too, Mary. You cooked. I'll wash the dishes." Sarah motioned them toward the table.

"Danki, but you came to visit with Daed and Jacob. Go visit with them. I'll take care of the dishes."

"Nein. We'll all pitch in to get them done faster. Jacob and I'll help, too." Caleb grabbed a dish towel. "I can't believe you were going to pass up the help, Mary."

Defiance glowed in Mary's eyes as they darted at Caleb. But she remained silent.

Sarah took a step back after the last dish found its way to the cupboard. She understood Mary wasn't going to let her, or probably any woman, into her kitchen. If Caleb made Mary step aside for a *frau*, she'd do it, but begrudgingly.

After Jacob finished sweeping the floor clean of crumbs and set the broom away, he ran to Caleb. "Now, Daed?"

"Jah. Now we take Sarah on the tour." Caleb opened the door and swept his arm toward the outside. "Your tour is about to begin, Frau Gingerich."

They walked her around the flower and vegetable gardens, then stopped by the barn for her to meet Tiger, the cat. When he rubbed against her leg, she picked him up. "You're a real beauty."

He purred in response.

Jacob tugged at her arm as excitement set his feet to prancing. "Come on, we have a surprise." Jacob walked her to the pen where the newborn calf laid next to his *mamm*.

"Oh, he is gorgeous." Sarah gave Caleb a glance when he stood next to her.

The cat jumped out of Sarah's arms, squeezed through the board fence and rubbed up against the calf.

"Ah, even Tiger likes him." The innocence of the animals warmed her heart.

"There's one last place to see. I'll give you a hint." Jacob rubbed his chin with his hand like he was deep in thought. "It's a great spot on a hot day."

Sarah looked up toward the sky as if really pondering the question, then dropped her gaze back to Jacob. "I have no idea what it is. Lead the way."

Jacob traipsed through the grass and weeds along the bank to the grove of maple trees by the pond on the edge of the pasture. Jacob pointed to the water, his face beaming.

"Oh! What a wonderful place to relax on the grass." She looked around. "It's a beautiful farm, Caleb and Jacob, and so well kept."

Both their faces glowed with pride.

"I contract the fields of vegetables to canneries, and I grow extra to sell at the auction and market." He turned around and pointed to the north pasture. "And we have a few milk cows."

"*Jah*, I see but it looks like more than a few."

"About forty."

"The farm must keep you busy."

Caleb nodded. "*Jah*, it does."

She couldn't keep her eyes off him. He was a handsome man, with a charming way about him. Even with a beard, she could see his strong jaw. She liked his beard.

The New Order men kept theirs trimmed, while the Old Order didn't allow such things. Her stomach fluttered whenever Caleb spoke to her, as though she were a young girl who was in a courtship with a *bu*. Only, now it was a man with *kinner*.

"Daed, is it time for cookies?" Jacob turned toward Sarah. "I helped make them."

"Then I definitely want one." Sarah wrapped her arm around Jacob's shoulder. "Lead the way, Mr. Baker."

The aroma of freshly brewed coffee greeted them when they entered the kitchen. Mary had the cookies and plates on the table. "Mmm, smells *gut* in here. You are a *wunderbaar* hostess, Mary."

"Danki." Mary nodded as she pulled out a chair from the table and sat.

Dessert was light and quick. And Sarah was thankful. She finished her coffee and cookie, then brushed the crumbs from her skirt.

Caleb excused himself to go hitch the horse to the buggy. "I'll meet you out front in a few minutes, Sarah."

"Jah, danki. I'll be ready."

Sarah stood. "Goodbye, Mary. I enjoyed meeting you."

Mary didn't stand. "Nice to meet you, too, Sarah." Her tone didn't match her congenial words.

A cold shimmy worked its way up Sarah's back. Could it be more obvious? She wasn't welcome in Mary's house.

Chapter Five

The ringing of the doorbell pulled Sarah's attention away from the display case and stopped her urge to eat a pecan roll. Her brother walked through the front door. "Turner, it's *gut* to see you."

He sauntered toward her. "Likewise, sister."

She dashed around the counter and tugged him into a hug. "Where have you been the past few weeks?"

"The shop keeps me busy." He tilted his chin up and breathed deeply. "Mmm. I forgot how *gut* it smells in here. I'll take one of Papa's cinnamon-nut rolls and a cup of coffee."

"Hey, Turner." Hannah poked her head out of the kitchen doorway. "Quit being a stranger. We miss you."

"*Jah*, I'm watching my waistline. Trying to get healthier. Can't keep eating rolls every day for breakfast."

"Okay, but don't talk like that in here, or you'll ruin our business. It's a *gut* thing you're our first customer." Hannah laughed as she disappeared back into the kitchen.

Sarah smiled as she listened to their banter. Her unmarried friend had hidden her crush on Turner for years. If he knew, he'd never acted on it these five years since he'd been a widower. She had wanted to let it slip to him, but Hannah made her promise to keep it a secret.

"Here's your sweet roll. I'll bring your coffee to the table." A few minutes later, Sarah set the cup down in front of him.

"Can you sit a minute and talk?" Turner's face looked serious, like the time he told her that their *daed* had died.

She pulled out a chair and sat opposite him. "*Jah*, I can stay until customers start coming. Hannah is baking, so I have to cover the counter. We miss you. Stop more often, even if you don't get a roll and coffee."

"*Jah*. I'll try. Sarah, there has been talk around the community about you."

She stared at her brother. "What talk? You mean about the bakery or me?"

He lowered his voice. "Both. They're saying a New Order Amish man and his *bu* have been hanging around the bakery. Word is that you went to his farm. Is that true?"

Her stomach clenched. Melinda Miller saw her getting into Caleb's buggy, and evidently someone saw her at his farm. "*Jah*, but it's not what you're implying."

"You should never go to a man's farm by yourself. What were you thinking?"

"Jacob, Caleb's *sohn* broke Samuel's bears, and Caleb wanted Jacob to work in the bakery to make amends. His *mamm* died, and he was looking for..." She shifted in her chair.

"For what? A *mamm*? It looks bad for a woman to go to a man's farm unescorted. You know that. He's New

Order. You don't want to marry outside our church. You complain now about not seeing me. Our church would shun you. New Order approves the use of tractors, lawn mowers, inside flush toilets, mechanical milkers, refrigerators and telephones in their homes that are not in accordance with our *Ordnung*. They're too progressive. If I ever have a *kind*, I wouldn't want him hanging around New Order *kinner* of families that have these conveniences. They spoil their youngies with those contraptions and get them used to the outside world. Yet it's the Old Order that boasts around a twenty percent higher youth retention rate."

Heat worked its way up her neck and burned on her cheeks. Sarah clenched her fists. "We're only friends. You are blowing this out of proportion. I'm not leaving our church."

"Watch yourself, sister. Your actions reflect on me, too." His eyes turned cold and locked with hers.

She held his gaze. "I run a business. They're customers."

"Be careful, Sarah. You could get disciplined by the bishop. Then the Amish will avoid your bakery."

She held her shaking hands up, palms out. "Stop it."

"*Nein. I'm* warning *you*. There's been talk." His tone sliced the air like a sharpened knife.

Silence stretched out between them, then he moved his gaze from her to the plate sitting before him.

He took a bite of roll. "Not bad. Daed's were better."

Jah, of course. To her *bruder*, she'd never bake or run the bakery as well as Daed had. Sarah straightened her back. The door opened and she rose. She gave Turner a quick smile.

"*Danki* for stopping." She called back over her shoulder. Her stomach turned queasy. He was telling her to do something she didn't want to do. Now she knew how Mary Brenneman felt when Caleb wanted her to like the woman he brought home.

Betrayed.

The morning was exhausting. A long break at lunch improved her mood, but Sarah kept rehashing Turner's words in her head. How could she convince her brother and the bishop that she and Caleb were just friends?

She emptied the carafe, yanked the coffee-grounds' basket out of its holder and spilled the wet grounds on the floor. What a mess!

She wiped up the grounds, mopped the floor and brewed a fresh pot. When the doorbell jingled, a group of five women entered. They were tourists. It was obvious from the tour-guide pamphlets in their hands. Sarah held out a plate of sample cookies. "*Welkum*, would you like to try a cookie?" When a woman reached out to take one, she bumped the plate, sending it crashing to the floor and breaking to smithereens.

"Oh, I'm so sorry. I'll be glad to pay for the plate."

"That's not necessary. I break a lot of plates, too." Sarah hurried and swept up the pieces.

The woman purchased two loaves of bread, a cherry pie and two dozen of Sarah's new lemon cookies, which she raved about after trying the sample.

Ach, she must have felt guilty. She bought enough to pay for a dozen plates. "*Danki* for stopping by."

Ten minutes to closing, Sarah walked the last customer to the door and peeked out the window. Dark clouds bumped and gathered, slowly squeezing the light from the day. Thunder rumbled like the moan of creation and lightning sliced across the ominous sky.

Streams of rain covered the window while the brooding sky churned and howled. Horses' hooves sloshing through water pulled her gaze to the street in time to see a buggy skid to a stop in front of her shop. *Nein*. A stifled groan stuck in her throat.

Bishop Yoder jumped out, dashed to the bakery and pushed the door open.

"*Gut* afternoon, Sarah." He removed his hat, pulled a handkerchief from his pocket and wiped the water from his face.

"*Jah*, the same to you. You couldn't make it home before the storm broke loose?"

"*Nein*, but I wanted to stop by and talk to you anyway. It's almost closing, *jah*?"

"I was getting ready to flip the sign over."

He turned to the door and flipped the card dangling from a string. "Done."

"*Danki.*" The pit of her stomach dropped.

"Let's have a seat and talk." He swept his hand toward a table.

Heat burned her cheeks as she pulled a chair out and sat. Averting her eyes from his face, she studied her clasped hands in her lap. Was Turner right? Was he here to discipline her? Wait. How did Turner know? As the oldest male of their family and the owner of the bakery, had the bishop talked to him first?

She sensed the bishop's stare. *Nein*, she hadn't done anything wrong. After all, she had a business and needed to be civil to her customers. Even accepting an occasional dinner invitation to help heal a brokenhearted *kind* should be her right. She raised her eyes to meet the bishop's stare.

"Sarah, it has reached my ears that you visited a New Order man's farm, unescorted."

"Bishop, have you heard the old saying? 'Believe none of what you hear and only half of what you see.'"

"Do not fraternize with him, or you could find yourself disciplined. Some of their beliefs and practices are not in accordance with our *Ordnung*." His tone turned haughty. "Be careful, Sarah. Some think you need to confess."

"I'm not courting Caleb Brenneman. We are only friends. His *sohn* broke the bears that sat on the bakery's counter and he worked in the bakery for his discipline. The *bu* is still mourning the death of his *mamm* and having a difficult time adjusting. Little Jacob took a shine to me, and they asked me to dinner to say *danki*. That's all. I've done nothing shameful."

"As a young widow, you need a family of your own. Alvin Studer needs a wife and a *mamm* for his six *kinner*. It would be a good match for both of you." Bishop Yoder set his elbows on the table and clasped his hands as if he were praying. "It's not *gut* for a young woman to be by herself. You need an *ehemann*, *jah*?"

She knew the direction he was heading. There would be no discipline if she married Alvin. It was unsaid, but it was there between the words.

"Alvin is only a few years older than you."

"Twelve years." She glared at the bishop.

"And he would make you a *gut* spouse. Unlike Caleb Brenneman, Alvin is Old Order."

The rain burst from the sky in a torrential downpour.

Sarah glanced out the window. *Lord, please stop the rain so the bishop can go home.* "I don't *liebe* Alvin."

"After you're married, *liebe* will come, I'm sure." The bishop's mouth was set in a firm line.

A sliver of golden glow squeezed through the window blind. Sarah witnessed the sun peeking through the clouds. The rain had suddenly stopped. *Danki, Lord.* Sarah scooted her chair back and stood.

"*Danki* for stopping by, Bishop Yoder, but I've stood on my feet all day and I'm tired. You have given me much to think about." She strolled to the door and opened it for her guest.

He nodded to Sarah on his way out the door. "Alvin needs to get married soon." His deep, solemn tone grated on her ear.

His piercing gaze tried to rip through her resolve and jab at her heart. Did he think she was going to give up the bakery to marry a man whom she didn't *liebe* and take care of his six *kinner*?

Sarah shoved the door closed, maybe a little too hard. The bishop glanced back over his shoulder. She locked the dead bolt, then swallowed a lump of frustration. She wadded up the bishop's plan for her life into an imaginary ball and let it roll over her shoulder and down her back.

A pan banging in the kitchen startled Sarah. She turned as Hannah appeared at the kitchen door.

"Is he gone?" Hannah slowly moved into the front of the bakery.

"*Jah.*"

"I'm sorry. I overheard."

"I figured you had."

"What are you going to do?" Hannah wiped her hands across her apron.

"He threatened to discipline me, but I've no intention of marrying Alvin Studer."

"I'm afraid you two are going to butt heads," Hannah said, wearing a grave face.

Sarah nodded. *Lord God, what are You truly asking of me?*

On Saturday Caleb pushed the Amish Sweet Delights door open and followed Jacob inside. Sarah glanced up from arranging pastries in the display case and tossed them a weak smile. Her eyes darted to the tables, then back at them as they approached the counter. Had he said something to offend her? This wasn't her normal greeting.

Jacob sprinted behind the counter and gave Sarah a hug. "I've missed you."

She leaned down, patted his back and whispered, "Me, too, sweetie." He ran back around the counter to start his hunt for the perfect treat.

Caleb's heart began to thump as he approached Sarah. "*Gut* mornin'. I'll take a frosted cinnamon roll and a cup of coffee."

She nodded and smiled at him, but she had an air of coolness about her. The week was a long, busy one for him but daydreaming of seeing her today had gotten him through. Now she seemed disinterested or tired. His throat tightened. "Have you had a busy morning, Sarah?"

She pulled a roll out of the display case, placed it on a plate and pushed it across the counter toward him. She poured his coffee, handed it to him, leaned in and whispered, "At the corner table are the bishop and some Elders from my church. They're watching me and wanted to know about our relationship. They don't like that we're friends."

"We will go," he mouthed silently.

Jacob chimed in. "I'll have the cream-filled donut and milk, please."

"Good choice." Sarah smiled at the *bu*. "They are especially *gut* today. Why don't you get that empty table, and I'll bring it over." Jacob ran to the table and sat.

As she arranged their order on a tray, she whispered to Caleb, "*Nein*. Jacob might say something if you just leave. I'll refill coffee cups and talk a minute. Maybe you could leave after that."

He carried their treats to the table, sat and gave Jacob his plate. To the *Englisch*, the Plain communities were the same. But that wasn't true. The Old Order had a problem with many of the conveniences that his New Order used, and his church believed in evangelizing. The Old Order communities didn't agree with that kind of mingling. Caleb hadn't thought living in such close proximity to the Old Order would make that much of a difference. And it wouldn't have if it weren't for his continued relationship with Sarah.

Yet he enjoyed her company. They were friends. *That's all.* Jacob adored her. Sarah had mended the *bu*'s heart, and he didn't want to pull that stitching out.

Sarah waited a few minutes before walking around with the coffee carafe. She stopped at the bishop's table and refilled their cups. "I don't often get Elders in here. I hope you enjoyed your coffee and rolls and will come back. Abraham, I remember you teasing me as a child when you stopped by to see Daed. It's *gut* to see you in the bakery again." Sarah's voice carried and Caleb could overhear the conversation.

"*Jah*, I remember those days. I miss coming here and visiting with your *daed*," Abraham said fondly.

"I miss those days, too," Sarah agreed.

She moved to the next table and gave a friendly smile. "Are you visiting Kalona?"

The woman nodded.

"Yep, we have our tour guide right here." The man held up the newest Kalona tourist pamphlet.

"I've seen that. It is a *gut* guide. There's a lot to see. Be sure to stop by the artisan shop. It has many *wunderbaar* things. Have a *gut* day." Sarah flashed them her best smile.

She stopped at Caleb's table. "I'm glad to see you, Jacob. Is your garden growing tall with all the rain this past week?"

"*Jah*. Everything has come up, and we will soon have vegetables to eat. You should come out and see it."

Caleb could see her face redden.

"*Jah*, maybe Hannah and I can visit soon. I enjoyed seeing you both, but I need to get back to the counter. Have a *gut* day."

She turned to leave, but Jacob started to ask Sarah something. "*Nein,* Jacob. We need to be on our way. Have a *gut* day, Sarah."

A loud bang came from the kitchen. Sarah set the pot on the counter and ran to the back. Caleb and Jacob jumped up and followed her to the kitchen.

Hannah looked up, startled. "I'm sorry. The rack holding the pans came loose from the wall when I pulled a pan off. I hope I didn't scare everyone." Her voice quaked. Hannah bent and started to pick up the mess.

Caleb and Jacob hurried to help clear the floor.

"Don't worry about it. I'm glad you're not hurt." Sarah took some pans from Hannah and set them on the counter.

Hannah stood and placed her hands on her waist. "I meant to tell Turner when he came in the next time that the rack was loose."

"You could have gotten hurt." Caleb picked up a couple of pans and set them by the sink. "Let me know when something needs repair. It won't take long. I can do it when I'm in town."

Caleb looked at Sarah. "I'll fix the rack right now. Do you have a screwdriver and screws?"

She pulled a toolbox from the closet. "This should have what you need."

He pulled the step stool over and got busy. Sarah watched the counter out front but stuck her head back in the kitchen to see how the work progressed.

While Caleb rehung the rack, Jacob helped Hannah clean the floor of stuff that had spilled when the pans hit the stove and counter. Caleb was proud of the way Jacob had matured since he'd started helping at the bakery. It confirmed he'd made the right decision.

After securing the rack to the wall, Caleb examined all the cupboard doors and shelves. He poked his nose into the pantry and checked the organizer.

He stepped into the front of the bakery. "It's fixed, Sarah."

She glanced back in the kitchen. *"Wunderbaar."*

"I noticed there are a couple of loose cupboard doors and wobbly shelves. I'll come back another day when you're not so busy and fix them."

"That sounds *gut*."

Caleb put the toolbox away, tidied up, and on their way out Sarah handed Jacob a sack of cookies. "*Danki* for all your work."

He and Jacob grabbed their hats and headed for the front door. Caleb faced the corner table and nodded. The bishop nodded back but the Elders stared at him with stony faces.

The pit of his stomach flopped. It appeared they were determined not to lose one of their flock.

As they headed to the buggy, Caleb heard low voices speaking behind him. He glanced over his shoulder and locked eyes with the bishop. Next to him walked the Elders. Were they planning to have a talk with him? Caleb stubbed his shoe on an uneven spot in the sidewalk and almost stumbled.

Snowball was half a block down the street, and when the horse saw them, he shuffled his hooves around, ready to stretch his legs. As Caleb stepped into the buggy, he caught a glimpse of the men on the sidewalk. The bishop nodded as he passed. The Elders looked straight ahead as if they never saw them.

Jah. He got the message. Loud and clear.

Chapter Six

Sarah placed her elbows close to the table's edge, with her hands folded and propped under her chin. She couldn't decide which she dreaded more. The Elders and Caleb seated in the bakery at the same time or leaving at the same time.

Hannah pushed a steaming cup of cinnamon-spice coffee and a sticky maple-pecan roll in front of Sarah, and sat down opposite her. "You look like you've just given away your last kitten. Monday morning blahs?"

"I'm still worrying about the bishop and the Elders following Caleb out of the bakery last Saturday. The bishop wouldn't dare say anything to Caleb. Would he?"

"He might. He doesn't think the Plain community should have modern conveniences or be studying the Bible. To him, the Bible is for the church to interpret."

"What should I say to the bishop?"

"Nothing. Caleb can take care of himself. Eat the roll. It's delicious."

Sarah sniffed the gooey maple and toasted pecans smothering the yeast roll, then took a bite. "Mmm." She smiled and nodded.

"I knew you'd like it."

Sarah chewed and swallowed. "In some ways, I don't fault the bishop." She blotted her mouth with a napkin. "He's trying to keep his community happy and together. It's fine to introduce widows and widowers if they want someone to marry. I know Alvin wants a *frau*, but it's not going to be me." She took another bite of the roll.

"Why don't you ask Turner to talk to the bishop on your behalf?" Hannah suggested as she sipped her coffee.

"It's been three years since my *ehemann* died. I loved Samuel, but he had a take-charge attitude. I've enjoyed my independence and making my own decisions since he's been gone. I've been satisfied working in the bakery. I would have liked *kinner*, but I have *nein* intention of leaving my bakery or my faith."

"At least you were married. I can't even say that. It's a wonder Bishop Yoder isn't asking *me* to marry Alvin instead of you." Hannah dunked her pastry in her coffee. "Of course, if I'd quit eating these…" She chuckled and held up her roll. "I could probably snag a man, but I do love to eat and don't mind wearing a larger size."

Sarah settled back in her chair. "I don't love Alvin and don't want a man that hits his *frau*. Caleb is New Order, and I can't marry him or I'll be shunned."

"You need an *ehemann* to share your life. And maybe you could have *kinner* with another man. Who knows?" Hannah shrugged.

"If that happened, I would feel like I betrayed Samuel."

"Don't say that. Samuel would want you to be happy." Hannah took the last bite of her roll.

Sarah wiped her hands on a napkin. "Besides, I enjoy

the bakery. I don't know what I'd do without it. Caleb's only been a widower for a year. I'm not sure he wants a permanent relationship."

The doorbell rang and Sarah pushed her problem with the bishop to the back of her mind as she walked to the counter. Hannah shot her a smile as she cleared the table and scampered back to the kitchen.

Catching the door as the customer left, Caleb skirted around her and entered. His face drawn, lines covered his forehead, his eyes rimmed in red with dark circles below them.

Sarah rushed around the counter and motioned him toward a table. She set a cinnamon roll and coffee in front of him. "What's wrong, Caleb?" Sarah patted his shoulder and sat beside him.

"My *bruder* got hurt Saturday. I've been at the hospital ever since I heard. He's in the ICU in Iowa City. A drunk driver in an SUV hit his buggy. Peter has internal bleeding, broken bones, head injuries and he's in a coma." Caleb took a deep breath. "The *kinner* and I were there all day yesterday and last night. They were tired and bored, so I brought them home. I have a favor to ask, Sarah. If you can't or don't want to do it, I'll understand. But I was wondering if you could come to the farm today and stay with the *kinner* while I go back to the hospital."

"Sure, we're only open until noon on Mondays. Hannah can close up."

"Glad to do it." Hannah said as she walked toward the table.

Sarah started for the kitchen. "I'll get my bag while you finish eating. Then we can go."

In Caleb's buggy, Sarah tried her best to shrink out

of sight from the people walking on the sidewalk. When a buggy approached from the opposite direction, she tipped her head down.

This wasn't right. Why should she have to act like a thief in the dark when she wanted to help a friend? Yet was she prepared if someone from her church saw her and sent the bishop to her door again?

Sarah glanced at Caleb and noticed how close his body was to hers. *Ach.* She needed to take her mind off him. He hadn't said a word since they had climbed into the buggy. Worry lines etched deep in his face signaled he was thinking of his *bruder.* She gazed at the landscape, the sky painted with a veil of thin clouds and a light fog still hovering, concealing the low areas on the ground.

She hoped the clip-clop of the horse's hooves drowned out her pounding heart. His casual way of asking her to stay with his *kinner* felt as if he were courting her and she belonged here on the seat next to him.

She wiped those impossible thoughts out of her head and tried to enjoy the ride to his house. Jacob was waiting for them on the porch when they arrived. He jumped off the last step and ran pell-mell over the grass to reach the buggy when it stopped. Sarah stepped down and into two small arms, which hugged her around the waist.

He stepped back. "Sarah, can you stay all night?"

"*Nein*, Jacob. I'll be back before evening and take Sarah home. You must entertain her while I'm gone. Show her all the things we missed the last time she was on the farm."

"*Jah*, Daed. We'll have a *gut* time."

"I brought you and your sister some cookies from the bakery." She handed him the sack. "Please take them into the house." He ran up the porch steps and into the house, letting the door bang shut.

"I'll try to be back before dark, but if I'm not, don't worry. My driver can take you home."

"I'll pray for your *bruder.*"

Just then, a car pulled into the drive and stopped. "He's early." Caleb waved at the driver, hurried to unhook Snowball, said goodbye and climbed into the car. His face looked pale and fear pooled in his eyes. She knew that feeling well, as memories of Samuel's accident came flooding back to her. She could still recall her *ehemann* lying on the ground after his horse bucked him off, his skull crushed on a rock. The only thing she could do was sit in a chair next to his bed and watch him slowly die. She prayed Caleb wouldn't have to go through that with his *bruder.*

She'd stay as long as Caleb needed her to watch his *kinner.* Who could find fault with that?

Jacob came running out of the *haus* and skidded to a stop. "They're in the cookie jar."

Sarah tousled Jacob's hair. "So, what should we do today?"

Jacob's mouth broadened with a smile. "I'm going to take you to see Tiger first. I want you to see how much he has grown."

"Okay. Just let me see if Mary needs my help with anything." She found her on the back porch, folding laundry. Sarah picked up a towel and took a whiff. "Mmm, I love the fresh, outdoorsy fragrance of laundry when it's hung in the sunshine."

Mary wrinkled her nose.

Sarah folded the towel and laid it on the pile. "Do you need help folding or help with anything else?"

Mary looked up and rolled her eyes, with no attempt at hiding her rude expression. "Ah, *nein*. I can do it. You didn't need to come. I told Daed I could handle this. I do everything when Daed's out in the field, including all his chores."

"I'm sure your *daed*'s just worried since he wouldn't be close and wanted an adult here."

Mary rolled her eyes again and huffed.

Sarah turned to leave, but Mary clearing her voice made her turn back around.

"Later, would you show me how to make Daed's favorite dishes, Rouladen and Black Forest cake?"

Sarah smiled. "Yes. I can do that. I'll go with Jacob for an hour, then come back and help you." She was surprised Mary suddenly needed her help, but at least it was a start.

Jacob escorted her across the barnyard, toward the barn. The breeze whipped her untied *kapp* strings around, pulling a few strands of hair loose from her bun. She straightened the *kapp* and tucked the wisps behind her ear.

Horse's hooves and buggy wheels on the road grabbed her attention. What if someone saw her here and told the bishop? Jacob took off running ahead of her, calling for his cat. Sarah hurried behind him, hoping to reach the barn before anyone saw her.

Jacob pulled the squeaky barn door open, then waited for her. When she grabbed the door, he ran in.

"Here, Tiger."

Sarah heard meowing.

Jacob disappeared behind a stall door and, five seconds later, jumped out, holding Tiger in front of him.

Sarah squealed. "Oh, he's grown so big. You must be feeding him well."

"*Jah.* He's a *gut* mouser, too. Do you want to hold him?"

"Ah, well, he's quite big. Why don't you just set him down, and I can watch him?"

Jacob lowered Tiger to the floor. Immediately the cat's ears perked up. His nose began twitching; he took a crouched position and crept along the floor so quietly, Sarah couldn't even hear him move. He rounded the corner and disappeared back into the barn.

"Tiger's probably on the scent of a mouse. I'll show you the garden, and then I have a surprise for you at the pond."

"Okay. But after that, I promised to help Mary make a new dish for supper."

They walked out into the barnyard. The garden was spread along the drive and back behind the house. Her eyes roamed over the rows of vegetables and the strawberry patch. "Your garden looks great, Jacob. *Nein* weeds. And your tomatoes are so tall."

"We started the tomatoes in the house in January. I watered them."

"They are very nice plants. *Gut* job."

"Come on. I have a surprise for you at the pond." Jacob hurried down to the edge of the water and pointed to the middle of the pond.

"Is that a duck?" she asked.

"*Jah.* She comes every year and Daed floats a nest for her to lay her eggs in. He said if I watch her closely, a few hours after the ducklings hatch, she'll walk them to the English River, where they'll be safe from predators."

"What a *wonderbaar* surprise. Now I need to get

back to the house to help your sister make supper." As she turned to leave, a buggy passed by on the road. She didn't see the driver's face, but he might have noticed her.

"I'll walk you back and then play with Tiger in the yard."

Sarah hurried to the *haus*, washed her hands and looked over the chuck roast Mary had cut into ten strips for the Rouladen. "You'll need to pound the meat to a quarter of an inch. I'll write down the recipes for the meat filling and the Black Forest cake."

Mary made the filling and spread it onto the strips, rolled the meat tightly into cylindrical shapes, then tied the bundle with twine and browned them. When done, she layered them in a Dutch oven to simmer until supper. Mary bent over the pot. "Mmm, it smells *gut*." She looked at Sarah and smiled. "I'm ready to start the cake."

Sarah handed Mary the recipe and helped her gather the ingredients. Then she watched as Mary made the cake and the filling. She topped it with whipped cream, cherries and chocolate shavings.

Sarah took a step closer and twirled the platter holding the cake. "Any bakery would *liebe* to have this in their display case to sell. It looks perfect."

Mary's face beamed. *"Danki."*

Sarah stacked the dirty dishes and carried them to the sink. Mary scooted ahead and stood in front of the sink. "I'll take care of the cleanup, Sarah. It's my supper. I want to do it all. You can talk to Jacob. I'm sure he's got something else to show you."

"I'd like to help you. It would take half the time with both of us working."

"I'll take care of it."

Jah, at least they got along for a little while, Sarah thought as she left the kitchen.

She wandered out to the barnyard, sat on the grass and watched Jacob play with his cat. He held a piece of twine and pulled it over the grass, and Tiger chased it around. They ran back and forth across the yard until Jacob ran to the garden and back.

"You two make me tired just watching you." Sarah patted the grass.

Jacob flopped onto the ground next to her. "I'm tired. Let's rest, Tiger." He told her about planting and hoeing the garden and what a big help he was.

The dinner bell rang at 7:00 p.m. Sarah sprang to her feet. "Your *daed* must be home. Let's hurry and see how your *onkel* is doing. I'll race you to the *haus*. One, two, three, go!"

Jacob outran her, continued up the porch steps and held the door open.

"You beat me." She panted as she entered the kitchen and looked around. "Is your *daed* here, Mary?"

"*Nein*. Since he was worried about Onkel Peter, he might stay late at the hospital. We'll eat without him."

"I'm sorry he didn't make it home to try your dinner."

"The leftovers will still taste *gut*. Sit. I'll say the prayer since Daed's not here."

It seemed strange to sit and eat without Caleb's presence at the head of the table. Sarah filled her plate and tried the Rouladen. "Mmm. It's delicious. *Gut* job, Mary."

Mary's face glowed with pride.

Sarah cleared the table and wouldn't take *nein* from

Mary this time. She planted her feet in front of the sink and stayed there, helping Mary wash dishes until the last one was placed in the cupboard.

Sarah wandered to the sitting room, sat in the wooden rocker and relaxed. She hadn't expected Caleb to stay so late at the hospital. Maybe his *bruder* had gotten worse.

She pulled her mending out of her bag and worked for an hour on repairing a frayed seam in an apron. She examined her stitches, then tucked it back in the bag.

At nine o'clock the *kinner* stepped into the sitting room smelling all clean with a lavender soap scent lingering on their hands "*Gut nacht*, Sarah." They chirped in unison.

"Sweet dreams, *kinner.*" As their footfalls drummed on the stairs, their hushed voices but distinguishable words floated back to Sarah.

"Why did you ask Sarah to help you with supper? Thought you didn't like her?"

"It's a *gut* thing you're not a snitch or I wouldn't tell you. 'Cause if I can cook well, Daed won't need to get married."

Stunned, Sarah stopped the motion of the rocking chair. Mary's words washed over her like a tidal wave. It wasn't going to be easy to win her over, if she ever could.

Sarah turned the lantern up, steadied the chair with her hands on the armrests and rose from the rocker. She strolled around the room. A quilt stand stood against the wall with two quilts laying over it. One had a double wedding ring pattern in green colors and the other had autumn-colored leaves set in blocks. The needlework stitching looked perfect.

Some handiwork that didn't look finished sat in a

sewing basket. The basket had blue fabric covering the lid, and underneath the fabric was cotton stuffing to make it a pincushion. A handle attached to the lid had *Martha* stitched across it. Sarah wandered back to the rocking chair and pulled a well-worn Bible off the end table. She noticed the inscription on the first page. *Presented to Martha Brenneman.*

Sarah pressed a hand to her chin. Martha's memory remained very much alive in this house. Her heart skipped a beat as her eyes took another quick survey around. Was Caleb ready to remarry? A smidgen of dread wrapped around her middle and inched its way to her throat. She turned the lantern out, sat in the rocker, laid her head back and closed her eyes.

"Wake up, Sarah."

A voice penetrated her hazy head. "What?" She opened her eyes slowly as she tried to erase the trailing effects of sleep.

Caleb stood before her, still wearing his coat.

"How is your *bruder*?" She stretched and sat up.

"He finally came out of the coma and is doing better. He's going to be okay."

"That's *wunderbaar* news, Caleb." She stood and smoothed the winkles out of her dress. "What time is it?"

"It's 4:00 a.m."

"What! I've been here all night. I need to get to the bakery. I should be starting the baking right now." She grabbed her bag.

"The driver is still here and will take you to Kalona."

"I didn't plan on staying the whole night at your home." Panic swept through her.

"I'm sorry, Sarah. No one will know." His annoyingly calm voice did not reassure her.

If the bishop found out, who knows what would happen to her this time. Her knees shook as she closed the car door.

The bishop might even ask her to explain her behavior, or worse, to confess on bended knee in front of the entire church.

Fear prickled the hair on her arms. Next Sunday, she could be facing community discipline.

Would they accept her explanation and give her a pardon?

Chapter Seven

Sarah slumped against the bakery's counter. Staying with Caleb's *kinner* until 4:00 a.m. had drained her. She inhaled a deep whiff of lemon bars, chocolate cake and a medley of pastries that assailed her senses. Even the sugary-sweet smell made her sluggish this morning.

She glanced at the clock, pushed away from the counter, meandered to the front door and turned the sign to Open. Tuesday was normally a slow day, and she hoped today was no exception. The steamy aroma of freshly brewed coffee wafted in her face as she came back around the counter.

Ach. A cup of medium-roast would perk her right up. Her hands cradled the cup as she sipped the rich black liquid. "Mmm."

The doorbell jingled. She turned and faced Elder Abraham Glick. "*Gut* mornin', Abraham. What can I get you?" She set her cup out of the way.

"If you have a minute, I'd like to talk with you."

Abraham had been her *daed*'s best friend and a man whom she'd more than once trusted with a secret. Like the time she skipped school to go fishing and he caught her at the pond. He said he wouldn't tell her *daed*. He didn't, but instead convinced her to confess.

"Would you like a cup of coffee and a cinnamon roll? It's on the house."

"Just coffee."

She set the cup in front of Abraham and sat opposite him. "What's this about, Abe?"

"Yesterday, I went past Caleb Brenneman's farm and saw you in the yard with his *bu*."

She drew in a deep breath. "Caleb's *bruder* was critically injured and in the hospital in a coma. He wanted to stay with him and asked me to watch his *kinner*."

"Sarah, the bishop warned you. I know Alvin's not at the top of your list of men to marry. But you need to avoid Caleb Brenneman. He's New Order, and nothing can come of it but trouble."

Her cheeks burned as she caught a hint of judgment in Abe's voice. "That's why watching Caleb's *kinner* shouldn't make any difference. I do not plan to leave my church, nor do I want disciplining. But I will help a friend in need, especially in an emergency."

Abe shrugged. "You don't want Bishop Yoder discovering you disobeyed his warning. If others know you went to his farm unescorted, they'll talk. Then you'll have to confess. I'm here as your friend, Sarah. Take care."

"*Danki*, Abraham, for stopping by." Sarah walked him to the door, unshed tears blurring her vision. She wasn't sorry she'd helped Caleb, but she was sorry for the chaos her actions had created for friends like Abraham when they were put into the difficult place of keeping a secret. Abe even took a chance by warning her. The bishop would expect Abe to report her.

All day she worked alongside Hannah in the kitchen as much as possible, trying to keep from watching and waiting for a visit from the bishop. Abraham's warning spun around in her head. She wasn't a child. She wasn't skipping work to go fishing. It had been an emergency, helping Caleb and his *kinner*.

Sarah glanced at the clock. One hour until closing.

A breeze swirled through the shop and a commotion at the door pulled Sarah's attention from cleaning the counter. Caleb and Jacob heaved a large toolbox over the threshold and plunked it on the floor. She propped her hands on her hips. "What are you two up to?"

"You helped me out while I was at the hospital, and I wanted to repay the debt. We are here to do repairs in the kitchen. Should only take an hour or so. I brought a helper."

"*Jah*, I see that." She surveyed the *bu*'s attire.

Jacob patted his tool belt, which drooped on one side while his other hand held it up at his waist. He pulled out a tack hammer and held it up. "I'm going to do a lot of work for you today."

"Then it's a *gut* thing you've come dressed like a carpenter. Follow me and you can get started."

"Sarah, before I forget. Mary was wondering if you could show her how to make strawberry jam." Caleb grabbed his toolbox and fell in line behind his *sohn* as they made their way to the kitchen.

"*Jah*, for sure and for certain, I can do that sometime." She watched as they started removing cupboard doors to replace the worn and loose hinges.

Hannah stepped to the sink and pointed to the faucet. "Can you fix this leak?"

Caleb examined the faucet, furrowed his brow and nodded.

Sarah showed Caleb where to place the new towel holder and ceiling saucepan rack, which she had stashed in the closet a month ago.

She ducked out of the kitchen and returned to the front to finish cleaning. After emptying the display case, she set the sheet pan of leftover baked goods in the cooler, then cleaned and sanitized the case like she did every night.

When she glanced in the kitchen and saw the faucet was fixed, she got the impression Hannah wasn't letting the guys leave until all the repairs were completed. She also noticed her friend had a pastry tray waiting on a table for them.

Sarah turned off the coffee pot just before closing and cleaned it. When the bakery was empty, Caleb and Jacob took a break and came to the front of the shop for their treat.

Caleb held up his brownie. "These are *gut*. So are the lemon bars."

Jacob nodded.

Sarah grabbed a napkin and wiped chocolate off one side of Jacob's mouth and lemon off the other side. The enticement was too great. She snatched a brownie off the tray and popped it into her mouth. When the doorbell jingled, she turned in time to see the bishop enter.

She cringed as she met him at the counter. "What can I help you with, Bishop Yoder? We are about to close."

"I wanted to talk with you, Sarah." He glanced at the table area.

"I'm having repairs done in the kitchen." She gestured toward the back. "The repairmen are here now. Could we do it another time, say tomorrow?"

"*Jah*, I guess it will wait until then." He scowled at her as he walked out.

Sarah followed him to the door, turned the dead bolt and flipped the sign to Closed.

As she headed back to the table, a knock sounded on the door.

Startled, she slowly twisted around. She blew out a long breath and ran to the door. "Bertha, we're closed."

"*Jah*, but I was wondering if I could give you a special order for tomorrow."

"Of course. Come in." Sarah took the order, ushered Bertha out and locked back up while Caleb and Jacob returned to the kitchen. She gazed out over the near-empty street, anxiety washing over her. The bishop's visit flashed back to her. What could he want? Had he too found out about her going to Caleb's farm? Helping someone in need *was not* wrong. So why did her insides whisper something different?

She glanced toward the kitchen, where Caleb and Jacob were finishing their work. Would the bishop make her choose between the Brennemans and her faith? A dread wrapped around her heart.

Sarah had a mess to clean up, and she didn't mean just the kitchen. Before meeting with the bishop, she had to decide what mattered most: Caleb and his family, or her faith and her family…

She let out a deep sigh. They were only friends. Why did she have to give them up? *Jah*, she knew the bishop was afraid her friendship with Caleb would turn into something more.

The thing was…she was afraid it wouldn't.

If she chose her faith and her family, it meant life without Caleb and Jacob. She couldn't choose Caleb and leave her church or she'd be shunned.

Hannah entered the room brushing her hands over her apron. "What did the bishop want?"

"To talk to me. He noticed Caleb and Jacob were here and decided to wait until tomorrow."

Hannah glanced back at the open kitchen door and whispered. "Think he knows you went out to the farm and watched the *kinner*?"

"I'm sure he's heard a story embellished by people who think they know what's what. Two buggies went by while I was outside at the farm."

"I have some news to tell you before someone else does." Hannah wrapped an arm around her friend's shoulder.

Sarah's back stiffened. "What else are they dishing out about me? Your tone is scaring me."

"Sorry. It isn't bad news. Well, maybe bad for me, but *gut* for your *bruder*. I heard Turner has been seeing Naomi Flickinger."

Sarah gasped. "I can't believe he didn't tell me. Courting is supposed to be secret, but I'm his sister." Sarah pressed a hand to her heart. "*Nein.* I don't believe that."

"Who knows? Maybe it's not true," Hannah said. "Maybe he's making her cupboards or hanging new doors."

"*Jah.* We'll see. They could be talking about Turner like they do me. The gossips need someone to wag their tongues about since it's a small town and they have nothing else to do."

"What are you going to say when the bishop comes

back? Have you decided?" Worry threaded through each of Hannah's words.

Sarah froze. "I've delayed making the decision, hoping it'd take care of itself."

"Oh, Sarah." Hannah folded her friend into a hug and held her there for several minutes. "If the bishop decides upon discipline, and you don't confess, the Amish won't come to the bakery."

"I know, but we get hundreds of tourists, at least during seven months of the year, and maybe longer if it's not too cold during the holidays. I'm praying for a long tourist season so I can save enough money for the winter months."

"You know...if you're shunned, I can't work here." Hannah's voice quaked.

Silence stretched out between them. "*Jah.* I was trying not to think about it. The man is Amish. So why should it be such a big deal?"

"He's New Order, and a lot of what they believe is against our *Ordnung*," Hannah whispered.

"I'm not marrying Alvin. I just can't." Tears clouded her vision. She blinked them back. "Why should they bully me with something so important? It's as if they're not thinking of my needs, only his. I know our faith believes we must give of ourselves to our community, but not my whole life."

Sarah never thought it would go this far. Never thought she'd see Caleb again. Blindly she hoped Alvin would give up.

Caleb's footsteps echoed over the flooring as he stepped to the side to maneuver his toolbox through the kitchen doorway. As he walked toward the front of the bakery, his tools clanked in the toolbox.

Hannah wrapped an arm around Sarah's shoulders and squeezed. "I'll go talk to Jacob and finish in the kitchen so we can go."

Caleb wore a confident smile. "All done. The cupboard doors are now solid. The racks are up, and we work cheap. A dessert should finish the payment."

"Okay, but I owe you more than that, Caleb."

"*Nein.* You were at the house all day and night with my *kinner.*"

Jah, and Abraham would never let her forget it…unless she confessed.

The question was, would the bishop forget it if she confessed? Or would he insist she marry Alvin?

Caleb stood so close to Sarah, he could reach out and touch her. *Nein.* Pull her into his arms and press a kiss to her lips. Sweat beaded on his forehead. He set his toolbox on the bakery floor and blotted his brow with his shirtsleeve.

His tongue felt like dried shoe leather with Sarah so near. He wasn't sure he could even form a word. He raised his gaze from her lips to her eyes.

Sarah's voice hitched a bit. "I set the desserts in the cooler in the kitchen. You can take your pick."

Caleb followed Sarah to the cooler and let a cool blast of air hit him. He drew in a deep breath. "What I'd really like for my dessert is to go on a picnic with you Sunday afternoon."

She smiled at him. "Do you want me to bring the dessert then, or will you take it now?"

"Bring it to the picnic. Jacob and I will fetch you early Sunday morning so you can attend Sunday school with us."

"I'll be ready." A blush rose to her cheeks, but it made her look even more fetching to Caleb.

Sarah locked the bakery door and hurried to catch Turner at his woodworking shop. As she drew closer, a faint light was visible in the back of his building. She knocked on the side door and tried the handle.

Locked.

She knocked harder. He lived in the back, and the light was on, so he should be there. Maybe he'd stepped out?

She tapped louder.

Faint footsteps came toward the door, and then it opened. "Sarah, what are you doing here?" Turner's voice sounded surprised.

"If you have a few minutes, I need to talk with you."

"If it's about repairs, I'm working on a big order, so I can't do them right away."

"*Nein.* A friend did the repairs. Can I come in a minute?" Turner stood in front of the doorway, as if he were too busy to see her.

"For a minute. I'm still working in the shop." He stepped back.

"Bishop Yoder is pestering me about marrying Alvin Studer. I don't want to marry Alvin. I heard he hit his late *frau.*"

"Don't believe that. Alvin is a quiet man. A hard worker. He owns a large farm and hires many youngies to help him work it. He'll make you a *gut ehemann.* Stop worrying. You won't need to run the bakery anymore."

She gasped. "I *liebe* the bakery. I don't plan to quit working there."

"What are you here for then?" His abruptness cut her off. He huffed so hard, it stirred the hair at her temples.

"The bishop stopped by before closing, but with so many still at the bakery, I told him to come back to-morrow. You should know, when Caleb Brenneman's *bruder* was in an accident and in a coma, I went to his farm and watched his *kinner* while he went to the hos-pital and sat with his sister-in-law and *bruder*. I think Bishop Yoder either wants to discipline me or wants me to marry Alvin. I want you to tell the bishop that I'm not going to marry Alvin."

Turner squinted at her against the darkened hallway. He lowered his chin and focused back on her. "Alvin is a decent man. He's in our Order, and Caleb Brenneman is not. You should help people in your own district and let Caleb's church help his family."

Sarah stepped back. She couldn't believe he had said that. He was as strict as Daed. Daed had insisted she marry Samuel but she hadn't minded. He was a *gut* man, a fair man, but a typical strict Amish man.

"I will not talk to the bishop for you, Sarah. Get that out of your head. I warned you about your actions. Now you must deal with the consequences."

She opened the door, slipped through and closed the door behind her. When they were *kinner*, Turner had always stood up for her.

Apparently not anymore.

Chapter Eight

Sarah carefully turned the bakery sign to Open and glanced up the street to see if the bishop was heading in this direction. Ominous dark clouds hung overhead and a cold April drizzle coated the lamppost. It looked black and sinister as it covered the sidewalk and street.

She craned her neck. No one was out driving yet. Maybe the inclement weather would force the bishop to cancel his visit.

Sarah poured herself a mug of coffee, took a sip and checked the front window. She jerked back, almost spilling the hot brew. The bishop had parked his buggy and was heading toward the bakery door.

He slipped off his coat and hat and hung them on a hook. He motioned to a table. "Sarah, join me."

She gulped a mouthful of coffee, dribbling a few drops out the corner of her parted lips and down her chin. She grabbed a napkin and blotted the moisture. Her body reluctantly moved, like the time Daed had asked her to pull a switch from a tree so he could discipline her.

She poured the bishop a cup of medium-roast, hoping

it would help soften his mood. "Bishop Yoder, I wasn't sure anyone would risk the streets today." She set the cup in front of him. "Haven't had any customers, but I have plenty of coffee."

He glared at her as she sat opposite him. "Alvin should be here soon."

His words knocked the wind out of her. She dragged in a ragged breath and tried to calm her racing pulse.

The bishop reached out with his fingertips and tapped the table twice. "We live our lives for Jesus Christ. As Christ gave up his life for us, we too must sacrifice. We must yield our will to *Gott*'s will."

Jah, she understood that, but how did the bishop know that *Gott* wanted her to marry Alvin?

The bishop straightened his back. "To be part of the church district means we must give up what is personal and selfish. We live in a community and give of ourselves to that community."

She gulped. "Bishop Yoder, I don't want to be Alvin's wife. *Ever.*"

"You don't believe in community?"

"Of course I do. I work at church events and at barn raisings. When someone is sick or injured, I help."

"Jah." He nodded. "I understand. You just need to spend time with Alvin because you do not know him well enough. That is perfectly normal. Get to know him and his *kinner*. You'll feel differently."

Sarah stared at the bishop in disbelief. *He's insisting I court Alvin!*

The bakery door opened and out of the corner of her eye, she could see a man enter. Her heart raced.

Alvin.

Her whole body went numb as Alvin slipped around behind her.

He pulled out the chair on her left. "*Gut* mornin', Sarah." The words fell off his silky tongue.

"*Jah.*" It was the only word she could form out of her mouth.

"Alvin was wondering if you would grant him permission to court you," the bishop blurted out.

She was stunned. How could she reply to that? Did she disobey the bishop and not give Alvin a chance?

Daggers stabbed at her heart as she slouched against the back of the chair. If she courted Alvin, she couldn't see Caleb and his family again.

The door banged open and Bertha Bontrager burst through like a bulldozer. She removed her bonnet and hung it on the coatrack. "It's not fit for car or buggy this morning." She laughed.

"Mornin', Bertha. I thought maybe you'd pick up your order later today or tomorrow with the weather so bad." Sarah rose from the table and nodded at the bishop. "I'll just be a minute."

Sarah pointed toward the kitchen. "Your order is in the back."

"No hurry."

When she returned to the front of the bakery, Bertha was sitting at the table with Alvin and the bishop. She sat the order on the table. "Coffee, Bertha?"

"*Jah.* And a cinnamon-swirl roll, please."

Sarah took her time pouring the coffee. There was one large swirl, the last one made. She had been planning to save it for a male customer that came in, but it'd take a woman a while to eat.

Sarah slid the cinnamon swirl on a plate and placed

it and a cup of coffee in front of Bertha while she listened to her describing the slick and dangerous conditions of the road coming into town. Brushing off the temptation to disappear back into the kitchen, Sarah silently prayed Bertha would stay as long as Alvin did.

Fifteen minutes later, Melinda Miller bumped the door open with her hip. She held her *boppli* in her arms and tried to keep the blowing rain off their faces while she maneuvered over the threshold.

Danki, Lord. Sarah stood and rushed to help Melinda.

The bishop pushed his chair back, scraping the floor with its wooden legs, tipped his hat to Sarah and headed out the door.

"Have a nice day, Bishop Yoder." Sarah almost sang the words but reined in her glee.

As Alvin pushed back his chair, Bertha stood with him. "Later today, I'll bring a casserole by for those six *kinner* of yours."

Alvin smiled and nodded. "*Danki*, Bertha."

After the bakery was empty, Hannah stepped out front. "Go on a buggy ride with Alvin and explain how you feel. Tell him you're still in love with Samuel."

"*Jah*, like that's going to stop him. He has six reasons and a houseful of work not to care what I think. He might not care if I like him or not."

Caleb's heart galloped when Sarah sat next to him. The buggy swayed as it hit a bump, and he hoped it would move her closer. He liked the feel of her sitting next to him.

When they arrived, he introduced Sarah to everyone at Sunday school. The women had brought breakfast casseroles, biscuits and jam to eat before they started their Bible study. Sarah mingled with the women. She knew most of them, probably from the bakery. Sarah expressed an interest in learning about assurance of salvation, something the Old Order didn't view as necessary, and he hoped she would keep coming back to Bible study. Maybe it would persuade her to join his church.

Yet if his *tochter* didn't accept Sarah, he wasn't sure what he'd do. He wanted his *kinner* to like the woman he might choose as his *frau*. He'd wait until after the picnic with his *kinner* to get Mary's reaction.

He leaned closer to Sarah as he shared his lesson book and Bible with her. She smelled of lilacs and springtime. She read scripture and discussed it with the group. She listened to the others and contributed from her experience. Her faith was sound and he could tell she had a deep *liebe* for *Gott*. When they stood to leave, everyone invited her to come back again.

Deep inside Caleb, tiny sprouts of feelings for her had blossomed.

Sarah tilted her head back and let the sunbeams shower her with warmth. The *kinner* were excited about the picnic. Mary acted less sulky and even chatted with her the whole time they laid out the picnic. It wasn't much, but she hoped it was a start to friendship.

When the picnic was over, Sarah hurried to wrap the food and place it in the basket while Caleb and the *kinner* set up the volleyball net. "Girls against guys," she yelled out.

"Jah," Caleb grinned. "If the girls lose, they have to make the guys their favorite meal with dessert."

Jacob squealed. "We are going to win, Daed."

"Okay," Mary chimed in. "But if the girls win, they get to pick a chore the guys have to do for them."

Caleb nodded in agreement. "Girls can go first."

Sarah served the ball over the net and Caleb returned it. Back and forth it went. First one team scored a point, then the other.

"You hit like an old man, Jacob," Mary teased.

"I do not." Jacob smacked the ball with all his energy and watched it sail over Mary's head to win the guys a point and the game.

Sarah checked the time. "I've had a great afternoon, but I need to get home. Pick a day this week, and Mary and I will make dinner."

On the way home, Sarah stole glances at Caleb, while his attention focused on maneuvering the buggy along the rough road. He had his straw hat pulled low over his forehead, shading his square jaw and powerful chin. His beard looked freshly trimmed and attractive. Her heart nearly skipped a beat.

Caleb talked to her about the farm and the progress of his crops. "They should yield a nice profit." Sarah nodded at his announcement. She smiled at the notion that they acted like a married couple.

When he pulled the buggy to a stop at the back of the bakery, she stepped out, foreboding churning in her stomach. If the bishop threatened her with discipline, she might not be able to see Caleb and his family again. And just when Mary seemed to be warming up to her...

The next Sunday, Sarah sat on the bench after the preaching, waiting for the publishing of the banns and the public announcements.

The preacher glanced from side to side at the filled benches. "I have a joyous announcement to make. Turner Lapp and Naomi Flickinger will be married in two weeks."

Sarah grabbed Hannah's hand and noticed a tear roll down her friend's cheek. "I'm fine, Sarah," Hannah whispered, as she flicked the moisture off her chin.

After the meal, Sarah dropped Hannah off at home and then proceeded to her apartment. Maybe Turner would stop by to invite her to the wedding, as was the custom after the announcement in church. No doubt, they planned a small wedding since they'd both been married before. Finally at 8:00 p.m., she couldn't wait for Turner any longer. She blew out the lamp and tucked herself in for the night.

On Monday morning, Sarah waited as Noah Mullet, Naomi's *bruder*, and two other men placed their morning orders at the bakery counter. One by one, each man took his sweet roll and coffee and sat at a table. When the shop had cleared of patrons, Noah called out, "Sarah, come over here and sit a while. Your *bruder* will be here any minute."

Sarah could feel tension, excitement or something brewing with these men. Were they going to play a joke on her *bruder*? The men had all been friends with Turner for a long time, and often in school had included her in their pranks. What could they possibly be up to? She sat next to Noah. "What's going on? You guys look like you are going to play a joke on someone." When the bakery door burst open, the words caught in her throat.

Turner hurried in and pulled up a chair. "Taking a break, sis?"

"*Jah*. Noah asked me to join them. Sorry if I'm intruding on a *buwe* thing." She started to stand.

"Ah, come on, Sarah, stay and talk." The guys at the table coaxed.

"*Jah*, you're not intruding." Noah waved his hand in a motion for the others to quiet down. "Turner, have you told Sarah your surprise?"

Turner shot Noah a frown. "Sis." His voice shook. He started poking at a crumb on the table, until he slowly brushed it over the table's edge.

"What is it?" He was making her nervous.

Then he let out a hoot. "Naomi and I would like you to help at the wedding, and she would like you to spend the night and get to know her family."

Sarah let the requests soak in. She felt like a traitor to Hannah, but Naomi was going to be her sister-in-law. Of course she would have liked it better if he'd picked Hannah for his *frau*. But she knew that would never happen. "*Jah*, of course I'll help. Whatever Naomi wants me to do. I wish you had told me you were getting married. It seems others knew it before me."

Sarah stood and swept her eyes over the table of men. Guess it was a joke. She was probably the only person in town who didn't suspect her *bruder* was going to marry Naomi. Even after Hannah mentioned it, she didn't want to believe that he wouldn't tell her. Tears welled up in her eyes as she headed for the kitchen. It didn't feel like she and Turner were family any longer.

She grabbed the rolling pin, took the dough she had resting, rolled it flat, scooped up the piecrust and lined a pie dish. She glanced at Hannah. "Did you hear?"

"*Jah*. Now you will have a sister."

"You'll always be my sister, Hannah." Sarah heard

heavy footsteps approaching the kitchen doorway. Turner slowly walked to her work area.

"I'll go out and watch the front," Hannah said. "Turner, I'd love to help Naomi family's get ready for the wedding, too."

"*Danki*, Hannah. That would be nice." He waited until Hannah had left the kitchen. "Sarah, why did you run off like that?"

Her heart pounding like a blacksmith's hammer, she laid a hand on her chest as if to stop the banging sound that echoed from her chest to her ears. "Turner, everyone in town knew but me. Why the secrecy? You couldn't tell me?"

"Once I get married and we start a family, I won't have much time to help do repairs at the bakery. I was hoping you'd marry Alvin, then I wouldn't have to worry. But you seemed so against Alvin, I didn't know how to approach it with you. As it is, I'm trying to save money, working every waking minute and taking extra orders. You should think about marrying Alvin so you will have someone to take care of you."

"I see. Someone to take care of me. Alvin has a big farm with hired help, six *kinner* that need caring for with lots of dirty laundry and meals that need cooking, but *I* am the one who needs taking care of!" She turned back to her pie. "Get out of here, Turner, and leave me alone."

Sarah trotted to the stove and stirred the pan of rhubarb that was simmering for the pie. Like the wispy plume of steam rising from the fruit, silence filled the air.

"You're a stubborn woman, sister."

Turner's footsteps trailed off as he headed to the front

of the shop. Sarah dropped to her knees and prayed. She took a long look at the height, breadth and depth of her problem, and knew what she had to do.

Chapter Nine

Sarah woke in a sweat and gasped. It was Turner's wedding day. A shiver of fear swept over her heart. She'd have to dodge the bishop and Alvin all day. What if the bishop acting as Alvin's *Schtecklimann*—go-between—tried to corner her to set a wedding date? *Ach*, she'd have to avoid them, or give a firm *nein*.

She pushed herself out of bed and slipped into her dress. She'd promised to help her sister-in-law-to-be get ready for the wedding.

It was time her *bruder* remarried. His *frau* had died several years ago. In school, he'd teased Naomi, but when they started to go to singings, Ethan had asked first to take Naomi home and Turner had lost his chance. Sarah remembered how he'd moped for months, until he met his late *frau*. Now he'd have a second chance at happiness with Naomi.

Sarah placed the wedding cake she'd made in the buggy, hitched her horse, King, and stopped on the way to pick up her friend. "How are you doing, Hannah?"

"I'm telling myself that Turner is my *bruder* and I must be happy for him and Naomi." Hannah settled herself in the seat and set her cake on her lap. Her cake would be only one of many decorated cakes baked by close friends.

She reached over and gave Hannah's hand a quick squeeze. Sarah swallowed the lump in her throat, shook King's reins and changed the subject. She pointed out yards with beautiful tulips, daffodils, snowball trees in bloom and bushes with bright red leaves.

While Sarah turned the buggy slowly into the driveway, Hannah braced the cakes with her hands. Naomi's *daed* ran over, helped them down and then climbed into the buggy to hand them the cakes.

Sarah led the way to the living room, which was cleared of furniture, and set her cake on an *Eck* table—V-shaped tables, placed in the corner for the bridal party. Hannah hesitantly set hers down, too. Sarah glanced at her friend and noticed tears shimmering in her eyes.

"I'm so sorry, Hannah. I know how this must hurt."

She drew a deep breath. "I'm fine." Her voice shook a little as she swiped her hands down her apron as if fighting for composure.

"Come on." Sarah patted Hannah on the shoulder. "Let's help in the kitchen until it's time for the wedding. That'll keep our minds busy."

Sarah helped prepare food and made sure the tables were set and the breads were sliced. At 9:00 a.m., the bridal party were already in their places and the singing had begun.

At the ceremony, Sarah watched the happy couple. Naomi looked *wunderbaar* in her new green dress that brought out the specks of jade in her hazel eyes. Turner gazed at Naomi with admiration, and joy radiated from her face. They made *liebe* look easy, Sarah decided. If only her *liebe* life were as simple as theirs appeared.

After dinner, Sarah slipped off to the kitchen to help with cleanup and keep out of Alvin's sight. When she ventured to the living room to clear tables, Alvin called her name, but she pretended she didn't hear and dashed back to the kitchen, carrying plates.

In the late afternoon, Sarah watched the happy couple visit with their guests. Naomi ran over to Sarah, hugged her and whispered, "*Danki* for helping, sister-in-law."

"You're welcome. I'm happy for both of you." Sarah gave each of them a kiss on the cheek when Turner strolled over to them.

"Your wedding is next, *jah*? Then I can help you." Naomi's eyes crinkled with excitement.

"It won't be anytime soon." Sarah shot Turner a smirk.

He turned back to his *frau*. "We need to see other guests."

Sarah picked up empty cake plates and stacked them until her hands were full. The pile teetered and tipped toward her a little too much until they dumped crumbs on her apron. She set the stack on a table, pulled her apron away from her dress and brushed the crumbs onto a plate. Sarah noticed a man approaching and looked up into Alvin's smiling face.

Ach—caught.

Laying her shaking and soiled hands on her apron, Sarah glanced into his eyes and their unnerving glint. She flashed a smile. "There you are, Alvin. I was wondering when I'd see you. I've promised Naomi and her *mamm* I'd stay here tonight to help with the cleanup and to get better acquainted with my extended family."

"*Jah*, I understand." The glint disappeared from Alvin's eyes and his chest deflated with a sigh. "I'll see you later, Sarah."

She grabbed some leftovers and hurried to the kitchen before he thought of something else to say.

A twinge of regret poked her. *I must tell him soon I'm not going to marry him.*

"I heard that. You lied to him."

Sarah whipped around. "No, I didn't, Hannah. They asked, and *jah*, I might stay." She handed Hannah a stack of dirty dishes.

"You need to explain to Alvin how you feel. He's a reasonable man."

"Maybe, but I can't chance it."

Hannah set the empty bowls and platters next to the sink and set glasses and silverware in the sudsy water. She pushed up her sleeves and began washing glasses. "What are you afraid of?"

Sarah glanced at the ceiling and took a few steps closer to Hannah. "That the bishop and Alvin will set a date for the wedding, announce it in church and force me to marry him or leave town. You are a lot more trusting than I am, Hannah. Maybe because you've never been married and had someone make all your decisions for you."

The wood flooring squeaked behind Sarah.

Hannah stopped washing dishes, turned around and gasped. Her eyes darted from someone behind Sarah to Sarah.

Sarah placed a hand on her throat. *It must be Alvin.* Well, at least now he knows, but she didn't mean to hurt his feelings. She pivoted slowly, like a rusty nut on a bolt.

Caleb stood there, holding a tray of dirty glasses and plates. "I saw you dart through the house, picking up dirty dishes, and thought I'd help you out."

Sarah's stomach twisted. "What are you doing here, Caleb?"

"I know Naomi Flickinger's *daed*. He even got me a *gut* deal with Turner on replacing my kitchen-cabinet doors. I've been thinking about sprucing up my house. It's time. I thought I might bump into you here."

"Turner is my *bruder*." Her voice squeaked.

"Ah, with different last names, I had no idea he was kin to you." His voice wavered.

Several women bustled into the kitchen and interrupted Caleb, their arms and hands burdened with dishes and food to store. Sarah searched Caleb's face, his eyes throwing an icy stare toward her.

He nodded and set the tray on the table. "Nice to see you again, Sarah," he said and walked out.

Caleb swallowed hard as he headed out the door. He glanced around at the cloudless deep blue sky. To him, the blue only reflected the bruising of his heart.

His heart pounded against his chest, trying its best to punch its way out. His palms drenched in sweat, he'd almost dropped the glassware. He'd planned to toss out the dirty paper napkins, but all he wanted was to get as far away from Sarah as possible.

So, the beautiful Sarah had an admirer. Alvin.

Of course a woman like her, who could pluck a star from the sky, had someone courting her. Most assuredly, Alvin was Old Order, so there was no conflict with church affiliation. He knew that was the biggest problem for him and Sarah to overcome. She didn't want to change churches, and neither did he. He'd thought he could convince her otherwise when he took her to Sunday school and Bible study.

On his way to the buggy, Caleb tried to force a smile to all those he met. It was difficult to do so with a stabbing pain in his gut. Sarah had an obvious attachment to Jacob, and in befriending Caleb, had he mistaken it as affection aimed at him? His face still burned with embarrassment.

"Fool," he mumbled through gritted teeth as he climbed in the buggy. "You're a fool." He pointed Snowball toward home.

He trotted Snowball a little faster than usual for a few miles. He lightly pulled on the reins to slow the horse. "Whoa there, settle down, boy." The steed evidently sensed his agitation. Why should he take things out on his horse because he took a browbeating of his own making?

It was time he stopped daydreaming about Sarah Gingerich and erased this infatuation from his head and heart.

Sarah knocked on the door to Caleb's house.

No answer.

She knocked again.

Silence.

She hadn't seen Alvin or Caleb in a couple of weeks—not since the wedding. Previously both of them had sought her out. Now neither one came around. Of course, summer meant hard work for farmers. Some vegetables planted early would be ready to harvest. She had noticed on the ride to his farm that trucks and wagons from canneries waited for produce. That roadside stands, farm markets and women wanting fruits and vegetables for canning and freezing would be waiting too. Caleb, no doubt, was very busy.

One last knock.

Sarah heard footsteps approaching the door, too light for Caleb, but too heavy for Jacob. The door swung open and Mary stood before her, looking frazzled and nearly worn out.

"Your *daed* told me you'd like to learn how to make jam. It's the perfect time, since strawberries are in season, if you'd like me to show you?"

Mary shrugged.

"Four hands are better than two." Sarah raised her brow.

"Could you show me how to can vegetables, too?" Mary asked.

"*Jah*, be glad to help. Ready to start now, or is another day better?"

Opening the door wider, she allowed Sarah to enter. They tackled the jam first. When they finished with that, Mary pointed to the big pot of string beans waiting in the corner.

"I picked them yesterday. There should be enough for eight quarts." It saved time that Mary had thought to wash and sterilize the jars the day before.

"Do you have much experience with canning, Mary?" She replied that her *mamm*'s sisters had helped. When Mary asked questions to learn, Sarah tried to teach her all she could.

An hour later Mary's tongue had loosened. "Are you

and my *daed* courting?" Mary kept her voice even. "He never mentions you anymore."

Out of the mouths of young'ins. Sarah stayed silent, hoping that would signal Mary to drop the subject.

"Are you two still friends?" Sarah couldn't decide by Mary's tone whether she was glad or not.

Apparently she decided Sarah wasn't going to answer, but Mary was in a mood to talk. "I'm fourteen on my next birthday."

"Oh? Not much longer until sixteen. Are you looking forward to attending your first singing?" Sarah held a jar as Mary filled it with beans.

"I'm a little nervous."

"Is there a special *bu* you have your eye on?"

"*Nein.* When I asked Daed questions, he said I'm too little to worry about it."

"He might not want to see his little girl growing up so fast. Give him time. He'll get used to the idea."

"He and Mamm were so much in *liebe.* I can't imagine why he wouldn't want that for me." She looked at Sarah thoughtfully. "Mamm was a good cook and a loving person. We all missed her terribly at first, snapping at each other and not wanting to touch anything in the house of hers. Then we decided it wasn't what she would have wanted."

Sarah's heart fell. Maybe Caleb wasn't ready to recommit.

"I know what you're going through, Mary. I lost my *mamm,* my *daed* and my *ehemann,* Samuel, all within two years. It's hard to lose loved ones. I felt like I was numb inside for a very long time. Nothing seemed right. Then one day, the grief lessened and I moved on."

"Exactly." Mary held up the spoon dripping with hot

liquid before dumping its content into the jar. "Mamm would have wanted us to get on with our lives. Last week, I finished some sewing she'd started. Before, I didn't have the heart to move her mending, let alone finish it. Suddenly it just seemed like the right time."

Sarah nodded and sensed Mary was getting through the grieving process.

Three hours later, heavy footsteps tromped up the porch stairs. Then stopped. Sarah straightened her back and squared her shoulders. Had Caleb recognized her buggy?

The door opened and Caleb stepped in. *Jah*, he must be surprised to see her. She glanced over and met his gaze.

He nodded and hung his hat on the hook. "What are you doing here?"

Sarah noticed Mary's head jerk. "I helped Mary make jam, as I promised."

"Oh." The word fell flat. He fetched a cold drink of water and took a sandwich that Mary had made a while ago out of the icebox.

"Is Jacob with you? I thought I might see him while I was here."

"He'll be in shortly. He stopped to see how Tiger's kittens were doing."

"Tiger fathered kittens?"

"*Nein.* Tiger is the *mamm*. Jacob named her, and I never paid any attention." His voice trailed to a whisper.

"Oh. I see."

Caleb set his empty glass down and headed for the door. "*Danki* for helping Mary." He closed the door and tromped down the porch steps.

Sarah had hoped to find some time alone with Caleb

to explain about Alvin, something she should have done earlier. But it didn't look like he was in a mood to listen.

Caleb stomped into the barn. "I appreciate Sarah keeping her promise to Mary, but she doesn't need to feel obligated to us," he mumbled.

"Daed, are you talking to me?" Jacob came out of a stall, Tiger following close behind.

"*Nein.* I'm just talking to myself. Sarah is at the house, helping Mary make jam. She wanted to see you."

"*Danki.* Come on, Tiger. Let's take one of your babies to show her. She might want to keep one."

"Jacob, do not pester Sarah to take a kitten if she says *nein.*"

"I won't." Jacob ran out the door and banged it shut.

Caleb shook his head. That *bu.* He grabbed the scythe and sickle, and sharpened their blades until they had a fine edge. Weeds were tall and he needed to get them cut. He took off his hat and wiped his brow with his sleeve. Why had Sarah come to the farm? To help Mary? Maybe she was no longer courting Alvin. Or she could have wanted to talk to him privately, but he didn't wait long enough to find out.

Nein. If she wanted to talk, she could have said something. Although, she did honor his request to help Mary. He should have at least said goodbye. Caleb hurried out the barn, banging the door closed. He saw Sarah heading to her buggy and ran across the barnyard. "Wait. There's something I want to ask you."

Her face brightened as he approached.

"Are you and Alvin courting?" he blurted out.

"What makes you think that?"

"I overheard you and Hannah talking at Naomi and Turner's wedding."

"Then you misunderstood. Our bishop likes to matchmake the widows and widowers. He tried to match Alvin and me. Bishop Yoder thinks we should court, but I have no intention of courting Alvin."

Sarah paused and Caleb noticed she had a strained expression.

"Hannah thinks I should be honest with Alvin and tell him I'm not going to marry him. But I don't want to be alone with Alvin in a buggy to tell him, and it's awkward with others around."

"Has this been going on the whole time we've known each other?"

"Well...not the whole time."

"Didn't you think you needed to be honest with me?" Caleb's voice tightened.

She took a step back, closer to the buggy. "I was hoping to resolve the situation with Alvin before it got out of hand."

"Before it got out of hand? You don't think it's out of hand now? Surely I made my interests known—taking you to my church, on a picnic, and asking you to supper."

"I thought if I ignored Alvin, he'd get discouraged and find someone else. Then I wouldn't have to worry about hurting his feelings."

"And you didn't care about hurting mine?"

"*Nein.* You're twisting my words. I didn't mean that. I was hoping to spare your feelings by not telling you. Apparently that didn't work."

"Sarah, honesty is the basis of any relationship. Without it, relationships fail."

Caleb headed toward the house. He heard Sarah climb into her buggy and click her tongue. "Giddyap, King."

The wheels crunched over the rocks as the buggy and Sarah drove out of his lane and out of his life. When he turned, his heart was beating wildly, and she'd disappeared behind the grove of trees.

What had he done? He didn't want her out of his life. If she had told him about Alvin, would he have believed Alvin meant nothing to her?

Caleb watched as the buggy stirred up dust, then dissolved into nothingness, like his chance for *liebe*.

Chapter Ten

Caleb banged around in the barn, cleaning the stalls with a pitchfork and tossing soiled straw in a manure spreader.

"Meow."

He glanced over at Tiger and her kittens eyeing him as they always did when it was almost time for milking.

"Meow…meow." One complaint after the other.

"Shoo. Get out of the way."

Bracing the pitchfork prongs against an area that had muck stuck to the floor, he pushed hard to loosen the mess. Then he watched spiders and bugs run across the planks and escape through cracks in the boards. Caleb poked, pulled and shoveled the pitchfork along every inch of flooring.

Thoughts of Sarah crept into his mind and whirled through his head. The thing he disliked most wasn't that Sarah hadn't told him about Alvin. It was his reaction. It made him jealous to think another man pushed so hard to get her. All this time, he'd taken it slow so Mary and Jacob could get to know her. Of course Alvin wanted her for his *frau*. She was beautiful, kind, good with *kinner* and a great cook. Who could ask for anyone more perfect?

Sarah burrowed into his mind and his dreams, and disrupted his work. She mentally tagged around with him every hour of every day. He walked over to the wall and hung the pitchfork and shovel on their hooks. Then he headed toward the house.

His gut twisted in turmoil. Had he sent her away, into the waiting arms of Alvin? His heart cringed with each step he took. *Fool!*

A chilly breeze swept over him and raindrops pelted his head and shoulders. He should have made his intentions known to Sarah, but he wasn't ready to propose. Not yet. He didn't want to force Mary to like Sarah. He knew he couldn't, even if he tried. Mary was stubborn. More than likely, she took after him. Even after she helped Mary make jelly and can vegetables, Mary hadn't warmed up to Sarah.

Agonizing over Sarah, Mary and the whole situation had robbed him of sleep for two nights. If he did doze off, images of Sarah in Alvin's arms gave him nightmares.

A gust of wind hurled rain at him, knocking his hat off and spraying water across his face and clothing. Caleb snatched his hat from the ground and took off running toward the porch. Taking the steps two at a time, he reached cover just before sheets of rain poured from the coal-gray sky. A cold tremor shook his body. What if he couldn't take her on another buggy ride or picnic?

The thought nearly stopped his heart. He sat on the porch swing to sort it out, but how could he search his heart when she had taken it with her?

* * *

Sarah finished refilling her customers' cups, then started a fresh pot of coffee. During midafternoon, the traffic coming into the bakery slowed, giving her time to tidy up.

The doorbell jangled, but she wanted to finish arranging the baked goods in the display case before she waited on the customer. Straightening up, she braced her hands on her hips. "May I help you?" She froze when she saw it was Caleb.

"I'm sorry I didn't take your news very well," he whispered.

Relief rushed over her. "I should have told you, but we never really had an understanding. I thought it forward to presume we did and try to explain about Alvin."

Caleb glanced over his shoulder, as if something or someone was waiting for him, then back at Sarah. "I have errands to run. I'll come back at five and pick you up. We'll go for a ride, away from stretching ears."

He melted her insides with a smile, giving her gooseflesh on her arms. "*Jah.* I'd like that." Her heart fluttered. "See you later."

She watched him stroll out the door. This time she'd be honest with him.

She closed the shop a few minutes early, ran upstairs and changed into a fresh dress. He arrived right at five o'clock and helped her into the buggy. She fluffed her dress around so it lay in neat folds.

"Giddyap, Snowball." He glanced at her across the seat, his voice deep and rich. "You look lovely, Sarah."

"*Danki.*" Her pulse thudded in time with the horse's clip-clop. He reached over, laid his hand over hers and gave a soft squeeze. A mixture of joy and fear coursed through her veins. What had really changed? Nothing. But it felt like everything had changed.

"Let me speak first." His voice was warm and laced with excitement.

"Okay."

"You're right, we have never had an understanding, but I think you care for me. Is that true?"

"Jah," she said slowly.

"More than just as a friend?"

She hesitated. A smile twitched at the corners of her mouth. *"Jah."*

"Gut. Until we figure out how to get around being from different Orders, can we just have an understanding that we want to see each other?"

Last evening she'd slept fitfully, consumed with the fear of never seeing Caleb and his family again. Now that fear lunged at her throat. She looked out of the buggy and into the one passing on the opposite side of the street. It belonged to Bishop Yoder, and he was staring straight at her.

"Sarah." Caleb snapped her attention back to him.

"Jah. That meets my approval, but as far as the bishop goes, I'm not sure he would agree."

Caleb's desire to have an understanding wasn't exactly what she wanted, but she knew it was the best he could do. She cleared her mind, then gazed out at the field of dark green cornstalks and breathed air with an earthy smell. White and yellow flowers dotted the roadside, and on some stretch of banks, farmers had sown prairie grass that had grown tall and waved invitingly in the breeze.

"We'll stop by and check on the *kinner* before I take you back to town."

Sarah stayed in the kitchen with Mary while Caleb and Jacob went out to do chores. She tilted her head back and inhaled a deep whiff. "Mmm. Something smells *gut*, Mary."

"It's beef stew with vegetables and gravy." Mary pulled some spices out of the oak spice rack and shook them into the boiling concoction.

"That's a lovely spice rack. Did your *daed* make it?"

"*Jah.* On the back, Daed carved, 'You are the spice of my life.' On the oak chest in their bedroom, he carved, 'I'll *liebe* you forever and ever.'"

She stirred the stew and set the spoon on a holder. "He made Mamm the sideboard and the table, too. They have a verse carved on their bottoms, but I can't remember what they say."

A sudden chill ran through Sarah's spine. Apparently Caleb had *liebed* Martha very much. Could he ever *liebe* her as much as he had his late *frau*? Could he set Martha's memory aside or push it into the back of his heart while he let his life go on with another woman?

If she did marry Caleb and moved in here, would she have to share his late *frau*'s house with her? Have constant reminders of Martha everywhere she looked? Would Sarah have to measure up to Martha in his *kinner*'s eyes?

"Sarah," Bishop Yoder called from across the lawn sprawled with congregants after preaching on Church Sunday.

Sarah cringed.

"I'll meet you in the buggy," Hannah said as she retreated far from their paths.

The bishop hurried as best he could with someone

either stopping him to talk, greeting him or asking him a question. He wove his way through the throngs of people and breathlessly made it to the tree where Sarah had not budged an inch since he called out her name.

She clenched her fists. *I should have feigned a headache and left after the preaching.*

"We need to set a date for your wedding to Alvin," the bishop blurted.

Sarah straightened her back and sucked in a deep breath. "Bishop, I do not want to marry Alvin. I don't like him."

The bishop stared at her with cold, steely eyes. "You haven't tried. Go for a buggy ride with him so you can get to know him."

She stood with her lips pressed tightly for a long while. Then she found the courage to speak. "*Nein.* Caleb Brenneman and I have an understanding."

"What did you say?" His voice rose with an edge to it.

"At the appropriate time, we will make a commitment to one another." After she said it aloud, it sounded strange even to her. Exactly what did that mean? He never really used the word *marry*. At the time, his words had sounded like a commitment. But now she wasn't so sure.

He laughed. "Is that what he said to you?"

She nodded. Moisture started trickling down her forehead and onto her brows.

"He did not tell you he would change to our more orthodox affiliation, did he?"

"Well, we haven't really discussed it."

"*Nein*, I imagine he hasn't. You need to discuss it, Sarah. Remember, you can't leave the church. He must rejoin the Old Order. What is he waiting for? I'll tell you what—for you to get used to his ways and their softer lifestyle. Ask him, Sarah. You'll see."

She glared at the bishop. She had fallen for Caleb and hoped he felt the same about her. Enough so he would change to the Old Order. *Nein*, Caleb had never mentioned it. She'd been lying to herself thinking it wouldn't make a difference to Caleb. That he would eventually offer to change. Only he hadn't, at least not yet.

"Sarah." The bishop jarred her out of her thoughts. Glaring at her, he said, "You must choose. But remember, giving up your church means shunning."

Jah, she had much to think about.

Sarah puttered around the apartment, watering plants and trying to decide how to approach the subject again with Caleb. A few weeks ago, every day seemed the same, but life was simpler. She had the bakery, and helped with church events and community projects. Now her life felt like it was being tossed around like a ball hanging on a string from a paddle.

The garden was always the place where she did her best thinking. Sarah unhooked her gardening smock and pinned it to cover her dress. After grabbing her tools from the closet, she headed downstairs and out back to till the garden. Sarah lowered her knees to a mat, pressed the blade of the hoe between each row and uprooted every annoying thistle and weed.

She worked until almost dark, clearing the path and loosening the soil between the rows of carrots, cabbage and lettuce. She took a sniff of the fragrant parsley and cilantro. "With a *gut* clean bed around you, you will flourish."

She weeded and watered the tomato plants. They would soon have red fruit. She was glad now she'd started them in the winter.

The hard physical movements drained her energy, and she still hadn't come to a decision. The bishop's words haunted her. As hard as she tried to forget them, they fought their way back to the forefront. She hated to admit it, but the bishop was right. Caleb knew the problem. He had to join her church, not the other way around. *Jah*, he took her to Bible study and to meet his Sunday school class so she would get to know them, like them and want to join them.

If the bishop had found out that she'd attended a function with the New Order community, he would have disciplined her. And rightly so. Caleb wanted to sway her to his side…his church.

She hadn't realized it before. It was as plain as a sign tacked on a tree.

Chapter Eleven

Sarah stayed busy the next three weeks, testing recipes
for her cookbook and neglecting her garden. She made
room in the display case for the three batches of new
cookie recipes she'd developed—spiced apple, spiced
oatmeal raisin and vegan carrot—and then added the
announcement to the chalkboard. She cut up several
cookies of each kind and laid the small pieces on a plate
and set the plate at the front of the counter.

Throughout the day, she received compliments on
her new recipes. At the end of the day, she cleaned the
display case and realized the new cookies had sold out.
Ach. They liked them!

Sarah pulled out the empty trays, carried them back
to the kitchen and waved them in front of Hannah.
"What do you think of this?"

"Congratulations. Now, how about creating a new
cake recipe or two?"

"I've been toying with a couple of ideas."

Sarah carted out the ingredients for a new pista-
chio-crunch cake. She stirred them all together and
popped the two layers in the oven. Grabbing a pen,

she made updates on the recipe card until the bishop'
words forced their way into her head again. She hate
to admit it, but he was right. Either Caleb or she had t
give up their church.

If neither of them wanted to change to the other per
son's church, they needed to end their relationship. Th
trouble was, she had grown very fond of Jacob…an
Caleb.

Sarah pulled the cake pans out of the oven and se
them to cool. She finished cleaning the bakery, an
just as she reached out to flip the sign on the front doo
to Closed, a nose poked against the glass door. Sh
jumped back and laughed. The door pushed open an
she wrapped Jacob in a hug.

She straightened her posture and smoothed her skirt.
Her attention darted to Caleb. "It's closing time. I'm out
of coffee and rolls."

"That's okay, we didn't come to eat." Caleb motioned
to his *sohn* to speak.

Jacob looked down and scuffed the toe of his shoe
on the floor like he was kicking a rock. "Sarah, I never
get to see you. Can I come and work in the bakery?"
His voice wavered.

Her heart melted. "I miss you, too, Jacob." When he
faced her, loneliness dampened his eyes, but she had
the perfect way to dry them. "Your garden is spotless
and mine is in desperate need of care. How would you
like to help me weed and prune bushes?"

Jacob let out a silly laugh. "I will have your garden
spick-and-span in no time at all."

"How about Monday afternoon?"

Jacob looked at his *daed*. Caleb nodded. "We'll come
by after lunch."

* * *

On Monday, Jacob hoed between the rows of vegetables, weeded around the tomatoes, and then grabbed the hose and watered the garden. When he finished, he weeded her flowers in the corner of the yard, carried buckets of water and thoroughly drenched each plant.

Caleb had brought his work gloves. As fast as Sarah could trim the bushes, he gathered the bush clippings and weeds from Jacob's work into a nice pile. She drew a quick breath at the touch of his hand cupping her elbow. "Let me do that for a while. Your arms and shoulders must be getting tired."

Sarah heaved a sigh. "I suppose so. The yard work has gone unattended far too long. Thank you and Jacob for all your help."

He nodded. "My pleasure."

"Mine, too, Daed. I'm a big help."

"Indeed you are," Sarah assured Jacob.

Tears threatened to fall at their sweet words, but Sarah choked them back. "It is very nice of you both to help me." She waited for Caleb to speak and say something like "you need an *ehemann*," but he didn't. It would definitely be a lot easier if she did have an *ehemann*. But one of her choice. Not chosen for her by the bishop.

Sarah propped her hands on her hips. "I just have one question. If we work hard together, we should also have fun together. What should we do? Go fishing and take a picnic lunch?"

Jacob's eyes grew big. "*Jah*. Let's do that." His gaze drifted to his *daed*. Caleb slowly let a smile play at the corners of his mouth. "Let's have our outing on Sunday afternoon."

Sarah brightened. It would be nice having the whole afternoon with Caleb and his family. And maybe it would give her an opportunity to talk to Caleb alone and ask him if he would change to Old Order.

She locked the door behind them. A giddy sensation welled deep in her heart. She didn't know how she and Caleb would solve their faith difference, but it just had to work out.

Before the bishop declared her shunned.

Sunday was here in no time. Mary had made plans with friends, but Jacob was up just after dawn. Caleb flooded a patch of ground with water and Jacob sat waiting. Caleb finished the chores and gathered their fishing poles and bucket then wandered over to Jacob, where he was digging up worms. "I can almost taste those fresh fish right now."

Jacob smacked his lips. "Me, too. Can Sarah stay for supper?"

Caleb's feet stuttered to a stop. "I don't know, Jacob. It might be too late by the time we get back." Caleb's stomach twisted into a knot. He couldn't tell his *sohn* that Sarah's bishop wouldn't allow that type of behavior from a single woman.

"Maybe another day." Jacob grabbed the bucket of worms and carried it to the buggy.

Caleb stowed their fishing poles on the floor of the buggy. "We should hurry. Sarah will be expecting us."

Sarah was ready to go with a picnic basket all packed when they pulled up in their buggy. Jacob held a bowl of cookies while Sarah climbed in and settled on the seat. "Guess what, Sarah?" Without waiting, he rushed on. "Daed and I dug worms this morning, and they are ready to go to work."

"*Gut.* I'm hoping you will show me how to fish. It has been a long time since I last held a pole and cast a hook in the water."

Jacob puffed his chest. "I'll put the worm on your hook and show you how to cast. It's easy."

Caleb nodded. "Jacob is an experienced fisherman. The last time we visited the English River, he caught two bluegills and one catfish to my one bluegill."

Jacob removed his hat and twirled it around in his hand like Caleb often did. "I'm the bestest, huh, Daed?"

"Indeed you are." Caleb parked the buggy under a tree along the bank of the river. While Sarah spread out the lunch, Caleb and Jacob found just the right spot to throw their lines in the water. They laid out their poles, tackle box and stringer.

Sarah laid a blanket on the ground and sat the picnic basket on one corner to hold it down when the breeze kicked up. She set the sandwiches, chips and salad in the center with the paper products. "Why don't you guys have a bite to eat before we start fishing?"

Caleb smiled as Jacob hurried to the blanket to sit next to Sarah. That left Caleb sitting on the opposite side, with the food in between them. But the more he brought Jacob to see Sarah, the more attached Jacob became to her. Which meant he needed to approach the subject of Sarah changing to New Order and soon. Of course that would mean he'd have to ask her to marry him. Was he truly prepared to do that?

Jacob chattered away. "Sarah, if you catch a catfish, you have to be very careful because their fins are sharp. But don't worry, I'll help you."

"*Danki.* I would really appreciate that."

"We didn't bring any minnows, only worms and bobbers." Jacob finished his last bite of sandwich. "I'll put the worm on the hook for you because it has to be done right or he can slip off and get away."

"My, you are very knowledgeable. I'm glad you are here to help me."

"Daed, can we fish now?"

Sarah gestured to the river. "Go ahead while I pack up the rest of our lunch, then I'll be right there."

Caleb opened the bucket of worms, and he and Jacob put the wiggly things on their hooks. Jacob walked down the bank and stepped on a rock by the river, then stepped farther out onto another rock. "Be careful, Jacob. The rocks will be slick."

"*Jah,* I am." Jacob's feet wobbled. His hook and line swung back and forth.

"Jacob, watch the hook," Caleb yelled as he threw down his pole and ran toward the *bu*.

Jacob reached up, grabbed the swinging hook and line, and caught the hook deep in his finger. "Ouch!"

Caleb grabbed Jacob and whirled him around to the grassy bank as Sarah ran down the slope. "Hold the pole, Sarah, while I grab the tackle box."

She dropped to her knees, put one arm around Jacob's shoulders and held the pole with the other. Caleb cut the fishing line, threw the pole on the ground and carried Jacob up the bank. "Sarah, sit and hold Jacob while I take out the hook."

"*Nein*, Daed." Jacob screamed. "It hurts too much."

Sarah's stomach turned a somersault as she sensed Jacob's pain from the tensing of his body. She held Jacob protectively and tossed Caleb a warning look.

Caleb's voice turned soothing. "Jacob, calm down and listen to me. The hook is all the way in past the barb, so I cannot pull it out the same way it went in. I need to cut off both ends, then push it through your finger. It is a small hook, so it will only go in a little ways. We have talked about this before. Will you be a big *bu* and let me work? It will only take a minute, and Sarah will help you hold your hand very still."

Jacob sniffled and tears rolled down his cheek. "Okay, but hurry."

He patted Jacob on the shoulder. "I will." He looked at Sarah. "Steady his hand."

Caleb cleaned the area with antiseptic and dried the finger. He pushed the hook through the pad of Jacob's finger, guiding it out the side while Jacob only let out a whimper. He cut off the barb and eye, then pulled the shank out with the pliers. Jacob moaned but did not move or cry. Caleb held gauze on Jacob's finger until the bleeding stopped, then cleaned the area and bandaged the fingertip.

When Caleb finished, Jacob leaned back against Sarah and sobbed.

"Jacob, you are a big *bu*." Caleb's voice was soft, yet firm.

"Caleb, I'll take care of Jacob while you pack up the buggy."

Sarah hugged Jacob close and whispered in his ear. "If you need to cry to release the pain, then you cry. That's why *Gott* gave us tears." She rubbed his back with the palm of her hand until exhaustion tackled his body and pulled him into a restless sleep. Tears filled her eyes and emotion clogged her throat. She was proud of this little man for holding perfectly still as Caleb had pushed the hook through his finger. Not many grown men would have been able to stay perfectly still and not let out a yelp. But this small *bu* proved to be as strong-willed as a man.

She blotted her tears and held this sweet little soul, wishing he were hers. It was harder each time she saw Jacob to let him go home without her. Yet she had no choice. She had planned to bring up the subject of their churches with Caleb, but now was not the time. But how could she let this frail *bu* go home? Would Mary comfort him?

Jacob tossed his head back and sobbed. "I want my *mamm*. Are you my *mamm*?"

Sarah jerked her head up and looked at Caleb as he approached. His startled eyes locked with hers. She patted Jacob's head and held it close to her. "Jacob, I am so sorry this happened. I will drive out tomorrow just to see you and spend the whole afternoon taking care of you."

Jacob's sobs quieted and his shoulders slumped in total surrender, trusting her to his care. Apparently he accepted her words as a motherly gesture.

Caleb lifted Jacob off Sarah's lap and set him in the buggy while Sarah gathered her picnic basket. After she climbed in, he stowed the basket on the floor by the seat. He tapped the reins on Snowball's back, and the horse set to work with a jerk of the buggy. "I'll take Sarah home to the bakery, Jacob. Then I'll get you home."

"*Nein*. Sarah wants to come home with me. Don't you?"

Sarah hesitated. "Is Mary home?"

Caleb shrugged. "She should be, but she might still be with her friends."

"Let's take Jacob to your house. I can tuck him into bed and sit with him for a while before you take me home."

Caleb glanced at Jacob and nodded.

The few miles to Caleb's farm seemed like an eternity. While Caleb helped Jacob into bed, Sarah heated a glass of milk for him. She tiptoed into the room and sat in the chair that Caleb had pulled next to the bed. "I'll stay with him for a while, but Mary has returned home."

"*Gut.* I'll do chores, then take you home."

She nodded but kept her gaze firmly on Jacob. When Caleb left the room, she leaned back in the chair, her pulse pounding with fear. It nearly tore a hole in her heart to see Jacob in pain.

How could she ever leave this little *bu*?

On Monday Sarah left the bakery early after instructing Hannah to close. She hitched King, treated him to a slice of apple and patted his nose. "Your legs will get a *gut* stretching today."

Caleb hurried out of the *haus* when she arrived. "Jacob's been wondering when you'd get here."

"How is he?"

"I think better than he wants to let on, but his finger looks swollen."

"*Ach.* I'll take care of that right away. His finger is probably throbbing."

Caleb held the door for Sarah as she dashed through. Mary stood at the sink and turned as she entered. "*Hullo*, Mary."

"*Hullo.*"

Sarah sprinted up the stairs and tapped lightly on Jacob's door.

"Come in," his tiny voice whispered from the other side.

She darted in, felt Jacob's forehead and examined the finger. "No fever, but I'll wrap some ice in a cloth and get that swelling down."

He jerked his hand back. "Will that hurt?"

"*Nein.* It will feel much better when the swelling is gone." She hurried to get the ice and returned in minutes. She propped his hand and gently applied the cold compress.

Jacob's eyes looked weary but he smiled. "I like it when you take care of me, Sarah. When I'm better, I'll help you with your garden."

Sarah grinned. *Jah,* the more time she spent with Jacob, the more she didn't ever want to leave his side. If the bishop found out about her two trips out here when he'd strictly forbidden it, she would surely be disciplined.

Chapter Twelve

The bell on the bakery door rang loudly in late afternoon as Jacob burst through, ran straight to Sarah and gave her a big hug. "*Danki* for coming to visit me when I hurt my finger."

"I was glad to do it. Since this is your first visit since the accident, you may pick out a special treat on me."

While Jacob searched the display case, Caleb stepped forward. "Mary's birthday is Sunday, and I was wondering if you'd make her a cake. Strawberry is her favorite. We'll have a small gathering for her in the afternoon at about four o'clock. Hannah's also invited."

"Sure, I'd be happy to do that for Mary."

"*Danki.* She won't be expecting it. Did you hear that, Jacob? It's a surprise."

"*Jah.* I won't tell."

Caleb pointed to a roll. Sarah pulled the cinnamon swirl out of the case, placed it on a plate and poured his coffee. By then Jacob had selected a Bismarck with powdered sugar on top.

When Sarah had a minute, she stole away from the

counter and sat next to Jacob. He held up his finger. "See my scar?" A little sadness edged his words.

"Oh my, that is a handsome scar, and you have a great story to tell about getting it."

Jacob looked at his finger with a proud glint in his eye.

"And it is *gut* to see that it has not hurt your appetite," she said as she glanced at his clean plate. "Caleb, King needs to have his legs stretched. Maybe I could drive out after I close and pick a few strawberries."

"After Jacob and I run a few errands, we will start home. You can pick as many as you want."

After locking up and hitching King, Sarah headed the buggy down the road toward Caleb's farm. The summer breeze twirled the strings of her prayer *kapp* and rustled the leaves on the cornstalks. The musical sound of King's hooves clip-clopping on the road, the birds singing and the bees buzzing by made the three-mile trip seem short.

The soaking rain from the day before still blanketed the ground, giving off an earthy smell. How she loved the country. She hadn't traveled outside of the Midwest and didn't want to. She couldn't imagine leaving all this behind.

When she met a farmer on a tractor pulling a wagon, she tugged the reins, maneuvering King to the far side of the road in case the vehicle's noise disturbed the horse. But it didn't. King was a well-disciplined horse.

Sarah guided the buggy into Caleb's barnyard, stopped and looked around as she stepped from her buggy. Caleb's farm was quiet. She didn't see Caleb or Jacob. Not even Tiger and her kittens were around to greet her.

She walked through the strawberry patch, hoping to find at least a few plump red fruits for Mary's cake. *Jah*. She pulled one from the plant and popped it in her mouth. *Mmm*. They would taste *wunderbaar* in Mary's birthday cake.

Ach. She'd forgotten a container for the strawberries. Mary wouldn't mind if she borrowed one. She strolled to the back porch and knocked on the door.

No answer.

She knocked again and listened for footfalls.

The breeze rustled a nearby field of grain, birds chirped and grasshoppers jumped through the grass, but silence creeped from the *haus*.

She turned the doorknob and the door swung open. "Mary. Are you home?"

Sarah stepped into the kitchen, listened, but the only sound was the ticking of a clock.

Poking her nose in the cupboards first, she looked around for a container. Only dishes sat on the shelves. She opened the pantry door and found a small empty box that was the right size stacked on top of other containers. She'd return it before Mary even noticed it was missing.

The tidiness of the *haus* caught her attention. She surrendered to curiosity and entered the living room. How did a thirteen-year-old girl manage to keep the house so clean and neat with all the other household chores?

Sarah understood how Mary missed her *mamm*. She missed hers, as well. A young woman needed a *mamm* to fuss over her, to help her prepare when she got married and to be there when she had her first *boppli*.

She strolled around the living room, looking at Martha's quilt rack, her mending and her basket of scrap material from quilting. Suddenly an idea popped into her head for a gift to give Mary for her birthday that would remind her every day of her *mamm*.

On Sunday, after preaching and the noon meal were finished, Sarah climbed into her buggy and flopped on the seat. "I had no idea that Alvin Studer and Bertha Bontrager were getting married until the banns were read today. No wonder I haven't seen the bishop or Alvin lately."

Hannah settled on the seat next to her. "You don't sound happy. I would think you would be shouting for joy." Hannah's voice rose in puzzlement.

Sarah didn't want to marry Alvin, but somehow the loss of him hit her hard. She was now envious of him, of what he had. She was happy for them, and imagined Alvin was getting ready right now, as was the custom, to ride around, inviting his family to the wedding.

"Don't be silly, Hannah." But loneliness drained Sarah's heart until it seemed as hollow as an old dead log. "I'll stop by the bakery and we can pick up the cake and mints and head out to Caleb's farm."

Sarah trotted King at an easy pace. Hannah held Mary's birthday cake on her knees and the mints she'd made sat on the seat between them.

"Don't hit a bump. I don't want to spoil your cake." Hannah shot her a warning look.

"You must be planning on a big piece. Strawberry is one of your favorites, too." Sarah tossed her a smile.

"Not this time. I decided if I were ever going to catch an *ehemann*, I'd have to lose some weight. I started my diet and have lost ten pounds so far."

"Hannah, I'm so proud of you."

Hannah smiled proudly as they pulled onto Caleb's farm.

Caleb watched the buggy approach, waited and helped them down, then escorted them into the house. "Mary, look who's here."

Caleb introduced Sarah and Hannah to his *bruder*, Peter, and his *frau*, Lillia. They greeted each other.

Mary's eyes glowed when Sarah uncovered the cake. A two-layer cake covered in frosting with strawberries and whipped cream on top.

"It's a *wunderbaar* cake and looks delicious," Mary gasped. *"Danki."*

Lillia agreed. "Looks *gut*."

Caleb smiled at Sarah and gave her a wink. "Let's set the table, and I'll get the ice cream. Sit, Mary. It's your birthday. We'll handle this."

"I want a big piece." Jacob scooted out a chair and plunked himself down.

"Of course, and I hope you try one of my mints, too." Hannah held the plate out to Jacob, smiled and nodded toward the mints.

He took a red one. "Mmm. That tastes like strawberries."

When they finished eating, Sarah pulled Mary's gift out of her bag. "Mary, this is for you. I took some of the scraps left over from your *mamm*'s leaf quilts and made a Bible cover and sewed one of her leaves on top."

Mary gasped and her face turned red. "You had no right! You took them without permission! How could you? I had plans for those scraps." She raked the legs of her chair back over the flooring as she stood, then ran out of the house, letting the screen door bang behind her.

"Daed, tell Mary she can't slam the door."

"Mind your business, Jacob. It's not your job to worry about Mary's actions."

"Jacob, I've heard a lot about Tiger and her kittens. Could I see them?" Hannah popped a mint in her mouth and stood.

He nodded, jumped off the chair and headed for the door. "You're going to *liebe* them. If you want one, I'll give it to you."

"Jacob," Caleb said stiffly.

"Okay. You don't *have* to take one." Hannah followed Jacob out the door.

"We must be going, *bruder*. Tell the *kinner* we had to leave." Peter patted Caleb on the back. "It was nice to meet you, Sarah."

Lillia gave Sarah a smile. "Don't worry, Sarah. Mary will get over it."

When the door closed, Sarah turned toward Caleb. "I'm so sorry, Caleb. They were scraps. I'd *nein* idea how badly it would hurt Mary. I thought she would like it."

"I'll talk to Mary. It was a shock. If you hadn't told her where they came from, it would have been a year before she noticed. She was very close to her *mamm,* and it hit a sensitive spot." He glanced at the door Mary had slammed. A line of worry etched across his forehead.

"I hope she doesn't think I was trying to steal the position that her *mamm* holds in her heart. That wasn't my intention."

"She'll get over it." Caleb's soothing voice wrapped around her like a hug.

Sarah stepped back. Her mouth was like a desert and all her words had dried up. She'd messed up badly.

Mary would never forgive her.

The next day, Sarah coaxed King into a faster trot as the buggy neared Caleb's farm. Drizzle changed to light rain when she turned into his drive. The wind kicked up, blowing dirt out of the fields and filling the air with a wet, muddy smell. The sky darkened with black clouds tumbling and rolling overhead. She tugged on the reins. "Whoa, King."

Caleb ran from the house and helped her down. "Go on in, and I'll put King in the barn."

She hurried up the steps and waited on the porch. She removed her cape and shook off the moisture, wishing it were that easy to shake away the mistake she'd made by taking Martha's scraps of material.

Caleb jumped the porch steps two at a time. "What brings you out here on a messy day like this?"

"I couldn't sleep a wink last night. I'm still fretting over how I hurt Mary. I saw the basket of scraps and thought she'd like the cover if it reminded her of her *mamm*. My heart is still aching over that stupid mistake."

"Don't beat yourself up, Sarah. She needs a little time to think about it. Mary would rather cook and clean than sew. I think she left the scraps sitting in the living room because they reminded her of her *mamm*, and she didn't know what else to do with them. You did nothing wrong. Someday, Mary will treasure what you did for her, but maybe not today." He shrugged.

"We talked a little when we canned, and it sounded like she was getting through grieving her *mamm*. I thought it'd be okay, but I should have asked. Can I talk to her?"

"She's in the kitchen." Caleb smiled and held the door open.

Sarah walked in slowly, as though she were a child going to the teacher for a scolding. She crossed the large room and stood by the table, propping her hip against it for support. Mary remained at the stove, cooking something that smelled like chicken and dumplings. If she heard her enter, she never acknowledged Sarah's presence.

"*Hullo*, Mary. I wanted to tell you again how sorry I am. If you want, I can pull the stitching from the cover and put the scraps back."

"That's not necessary. I thought maybe one day I'd think of something to do with them, but it's a nice cover." Mary remained facing the stove.

"When you're ready to can vegetables again, I'll be more than happy to help."

"*Danki* for the offer." Mary kept her back toward Sarah.

One thing was for sure and for certain.

Mary would never forgive her.

Chapter Thirteen

After the next preaching, Sarah hurried to disappear from Bishop Yoder's sight. She kept a brisk pace, turned the corner and headed for the door.

"Sarah." His footsteps thumped closer with each stride.

The thought of surrender had never occurred to her before, but his persistence had worn her down. She frowned, then stopped and turned around. "Bishop, did you call my name?"

"*Jah.* And after I did, it looked like your step had a livelier spring to it toward the door."

"Sorry. Thoughts preoccupied my mind. What did you need to see me about?"

"Do you know Ezra Smith?"

Exasperation sent a chill charging through her, but she shook it off. "I've seen him, but I don't really know him."

"He is a widower with two small *kinner*, and he'd like to meet you. How about tomorrow?" His rigid stance spoke volumes.

"*Nein*, Monday is not good. Tuesday is better." She started easing toward the door.

"He'll stop by the bakery, and perhaps he'll ask you on a buggy ride."

Sarah glanced over the bishop's right shoulder and noticed others gawking and seemingly edging in their direction. "I'll bake something special and look forward to meeting him."

The bishop's mouth practically hit the floor in surprise. Then he cleared his throat. "Have an enjoyable day."

"You, too, Bishop." She headed to her buggy, where Hannah waited, wearing a smile.

"What was that all about?"

"I think the bishop and I might have come to some kind of an understanding, although he doesn't know it yet."

Hannah raised a brow. "What does that mean?"

"You'll see soon enough."

Sarah guided her buggy up Caleb's driveway. The crunching of gravel under the wheels appeared to snag Caleb's attention from watering his garden. He dropped the hose and hurried to meet her.

"*Gut* mornin'. You're here early." His smile warmed her heart.

"*Jah*. Is Mary ready to can tomatoes?"

"They are already in a hot-water bath." He gave King a pat.

"*Ach*. I'm late. Canning is an all-day ordeal, so I'd better get to it." She handed him the sack of bread and cookies she had brought, latched on to his offered arm and stepped to the ground. "There's a basket with potato salad and fried chicken on the floor of the buggy. Please bring it in."

"*Danki* for helping Mary." His words tangled in the sounds of her grabbing the sack and running for the house.

Sweltering heat hit Sarah in the face as she entered the kitchen, and the smell of cooking tomatoes permeated the air. She sat her sack on the table and then stood next to Mary at the stove. Plumes of steam rose from the kettles of simmering fruit. The breeze streaming through the open window did little to cool the room.

Caleb set the basket in the propane-powered refrigerator and tossed Sarah a smile on his way out the door.

"Mornin', Mary. I'm ready to work."

"Mornin'. Sure you want to? It's really hot in here." Mary grabbed the towel slung over her shoulder and wiped the dripping perspiration from her face.

"*Jah.*" Sarah pushed up her sleeves, grabbed a spoon and started packing the mason jars Mary had already washed and sterilized.

She'd worked nearly an hour, and Mary hadn't said two words to her except what the work required. Guilt inched up Sarah's spine. It was crystal clear. Mary would never forgive her for taking the fabric scraps and making the book cover.

Beads of sweat rolled down Sarah's back. She walked to the window and stood in front of the breeze for several minutes.

Mary looked at her and smiled. "Hot?"

"*Jah.*"

"Me, too."

At four o'clock, the jars filled, Sarah helped Mary clean the kitchen. "I'm exhausted." She tidied her dress, wiped off splatters, and washed her face and hands. "Let me know when more tomatoes are ready to can."

"*Danki* for your help." Mary's no-nonsense attitude made it plain she'd tolerate her presence, but she'd no longer confide in her.

Sarah pulled her potato salad and chicken out of the refrigerator and placed them on the table next to Mary's marinated, sliced red tomatoes and a loaf of bread. While she set the plates and silverware on the table, Mary rang the dinner bell.

Judging from the silence at the table and the small amount of food on the plates, it was too uncomfortable to eat in a sweltering-hot kitchen. Jacob picked at his chicken and barely touched his potato salad. "Jacob, do you like the dinner?"

"I'm too hot to eat. Since you canned tomatoes with Mary, can you help me with the garden?" Jacob puffed out his lower lip. "You never help me."

"Jacob." Caleb's firm tone held a warning.

Jacob kicked the chair. "It's not fair! She never comes to help me anymore!" He jumped off the chair and ran out the kitchen's screen door, letting it bang twice before it shut.

"Jacob, get back here," Caleb bellowed. Jacob sidled up to the door. "Apologize to Sarah right now."

His chin almost touched his chest, but his brooding gray eyes peered up. "I'm sorry, Sarah." He ran down the porch steps and headed across the lawn.

Sarah followed him out the door. Jacob was right. She'd spent a lot of time with Mary, but she couldn't spend much more time at Caleb's farm or someone would find out and tell the bishop. "Jacob, wait."

"That's okay." But his shaky voice told her it wasn't.

* * *

Caleb laid a warm and soothing hand on her shoulder. "He'll get over it. We'll think of some way you can spend time with him." He winked. "I'll hitch King up for you."

Sarah blew out a heavy breath. "Tell Jacob I'll help him next time."

As he tightened the girth around King, a worry hovered in the back of his mind. Eventually the bishop would hear of her visits to his farm. *Nein*, they had to think of other ways to spend time together, and Sarah would have to quit helping Mary.

Caleb waited in the driveway with the buggy.

Her steps were slow but sure to where he waited. He took her basket and set it on the seat. "You look tired."

"*Jah*. The heat and the canning sapped my energy." A moment of silence settled between them as they watched a few robins scamper around, looking for their supper.

"I'll stop by one day this week." He backed away from the buggy.

"That'll be nice." The breeze picked up and snapped the tie strings to her prayer *kapp*. "Sure, now the wind blows, when we're *done* canning."

Caleb laughed. "Sounds like you think the breeze schemed against you and Mary while you canned."

She chuckled. "I didn't mean it quite like that." Sarah stepped into the buggy. "Caleb, I have something I need to tell you. Because of the incident with Alvin, I need to explain so there's no misunderstanding." Sarah let her gaze fall on his shirt. She lifted her chin and her eyes clouded with a mist.

"What's up?" Uneasiness tugged at his nerves. Was something said when he left the kitchen?

"The bishop donned his matchmaking hat again. He wants me to spend time with Ezra Smith. He is a widower with two *kinner*. I have no desire to marry him, but I wanted to show the bishop that I believe in supporting my community."

The smile slid from his face. His heart dropped to his feet. He froze. He stared at her. Gott, *You took away Martha and now You're taking away Sarah.*

"I must trust *Gott* to guide my heart and my head, but know that this is only to appease the bishop."

He fought to find his voice. "*Jah*, I understand." His voice cracked. "It's hard when your religion is based on community. You must decide what is right for you, but I will miss your company."

"Please let me know when Mary is ready to do more canning. She's still young and should have help with such things."

"*Danki* for your thoughtfulness, Sarah."

He held out his hand to her. She grasped it and squeezed. When he took it away, it was as if a cool breeze had swept over his heart. He would miss her warm touch.

Caleb watched as Sarah's buggy drove away, kicking up dust that swirled around and drifted away. His chest ached as if she'd torn his heart out, wadded it up and tossed it into that dust cloud. He gulped a deep breath of air. The strength drained from his body. He tried to take a step, but couldn't. Not yet. Not until she was out of sight. It was silly the way his insides did somersaults whenever she was near and felt like a hollowed-out log when she left.

Jah, he needed to get a moment alone with Sarah and

ask her if she would change to the New Order. Then he'd know what to do next.

The first of July, but he felt like it was January in Iowa and it was twenty below zero.

Sarah rose early to get a head start on baking. She paused for a moment to review Thursday's list. Yesterday, for the first time, the bakery had sold out of baked goods. She mixed up the yeast rolls, increased the recipe to make three dozen more, covered the bowl and set it aside.

Footfalls across the bakery shop's floor soon found their way to the kitchen. Hannah plopped her hip against the table. "I was practically up all night, helping Mamm and Daed pack for their trip to Missouri. Thanks for starting the baking on your own. I'll work hard to make up for being late."

"Gut." Sarah pointed at the list. "You can bake the cookies. I promised the bishop to make something special for Ezra's visit." Hannah nodded and headed to her work area.

Sarah mentally reviewed the recipes while she loaded her arms with the ingredients to make apple fritters and an apple strudel. Men had a hard time resisting fritters and strudel. She dumped it all on her workspace, then fetched the ten-pound bag of apples and set it on the sink.

While Hannah started the cookies, Sarah peeled, cored and diced apples. She stirred up the strudel, added part of the apples and popped it in the oven. She made the fritter batter with the remaining apples. After grabbing a pan from the rack, she heated the oil and dropped the fritters in until they were golden brown. After they cooled, she drizzled a glaze over top.

Midmorning, the bakery door opened and Ezra Smith timidly entered and gave her a shy nod. He wandered casually in front of the display case as if trying to make a decision, and every so often glanced her way.

She smiled at his attempt to make this visit look casual. "*Gut* mornin', Ezra. *Welkum.*"

Hannah peeked around the doorway but disappeared back into the kitchen.

"It all looks *gut*, but I will take an apple fritter and a cup of coffee." He paused. "And two of the chocolate-frosted cake donuts to take home."

Sarah handed him the sack of donuts. She placed a fritter on a plate and a sugar cookie on another, poured two cups of coffee, and set it all on a tray. She led the way to a table and set her coffee and cookie across from him. "I'll keep you company, if you don't mind."

Ezra pulled out a chair for her and one for him. He slid his hat on the empty seat nearby.

Sarah sipped her coffee and settled back in the chair. Ezra had a handsome face with a wide jaw, but it gave him character. His sandy-colored hair looked *gut* with his sun-bronzed face.

"This is a delicious fritter, Sarah. Did you make it?"

"*Jah. Danki.*" She folded her hands in her lap.

He nodded to her plate. "*Datt*'s a cute sugar cookie in the shape of a dog." Ezra's eyes sparkled and little crinkles etched around them when he laughed.

"Hannah likes them. She's my assistant. It reminds her of her dog, Mint-Candy."

He chuckled. "*Datt*'s a funny name for a dog."

"When you see Hannah, ask her how he got his name."

"My *kinner* are home with my sister." He pointed to a sugar cookie. "They would like your bakery very much."

"*Jah.* Most *kinner* do."

He propped an elbow on the table and leaned closer to her. "My large farm keeps me busy growing vegetables to sell at the canneries and at auction. I also raise hogs and cattle. If I have more *sohns*, I could buy more land and expand my produce. Then the farm would be large enough to support more than one family."

Ezra smiled shyly. "I hope to find a woman who shares my interests."

The heat burned on her cheeks. She glanced down at the table instead of into his deep brown eyes.

"Ah, Sarah, don't blush. We are friends, talking. *Jah?*" His voice was smooth as whipped cream.

Ezra had shared his hopes and dreams already, unlike Caleb, who often drove her the three miles from his farm to town and hardly said two words to her. She already knew what Ezra wanted but hadn't yet discovered what Caleb saw for his future.

In all fairness, though, Caleb was a typical farmer, who drove slowly, gawking at his neighbors' fields and comparing them to his own. He measured his farm's growing progress during the season against other farms around his. Ezra might do the same, but he also communicated well.

"Sarah?"

"Sorry. I was thinking about how much work you do. *Danki* for stopping in today."

He smiled. "Even a farmer has to take time off. That

gives me an idea. Tomorrow, I'm taking my *kinner* to the Washington County Fair. I'd like for you to join us."

She'd never been to a fair before. Daed would grumble he was too busy for that kind of nonsense. She'd known others who visited the fair and raved about all the fun they had. "I'd like that very much, Ezra." Then a twinge of regret pierced her, but it was too late to take her answer back.

"See you at nine tomorrow morning, and wear comfortable shoes." He grabbed his hat from the chair and flashed a broad smile before he nodded goodbye and walked out the bakery door.

Chapter Fourteen

Friday dawned with a cloudless blue sky, giving Sarah the inspiration to pack a light lunch for a picnic at the fair. At five minutes to nine o'clock, she carried her bag out to the porch and sat on the step to wait. The rented vehicle and driver arrived on time. Ezra opened the back door, and she slid in next to a couple of sandy-haired cuties who were the spitting image of their *daed*.

Ezra hopped back in the front of the SUV next to the driver, turned around and looked at his *kinner*. "This is Beth and David." He tilted his head toward Sarah. "This is Sarah Gingerich."

She smiled. "Nice to meet you both."

"Miss Sarah, are you excited about going to the fair?" Beth's amber eyes sparkled as she spoke.

"Very much so. I've never attended the fair before." She pressed a hand to her stomach to stop the fluttering of a giant butterfly.

"Really?" Ezra said. "Your folks never took you?"

"*Nein*. They were always too busy in the bakery."

"You'll have a *gut* time. I'm glad I'm the one who gets to show it to you," Ezra said.

Sarah swallowed a sigh. Was he getting interested in her already? Had she misled him?

Ezra talked to her for a while, then started talking to the driver about farming. The *kinner* acted as if they had forgotten she was there and started discussing what they wanted to do and see first at the fair. She relaxed in her seat and enjoyed the scenery for the twenty-minute drive to the fairgrounds.

They stepped out of the SUV, and Ezra arranged a time for the driver to pick them up. He swung his arm with a sweeping movement toward the midway. "Sarah, the fun awaits you." Ezra stayed close beside her as the *kinner* walked ahead. After a short distance, the *kinner* stopped to look at a game of chance, but Ezra motioned them along.

When they came to the cotton candy vendor, David gave Ezra a puppy-dog look. "Daed, please, can we have some?"

Ezra paid and the man handed David and Beth each a stick of what looked like swirls of spun cotton wrapped around it. He held a stick out to Sarah. She shook her head. "I've never eaten it before. I don't know if I'd like it."

Ezra took the stick. "You've never had cotton candy? Now's your chance. We'll share." He grabbed a hunk, and pulled it off. "See, like this," he said, and stuffed it in his mouth. "Your turn."

She pulled off a small, sticky amount and stuck it in her mouth. "Oh. It's delicious and practically melts in your mouth." She smiled. "That was fun to eat. What is it?"

"Spun sugar." Ezra's tongue had a tinge of blue coloring. "Whenever we go to the fair, we buy it. It's a once-a-year treat."

Sarah ate a couple more bites. "That's really sweet. Think I'd better quit eating, or I'll get sick."

"Let's keep moving." Ezra started walking down the midway, nibbling the cotton candy until they reached the end of the road. "Let's head to the barns and see if the judging is over."

He offered Sarah the last bite of cotton candy. She shook her head.

He popped the rest in his mouth and threw the stick into a garbage barrel sitting along the midway.

Sarah walked alongside Ezra as they entered the first barn and sauntered over to a pigpen. She wrinkled her nose at the barn's odor and swatted at a fly that buzzed near her face.

Ezra leaned over a fence. "The fair judge looks for leanness and muscling." He pointed to the hog and glanced at Sarah and David. "The back-fat depth of a show hog is ideally less than for a commercial hog." He patted the animal. "They want to see deep loin muscle."

Ezra explained the strict regimen it took to raise the animals. His *kinner* nodded. David asked a couple of questions and Ezra patiently answered. Sarah smiled as she listened to him teach his *bu*. He was a good *daed*, a kind man, and he'd make some woman a *wunderbaar ehemann*. She just wasn't sure that woman was her.

Sarah watched a couple of *buwe* who she guessed hadn't shown their animals yet. They scrubbed the hogs with a brush and water, rinsed and repeated. When water splashed her way, she stepped back and onto the foot of the person standing directly behind her.

She whirled around, swishing her hands over her

dress to brush the water off. "I'm so sorry. I didn't know…" She stopped in her tracks and gazed into Caleb's eyes.

Caleb's gut clenched as he gawked at Sarah, and Ezra Smith standing next to her. The shock of seeing them together sent his heart racing until he gained control.

Ezra held out his hand. "Nice to see you, Caleb. Are you enjoying the fair?"

He swallowed hard. "*Jah*. Very much." *Until now.*

"Why didn't you come to the fair with us?" Jacob ran to Sarah and hugged her.

"She is with another friend, Jacob." Caleb gently pulled his *sohn* to his side.

"But Daed…"

"Hush, Jacob. Adults are talking." Jacob pressed his lips in a straight line.

Ezra's gaze bounced from Caleb to Sarah. "Do you two know each other?"

Caleb noticed the blush rising on Sarah's cheeks. "*Jah*, from the bakery. Mornin', Sarah."

"She's a *wunderbaar* baker." Ezra smiled down at Sarah with a twinkle in his eye.

"*Jah*, she is indeed. I promised Jacob and Mary we'd head to the horse barn next. Have a *gut* time at the fair, Sarah."

Mary glanced from Sarah to Ezra, turned to Caleb and raised a questioning brow.

"But Daed, I want to stay with Sarah."

"Sorry, Jacob, but we have a tight schedule to keep before our driver returns." He gave a firm tug on Jacob's arm and headed toward the horse barn. When they were finally out of sight, he released Jacob's arm.

"Why didn't we ask Sarah to come with us to the fair?" Jacob sniffled. "I want her to have fun with us."

"I'm sorry. I didn't think of it." Sarah had been honest with him. Yet he hadn't imagined seeing them together would hurt so much, as though a bull were goring him and ripping his heart out. He gulped a breath of air.

He hurried his *kinner* along until they were safely in the horse barn. They visited every stall. Usually, this was the best part of the fair for Caleb, but today the joy of the judging had gone flat, like a popped bubble. "It's getting late. We need to move on."

They entered the 4-H building and walked around, viewing the project winners of horticulture, gardening, crafts and baking. Ugh. The cakes reminded Caleb of Sarah and all the memories they'd made together. Heat crept up his neck and onto his cheeks. His face burned at the thought…of her…with Ezra.

Caleb put a hand on Jacob's back and tried to push him along. The *bu* sulked, with his arms crossed in front, and dragged his feet in the dirt as he walked. Occasionally, he'd kick a rock or stick in his path. He'd let Jacob down. "Jacob, how about some saltwater taffy? *Jah?*"

A smile played at the corners of the *bu*'s mouth as if he might be fighting it, but the charm of the soft, tasty candy was too much to resist.

He allowed Jacob to select the flavor—a bag of assortments: vanilla, banana, peppermint, strawberry, orange and licorice. After he paid, Caleb whirled around just in time to catch a glimpse of Ezra and Sarah heading their way. He quickly steered Jacob and Mary in the opposite direction. His heart was shredded to pieces.

When they neared a food stand, his stomach growled

at the greasy aroma. "How about a burger and some lemonade?" Mary nodded and Jacob's smile reached from ear to ear.

Caleb took a bite of his burger, but could barely get it down. He had little appetite, but Jacob seemed to have completely forgotten about Sarah. He wished he could do the same.

He glanced at his pocket watch and relief washed over him. "It's time to meet our driver." Weaving through the crowd on the midway, Caleb led the way around people entering through the front gate as they maneuvered to get out.

On the way home in the car, he heard Mary and Jacob in the back seat, crinkling the saltwater taffy paper and reminiscing about the fair with candy stuffed in their mouths, muffling their speech. The driver had his country music station cranked up, listening to the top one hundred songs in the country. *Danki, Lord.* The loud music meant he didn't have to hold a conversation. That suited Caleb just fine. His heart was still turning cartwheels at the sight of Sarah and Ezra together.

If he couldn't offer her a proposal of marriage, he had to step aside. Yet losing her gnawed at the edges of his soul.

When they finally arrived back at the farm, the *kinner* raced for the house, and Caleb traipsed to the barn to do chores. As he started preparations for milking, Tiger and her kittens scurried around underfoot.

"Shoo, Tiger. You're not getting any milk." He waved his hand in a swishing movement. They scattered, no doubt sensing the agitation brewing in his gut.

Lord, why did You put Sarah in my life if You were only going to take her away again? He didn't know what his future held, but it appeared that Sarah wasn't part of God's plan for his life.

The next morning, Caleb forced himself awake from a nightmare he was having about losing Sarah. He jumped out of bed, ate and stayed busy weeding vegetables, repairing farm equipment and preparing his numb heart for a life without Sarah. When he finished his chores, he hung the tools on a hook in the barn and headed for the house. He stopped and gazed around the farm, at the *haus*, barn, garden and out across the field. This was his world, and he'd started envisioning Sarah sitting with him on the porch in a rocker someday, sipping lemonade and making plans for the future. A lump lodged in his throat.

He tromped across the grass, toward the porch.

He glanced over his shoulder at Tiger and her kittens following behind.

Jacob ran out of the house and skidded to a stop in front of him. "Daed, when is Sarah coming to visit again? I want to show her how much the kittens have grown."

"Sarah is very busy running her bakery."

Jacob's eyes widened and a smile stretched across his mouth and lit up his face. "*Jah.* Can we go to Kalona and visit her? I'd like a brownie."

"I'm busy today—maybe another day."

The happy glow slid from Jacob's face. He crossed the barnyard, his shoulders slumped and the cats parading behind him all the way to the barn.

He hated to disappoint Jacob again, but he couldn't face Sarah just yet. What would he say to her?

As he reached the house, he felt guilty that he hadn't

asked Sarah to the fair, and likewise that he'd refused to take Jacob to see his friend.

Maybe a cupcake would taste *gut* right about now…

Sarah peered up as the door opened, sending a blast of warm air throughout the bakery. "*Ach*, it's *gut* to see you all."

Ezra and his two *kinner* strolled to the counter. He motioned to the baked goods. "You can have one treat each."

They each pointed to a cookie and Sarah placed them in separate bags. She handed David the chocolate chip and Beth the sugar cookie.

Hannah teased the *kinner* by holding out a tray of candy to them. They looked at their *daed* frowning at them, then back at Hannah and shook their heads.

When Ezra wasn't looking, Hannah took two pieces of candy and plopped one in each of their sacks. "Would you like a glass of fresh lemonade to drink at the table?" she asked loudly, to cover the sound of rustling sacks.

They smiled and nodded.

Sarah got a kick out of watching her friend interact with the *kinner*. She'd make a *wunderbaar mamm*. Hopefully, someday, a *gut* man would sweep Hannah off her feet.

"I think I can get two more cookies to go along with the drinks," Hannah whispered.

David's eyes widened.

Ezra stood at the opposite end of the display case, looking at the pie, but kept stealing glances at Hannah. He looked up at Sarah and pointed to a piece of cherry pie. "And a glass of lemonade."

"Have a seat. I'll bring it to the table." Sarah cut a

slice of pie and fixed a plate of assorted cookies while Hannah put five glasses of lemonade on a tray. They carried the refreshments to the table for a much-deserved break.

When Sarah finished her lemonade, she walked toward the open window. "The breeze feels like a kiss of fall. I could stand here all day."

When the *kinner* were finished, Hannah coaxed them to the counter to try cookie samples.

"Ezra." Sarah brushed the crumbs from her cookie onto her napkin and placed it in her empty paper cup. "I'm sorry, but I only want a platonic relationship."

He looked away, then back at her. "*Jah.* Okay."

Ezra didn't seem too upset. Maybe that explained his stolen looks at her friend. Hannah was a lovely woman.

The sound of hooves on the pavement drew Sarah's attention to a buggy pulling up out front. "Time for us to get back to work. Have a *gut* day, Ezra."

"*Jah.* You, too." His *kinner* followed Ezra out the door just as an older Amish couple entered.

Sarah waited on the customers. When they left, she started to clean up while Hannah packaged day-old cookies a dozen to a bag. "You didn't even snitch a cookie to eat."

"*Nein.*" Hannah shook her head. "I'm faithful to my diet. I've lost twenty pounds and two dress sizes, and plan to lose twenty more."

"I think Ezra noticed. He was stealing glances at you."

"*Nein.* He's here to see you."

"We are only friends. I've made that very clear to him."

"You didn't do that with Alvin."

"Alvin was different. I don't think it would have made any difference with him. But Ezra is a kind man, with sweet *kinner*."

The door burst open and Jacob ran in ahead of Caleb and Mary. He enveloped Sarah in a hug, then Hannah. "Why don't you come out to the farm anymore? Tiger and her kittens miss you."

"I bet the kittens are getting big." She measured out a distance with her hands.

He shook his head. "Bigger."

"Jacob." Caleb flashed his warning expression. Apparently he wasn't supposed to have asked her to visit.

The *bu* nodded, then scampered to the front of the display case. "Tiger is teaching them to be *gut* mousers like her."

"Ah. *Datt* is *wunderbaar*," Hannah chimed in.

Caleb quietly browsed the display case, his back stiff and his shoulders squared. *Jah*, Jacob must have pestered him to come.

"Everything smells so *gut*." Jacob looked around and his eyes locked onto his favorite. "Mmm. Chocolate chip cookies."

"I will get you all a cookie and lemonade." Hannah filled plastic cups with the ice-cold beverage and dotted a plate with an assortment of cookies.

Sarah meandered over by Mary. "Let me know when you're ready to can again, and I'll help."

"*Danki* but Aent Lillia said she'd help me next time." Mary kept her gaze focused on the shelves of sweets.

"That's nice." Only, Sarah wanted to be the one to help her. She was hurt by the rejection, but a thought occurred to her. Maybe Caleb felt rejected when he saw her with Ezra at the fair, and that was the reason for his standoffish attitude.

Hannah set the tray with the lemonade on a table. The *kinner* sat down and each took a cookie.

Sarah waited while Caleb stared at the baked goods, but the silence stretched into awkwardness. *Jah*, his feelings must be hurt. She'd tried to spare him by telling him about Ezra, but obviously she'd handled that badly. She shouldn't have gone to the fair with Ezra and his *kinner*.

"The cinnamon-raisin bread looks *gut*." His words almost sounded like he choked them out.

"It is. Very *gut*. Hannah made it."

He lifted his eyes and met her gaze. She leaned over the counter. "Caleb, I'm sorry if I made things difficult between us. I told you the bishop had his matchmaking hat on. Ezra and I are just friends." The thought of sitting next to Caleb in the buggy flashed through her mind, followed by the horrific idea that if he believed their relationship was threatened, he might abandon it.

Caleb shuffled his feet a step closer to the counter and swiped a hand down his beard. "Sarah, I understand. You *should* accept invitations. We don't have a commitment. When I saw you there with Ezra, it took me by surprise, that's all. I hadn't planned to bump into you at the fair."

She walked around the counter and stood next to him. Her heart drummed wildly in her chest at his nearness.

He stammered. "Sarah, would you like to attend Sunday school again with me sometime?"

"*Jah*. I look forward to going."

Chapter Fifteen

The bakery door opened, interrupting Sarah's scrubbing of the display case. *Ach*, it was almost closing and the few remaining baked goods were in the cooler. She raised her shoulders and gasped when she saw her brother. "Turner, why the serious face? Something wrong?"

"Come sit with me. I need to talk to you." He scrubbed his hands over his face before facing Sarah. "I hate to do this."

"What is it?" She sensed something dreadful had happened. "Is it Aent Emma?" She'd already had one heart attack.

He leaned forward in his chair, shook his head solemnly, braced his elbows on the table and intertwined his fingers together under his chin.

"Is this about Caleb Brenneman?" Fear seized her heart.

"Nein." Turner dropped both hands so they hit the table palms down and made a loud thud. "Sarah, I've sold the bakery, all the contents and the name. I've

signed the purchase agreement and will sign final papers next week, in the lawyer's office."

Her mouth dropped open, and a loud cry escaped before her hand covered her mouth. A cold numbness slowly consumed her body.

When the shock subsided, she lowered her hand. "I can't believe you sold the bakery out from under me." Sweat clung to her palms.

"I didn't want to. But Naomi is pregnant and the apartment above the woodworking shop is dusty, noisy and no place to raise a *boppli*. The money from the sale of the bakery will go toward building a house. This old bakery and structure won't bring much, probably just enough to build a small, modest *haus*."

"Then why sell it when you know it means so much to me? I have to support myself. You're putting me out on the street."

"I thought you and Ezra Smith were getting married. People saw you at the fair together. You missed your chance with Alvin."

"Unbelievable," Sarah snapped at him. "Do you *liebe* Naomi?"

"Of course I do. What does that have to do with this?"

"You and Naomi are madly in *liebe* with each other. But you thought I should marry Alvin, a man I dislike, and take care of him, his *haus* and his six *kinner*."

"You would have grown to *liebe* him like Mamm and Daed. Theirs was an arranged marriage."

She gasped. "How long do I have before I have to move out?"

"You have thirty days from next Monday."

"Is he buying all of the ovens and the pans that Mamm and Daed originally had in the bakery?"

"*Jah.* You should have them and the shop all cleaned by his possession date."

"I'll let you know when I'm moving." She pushed her chair away from the table, her eyes averted from Turner, and stomped to the door. "*Danki* for giving me notice, Turner. Now please leave. I have a lot of thinking, planning and packing to do."

"Listen, Sarah." He made his way to the front door. "Don't be so huffy. It's time you remarried anyway."

"You don't have the right to tell me when to get remarried and neither does the bishop. Was this his idea?"

"Of course not. He had nothing to do with this. Our faith requires that a woman think about her family, church and community before herself."

"*Danki* for the reminder. I know the sacrifice women must make, Turner. I'll tell you right now, I'm not marrying a man I don't *liebe* or care for just to have a roof over my head. Please leave. I have things to do."

She locked the door, turned out the lights in the front and made her wobbly legs carry her to the back of the bakery. Hannah stood in the middle of the kitchen floor, her mouth open and tears rolling down her cheeks. Sarah rushed into her friend's waiting arms.

Hannah rubbed her back soothingly. "What are you going to do? You can come and stay at our farm. Mamm and Daed would love to have you."

Sarah stepped back and wiped the tears from her cheeks. "I need to think about it. I'm going to be open for a couple more days to say goodbye to our customers. They have been faithful, and I want to thank them. Go home, Hannah. We'll talk tomorrow. I'm exhausted and my heart is ripped in two. I can't even think right now."

The pity in Hannah's eyes sliced through her every bit as much as Turner's words. Sarah was grateful that he had let her live here and operate the bakery as long as she had. She just hadn't prepared herself for the day he exercised his right to sell.

Wandering throughout the bakery, Sarah swiped her hand across the stove, touched the counters and cabinets. She caressed the Best Bakery wall plaque with her fingertips. Daed had received it from the town for giving away baked goods to charity. Sarah remembered all the fun her family had had here. Not just work, but laughing and talking about the future. Her chest swelled with pain.

Since she was a small girl, she'd watched her parents work in the bakery. The recipes never existed on paper, to avoid theft. They'd taught Sarah each recipe, and she had tucked them away in her memory. The Amish Sweet Delights bakery was a favorite tourist attraction in the Kalona area. Now all that her parents had worked for was gone.

She tried to drink in all the memories. How had the new owner seen inside the bakery? Had he come in and bought something? Turner had a key. He must have let him in when she'd closed for the night. Would Turner have done that?

Jah, he must have.

She crossed her arms in front of her and stared out the window, into the darkening sky, into the unknown. What did Daed constantly quip when she'd fallen and skinned a knee? *Buck up, you're tougher than that, tochter.*

Nein home and *nein* prospect of a job kept spinning around in her head. She had some money saved up. Turner hadn't charged her rent, so her savings had grown into a tidy sum, and she had money from the sale of her and Samuel's small *haus*.

The queasiness in her stomach overwhelmed her for a moment. Maybe she'd hook up King and take a drive in the country to clear her head.

She knew the Amish custom—girls married, the older boys were given money to start a business and the youngest boy inherited the property. In her family's case, Turner had been the only *sohn*. She just never thought he'd sell the bakery out from under her. Not Mamm and Daed's bakery. The bakery was part of her soul like a family homestead.

It was hard to believe that her *bruder* actually expected her to marry someone she didn't *liebe*.

Sarah drew in a deep breath, locked the back door and trudged up the stairs to her apartment. To make a plan…for her future.

After Daed's death, she unquestioningly took over managing the bakery. She wandered over to her sitting room window, laid her hand over the back of Daed's rocker and gave it a push. He often rocked in the chair when he had a problem to ponder. She smoothed the back of her skirt as she sat in the chair.

What was she going to do? There was an empty building in Kalona, next to the Knit 'n' Sew shop. She could call the Realtor and ask to walk through it. To open a new shop in town meant competing with her old bakery. Since Amish Sweet Delights was in the Kalona tourism guide, they would get most of the tourist business. The town only redid the guidebooks every few years. Could she even compete with Amish Sweet Delights? She usually talked to Turner when she had a problem. Not this time.

She changed into a fresh dress, hitched King to her buggy and headed for the country. To clear her mind and, like Daed would say, reseed. She had to move on, figure out where to go, what to do next…for the rest of her life.

Caleb opened the door. "What a delightful surprise, Sarah. Come in."

"*Nein.* Would you mind coming out and sitting on your porch so we can talk privately?"

He closed the door and escorted her to the porch swing he'd made. "Something wrong?"

She filled him in on Turner's visit and the sale of the bakery. "Turner had the right," she emphasized. Her voice broke twice but she made it through telling him about their conversation.

He wrapped his arm around her shoulders and squeezed. "What are your plans? Where will you live?"

"Hannah said I could stay with her and her folks."

"You're a *wunderbaar* baker. You could work for someone else, maybe even the new owner."

"*Nein.* I won't do that."

"Okay. I understand. Rent a shop or buy a building and start a new bakery?"

"If I opened a regular bakery, the commercial ovens each would cost between five and twenty thousand. I would also need a cooler and display case." Her hands fidgeted in her lap and pulled at a loose thread in the hem of her apron. "Guess I'm scared of failing."

"Everyone loves your baking."

"*Jah*, but I'd have to compete with Amish Sweet Delights. Turner sold the name, along with the bakery and its contents. Therefore, my bakery reputation will not follow me. My local customers may come back. Tourism creates a huge boost to sales. But the tourists visit the bakery listed in the tour books and brochures. The town only updates and reprints the tourism books every few years."

He turned toward her as much as he could in the swing. "I can help you hunt for a *haus* or shop and lend you money."

"*Danki.* But I don't need your money. I just wanted to get out of the bakery and think. We're open Monday and Tuesday, maybe Wednesday. I want to say goodbye to our loyal customers."

"If you start your own business, I know you'll succeed." He covered her hand with his and squeezed.

"*Danki* for the encouragement." A weak smile tugged at her mouth.

Caleb couldn't imagine a *bruder* doing that to his unmarried sister, even if he did have the right. He couldn't ask Sarah to marry him. At least not yet.

Something about this woman brought out his protective nature. But what else could he do to help Sarah?

Sarah gazed out over Caleb's farm and drew a deep breath. She'd bared her soul to this man. He was a sweetheart to listen while she unloaded her burden. His encouragement, his strength and his confidence seeped through her. Uplifted her.

She hoped he hadn't judged Turner. He was her *bruder,* and she would *liebe* him according to *Gott*'s will. She understood that property went to the youngest male of the family. The bakery was his to do with as he wished. She would not harbor ill thoughts of him.

Caleb was a safe refuge while *Gott* was letting her wander. She blotted a tear in the corner of her eye with her fingertip. Like Moses in the desert, she had to figure out what *Gott*'s will was for her life.

"What do you think you will do?" She could sense Caleb measuring his words. Was an idea going through his head? Maybe a marriage proposal. *Nein*, he wasn't ready for a commitment yet.

"I'm thinking about renting a *haus* in Kalona and putting in a home bakery. I reviewed the laws, and it is fortunate that I live in Iowa. It is one of the few states that allow home bakeries. I'm just limited to the amount the home bakery can earn. Still, I can gauge if I'll get enough business to open a bakery here in town." She rested her head on Caleb's arm, lying over the back of the swing.

Caleb tapped her arm. "What would you call a new bakery?"

She leveled her gaze at him and tried to smile. The idea appealed to her the more she talked about it. "I hadn't really thought about it—maybe Sweet Daed's."

"I like it." His sage-green eyes sparkled as he nodded.

They swung back and forth in silence a few minutes. Her heart swelled with *liebe* and appreciation for Caleb. He was a *gut* soul mate, with a listening ear. He sprinkled in just the right amount of advice and sweetened it with encouragement. His arm wrapped her in warmth, while his strength penetrated deep into her heart and spirit.

She let out a long sigh. *It's in* Gott's *hands. He ap-*

parently has a new direction for my life. Straightening her back, she lifted her chin. After the shock of Samuel's death and Turner selling the bakery, she had never been more ready to get on with her life than now.

Chapter Sixteen

Monday dawned with a brilliant sun forcing its way through angry gray clouds. Sarah took that as an encouraging reminder from *Gott* that He can do great things. She wiped the bakery's chalkboard clean and wrote a notice along with the daily special.

> Bakery sold. New owner to take over Amish Sweet Delights on September 1. Today through Wednesday, FREE coffee with the purchase of any one item.

She unlocked the door and flipped the sign to Open.

Within minutes, the first customer entered and stood in front of the sign. "I'll miss your bakery, and my husband will miss your cinnamon rolls. He takes one every day to work and eats it on break."

"*Danki.* I'm sad about leaving, but Turner owned the bakery and decided to sell."

Later in the morning, she overheard a couple of jean-clad customers grumbling about Turner selling the shop out from under her. *Jah*, the gossip had started. She pretended not to hear but could detect the mood in the bakery had turned somber.

She pasted on a smile. By noon, it became harder to mask her breaking heart. When the doorbell jingled, Caleb's gaze met hers. His wink of encouragement and his smiling face boosted her morale and warmed her spirit.

Jacob followed close behind his *daed* and hugged her with tear-filled eyes. "Daed said you sold the bakery and this was your last week. I can't come to see you anymore or work for you?" His voice quivered.

"Of course you can. I just won't be here, in *this* shop. When I move, I will need your help."

"Where will you be?"

She glanced up and noticed the patrons at the tables were watching her and undoubtedly listening to their conversation. "I'll let you know when I move. I have a surprise for you," she whispered. "You can have anything in the bakery. It's on the house."

"What does that mean?" he whispered back.

"It's free because you are my special friend. Your *daed* can have a free cup of coffee if he buys something." She glanced at Caleb.

He raised an eyebrow. "I'm not a special friend?"

She smiled.

Caleb pointed to a cinnamon roll. "How are you doing? Have you made plans yet?"

Sarah pulled the roll out of the case, placed it on a plate and poured his coffee. "*Jah.* I'll spend the next week here cleaning and getting it ready for the new owner. After that, I'm moving into a *haus* I've rented here in town and will start a small bakery. The drawback is a home bakery can only earn twenty thousand dollars a year." She flashed him a broad smile. "I was hoping you'd help me move."

"*Jah*, just let me know when."

She squared her shoulders. "There's a peace in me that *Gott* is leading me down a different road and into a new chapter of my life. Strangely, when I updated the bakery chalkboard this morning, a thread of excitement wove through my veins about this new journey. I'm actually getting anxious to see where His Spirit leads me. I thought *Gott* had abandoned me. But maybe He waited until He'd softened my heart and curbed my stubbornness before I could take the next step in my life."

A little guilt tugged at his gut. After Sarah settled into her *haus*, he needed to approach her about changing to New Order. Now she had enough dealing with the bakery. He didn't want to upset her with another big change. Not just yet, anyway.

Sarah waited on everyone in line at the counter. When she snagged a break, she wandered to the tables with the carafe of coffee, refilled cups and sat by Jacob and Caleb for a minute.

Jacob threw his arms around Sarah. "Don't move too far away, please. I will miss you too much." Moisture pooled in the corner of his eye.

Sarah held him tightly. It was her worst fear that she'd have to leave Jacob when she couldn't find a vacant shop. "I'm renting a *haus* in Kalona so I'll be nearby," she whispered. His body stopped trembling. He relaxed his shoulders and blinked back a tear.

"Can I help you pack?" His tiny voice quivered.

"Of course. Hannah and I could use your strong arms."

Jacob held his right arm up, bent it at the elbow and flexed his bicep.

"Wow," Hannah gasped as she approached from the kitchen door. "You are strong."

Jacob laughed and nodded as he put his arm down. "I do a lot of farm work."

"I have some business in town on Saturday. I'll drop Jacob off in the morning," Caleb offered.

When the doorbell sprung to life, she headed back to the counter, and Caleb and Jacob waved on their way out the door. A pang of sadness squeezed Sarah's chest as they walked out of the Amish Sweet Delights bakery for the last time.

Tuesday was double the business of Monday. Every chance Sarah had, she ran back to the kitchen and helped Hannah with the baking.

Wednesday tugged on her heart—her last day to have the bakery. Tears blurred her vision for the whole eight hours. "Hannah, the past three days we've had more business than we've generally have in six days. There hasn't been this much business since Daed was alive."

Hannah nodded in agreement. "It feels like your *daed* died all over again."

"*Jah.* It touches my soul to witness how the community appreciated the bakery." She had helped Hannah bake all day to keep up with sales.

At 5:00 p.m., Sarah closed the front door, locked it and flipped the sign for the last time. A chill swept over her.

Her parents' legacy…gone.

Her dream…gone.

Tears ran down her cheeks and dripped off her chin. She reached for the counter to steady her step. Hannah ran from the back of the bakery, wrapped her arms around Sarah, and held her until she quit sobbing and shaking.

"I'm okay, Hannah. *Danki* for being my friend and helping me all these years."

Tears welled up, but she blinked them back. Tomorrow, she'd set her feet on a new path.

Sarah awoke in the middle of the night with a to-do list whirling in her head. She sat up and reached for the flashlight on the bed stand. Her loose hair tumbled off her shoulders, fell past her waist and rested on the bed. She pulled her hair to her left and drew it over her shoulder so it wouldn't catch when she leaned back. *Ach, Lord, my long hair is an outward symbol of submission to You. But it does get in the way sometimes.*

She plucked her prayer book from the drawer of her nightstand, took out the marker and settled back. After reading only a couple of pages, her mind drifted back to the tasks that needed to be done before she moved. Returning her book to the drawer, she rummaged in the back until she found a pad and pencil. She jotted down boxes, twine, cleaning products, then wrote down what cleaning she'd already done and what remained for her to do. Her brain raced from one thing to another, pushing sleep out of her head.

She reviewed the lists. She'd pack away some of her own pans that she wouldn't need until she started her own bakery and noted that in another column.

Sarah glanced at the clock. It was now 3:00 a.m. She rubbed her forehead to clear the fog out of her brain, but it didn't help. Maybe a short break would refresh her mind. She rested her head back against the headboard.

Ringing blasted in her ears and roused her from a deep slumber. She reached over and hit the alarm button. A glance at her to-do list propelled her out of bed. She threw her dress on, pinned her hair up in a bun, slid on her prayer *kapp* and headed to the bakery.

Sarah scooped medium-roast into the coffee maker, added water and started the brewer. She glanced around at the chaos of boxes and cleaning products, but the idea of owning her own bakery boosted her energy level. Stuff she considered hers, she started packing in cartons and pushing to the side.

The back door opened and closed. "Is the coffee hot?" Hannah shivered. "It's chilly out there."

"Hot and strong. Your cup is ready."

Hannah gave her a hug. "How're ya doing today?"

"Better."

Hannah pulled a chair away from the table and collapsed into her usual morning heap. "Thanks for having my coffee ready."

"I made a list of things I had to do this morning. That was on it."

Sarah poured a mug of brew for herself and sat at the table. She took a couple of sips and cradled the mug in her hands. Glancing around the bakery, her heart felt as empty as the pantry. How was it going to feel not coming here every day?

The bakery her folks had cherished would belong to someone else. Everything that was familiar. Gone.

Well, almost.

Since Mamm and Daed's recipes didn't exist in written form, the new owner wouldn't get those. She set the mug down. Surely Turner couldn't make her write them down. Could he?

The front door whooshed open and closed as Jacob entered. "What happened to the bell?"

Sarah swallowed a gulp of coffee. "I took it down and packed it."

Jacob hung his hat on a peg and tossed her a sympathetic smile. The little *bu* had a way of sprinkling her day with sunshine even when it rained.

Sarah motioned to the stacked pots and pans, then to the cartons. "You can pack all those pans, Jacob." He set to work and packed five cartons before his *daed* stopped to pick him up.

Jacob wrapped her in hug and Sarah sensed by his squeeze that he felt her grief through the anguish of losing his *mamm*. A *bu* still grieving his *mamm*'s death understood her pain. She laid her head on his tiny shoulder and blinked back a tear.

Caleb wrapped them both in a hug. "Do you need anything?"

She shook her head. All she really needed was these two in her life. With their love and encouragement, she could deal with losing her bakery.

Sarah wandered through her rented *haus,* trying to imagine living here. She'd lost the bakery, the one place she'd called home. Tomorrow was moving day. Her life, like stale cake, was crumbling.

After cleaning the cupboards, flooring and walls, Sarah returned to her apartment. She unhitched King and walked up the sidewalk, admiring the yellow and gold chrysanthemums that waved in the warm fall breeze in the garden her *daed* had started. Sarah headed upstairs, pulled out some empty boxes and packed the last of her possessions.

At bedtime, images of being alone the rest of her life ran through her mind for hours. The bakery had given her life a purpose. But now? A hollowness settled in her heart.

Sarah lay in bed with her life seemingly out of her reach, like the tiny star shining through the window. She stared into the darkness and closed her eyes.

Dawn crept into the room until Sarah forced her sleep-deprived eyes open, heaved her body out of bed, dressed and wandered down to the bakery for one last goodbye. Her heart pounded while her eyes fought back tears. She unlocked the door and stepped in for the last time.

Sarah roamed around the kitchen, soaking up the essence of the past, sliding her hand over the cupboard doors that gaped open to air the scrubbed shelves. The aroma of Lysol and ammonia still hung in the air and stung her eyes.

She walked out of the bakery and locked the door for the last time.

Now she had to trust *Gott.*

Chapter Seventeen

Caleb's footfalls echoed in the empty room as he inspected the paint job he'd done on Sarah's rented *haus*. The cream color she'd selected for the kitchen reflected the sunlight and brightened her work area. The bedroom's pale yellow walls cast a cheery glow about the room. She'd appreciate that. Where was she, anyway?

He searched upstairs, and wound his way through the first floor to the kitchen. She wasn't downstairs either. He peered out the window. Sarah sat forlornly on the back stoop, elbows propped on her knees, with hands clasped under her chin. She looked deep in thought.

Caleb stepped down off the stoop and sat next to her. "You okay?"

"I will be." Her voice wavered. "I feel as empty as the house."

He wrapped his arm around her and pulled her close.

She leaned her head against his shoulder. "I appreciate all your help and support, Caleb." She laid her hand on his and squeezed. The warmth of her soft skin felt good against his. His heart swelled with *liebe*. He wanted to take away her hurt, but he had no words that would do that.

Caleb recognized the squeaking breaks of the *Englischer*'s truck they had loaded her belongings in, and heard it pull into her drive. "Ezra and his friend are here."

She nodded and sat up straight. "*Danki* for asking them to move my furniture."

The sensation of her scooting away from him sent a lonely shiver through his body. He could multiply that feeling by a thousand if she moved to another town.

Caleb stood and helped Sarah to her feet. He placed his hand on her back as she stepped up on the stoop. His heart twisted tighter and tighter with *liebe* for this woman. Ever since he'd seen her with Ezra at the fair, he couldn't keep from thinking about her, dreaming of her. Worrying about losing her.

But he couldn't ask her to marry him until Mary accepted the idea and Sarah agreed to change to New Order. And he couldn't ask her to do that when she'd just lost her bakery.

He opened the back door for Sarah. "I'll go help unload the truck."

When they entered the kitchen, she headed toward the coffee pot. "I'll have coffee and sandwiches for all of you when you're done. The boxes are marked. I'll be there in a minute to guide the furniture to its place."

They worked all morning, bringing in boxes, crates and furniture, creating a maze of passages. Little by little, the mess disappeared as she directed each piece of furniture to its rightful spot. By noon the *haus* looked great, and she could spend the night in her own bed.

After Ezra and his friend left, Caleb helped her move

furniture and uncrate furnishings. While she washed dishes and put them away, he hung a coatrack, tightened a doorknob and attached her spice cabinet above the stove.

The next morning, Sarah finished unpacking her clothes and placed the linens in the upstairs closet. Her next task was to tackle the mess in the kitchen. She pushed the labyrinth of boxes to make a path from the table to the stove. She plopped her hands on her hips, looked around and cringed at the mountain of work left to do.

The sudden knock on the front door startled her. It sounded like a tapping. Were there woodpeckers around?

She hurried through the maze of cartons and flung the door open. *"Ach."* Sarah's lip quivered at the sight of her friends. Caleb, and Jacob, standing next to Hannah. "I'm so glad to see you. Come in."

"Hope you don't mind, but Jacob insisted on coming to help you unpack boxes. I'll help, too, after I run an errand." Caleb said as he took a step back toward his buggy.

"Of course we can use Jacob's help," Hannah responded. "That tool belt he is wearing will come in handy today. We will get a full day's use of him."

"I'm ready to start right away." Jacob slid his hammer out of his tool belt and held it up. "It's *gut* for knocking on doors, too." A mischievous smile spread across his face. "Did you get a dog, Sarah. There is one lying under the tree?"

"Nein, that is my dog, Mint-Candy. He followed me to work." Hannah shook her head. "He's a lazy dog and will sleep all day until I go home."

Sarah chuckled as Jacob and Hannah talked and followed her inside. She pointed to the boxes marked Kitchen. "While I clean and arrange the pantry, if you two could unpack, wash and arrange the dishes in the cupboards, I would greatly appreciate it."

They worked all morning. Jacob found a loose handle on a drawer. He pulled his Phillips screwdriver out of his belt, gave the screw a few twists and a grunt at the final turn.

"Good job," Hannah praised, and Jacob's face beamed.

Sarah's throat tightened at the way this little *bu* bloomed when encouraged. "Who has an idea for a name for our new home bakery? I had thought about Sweet Daed's, but I'm open to other suggestions."

Silence ruled the kitchen as thought waves flew around, dodging an occasional pan banging.

Jacob brushed his hands across his trousers. "I could think better if I had a cookie to eat."

"You could, huh. Help yourself." Hannah chuckled, "So, that's the problem with these hips. I am thinking too much."

Sarah stifled a laugh while listening to the two of them banter.

Jacob stuck his hand in the cookie jar and retrieved a large chocolate chunk cookie. He took a bite. "I have it!" Crumbs flew from his mouth as he spoke. "Let's call it The Cookie Box."

"I *liebe* it." Hannah chuckled.

Sarah gasped. "Me, too. That's it. We'll need to advertise. Maybe post some flyers around town. Hannah, ask your friend to make us some posters to tack around town, and a web page."

"*Gut* idea." Hannah poured three glasses of lemonade and pulled three cookies from the jar. "We need to celebrate first." They cleared a spot on the table, held their glasses up and clinked them together. "To The Cookie Box."

Sarah grabbed a pad and pencil. "Let's get started. We need to apply for the license and get an inspection. I'll ask Caleb to build us some tables and racks for our baked goods."

On opening day, Sarah hung the *Welkum* sign and unlocked the dead bolt on the kitchen door of The Cookie Box. She turned and squealed. "We're open!"

Hannah embraced her friend. "It's all ours." She whirled Sarah around in a circle, like she had when they were girls.

"Stop, Hannah, I'm getting dizzy." Sarah plopped into a chair to catch her breath. "I can't believe how *gut* it feels to own a bakery again, even if it's only part-time."

Horses' hooves and buggy wheels churned to a stop in front of the *haus,* indicating the bakery might have its first customers. Sarah stood and took a quick glance around to make sure everything was ready.

Melinda Miller opened the door and strolled in with a smile stretching across her face. "I'm so glad you're open for business, Sarah. I've sure missed buying my bread at your bakery." She took a deep breath. "Mmm. It smells delicious in here. Two loaves of whole wheat and one white bread."

Sarah smiled. "It's good to see you, Melinda. *Danki* for supporting us." She bagged up her order and before she was through, two more customers had walked in and were looking around.

By the end of the day, several of their old customers had stopped in and made purchases. Sarah hadn't been sure how much they needed to bake for The Cookie Box. As it turned out, the guess was a *gut* one.

Peeking out the window at closing time, Hannah watched the last person drive away. "Yeah! We got several of our old customers back."

Sarah twirled around with her arms in the air. "We did." She scooted to the coffee pot, poured two cups and handed Hannah hers. Sarah held her cup in the air.

Hannah clinked her cup to the other. "I'm happy for you, Sarah. The bakery's going to be a big success."

A loud knock caught their attention. Hannah nodded toward the door. "Go answer, Sarah, and I'll make a pie for tomorrow."

Sarah set her cup on the table, opened the door and threw her arms around Turner. "*Danki* for stopping by for our opening. I didn't expect it. Would you like a cup of coffee and a roll?"

"*Nein.*" He removed his straw hat and turned it around in his hands. "I would like to have a private conversation with you on the porch."

She motioned to the door and followed him out. They sat in the two rocking chairs that Hannah's *daed* had made her for the porch.

"Sarah, have you been talking about me?" Her *bruder* was never one to beat around the bush.

She stared at Turner, baffled, and then stumbled for the words. "What? *Nein.* What are you talking about?"

"Since your bakery closed, my woodworking busi-

ness has declined. Ken Johnson, Amish Sweet Delights'
new owner, said his business also took a downturn."

Sarah didn't know quite what to say. Their businesses
were declining and they blamed her. A prickly feeling
inched its way up her back. "I have said nothing about
you or Mr. Johnson. People make up their own minds.
They don't need me to tell them what they like or dislike." She stood and propped her fists on her hips.

"If you don't have anything else to say to me, I need
to get back in and help Hannah."

Turner stared at the hat in his hands and didn't reply.
He stood and headed for his buggy.

She stomped into the kitchen and shoved the door
closed.

Hannah looked up. "Problem?"

"He said the Amish Sweet Delights business and his
have declined since he sold the bakery and wanted to
know if I've been gossiping about them." Sarah paced
back and forth across the kitchen floor. "I haven't said
a word."

Hannah looked up from rolling a piecrust. "Daed
said there is talk in the community. People liked that
you ran your *daed*'s Amish Sweet Delights and they
liked your baked goods. Some have tried the new bakery and said their baked products aren't as *gut* as yours."

"Maybe if Mr. Johnson and Turner are blaming me,
they have a guilty conscience," Sarah sniffed.

Hannah dumped the apples she had already cut and
spiced into the pie shell and placed strips of woven
dough over the top for a crust. She pinched the edges of
the dough and set it in the oven. "Daed said that some
folks around town, like Lazy Susan, didn't like that
Amish don't make at least some of the products for the

Amish Sweet Delights bakery. Susan said it makes her café and all the businesses in town look bad, like their goods aren't authentic."

Sarah stood at the opposite end of the table from Hannah. "Really? How do people know that an Amish woman is not helping with the baking?"

"Someone asked Mr. Johnson. He told them he was trying to find an Amish woman, but in the meantime, he and his wife were doing all the baking."

"Why didn't you tell me that before, Hannah?"

"For the reason you just spoke of—so Turner couldn't accuse you of starting the gossip. But he did anyway. Sorry. I should have told you earlier."

Sarah pulled a chair away from the table and sat. "I never dreamed our baked goods were *that* much better."

"We are both terrific bakers." Hannah chuckled and sat next to Sarah. "I'm still shocked Turner sold the name of the bakery."

"*Jah*, me, too. I don't even know how Turner and this man met. Turner inherited the bakery and all the contents, so it was his right to sell it and the name."

"How about the recipes?"

"Mamm and Daed never wrote them down. They taught me from memory. Turner knew that. He never baked, so he never learned them."

"Could he make you give them to Mr. Johnson?"

"I don't know. I hope not." Sarah wrung her hands.

Caleb walked across Sarah's porch. Jacob followed but bumped the door. "Quiet, Jacob. Be careful."

"Sorry, Daed. With my arms full, I lost my balance."

Caleb opened the door and poked his head in. "Mmm. Smells *wunderbaar* in here."

Sarah laughed. "What are you two up to out there? Come in."

"*Nein*, Jacob wants you and Hannah to come out. He has a surprise for you." Jacob giggled and scuffled around on the porch.

Sarah dried her hands while Hannah headed for the door. Hannah stepped out on the porch and roared with laughter. "Sarah, come see."

Caleb held the door open, his eyes feasting on every move Sarah made. She walked by cautiously with a smile pulling at the corners of her mouth.

"Oh, how cute. Tiger and her kittens have come for a visit, but Mint-Candy doesn't seem to like them."

Hannah laughed. "I'll give those cats a big dish of milk if they can get a rise out of that lazy dog. The walk over here seems to have tuckered him out."

Tiger and her kittens jumped and chased each other around the yard as if they'd never seen grass before. Mint-Candy lay in a ball, his eyelids closed. Some of the kittens nipped at his tail and others chewed on his feet. One kitty went nose to nose with Mint-Candy, but the lazy pup didn't seem to care.

"That's a funny name for a dog." Jacob patted the terrier.

"*Jah*—" Hannah scratched the dog's ears "—there is a story behind it. When the dog was young, Daed had bought a box of mint candy. This little ball of fur climbed onto his chair and got the box of candy off the end table and ate all of them and chewed up the container. He smelled like mint for days."

Jacob laughed until he fell on the ground beside Mint-Candy.

Hannah bent down beside Jacob. "We kept calling

him that and the name stuck. He likes to take naps. Don't think even a summer's storm could chase him from his spot." Hannah turned to head back into Sarah's house. "I'll bring out a pitcher of lemonade and some cookies."

Jacob laughed and played with the kittens.

Caleb motioned to Sarah. "Shall we have a seat?"

Sarah pulled out a chair by the table Hannah's *daed* had made for her porch. "What brings you two to town on a beautiful September day?"

"Errands, and I promised Mary I was going to mention to you that she plans on canning tomatoes again on Monday."

"I'll be by to help. I'm still hoping to repair the damage with Mary. At least she likes me to help her can tomatoes, so that gets me in her kitchen. Maybe I can earn her forgiveness someday."

Caleb reached over and squeezed her small hand, lying on the table. Her soft skin teased the tips of his fingers and sent a streak of warmth straight to his heart. The breeze had caught a few strands of Sarah's dark brown hair and danced them around her cinnamon-brown eyes. The soft flutter like a bow on a violin plucked at his heartstrings. If anyone could replace Martha in his heart, it was Sarah.

The thought of a commitment sent a jolt bolting through him. *Nein.* Not yet.

Chapter Eighteen

Sarah woke at dawn on Saturday determined to get an early start on baking. She stood at the sink, the sun's bright yellow beams streaming through the window while she washed a stack of pans. On the weekend, it would be nice to have Jacob's help. Maybe she'd mention it to Caleb. She missed that little *bu* and the joy he brought her.

She stirred up a batch of peanut butter cookies and glanced at Hannah, whose nose was stuck in a recipe book as she hummed a hymn from the *Ausbund*. Her friend never went this long without talking; she always had some tidbit of news to share.

Hannah zipped around the kitchen in her new dress that looked two sizes smaller than her old one. She never mentioned her additional weight loss. But Sarah suspected that Ezra stopping by every Saturday and flirting with Hannah had something to do with her good mood.

Sarah rolled the dough into walnut-sized balls, dropped them onto the baking sheets, pressed them down, popped them in the oven and set the timer. The heat from the oven made the small kitchen hot. She picked up a pot holder and fanned it past her face, but it had little effect. She poured herself a glass of lemonade and strolled out onto the porch to enjoy the warm fall day.

The breeze rustled the hem of her dress as she walked to the railing. The air blew across her skin, cooling and refreshing her. She propped one hip against the railing and looked up to heaven. *Your scripture revealed that You have a plan for us, but where's mine,* Gott? *I have no family and no future. Where do I go from here, Lord?*

Silence. Not even a bird was singing.

The timer rang. She sent a final glance heavenward, then hurried back in, pulled the cookies out of the oven and set them on a rack to cool.

At noon, Hannah's folks walked in, letting a draft from the outside follow them in. Sarah tossed the happy wanderers a smile. "*Welkum* back, Edna and John. How was the trip to Missouri, and your visit with your *sohn* and his family?"

"Oh, Sarah, what fun we had!" Edna gushed.

Hannah hugged her *mamm* and *daed.*

"Oh, you wouldn't believe what a *wunderbaar* time we had. It brought tears to my eyes to see them, and we hated to leave." Edna sat and filled them in on the trip.

"I'd like some tea and cookies," John chimed in when his wife paused. "Carrying all those suitcases upstairs was hard work."

Sarah made tea and set a plate of cookies on the table. Edna chattered, spilling the news on everyone and everything going on in Seymour, Missouri.

John wiped his brow with a hanky, took a cookie and smiled. "I longed the whole trip home for one of Hannah's cookies. No one makes a tasty *makrone*, macaroon, like her." He licked his lips.

"Hannah, dear, your father and I would like a few words with you," Edna said after she took a bite of cookie and a sip of tea.

Sarah stood. Edna's tone let her know they had a family matter to discuss. "I'll let you visit." She busied herself in another area of the *haus* until she heard Hannah's parents leave.

When Sarah entered the kitchen, Hannah's face was red and her eyes were puffy. "What's wrong?" She rushed to Hannah's side and enveloped her in a hug.

"*Jah*, everything is wrong." When a customer opened the door, Hannah stepped back from her friend. "Tell you later," she whispered.

When the last customer left, Sarah poured two glasses of lemonade and carried them to the table. "Come and have a seat." Hannah's face looked tense, and her hand shook hard enough that the lemonade sloshed over the top.

"What is it, Hannah? You look worried. Is something wrong? Is your *mamm* or *daed* sick, or your *bruder*?"

"No one is sick. My folks are getting older, Daed's arthritic hands hurt and it makes it difficult for him to farm by himself. They are both tired of the cold and snowy Iowa winters. They want to move south to Missouri." Her voice wavered with concern. She took a sip of lemonade.

Sarah's stomach clenched as she waited for Hannah to regain control.

Hannah drew a deep breath and blew it out. "My *bruder* wants them to sell the farm, move to Seymour and live in the *dawdi-haus* on his farm."

"Ach." The gravity of Hannah's words settled over Sarah. "Are they going to move?"

Her friend twisted her glass on the table's surface, stopped, and slid her fingers up and down the condensation clinging to the outside. Hannah's brown eyes peered up and met Sarah's gaze.

"I have to move to Missouri with them, Sarah."

Hannah's words covered Sarah like a cold blanket of snow. She let the words float on the air to make sure she heard them correctly. "I see."

"I'm so sorry, Sarah. I won't be here to help you with the bakery anymore."

"Nein. That's okay. When do you go?"

She told Sarah all the details. "We move at the end of the year. They already have a buyer and Daed agreed to let him have the farm in December."

Sarah settled back in her chair to let the shock sink in. She hadn't expected it to be quite so soon. "I will have to find someone to replace you."

An unchecked tear rolled down Hannah's cheek. She snatched a tissue from her pocket and blotted the moisture. "I'm so sorry, Sarah."

"I know you are. Don't look so glum. It's not the apocalypse."

Hannah's laugh shook with tension. "I'm going to miss you, Sarah. I didn't want to go, but Daed said it was unacceptable for a single woman to live by herself."

"You could stay with me."

"Nein, it's not the same. You're a widow, but since I've never been married, Daed forbids it."

"Jah, he's right. I'm going to miss you."

Hannah nodded. She took her glass to the sink and started washing dishes.

After Hannah went home, Sarah drank the rest of her lemonade and sat in silence. What was she going to do without Hannah?

Gott, You have taken everything from me. What do I do now?

Morning came too soon after her restless sleep. Sarah pushed herself out of bed, hurried to get dressed, hitched King and trotted him all the way to the Millers' farm for the preaching service. Preaching was at the Millers' farm this month. Hannah usually rode with her but when she stopped at her house, Hannah claimed she had a headache and stayed home.

Sarah sat on a bench and prayed, hoping it'd ease the pain of losing Hannah and her folks. She closed her eyes and swallowed the glumness in her throat.

Her life had changed directions again. *Move on. Don't cling to the past. Look forward to the future.* She took a deep breath and blew it out.

But she knew she needed to trust Him.

Bishop Yoder's preaching about losing a kindred soul, as well as his testimony, touched her heart and filled it with peace. She was still reeling from the inspiration when they read the banns and announced Ezra Smith and Hannah Ropp's names. They were getting married…in two weeks!

I can't believe Hannah didn't confide in me. Courting was usually a secret, but she was Hannah's best friend.

After church, Sarah ate her meal in a hurry and hitched her buggy. She urged King into a fast trot, jingling the harness rings and sending his hooves pounding on the roadway. Her heart thumped her ribs the whole way to Hannah's *haus*.

John Ropp was standing in the barnyard when she arrived. Preparation had already begun for the wedding in two weeks. "You must have heard the good news." He smiled as he held King's reins so Sarah could step down from the buggy. "I'll put King in the barn to cool off. He looks hot." John patted the animal to calm him.

She ran into the Ropp *haus* and knocked on Hannah's door.

She heard Hannah giggle. "Come in."

"Headache, huh?" She ran over and smothered her friend with a hug. "Congratulations. You kept the secret from me, of all people."

"I wanted it to be a surprise. You should have guessed by the big garden Daed put in." A tear ran down Hannah's cheek. She snatched a hankerchief from the bureau drawer and blotted both eyes.

"I'm so happy for you, Hannah. Are you moving to Missouri?"

"*Nein.* Ezra and I are staying here. Mamm and Daed won't move until after the wedding."

"That's an answer to my prayer. I can hardly believe it."

"I'm not going to Missouri, but Ezra's farm is at least thirty minutes away, so we probably won't get to visit often. Since you're staying in Kalona, I can stop by when I'm in town. But I'm really going to miss Mamm." She sighed.

Sarah put a hand on Hannah's back. "You can call her from the phone shed and write letters. Besides, you'll be so busy with his *kinner,* you won't have time to get lonely or bored."

"*Jah*, you're right." Hannah sucked in a breath. "I'm

so excited. Let's go downstairs on the table and start planning the wedding with Mamm."

They tore down the stairs and ran to the kitchen like they did when they were *yung*. "Mamm, sit and help us plan the wedding."

The three of them worked out the details and made a list of things to do: need postcards for invitations, scrub floors, get benches and tables, polish silverware, borrow dishes, make up dinner and supper menus. And clean the *haus* from top to bottom.

This listing went on and on until the afternoon melted into evening. "I need to get home and get some sleep. I'll see you tomorrow."

On the way home, a giddy notion slipped into Sarah's head. She smiled and pretended for a moment that it was her and Caleb's wedding. When she finally got to bed, sleep did not come easy.

The next day, Sarah returned to Hannah's *haus* to help with preparations. "What's next on your to-do list?"

Edna frowned. "Are you sure you want to do it?"

Sarah looked at the list. "It looks like I've just volunteered to wash the borrowed dishes and polish the silverware." She drew in a deep breath. "I better get started."

Edna patted her on the back. "It will be a big help. I have so many things to do, and John is frantic. Hannah is in her bedroom, working on her wedding dress. That leaves me to do everything else. My cousins won't be by until this afternoon to help." Edna sighed and went off into the other room.

A knock on the door startled Sarah. She glanced around. "Edna?"

No answer. She dried her hands on a towel and hurried to the front door.

It was Caleb and Mary. "*Hullo!* What are you doing here?"

Caleb smiled. "We came to offer our assistance."

"Mary, why don't you go upstairs? Hannah would *liebe* to see you. She's in her room, first door on the right. Caleb, John is frantic with work. He'll *welkum* your assistance."

"Jacob is already helping him. He's picking up sticks in the yard."

"*Gut.*"

"It was the least I could do after the incident at the fair when I thought Ezra and…well, you know."

She nodded. "Do you remember what you told me once?"

He shook his head.

"In order for a relationship to work, trust has to come first."

Caleb blushed as he smiled at Sarah. "*Jah*, now I remember."

As he walked beside her back into the house, Sarah's cheeks flushed, as well. All these wedding preparations had a way of turning one's mind to thoughts of marriage and weddings.

She wondered if she and Caleb would ever stand before the bishop together, but Caleb had never mentioned the idea of marriage. A prudent woman would walk away from this relationship and chalk it under nothing more than friendship. But what more romantic place was there than a wedding to give Caleb a nudge?

* * *

As Ezra and Hannah said their vows in Pennsylvania Dutch, butterflies fluttered in Sarah's stomach. When the bishop said a blessing and pronounced them *ehemann* and *frau*, Sarah's throat clogged. Hannah, her childhood friend, getting married was like another chapter in her life folded and tucked away. She would miss her friend.

The meal after the wedding consisted of roast duck, turkey and chicken with all the trimmings. When the chairs at the tables scattered all around the house were full, the bishop gave the signal for silent prayer. Then everyone waited for the first clink of silverware against a plate before beginning.

Sarah glanced at the cakes she and Mary had made and placed on the *Eck*, the bridal table. Mary had done a *wunderbaar* job; lemon cake was Hannah's favorite.

Sarah laughed as she sat next to Hannah at the table and squeezed her hand. "Frau Smith, you are radiant."

Hannah laughed. "I can hardly believe I'm married. I'm too excited to eat."

When it was time for the bride and groom to visit with their guests, Sarah wove her way through the crowd, looking for Caleb. Many of their customers from Amish Sweet Delights and The Cookie Box had come.

With all the people milling around, spotting him was hard. A couple of times, she caught a glimpse of Bishop Yoder, but headed quickly in a different direction. Except for one time when he called from a distance and told her he wanted to introduce her to Elmer Plank. *Nein.* She was through allowing the bishop to matchmake for her. She wouldn't hurt Caleb again.

Hannah's wedding gave Sarah a chance to talk to

so many people in the community she hadn't seen in a while. Later she caught sight of Mary carrying dishes into the *haus*, and hurried to catch up with her. "Mary, have you seen your *daed*?"

"He was talking to Kathryn Miller under a tree in the backyard." Mary shrugged.

Sarah wandered through the yard, talking to people as she went. When she rounded the corner of the *haus*, she spotted Caleb standing under the chestnut tree with Kathryn. Widow Miller laughed loudly at something Caleb said and touched his arm. He smiled back at her.

She waited a moment in the shadows. A sliver of distrust swept over her… Guilt prickled up her back. Trust was the very thing Caleb said that two people had to have. Relationships were built on trust.

Turning around, she headed back to the kitchen to help with the dishes. Mary stood at the sink, stacks of dishes on both sides. Sarah stepped between Mary and one of Hannah's relatives. "I'll help out so you won't be here all night."

The relative looked delighted at Sarah's offer.

Mary picked up a plate to dry. "I'm glad Hannah's staying in our community. She will probably miss her *mamm*. I still miss mine, but I like to talk to Hannah." Her voice choked with emotion. "It was a beautiful wedding. Hannah looked so in *liebe*."

Sarah wrapped an arm around Mary's shoulders and hugged her. Surprisingly, she put her arm around Sarah's waist and hugged back. She knew Mary didn't have many female relatives, and she could tell it would have been another loss for her if Hannah had moved.

After grabbing a dish towel, Sarah dried the next plate in the drain rack.

A short while later the door opened and Caleb, with Jacob in tow, sauntered over. "Mary, it's getting late. Are you ready to go home?"

She turned toward Sarah. "Anything else I need to do?"

"*Nein. Danki* for your help and baking the cake."

"Sarah, I'll pick you up Sunday so you can attend Sunday school with us." Caleb's eyes twinkled, and he gave a smile that made her knees turn to mush.

"*Jah.* Who could refuse a smile like that?" She threw the dish towel over her shoulder, perched her hands on her hips and raised a brow. She was falling for him, all right. Remorse pricked the back of her neck for having a hesitant heart when she saw him with Kathryn.

He hadn't said he loved her. Yet. But wasn't that what she was reading on his face? Was he only looking for companionship?

She still had so many questions. And not enough answers.

Chapter Nineteen

Sarah opened her Bible to Jeremiah 29, and searched for the answer to why *Gott* took away everything she loved. Would He take Caleb away, too? When she came to the eleventh verse, she read it over and over. *"For I know the thoughts that I think toward you, saith the Lord, thoughts of peace, and not evil, to give you an expected end."*

She had always believed that *Gott* had taken Samuel and her bakery from her, and had closed her womb. *Nein.* He wouldn't harm her.

Jeremiah 29:11 is saying that *Gott* cannot keep us from suffering, but He will share our burden and carry us through. He was there all the time. He'd given her Samuel's love. Hannah's friendship. It all boiled down to the fact that she had to trust Him.

A knock on the door startled her.

She glanced at the clock. *Ach*, Caleb. She slid her Bible and study guide into her bag and hurried to answer the door. "I'm ready. I'll just grab my things." She slipped her cape and bonnet on and locked the door behind her.

She settled into the buggy, beside Caleb. "I enjoy attending Sunday school and Bible study with your church group. Old Order still believes only the church should interpret scripture, so they don't encourage group study. It's probably one of the biggest differences in our Orders. That, and the use of mechanical conveniences. Yet Old Order has a better youth retention rate than New Order. Did you know that, Caleb?"

"*Jah.* It's a concern for us. Many think the youth leaving our Order is because we believe in evangelizing and going out into the community. It teaches the youth too much about the outside world and not about staying within *our* community. I worry about Mary and Jacob leaving the faith after they go through their *rumschpringe*." Caleb glanced her way with worry lining his eyes.

"Do you think you will ever change back to Old Order?" She hadn't meant to blurt it out, but she had to know.

"I need the use of the tractor and other mechanical devices, like the rototiller, bulk milk tank, and mechanical milker for farming." His face flushed red. "I can't change."

There it was. Her heart plunged to the floor. Her church and her family would shun her if she left the Old Order to marry Caleb. Neither of them was willing to give in. She drew a deep breath, met his gaze with a weak smile and reached over to pat his arm. "Jacob and Mary will stick with the faith—I'm sure of it. They'd miss you too much."

He took her hand and squeezed it lightly before letting go, but a cloud of uneasiness hung between them. Sarah shifted her weight and gazed out the window at the harvested fields. They looked as bare and bleak as her hope for a marriage to Caleb. "Since Hannah is married, I was thinking about moving to Iowa City and opening a regular bakery." A plan she'd just now hatched since chances seemed slim she'd be marrying Caleb.

Snowball held a steady pace as the buggy bounced over ruts in the country road. Finally, Caleb's voice cut through the stillness. "Tomorrow I'll get a driver and take you to Iowa City to start your search."

"You're a *gut* friend to do that for me."

"You helped Mary can tomatoes, and that's hard work in the heat. I'll be glad to repay the favor."

She gripped her bag. *He thinks he needs to repay the favor. That's all.*

What was the point of them spending time together if marriage wasn't in their future?

Caleb rose early and dressed. He'd slept restlessly, at best, with dreams of Sarah constantly waking him. Iowa City was eighteen miles away. By horse and buggy, that was almost an hour. He'd have to rent a car and driver whenever he wanted to see her.

He took a calming breath, rubbed a hand over his chest and tried to ease the ache. What was he going to do without Sarah? He could ask her to marry him and not wait for Mary and Sarah to work out their differences. Surely Mary would come to accept Sarah. The question was…could he convince Sarah to change to New Order?

The driver picked him and Jacob up on time, then headed for Sarah's *haus*. She was waiting at the door with her bag, spiraled notebook and pencil in hand, and an optimistic smile on her face. How could he convince Sarah to stay in Kalona? He stepped out of the car and held the door while she slid in, next to Jacob. He hopped back in front next to the driver.

"Jacob, I'm glad you are coming along while I look for a bakery. I value your opinion very much." She patted his arm.

"Why do you have to move to Iowa City? I want you to stay in Kalona and run The Cookie Box so I can visit you."

"Jacob. Sarah has lost Hannah and must make other arrangements." Caleb glared at his *sohn*.

Sarah handed a slip of paper with an address to the driver. "*Hullo.* I'm Sarah. We have an appointment with a real estate agent to look at a couple of empty shops."

He took the paper and nodded. "Eddie. Have you there in a few minutes, ma'am."

Soon they were walking around an old, dilapidated shop. She looked in closets, cupboards, nooks and crannies. She glanced at the ceiling and knocked on the walls.

Caleb took a deep breath. It would take her a year to fix this place up. He could help but he had farm work. Doing this much alone was impossible.

Sarah glanced at the real estate agent, Marge, who waved her arms around. "It's old but it has a charm to it."

Caleb snorted.

Sarah shook her head and Marge motioned toward the door. "The next building might be more what you had in mind."

Caleb cringed at the idea of Sarah staying alone in Iowa City. At the next spot, he glanced around at the expensive cupboards and counters and whistled. "What do you think of this place, Sarah?"

"It's a lot of money. I'd have to hire help in order to make enough to support myself and pay the rent. I'd have to charge a lot more than I did in Kalona." Discouragement hovered in her voice.

At the third place, he took her hand and helped her up the steps. Her palm was cold and clammy. He looked around the shop and whistled. "A fancy shop, *jah*?"

She nodded. Her forehead furrowed, and her eyes clouded with worry.

Jacob rubbed his hand over the brown marble counter. He blew out a big puff of air, trying to whistle. "*Jah*, this is *gut* and looks like an *Englisch* bakery. Can I come and stay with you? I'll work hard on Saturday."

"Jacob!" Caleb tossed him a cross face.

"I'd rather stay with Sarah." Jacob pouted.

Caleb regretted his outburst. He knew the *bu* was scared of losing Sarah. He was, too.

Sarah caught Jacob's hand and held it while they exited the building. Caleb wrapped his arm around her shoulder. "It's time we stopped for lunch. Let's go to a nice restaurant. We can rest and talk about some of the shops you wrote under the Maybe column on your notepad."

"That sounds *gut*." She said goodbye to Marge and told her she'd be in touch.

"Eddie, would you mind taking us to A Little Bit Country restaurant on Melrose Avenue? We'd like you to join us."

"No, thanks. I'll come back and pick you up in an hour. The missus will have a delicious dinner waiting for me, so I don't want to spoil my appetite."

The hostess seated them at a table by the window and handed them menus.

Sarah opened her menu. "Caleb, this is expensive."

"It's my treat. Order whatever you like."

She took a deep breath and studied the selection for several minutes. She laid it down on the wine-colored tablecloth and lightly rubbed her hand across the rich linen. "Nice."

"I'm glad you like it. Relax. Take that worried look off your face. They'll think we can't afford to pay."

She laughed. "I'll try."

Their waitress brought them water, took their orders and quietly stole away.

"You didn't find anything you're serious about today?" He could tell she was thinking about her answer.

"I have money saved, but it'll take a lot to set up the shop. It's expensive here. I'd have to charge a lot more for the baked goods in order to pay for the rent. I'd also have to hire several people to help me. So it's definitely something I'm going to have to think about before I make a decision."

"Wait until spring," Caleb offered, trying to make it sound sensible.

"If I waited until spring and needed your help, you'd be out working in the fields."

"Don't worry. I promise you, we'll figure something out. But take your time. This isn't a decision to be made lightly." He watched as she moved her silverware around and took a sip from her water glass. Her brow furrowed. *Jah*, she was mulling it over. He hoped she came to the same conclusion that he did.

The waitress brought their food to the table. "I'll stop back later. Enjoy."

Sarah took a bite of her sandwich. "This turkey on the homemade bread is delicious. It has tomato and melted cheese and some kind of sauce. How's yours?"

"Mine is *gut*. Jacob, is your sandwich tasty?"

"Nein."

Caleb read the hurt in the *bu*'s eyes. "Jacob, Sarah has to run her business, and there is already one bakery in Kalona."

"Jah. But I want her to stay. She can come live with us."

"Nein, Jacob. She cannot do that."

Sarah quickly changed the subject. "Even if I don't get a shop selected today, it was worth the trip to Iowa City just to eat here. This restaurant is charming."

The server stopped at the table with a water pitcher and refilled their glasses. "How are your meals?"

Sarah's face glowed as though she were a *kind* visiting a restaurant for the first time. *"Wunderbaar.* Could I see a dessert menu, please?"

"Sorry, the pastry chef quit and the new one hasn't started yet."

"Oh, that's too bad."

"Haven't I seen you before?" The waitress looked at Sarah with a scrutinizing eye. She glanced at her clothes, then at Caleb. "You look familiar. Wait a minute. Do you run that Amish Sweet Delights bakery in Kalona?"

"Jah, I'm Sarah Gingerich. I did operate the bakery, but my *bruder* sold it."

"Oh, too bad. Your baked goods were wonderful." She handed the water pitcher to another server before stacking their empty dishes on a tray. "Nice to see you again. Just in town, enjoying the day?"

"I'm looking at shops in Iowa City and thinking about opening a bakery here."

"Hope you find one. It'd be nice having your bakery close by."

Caleb paid the check and helped Sarah slide her chair back. He glared at Jacob and his sandwich with only a nibble out of it. "Since you didn't eat your lunch, don't ask for a treat later." He gestured to his *sohn* to lead the way to the door.

"Excuse me." A well-dressed man hurried toward them. "Are you Sarah Gingerich?"

She stopped and faced the speaker. *"Jah."*

"I'm Kenneth Gardner. I'm the restaurant manager. I've visited your bakery before. You make delicious desserts."

"Danki."

"My pastry chef quit and my new one doesn't start for four weeks. I was wondering if you'd be able to bake desserts for me for a few weeks. Either here at the restaurant, or if you bake them at your bakery, we could make arrangements to have someone pick them up."

"I live in Kalona."

"One of our workers is from Kalona, so he could pick them up on his way to work. We'd advertise them as Amish desserts. We'll call it a special for the holidays. Since we're located in the heart of the Amish community, our customers may like the change."

"I could maybe do it for a few weeks. What kind of desserts?"

Caleb could hear the excitement in her voice. He took a step closer to the door.

"Pies, apple crisps, brownies, cookies—that type of thing. Let's step over here and talk about it further. I'll introduce you to Mike Matthews. He'll be the one to pick up the baked goods."

When they left the restaurant, Caleb flashed Sarah a smile. "Congratulations."

Sarah held up a hand. "I'm still shaking. I can't believe it. It's only for a few weeks, but it made me feel *gut* they even asked. And with this arrangement, the baked goods are preordered. I'll need an organizer put in the pantry in my kitchen and some more shelves."

"Write out what you need. I'll pick it up and be over tomorrow to get started."

"I might do what you suggested, Caleb. Just stay in Kalona for the winter, keep The Cookie Box and work on my cookbook."

Caleb forced a grin from his face. It was all music to his ears.

Sarah stood back and surveyed the organizer and extra shelving Caleb had installed in her house. "*Wunderbaar.* I don't know how I'll repay all the work you do for me."

"No repayment needed. You're a friend, Sarah. I enjoy helping you."

His words struck her like a cold snowball to the cheek. Was he trying to tell her that's all she meant to him? A friend. She forced a weak smile. "I'd like to make you supper to repay you."

"Another time. I want to get home to Mary and Jacob." He gave a wave as he closed the door behind him.

She unpacked her saucepans from the storage box,

washed and hung them. The high-ceilinged room echoed as her shoes clomped across the wooden flooring. It reminded her of how empty the house was without Caleb's presence. She needed to stay busy and forget about such things.

She clutched her first order from A Little Bit Country to her chest. Working for a five-star restaurant was a *gut* move, even if the job was only temporary. If she opened a bakery in Iowa City, maybe they'd continue to give her business. That meant she needed to make them some very tasty desserts.

After pulling her supplies from the pantry, she started on the brownies. When those were in the oven, she stirred up the cookie dough and baked five dozen chocolate chip and oatmeal raisin cookies. Next she started a batch of yeast rolls rising. They didn't ask for the cinnamon rolls, but she'd throw them in as a *danki* for the orders and give them a sample. While those were set aside to rise, she made a chocolate cake and the apple crisp, then finished making the rolls.

Sarah packed all the desserts into boxes, which took until the wee hours of the morning. She set the baked goods on the table, sat in the rocker and waited for Mike Matthews, the man from the restaurant, to stop by.

The knock at her front door startled Sarah out of her snooze. She jumped off the rocker and found Mike on her front porch. "Mornin', Mike. They're all ready for you."

"Morning, Sarah. Fall asleep, didya?"

"*Jah.* Since I closed the other bakery, I'm not used to working late and getting up in the middle of the night."

He laughed. "See you in a couple of days."

She locked the door behind him and headed to bed for a little more sleep.

Two days later, she had a new order from the restaurant. Mr. Gardner's order included a note. *Thanks for the cinnamon rolls you included free last time. Our brunch crowd raved about them.*

It paid off. He'd ordered five dozen cinnamon rolls. For the next order, she'd include two dozen sample dinner rolls and a free apple strudel. This order would take all night. At times like this, she wished Hannah was still around to help her, but Hannah was happily taking care of her *ehemann* and his *kinner.*

When Mike knocked the next day at 5:00 a.m., he handed her a slip of paper. "Chef Randy loved your desserts. He asked me to give you the name and address of his publisher to get your cookbook published. You still have time to get them printed to sell for Christmas. Randy's *Little Bit Country Cookbook* sells out over the holidays in the restaurant gift shop."

"*Danki*, Mike." Sarah laid the note on the table and helped Mike carry the boxes to the car.

The next day when Mike dropped off the order, there was a note stapled to it. Besides their usual order, they'd added three apple strudels. She grinned. Free samples were always her best advertisement.

Sarah had hoped Caleb would stop by so she could share her exciting news with him. Each time horses' hooves clopped on the pavement in front of her *haus*, she peeked outside. But each time, the buggy passed by.

Why hadn't he come by?

With his stomach signaling time for dinner, Caleb finished his chores and headed to the house. He opened the kitchen door to black smoke engulfing the room. He ran to the stove, grabbed a pot holder and pulled the unattended frying pan off the burner.

Jacob ran into the kitchen. "What's that smell?" He wrinkled his nose and made a face.

"Looks like our dinner. Where's Mary?"

"She went outside."

"How long has she been gone?"

"I don't know. A long time. She told me to play in my room."

Mary slammed the back door and turned to face her *daed.* "*Ach.* Smells like burnt roast. I had the roast simmering in water. Guess it must have boiled dry."

"You can't leave food on the stove with a lit burner and go out of the *haus.* You know better than that, Mary." Caleb raised his voice. "Where were you?"

"Sorry. I just stepped outside for a breath of cool air. The kitchen was hot." Her tone was unapologetic.

"It takes a while for meat to boil dry. Why were you outside?"

"Talking to some girls. I walked with them down to the creek and back."

"That is a mile away. The meat is burnt and Jacob was here by himself."

"I'll fry some hamburgers." She slowed her words, but her voice shook.

"You'll do no such thing. Go clean up that mess, and Jacob and I will fix sandwiches."

After Mary and Jacob went to bed, Caleb sat and stared into the dark living room. He missed Sarah every second of every day. He rubbed his forearms. Even they ached for her.

Caleb glanced at the clock on the oak mantel as it

chimed midnight. *Jah.* Past time for bed. He pulled change out of his pocket, dropped it into a glass dish next to the clock and listened to it clink on the bottom.

He rubbed his hand across the mantel and looked at his fingers, then at the trail they left in the dust.

He wouldn't blame Mary if she decided to take an afternoon and read a book or visit with a friend. She deserved the time off. He was gone the whole day. She worked as hard as any woman, cooking and cleaning all day. But a dusty *haus* was puzzling, and out of character for her.

He whisked a finger across the sideboard, the end tables and the wooden chairs. They were all dusty. He scratched his head. Recently, meals had been lighter and simpler than usual. Now when she cooked a beef roast, she went outside while it cooked. She had burned food before, but he'd thought she was busy with the cleaning and laundry.

He stroked his beard. Something was going on with Mary. He could ask Jacob, but he attended school most of the day.

Was she interested in a *bu*? Maybe.

He'd never seen her talking to any *bu* at church. At least not that he'd noticed, but he didn't watch her every second. Should he ask her? Would she tell him what was going on if he did?

Sarah would know what to do.

Chapter Twenty

$\sim$

On Friday Sarah had the last order for A Little Bit Country restaurant all ready when she pulled the door open.

A weird sadness suddenly rushed through her. She enjoyed Mike's chatter, and seeing him every week. But that wasn't it. *Nein.* She enjoyed working for the restaurant. It gave her a feeling of pride, but if the bishop knew that, he would make her confess. It wasn't a conceited pride. The recipes for the desserts she'd sold the restaurant belonged to her, and not her *daed.* She'd always worked under her *daed*'s shadow. It was the reason she'd written the cookbook—to prove to herself she could do it.

"Mornin', Mike. Your order's ready. Has your new pastry chef started?"

"No. Not yet." He smiled and pulled a sealed envelope out of his pocket and handed it to Sarah. "I'm supposed to wait for an answer. I'll load the car while you decide on a reply."

Ach. Maybe they wanted her to keep baking a few more weeks. She unfolded the paper and read. Then sat and read it again. Excitement surged through her. "Tell Mr. Gardner I'll be in to see him tomorrow." Her throat tightened. It was a *wunderbaar* opportunity.

She closed the door behind Mike and stumbled to a chair. This was something she'd never expected. Pastry chef. Their new chef had found another job and wasn't coming. They were offering the job to her. She needed a job to support herself. If she bought a shop, it might be months, maybe years before she'd break even.

This was perfect…or was it?

She'd have to hire a driver to take her the eighteen miles to work every day. Maybe she could ride with Mike on the days he worked. Or she could rent an apartment in Iowa City. It was a *wunderbaar* opportunity, but could she leave Kalona? Leave Caleb and his family? She'd hardly ever get to see them.

Tears streamed down her cheeks and sobs heaved her shoulders.

Caleb knocked on the door and waited. He hunched over against the raw wind and pulled his coat tightly around his neck. As soon as the door opened, the warm air hit his face.

"Come in out of the cold." Sarah waved toward the table. "Have a seat. I have hot coffee to warm your bones."

"*Nein.* Let's not give the neighbors something to talk about. Why don't you come with me to Lazy Susan's café?"

Sarah slipped into her black bonnet and heavy cape, locked her door and hurried to his buggy.

When comfortably seated at the restaurant, she ordered coffee and one of Susan's cinnamon rolls. "I might as well try the competition."

Caleb smiled at her selection and ordered the same.

The waitress nodded. "Just take a minute."

"What brings you to town today? An errand?" Sarah asked. "It's a cold day to be out and about."

"I wanted to talk to you about Mary." He stopped abruptly at the presence of the server. She set the coffee and rolls down.

Caleb took a bite of roll. "They're not as *gut* as yours." He raised his brow. "You're the best roll maker I know."

"*Danki.* I appreciate your loyalty."

Caleb stirred cream into his coffee, the spoon clinking against the glass cup a little too much. He noticed her eyes darting from his cup to meet his gaze.

"Is there something wrong, Caleb?" She sat back in the chair.

"I wanted to ask you something about Mary."

"Mary?" A tone of surprise tinged her voice.

"When you helped her can tomatoes this summer, did she say anything about a special *bu* she might have liked?"

"A *bu*?" She gasped. "Why do you ask that?"

"Mary has been acting strangely lately."

"What do you mean?" She took a sip of coffee, looking over the rim of the cup at him.

"Clothes aren't getting washed when they need it. The living room is dusty. Last night's supper was burnt, and she left Jacob alone in the house."

"Mary doesn't say much to me about anything, unfortunately."

"You must have talked about something during canning."

"We talked and said it would only be two years and she would be attending singings. I asked if she was excited about that, and she said *jah*."

"So, she was talking about boys."

"Don't jump to conclusions. I asked if she liked a special *bu*. She said *nein*."

"But that was a few months ago. She could like one now," he insisted.

"Have you talked to her?"

"Nein." He picked up a spoon and stirred his coffee again.

"Tell her what you've noticed and ask if there is a problem." Sarah tapped the table with her fingertips. "Go home. Sit her down and talk with her."

"Maybe I'll give her a little longer and try to keep a better eye on her."

Sarah raised a brow. "She's a young woman. Maybe she bought a romance novel and lost track of time reading. Without a woman around to give her advice, maybe she's searching for answers on how to act around *buwe*."

He leaned back, took a deep breath and exhaled. "You're probably right. She's normally a responsible girl. I know it must be hard when she doesn't have an older sister or a *mamm* to tell her things."

"Mary is sensible. Just talk to her." Sarah reached across the table and patted his arm. "And now that we have settled your problem, I have some good news to tell you. A Little Bit Country restaurant has offered me the job of pastry chef, and I'm going to take it."

His heart nearly stopped. He drew in a deep breath.

His body wouldn't move. It was as if he were a frozen snowman. Her penetrating gaze thawed his shock. "Did I hear right? They offered you a job as a pastry chef."

"Jah." She gave a nervous laugh. "I can start whenever I want. I was hoping you could take me to Iowa City to find an apartment, and help me move."

He wanted to shout *nein!* from the top of a barn. But how could he? If he demanded she stay, what could he offer her? Neither of them wanted to change to the other's Order. Tears threatened his vision, but he lowered his chin and blinked them back. His heart was ripping in two. He swiped a hand through his beard. *"Jah.* I can do that. I'll miss you."

His chest hurt so badly, he could hardly speak. She was like his right hand. *Nein.* Not just his hand. Sarah was part of his soul, and she was ripping it apart.

"Have you started to pack?" he stammered.

She nodded.

"I'll take you home and come back tomorrow morning at eight with a car and driver to take you to Iowa City." He laid his money on the table and stood.

She chattered about her new job all the way back to her *haus.* He dropped her off and headed Snowball home in a slow trot that allowed him to decide how to tell Jacob the news. It would crush Jacob's heart to lose Sarah from his life. The knot tightened in Caleb's abdomen as he tried to decide how to come to terms with Sarah's decision.

He worried Mary was sneaking out with some *bu.* He didn't want to lose her. Not yet.

Instead, he was losing Sarah.

* * *

The Amish taxi pulled into Sarah's driveway on time. She grabbed her bag and darted out the door, adrenaline and excitement fueling her feet.

They arrived at the restaurant at 9:00 a.m. The old Victorian building was going to be a *wunderbaar* place to work. At least, it helped ease her aching heart to tell herself that. Remembering where Mr. Gardner's office was from her last visit, she started in that direction.

"I'll wait at a table," Caleb called as he headed that way.

Mr. Gardner's secretary escorted Sarah into his office and closed the door. He motioned toward the furniture. "Sarah, I'm so glad you decided to join us."

"*Gut* mornin'. *Jah*, I'm ready." She sat but held her back straight so it hardly touched the red brocade chair. Her hands rubbed the rich texture of the fabric. It looked too fancy to sit on.

He reclined behind his mahogany desk in his high-backed brown leather chair. "We had many compliments on your desserts. When the pastry chef decided he didn't want to move from Florida to Iowa, you were the first person that came to mind."

"*Danki*, Mr. Gardner." Her heart fluttered from the flattery.

After they settled on her salary, and her days off, they discussed her starting date. "I'm looking for an apartment in Iowa City, and as soon as I find one, I'll move. Meanwhile, can I work from home and have Mike pick the baked goods up? I'm hoping it won't take more than two or three weeks."

"That'll work." He stood. "I'll introduce you to Chef Randy. He'll show you around the kitchen. He has heard of you through the Amish tourism books and has tried your desserts. He's a big fan of yours and is very excited to work with you."

"*Danki,* Mr. Gardner. I'm excited about this opportunity."

But if she were truly excited about the job, then why didn't her heart agree?

Caleb was hoping it would take several visits to Iowa City before Sarah found an apartment. Instead, she found the perfect apartment about a mile from the restaurant. It was small but move-in ready. She'd have to store most of her furniture, but it wouldn't require much care if she worked late hours.

"I'll let you know when I'm packed. Could you ask Ezra's friend with the truck if he could help me move?"

"Of course."

"I have another favor. Could you keep King and my buggy at your place for a while? At least until I see how this job and living in Iowa City are going to work out? Mary can use the buggy, and King is a *wunderbaar,* gentle horse."

"Glad to do it. You'll need to come out and say good-bye to the *kinner* before you leave town."

"I'll do that when I drive the buggy out."

The memories of the *gut* times he'd had with Sarah came flooding back. His heart felt swollen and ready to burst out of his chest at the thought of never seeing her again. At least not often. He forced the lump in his throat away.

Her warm smile stayed with him all the way home. When he entered the *haus,* he checked on his *kinner.* They were both in their rooms. He sat in his rocker for a long while, staring around the room at Martha's Bible, her fabric scraps in the corner and her quilts.

He went to the pantry and pulled out the cardboard box he saved to carry Mary's canned goods and jellies to market. He packed all of Martha's things from around the house into the box and set it in storage.

As he climbed the stairs to his bedroom, several steps squeaked under his weight. He'd been so busy helping Sarah lately, he'd neglected his own home's repairs.

Caleb sighed. With her gone, he'd have plenty of time on his hands for repairs. But his heart wouldn't be the same without Sarah in his life.

Chapter Twenty-One

Her hands shaking, Sarah slowly slipped the harness on King and tightened the girth. "This is the last time I'll hitch you, at least for a while. I have to work and take care of myself." She rubbed his ears and mane, then glanced into his large brown eyes. He shook his head, snorted as if he understood and nervously paced the ground.

She slipped her handkerchief out of her bag, wiped away tears and blew her nose. "We best get on our way to Caleb's farm."

She climbed into the buggy and tapped the reins against King's back. The harness pulled taut as the buggy jerked to a start.

Sarah glanced up. *Gott, I can't believe that I'm on a totally different road for my life. I have no idea where You're leading me, but I'm going to miss Caleb, Jacob and Mary.* She gasped for a breath of air, then continued. *The agony is ripping my heart in two, but I must trust that You have placed me on the right path.*

When King pulled into the driveway, Jacob and Caleb ran out of the *haus* to meet her. Mary followed at a slower pace. Sarah smiled as Mary approached. Slow was better than not at all. Caleb helped her down. Jacob hugged her.

"Mary made us hot tea and rolls to share as your last sit-down with us. I'll unhitch King and put him in the barn."

"I'm going to miss you. Don't go," Jacob sobbed.

"Jacob, we talked about this." Caleb's stern face tossed him a warning.

"Please don't go!"

"Jacob, help me unhitch King while the women go inside."

Sarah caught the jerk in Mary's head as she looked at her *daed*. He'd called her a woman.

Mary led the way into the *haus*. "Living in Iowa City will be *wunderbaar*. Are you excited?" She banged the teakettle as she poured the hot water into the teapot, then set the basket of loose tea in the pot to steep.

"*Jah*, excited and nervous. I'll have no close Plain friends there. You can use King and my buggy."

"Really? *Danki*. Can I visit you sometime and stay a few days?"

"*Jah*, that would be fine, if your *daed* says you can."

Caleb and Jacob banged the door as they entered. They took their coats and hats off and placed them on hooks.

Jacob sat on a chair, his head down, lips poked out in a pout.

Mary set the plate of rolls she'd made on the table and poured the tea. "It's ready."

Sarah sat next to Jacob, but he still wasn't in a talking mood. She took one of the rolls and munched a corner. "Mmm. This is delicious."

"*Danki.* Caramel-pecan, Mamm's favorite."

"Your *mamm* must have been a very *gut* baker."

"*Jah.* She had many talents. So do you, Sarah. You're going to work at a fancy restaurant as a pastry chef."

"Think you'll like living in the city?" Jacob asked between bites and sniffles.

"Maybe, but I'll miss the country, and all of you, very much."

Sarah finished her tea and brushed a crumb from her skirt. She glanced at the clock and stood. "My driver should be here any minute. I don't want to make him wait."

"I'll go check." Caleb walked to the window and looked out. "He's here. I could go with and see that you make it okay."

"*Nein*, Caleb. That would be harder for me. The driver is taking me back to Kalona to get the last of my luggage and run a couple of errands before we leave for Iowa City."

They walked out to the SUV, and each one gave her a hug. "*Danki* for your *liebe* and friendship, and for your *wunderbaar* cooking, Mary." She climbed into the Ford and buckled her seat belt.

As the vehicle pulled away, she waved. Sarah gazed out the far window of the vehicle so Caleb wouldn't see her face. As soon as they were out of the driveway, she pulled out her handkerchief and wiped the tears from her cheeks.

Caleb's chest tightened. *You're a fool, Caleb Brenneman. You should have asked her to marry you. Now it's too late. She's excited about her new job as a pastry chef. You can't burst her dream.*

He walked to the barn and cleaned his workbench and tools. He trudged back to the *haus* and closed the door against the cold, brisk wind. Maybe a hot cup of coffee would soothe the knot in his throat.

Caleb hung his hat and coat on a peg and took a whiff of an unpleasant odor that permeated the air. "Mary, you burned dinner again, didn't you?"

She turned away from the stove. "Sorry, Daed. I only stepped outside for a minute."

"What's gotten into you, Mary?"

"Nothing."

"Daed, can we go see Sarah?" Jacob pouted.

"Sit and eat. We'll talk about it later."

"There are only chicken and vegetables to eat. Mary burned the potatoes."

They clasped hands and Caleb said the prayer. He examined the potatoes. A little scorched where they touched the pan, but still eatable.

"Yuck. These potatoes taste terrible. They make my tongue taste awful." Jacob gulped a drink of water.

"Why don't we go see Sarah in Iowa City tomorrow?" Mary took a bite of potatoes and ate them. She wrinkled her nose and shook her face at Jacob. "They don't taste so bad. You're such a *boppli*."

"Didn't think you liked Sarah. You just want to go to Iowa City." Caleb pointed his fork at Mary.

"I want to see Sarah and eat one of her cookies," Jacob chimed in.

"I want to see where she lives," Mary added.

Caleb dropped his fork, the metal clinking as it hit the glass plate. "You've never cared about Sarah. Why the change of heart?"

"That's not true. She made me a birthday cake and

helped me can vegetables all summer. She showed me how to cook several dishes. Why wouldn't I like her?"

"Why are you saying that, Mary, when you know you gave her the cold shoulder after she took your *mamm*'s leftover scraps to make a book cover?"

"I'm over that. I had wanted to make a memento to remember Mamm. But I probably would never have gotten it done, and the one Sarah made looks *gut*."

Caleb pushed his chair back, scraping the legs on the floor, and threw his arms in the air. "All this time you liked Sarah and never said anything?"

"I certainly don't like Widow Miller. Sarah is much better for a *mamm* than Kathryn. I can't believe you didn't ask Sarah to marry you."

"*Jah*, Daed. Marry Sarah. Then she can come live with us," Jacob squealed.

Caleb turned to Mary. "You like her now?"

"I like her and I can tolerate her a lot better than Kathryn. Kathryn has set her *kapp* for you. The way she bats her lashes when you're around." Mary rolled her eyes.

"What does 'set her *kapp*' mean, Daed?" Jacob raised puzzled eyes.

"Never mind, Jacob."

"Why hasn't the laundry been getting done, or the cleaning? Why is the food burnt now half the time?"

"I'm tired of doing all the housework. Soon I'll get married and have to do everything by myself. I want a life first. I want to go skating with my friends. I want to have fun."

"Mary, you shouldn't say things like that. Should she, Daed?" Jacob shook his head.

"Jacob, please. Mary and I are talking."

Caleb sat back and rubbed a hand across his forehead. It was hard work for a woman to manage a whole household, let alone a fourteen-year-old *mädel*. He should've hired help.

"I can't see my friends—there's no time. A few of us have been going down to the frozen creek and skating."

"And you leave Jacob here all by himself? What if he got hurt?"

"Exactly. If I go do anything, I feel guilty because I took a little time away from all this work." She waved her arms around. "It was nice when Sarah was here, helping mc. I know I shouldn't have gotten mad at her over those scraps of material. Mamm wouldn't have liked my behavior."

Mary raised her gaze to Caleb. "You let Sarah go. I thought you loved her. Go after her, Daed."

He headed outside. He needed some cold air to clear his mind. All this time, Mary had played games with him instead of being honest.

Nein. That wasn't the truth. She was truly hurt at first when Sarah took the scraps. Apparently when Sarah helped her and taught her like a *mamm*, she forgave Sarah. Then *Gott* healed her grieving heart.

He'd made a mess of things.

He heard the kitchen door close bchind him and two sets of feet walking across the porch.

"Daed, you need your coat. Are we going to get Sarah?" Mary asked.

"*Jah.* Get ready. You, too, Jacob." Caleb ran into the *haus,* grabbed his coat and hat, and threw them on while he raced to the barn.

"Hurry, Daed. Hurry." Mary yelled. "Before she leaves her *haus* in Kalona."

Caleb hitched Snowball to the buggy while the horse paced the ground in place as if he sensed the urgency. Caleb motioned and the *kinner* jumped in behind him. He tapped the reins on Snowball's back. The buggy lurched ahead as the horse set the wheels in motion.

When they turned onto the roadway, Snowball increased his gait to a full trot toward Kalona. The three miles to town seemed more like twenty to Caleb as he reined the horse to a stop. Sarah's yard and driveway were empty.

"Wait here." Caleb stepped down, hurried to the door and knocked.

No answer.

The man on the porch next door waved Caleb over. "She left a few minutes ago for Iowa City. If you hurry, you might be able to catch up with them. I heard her say she needed to stop at the bank, and she had to turn in the house key."

"*Danki* for your help."

Caleb headed toward Route 218 at the edge of town to wait for the SUV.

Sarah already missed Caleb and the *kinner* so much, her heart was about to burst. After she settled in to her apartment, she'd bury herself in work at the restaurant until she'd adjusted to life without the Brennemans.

Caleb was obviously not ready to remarry, and she understood that. Martha had only been gone not quite two years. Yet it was difficult seeing him when he didn't want a relationship, only a friend, a companion.

When the SUV slowed, she glanced out the window and noticed a buggy sitting along the side of the road with Caleb, Jacob and Mary waving for them to stop.

She tried to slow her racing heart. She'd probably forgotten something at their *haus*, or they just wanted to wish her well again. She stepped out of the SUV.

Jacob tore out ahead of his *daed* and Mary, skidding to a halt in front of her. He threw his arms around her in a hug and sobbed.

Sarah rubbed his back and whispered. "I'll miss you, too, Jacob."

"Don't you want to be my *mamm*?"

She froze.

What in the world was this *bu* talking about? How could she ever face Caleb? The heat burned on her cheeks.

Caleb and Mary hurried over and stood a few feet away from her and Jacob. Sarah glanced up. She drew a ragged breath and noticed the broad smiles on their faces. She patted Jacob's back as he continued to hug her.

Caleb took a step closer. Sarah's gaze met his.

Caleb's lips twitched and his eyes sparkled like precious stones. His eyes captured and held hers. "*Jah*, sorry, Sarah, but I imagine there are worse proposals than that."

Did he say what she thought he'd said? Did Caleb Brenneman just propose to her?

Caleb stepped forward and patted Jacob. "It's my turn. Let me give her a hug, too."

Jacob stepped back and rubbed his shirtsleeve over his eyes and down his cheeks.

Caleb wrapped his arms around Sarah and gave her a tender kiss. When he pulled away, he locked eyes with her and whispered, "*Ich liebe dich.* I love you, Sarah."

"*Ich liebe dich*, Caleb Brenneman." She looked over

at Mary's smiling face. "And I loved the way the whole family asked. I wouldn't have wanted it any differently. My heart is overflowing with *liebe* for you all. *Jah*, I'll marry you...for sure and for certain."

Cars were driving by with windows down and people clapping. Some held cell phones out the windows, taking pictures.

"Oh, no!" Mary laughed. "This is going to be all over the internet." Mary hurried and put her iPhone in her pocket, but not before Sarah witnessed the act. Their gaze met and Sarah gave Mary a wink.

Sarah stepped back. "I need to call Mr. Gardner and tell him I won't be taking the pastry chef job after all."

Caleb grinned. "Maybe you can bake for him until he hires a new chef."

Sarah nodded.

"Mary, I almost forgot." Sarah darted to the SUV, hurried back and handed the book to Mary. "I forgot to give you this earlier." Sarah wrapped an arm around Mary's shoulders.

Mary stared at Sarah for a few seconds and glanced at the book in her hands, *Baking the Amish Way* by Sarah Gingerich. She turned the front cover over and spotted a note written on the inside.

Sarah whispered the words to Mary. "To my darling girl, Mary. I treasure you in a very special way. May God always bless you and guide your footsteps. May your days always bloom with joy, like the flowers of the garden. And may you always cook and bake with love. Yours in a very special way, Sarah."

Mary raised tear-filled eyes to Sarah. *"Danki."* She wrapped her arms around Sarah and gave her a kiss on the cheek.

Sarah returned the hug and kissed the top of Mary's head.

"They're my *mamm* and *daed*'s recipes, and some I developed myself. Your copy is the very first one off the press. I made sure of that."

Sarah gestured toward the crowd gathering around them. "We made quite a spectacle. If folks didn't know what the Amish people were like, they got their eyes and ears full today."

"*Jah*, they did." Caleb sighed. "That's the thing with us Plain folk. We like to keep life exciting in a simple kind of way."

Sarah feasted her eyes on Caleb and pulled him close once again. "I'm never going to let you three get out of my sight."

"Does that mean you are willing to give up the bakery and come be a farmer's wife?"

"After I left your farm and before I even got back to Kalona, I discovered it wasn't the bakery that mattered to me. It was you, Jacob and Mary. The thing I want most in life—to be part of your family."

Epilogue

"Sarah."

Ach. She stopped and cringed. *The bishop.* Only fifty feet from her buggy. She turned and waited for him to catch up to her.

"Bishop Yoder, I'm married now. You certainly don't want to introduce me to another widower, do you?"

He laughed. "But every time I introduced a widower to you, he ended up married—to someone else. The only exception was Elmer Plank."

"*Jah.* Elmer is a really nice man." She nodded. "I'm working on introducing him to someone. We'll see how it turns out."

"Ah, *gut.* Then I can turn the matchmaker hat over to you. What I really wanted to ask was how you managed to convince your *ehemann* to join our church. I didn't think Caleb Brenneman would ever come back to the Old Order."

"Old Order has a better youth retention rate, and we want to keep the *kinner* close. Again, thank you, Bishop, for marrying Caleb and me last Thursday. We really appreciate you clearing your schedule."

"It's almost Christmas. You should be with your loved ones for the holidays." He turned to leave, then glanced over his shoulder. "I wasn't taking any chances on getting you two married." He winked at her. "*Gut* day, Sarah."

As he walked away, she chuckled. "You're an old softy, Bishop."

"Don't tell anyone that, or I'll deny it." He raised his hand in the air and waved.

Sarah hurried to the buggy, grabbed her *ehemann*'s hand and snuggled close to him. "Sorry you had to wait."

Caleb turned to her as he gave the reins a tap on Snowball's back. "What did the bishop want?"

"Oh, just to see how I liked married life."

"I hope you told him it is *wunderbaar*." Caleb smiled.

Sarah slipped her hand around his elbow and squeezed. "Of course, *liebling*."

"And you don't miss being a pastry chef?"

Sarah hesitated. "Maybe a little bit, but I'd rather be with my family."

The snow began to fall as Caleb turned the buggy into the drive. Sarah shivered. "It's cold. Who wants hot cocoa?"

Everyone said, "Me," at the same time.

"Cookies and cocoa in fifteen minutes." Sarah hurried into the house and shook the snow off her cape. "Mary, we'll need to start making Christmas cookies tomorrow."

"Have you talked to Daed yet about us opening a bakery?" She pulled out a saucepan and grabbed the milk.

"Not yet. I'm waiting for the right time." She glanced over at Mary as they worked side by side.

Mary set cups, plates and spoons on the table. "I'll fetch the cookies," she called out as she headed to the pantry.

Out of the corner of her eye, Sarah caught Caleb sneaking up behind her. He planted a big kiss on her cheek.

"I *liebe* you." His breath tickled her face.

"I *liebe* you, too." She turned around, wrapped her arms around his neck and pulled him close for a tender kiss.

"I'm going to like being married. And to think, I almost lost you."

"*Nein.* That was never going to happen. You just needed a little nudge." Sarah glanced around and noticed Mary had disappeared from the room.

"What? You had this planned all the time?" His eyes widened.

Sarah smiled. "Come on, everyone, the cocoa is hot."

Jacob pulled out his chair and sat. "Mamm, I'm ready for my snack now."

Sarah smiled at her new name—Mamm.

When Mary stood behind her chair, Sarah noticed she held something behind her back. Mary brought her hand in front and held up the book cover that Sarah had made out of Martha's quilt scraps. Mary folded the book cover back to display Sarah's cookbook.

"Now I'll always have both of my *mamms* right here, at my fingertips and in my heart, always."

Sarah ran and gave her a hug. "*Danki.* That is the best Christmas present you could have given me." Tears clouded her eyes and rolled down her cheeks.

Gott had been with her on this journey all along to give her what she needed. For sure and for certain, how could she ever have doubted Him?

* * * * *

SPECIAL EXCERPT FROM

LOVE INSPIRED
INSPIRATIONAL ROMANCE

Can the new teacher in this Amish community help the family next door without losing her heart?

Read on for a sneak preview of
The Amish Teacher's Dilemma *by Patricia Davids,*
available in March 2020 from Love Inspired.

Clang, clang, clang.

The hammering outside her new schoolhouse grew louder. Eva Coblentz moved to the window to locate the source of the clatter. Across the road she saw a man pounding on an ancient-looking piece of machinery with steel wheels and a scoop-like nose on the front end.

When he had the sheet of metal shaped to fit the front of the machine, he stood back to assess his work. He knelt and hammered on the shovel-like nose three more times. Satisfied, he gathered up his tools and started in her direction.

She stepped back from the window. Was he coming to the school? Why? Had he noticed her gawking? Perhaps he only wanted to welcome the new teacher, although his lack of a beard said he wasn't married.

She glanced around the room. Should she meet him by the door? That seemed too eager. Her eyes settled on the large desk at the front of the classroom. She should look as if she was ready for the school year to start. A professional attitude would put off any suggestion that she was interested in meeting single men.

LIEXP0220

Eva hurried to the desk, pulled out the chair and sat down as the outside door opened. The chair tipped over backward, sending her flailing. Her head hit the wall with a painful thud as she slid to the floor. Stunned, she slowly opened her eyes to see the man leaning over the desk.

He had the most beautiful gray eyes she'd ever beheld. They were rimmed with thick, dark lashes in stark contrast to the mop of curly, dark red hair springing out from beneath his straw hat. Tiny sparks of light whirled around him.

"I'm Willis Gingrich. Local blacksmith." He squatted beside her. "Can you tell me your name?"

The warmth and strength of his hand on her skin sent a sizzle of awareness along her nerve endings. "I'm Eva Coblentz. I am the new teacher and I'm fine now."

Don't miss
The Amish Teacher's Dilemma
by USA TODAY *bestselling author Patricia Davids,*
available March 2020 wherever
Love Inspired books and ebooks are sold.

LoveInspired.com

HARLEQUIN

*Heartfelt or suspenseful,
inspiring or passionate, Harlequin
has your happily-ever-after.*

With new books published
every month, you are sure to find the
satisfying escape you know you deserve.

SIGN UP FOR THE
HARLEQUIN NEWSLETTER

Be the first to hear about great new
reads and exciting offers!

Harlequin.com/newsletters